WOLF MARK

JOSEPH BRUCHAC

Tu Books

An imprint of LEE & LOW BOOKS Inc.

New York

For the Wolf People
who continue
to teach us

Text copyright © 2011 by Joseph Bruchac
Translation of Ahkmetova poems © 2011 by Joseph Bruchac

TU BOOKS, an imprint of LEE & LOW BOOKS Inc.
95 Madison Avenue, New York, NY 10016
leeandlow.com

Manufactured in the United States of America
by Worzalla Publishing Company, September 2011

Book design by Kelly Eismann
Book production by The Kids at Our House
The text is set in Minion
10 9 8 7 6 5 4 3 2 1
First Edition

Library of Congress Cataloging-in-Publication Data

Bruchac, Joseph, 1942-
Wolf mark / Joseph Bruchac. — 1st ed.
p. cm.
Summary: When Lucas King's covert-ops father is kidnapped and his best friend Meena is put in danger, Luke's only chance to save them—a skin that will let him walk as a wolf—is hidden away in an abandoned mansion guarded by monsters.
ISBN 978-1-60060-661-8 (hardcover : alk. paper) — ISBN 978-1-60060-878-0 (e-book)
[1. Supernatural—Fiction. 2. Spies—Fiction. 3. Shapeshifting—Fiction.
4. Indians of North America—Fiction. 5. Fathers and sons—Fiction.] I. Title.
PZ7.B82816Wo 2011
[Fic]--dc23   2011014252

If you're afraid of the wolf
stay out of the forest.

—Russian proverb

Wolf I am.
In darkness, in light.
Wherever I search,
wherever I run,
wherever I stand,
everything will be good . . .

—Cheyenne Scout's Song

Everything resembles the truth,
everything can happen to a man.

—Nicolai Gogol, *Dead Souls*

PROLOGUE

MOON

The mark is on the back of my left wrist. It's not that big. It could almost be hidden by a wristwatch. I've tried that. But the touch of metal against it for any length of time makes it itch at first and then burn. So rather than finding myself baring my teeth and growling at the annoyance and pain of it, I just do the next best thing. Long sleeves. All through the year even when the sun is blazing. Which is okay by me because I never feel hot.

The mark wasn't that visible when I was younger. Back when Mom was still here. But it's gotten darker every year. It really does look like an animal, like a German shepherd . . . or a wolf. Sitting on its haunches, its head is raised—to bay at the moon, I guess.

I can understand that.

Moon, Mom told me, was my first word. My dad wasn't around to hear it. I'm not sure where he was deployed then. But it was probably somewhere in the Middle East seeing as how that was almost seventeen years ago.

Moon, I'd say.

Again and again with my arms lifted as if I was trying to embrace it.

Moon. Moon. Moon.

MEENA

Friday morning.

Maybe from now on my life is going to be like that of any other kid my age. Maybe I really can have friends and not have to move to a new town every six months. Maybe things are finally going to be normal for me. Or at least as close to normal as any teenager's life can be after his mother dies and he's stuck in a run-down trailer with a father who has lost himself in the bottom of a bottle.

Someone pokes me in the side with the eraser end of a pencil.

I look over at the dark-haired girl in the desk next to me.

She furrows her brow in mock anger, jerks her head toward the front of the class where our French teacher is writing on the board, and mouths the words *Pay attention!* She holds up the pencil and turns it so that the sharp end is pointed toward me like a dagger.

If it really was a knife, I know four different ways to take it out of an enemy's hand before the attacker can take another breath. One would end up permanently cutting off the breath of whoever was threatening my life as I thrust that blade back into the assailant's throat.

I don't ever want to do that to anyone. And there's no way on God's green earth I'd ever do that to Meena. I control the twitch in my right hand, keep it flat on my desktop. I raise my eyebrows and put an exaggerated look of mock fear on my face.

Spare me, I mouth back.

Meena has to stifle a giggle at that, which brings a real smile to my face. I love it when she laughs, even more when I'm the one who made her laugh. Meena Kureshi. Even her name is musical. Plus she is the most beautiful girl I've ever met. Not that she acts as if she knows that. She's not stuck up or hung up on being pretty. It's just natural. But I'm going on too long about this. One of my faults.

Meena points with her pencil at the stapled sheath of papers I've placed facedown on my desk. She holds hers up. The usual A is printed in the upper right corner.

"What did you get?" she whispers.

I turn my essay over to display the B on top of it, which was handed back to me—as was Meena's—at the end of our last class. The comment from our English literature teacher is printed in large red letters underneath it.

BREVITY IS THE SOUL OF WIT

Once again I've just plain gone on too long about the subject. Meena nods.

Keep it simple, stupid, she mouths at me. Then she raises her left eyebrow and smiles—which makes it okay.

I don't mind Meena calling me stupid. She can call me anything she wants. We're friends, and that means more to me than

2

she realizes. I've had so few friends in my life—in fact, about as many as you can count on two fingers of one hand. I feel like I can tell her anything. Well, not really anything. That is a huge exaggeration. I mean that I feel as if I can trust her. And that is saying a lot. Trust is not something I was raised to either give or receive anywhere outside the circle of my family.

This fall is the start of the second year I've known Meena. We've been in a bunch of classes together. We usually end up being seated close to each other. First it was by alphabetical accident. Lucas King. Meena Kureshi. Now it's by choice.

Mine, mostly.

When Meena's really intent on something, her brow knits up. She puts her hand to her forehead and then brushes her thick hair back over her ear. Her hair flows like dark ocean waves. She doesn't throw her hair back the way a girl does when she's flirting. She just does it unconsciously, not even aware of how amazingly cool she looks when she does that.

They've turned off the air conditioning in the school. It's a cost-saving measure because of the budget crunch. The choice was between using less electricity or letting two more teachers go. The new county executive, owl-eyed Dr. Edmund O. (probably for "Overlord") Kesselring, has been promising that his new development initiatives—low to no tax on the new high-tech multinationals he's lured in to take over the deserted industrial complexes that ring the town—will fix everything. Like Maxico, the one that Kesselring is part owner of along with an elderly Romanian industrialist named Rogan Machescou. But aside from bringing in a wave of foreign students to our school, the children of those new industrialists like Meena and the other Pakistani kids, there hasn't yet been much difference. Imported labor has been introduced, rather than many new jobs for the locals. There's been little change here—only

3

a few pennies' worth. Rangerville High, for example, has only seen a trickle of money coming its way. Like alms for the poor.

So, when it gets hot like this on a late autumn day, the morning sun trying to burn its way through the shades drawn down over the windows of our French class, everybody just sits here and sweats.

Except for me. Sweating is something I never do. For some reason I always feel about the same temperature-wise. I'm always just on the edge of feeling chilled. Kind of like you feel just before you put on a coat. Although putting on a coat doesn't make that much difference for me. Even when I do vigorous exercise, I don't perspire.

Meena sweats. Not a lot. But little round beads of moisture form on her nose. They're like tiny diamonds. I want to reach out a finger and touch them. Or, even better, I long to lean close enough to feel her warm breath and then put out my tongue and gently lick off those salty gems.

Meena reaches over and pokes me with her elbow.

She thinks this look on my face means I'm daydreaming about riding my motorcycle or walking through the woods. Two of my favorite things, as Meena knows. The call of the road, the freedom of the wild, the healing purity of nature. It's not just that my over-written essay—which she read before I handed it in—was about all of that. It's something I've mentioned to her often. And she agrees with me, which is another reason why she's such a good friend.

"The place where I feel most free, it is in the forest," she said to me once.

I could have kissed her for that. Well, not just for that. But it's true. We need unspoiled places. We need to do something to control this so-called civilization that is killing the planet we live on. We need to get back to a more natural way of being, back to the wild.

4

Back to the wild. Just that one brief phrase makes me remember how it used to be with my parents. Whenever the three of us had time to do anything special together, we'd always go to the nearest wild place—like a national park or a state forest—and run its trails together. We'd find animal tracks, identify them, and figure out the stories those tracks told of what the animals had been doing.

"Tracks are maps," Dad would say. "Study them as if your life depends on it." Then he'd pause. "It might, you know."

Thinking of maps, Dad had this map that he loved. I'm not sure where it vanished to after Mom's death. It showed the locations of all the national parks and national forests and preserves in the U.S. and Canada. We'd use it to pick our vacation spots.

He and Mom also supported every environmental cause that you could imagine. Whenever we moved, which was often, Dad would always make sure he was on the mailing lists for his favorite causes. Even now, though he never opens them anymore, Dad still gets letters every week from the Sierra Club, the Rain Forest Alliance, the National Resources Defense Fund, and about a dozen others looking for contributions.

Mom used to joke that if you cut us we'd bleed green.

"Nope," Dad would say, "our blood may be different, but not that way."

Then they'd exchange a knowing look and laugh. I'd laugh along with them, thinking I understood. After all, even back then, before my age got into the double digits, I knew that we were very unlike any other family around us. It wasn't just because we were eco-nuts and moved all the time. How many other kids my age were taught martial arts and weaponry from the time they could walk? At the age of seven I could disassemble an AK-47 and put it back together blindfolded. How many other third graders had to memorize new codes for the locks on our doors and "safe" words to use in phone conversations with his parents every week?

Meena pokes me a second time.

"Dors-tu, sot?" she hisses. When she teases me she does it in French sometimes. We took third-year French together last spring.

Are you asleep, fool? is what she just asked.

"Merci," I whisper back. "Thanks. I'm awake."

But not really. At times, there's some part of me I can't explain that feels as if it's never been awakened.

No matter how many times I daydream about doing so, I'm not going to ask Meena to go out with me this weekend or even to take a ride on my bike. I'm going to do what I do every weekend, be alone. Now that my best friend Renzo is working long hours every weekend, trying to put enough money aside for at least a semester at community college in a year, I can't even hang out that much with him. I can take a long ride on my motorcycle. Alone. I can go for a run in the woods. Alone. Or I can just dream.

Dreaming is what I seem to do best.

DREAMING

My dreams? It's Sunday evening now and I'm thinking about them. I've been thinking about them all day, even while I was riding my motorcycle.

Here's the first one. My mother is still alive. My father is home and he's not drunk. We're still living in our last house and not an elongated aluminum box.

Our old house, back in Illinois where we used to live, was on a two-acre lot. There were woods behind it. That's the only similarity between the Sardine Can and our old place, that we're close to a forest. That's the one thing Dad can't seem to live without, being close to where it's wild, where there are lots of trees and a clear view of the night sky unpolluted by street lights. Plus being close to woods is useful when you need to make a quick exit unobserved.

The sweet full moon would rise like a giant silver balloon out of those woods. The house had seven full rooms. There was a living room, a kitchen, a dining room, their bedroom, my bedroom, Dad's den, and one bathroom. Three more than in the trailer. Mom and Dad and me together, and all of us happy.

That's the craziest dream. The one that came to me in my sleep on Saturday night. The one I tried to hold onto when I woke up this morning. The one that was gone when I opened my eyes.

Dream number two. Me and Meena are together on my Norton Commando. She's sitting behind me, her arms around my waist, her face thrust forward so her cheek is pressed against mine. That's the dream that kept coming back to me as I was riding this afternoon. It was so real that the next thing I knew I was in Meena's part of town, the newest development with the biggest houses. I almost turned onto the street where I know she lives. Maybe she'd be out front. Maybe her father would not be around. Maybe she'd see me and her face would light up and she'd wave and run to the curb. But I couldn't get up the courage to turn my handlebars that way. Instead, at the intersection, I went in the opposite direction, kicked it into fifth gear, and didn't look back.

But perhaps that dream isn't all that crazy. Meena has confided in me more than once—and lately, about once every day—about how restricted she feels in the role she's expected to play as a dutiful Muslim daughter.

"If I had your freedom, Luke," she said just yesterday, "I would get on that motorcycle of yours and just ride until I came to a place where I could do whatever I want."

She's told me that her goal is to be a scientist like her father, a profession that hasn't been that open in the past to women in her country. Whenever she has a chance to visit him at his work she jumps at it. That's not often, though, because the research he's doing—something, she said, to do with gene-splicing—is top secret and even family members are frowned upon as visitors.

"For a while," Meena said, "things were getting better for

women and girls. We even had a woman running our nation."

She paused then. I knew why. Since the assassination of that woman leader, things have been going from bad to worse in her country. I controlled my impulse to reach out and take her hand—and not just as a consoling friend. I sat there, listening, let her take a deep breath.

"But now," she sighed, "now with the Taliban gaining power, more doors are closing for women and girls than opening."

She made a fist and hit the top of the lunch table between us, so hard that trays bounced and half of my untouched green peas went flying. A few people turned for a moment to look—probably hoping for a fight to liven up the lunch period—then lost interest when they saw that violence was not imminent.

"It makes me so angry," she finally said, "the way they are trying to push us back into the dark ages."

So the first part of that recurring dream, Meena with me on my bike, isn't all that nutty. The insane part comes next when the scene shifts to the two of us sitting on a bench. My arm is around her shoulders while we watch the sun go down. I can't wait for it to get dark. I want to share everything with her, especially the night that I love so much. Meena's thigh is pressed against mine. Her left hand is on my arm. She's stroking the back of my left wrist with her fingertips, tracing the shape there like she's petting a dog. Little pulses of electricity spark at her touch. Her face is golden in the fading light. Her skin is smoother than silk. And that's all I intend to share of that dream.

Recurring dream number three is the one that seems most real to me. It has nothing to do with my family or Meena. I'm looking up at a cliff. My left wrist is throbbing—no, pulling at me as if someone or something was yanking a string tied to it. There's a cave way up near the top. It's a straight rock face and I've never done rock climbing before, but I'm about to scale it. I wake up, though, before I make my first move.

I wonder why that is. Why I wake up. Why I don't scramble up to that cave. It's not because climbing a sheer cliff would be all that hard for me. Although I make it a point to hang back and not even get close to the climbing wall in the gym, I could do it easy, eyes closed. I've always been stronger than I look, despite the fact that I'm thin. I stay away from sports, though. I've had it drummed into me that I need to keep a low profile. Never draw much attention to yourself.

I don't show off how fast I can run or much else that I'm physically capable of doing. That only caused me trouble once last year. The first day I arrived at RHS, four senior burnouts who made a racket out of bullying people tried their little routine with me. Would-be gangstas, sharks scenting a few fish. They came up just as I finished locking the ancient one-speed Schwinn bicycle I'd found behind our trailer. Dad must have loaded it into the U-haul without thinking. Or maybe I did. It's hard to tell. We were both sort of sleepwalking for weeks after Mom's sudden death, doing things automatically.

I'd looked at the bike. If I grease this, I thought, and put the chain back on, it'll probably work. I'd needed to get to school. The bus had missed our driveway and my father had been nowhere to be found. I could have walked the four miles—or run it—but the Schwinn appealed to me. It had been my mom's. Riding it might make me feel close to her. Of course, it was about as uncool in the world of a twenty-first century high school as being a fan of *The Partridge Family*. It made me look like a geek. An easy mark.

"Show us what you got in your pockets," snarled the skinny senior with a constellation of zits across his forehead.

"Protection insurance," the one with the reverse Mohawk

haircut explained in a bored but nasty voice.

They grabbed my arms. I shook them off like a dog shaking off water. All three went stumbling back about ten feet. I shouldn't have done that, but my reflexes got the better of me. I forced myself to hold back. I hoped no one else had noticed. But as I straightened up my hands were curled in front of me and I couldn't stop myself from looking down my nose at them.

Whatever was in my eyes stopped whatever they had in mind. They walked away.

"That was way sick," someone said.

I turned my head his way. A kid with dirty blond hair and a flat face. He was built like a stack of beach balls piled to the height of five feet eight inches. In one broad hand he held a bike chain that someone had left hanging on the rack. He tilted his head to the side and looked down at the length of heavy metal links.

I got it. He'd been ready to wade in and help me, despite resembling the chubbier half of this team of comedians in the old movies. Abbott and Costello.

I nodded my thanks. The blond kid's face opened into a half-moon grin.

"Name's Lorenzo. Renzo's what my buds call me."

"Renzo." I held out my hand to take his.

"You know you was growlin'?" he asked.

"No," I said.

Two weeks after that incident, I got my motorcycle license and Dad gave me his vintage Norton Commando. It was either a sign of how much he trusted me—or how little he cared about anything after Mom's death, even my drawing attention to myself by being a teenager on a cherry motorcycle. I hoped it was the former, feared it was the latter, but accepted it anyway. As it turned out, when I didn't react to the oohs and ahs that I got from some kids when I first pulled up with it in the school parking lot last year, people just got used to it. It was no big deal. I stayed low-profile, nearly invisible. Nobody aside from Meena and Renzo ever looked at me twice. Of course that was before the Sunglass Mafia arrived and started keeping watch on everyone. Seven Russian juniors and seniors. Word is that their families really are in the Russian mafia. For various reasons, I make it a point to avoid them.

Maybe on Monday I will take a chance. I will get up the nerve to ask Meena if she'd like to take a ride with me. There's no reason why I can't try to make at least part of one of my dreams come true. Is there?

3

UNCLE CAL

Monday morning.

There's a knot in my stomach the size of a fist.

I wake up as I always do, before the radio alarm goes off. I don't know why I bother to set it. I always open my eyes in time to turn over, hold my hand over the top of the radio, and count to five before the music comes on.

But this morning is not just as usual. I lay here. I don't get out of bed.

Remember that third dream of mine, the one I never finish? Last night I took a big step toward finishing it. I climbed the cliff.

And I went into that cave. It felt more familiar than the so-called living room of this tin can I share with the narcotized zombie currently inhabiting the body of my father. There was a metal-banded chest by the back wall. Just like *Pirates of the Caribbean*. Something in that chest was calling me, telling me to open it. That it needed me. I felt a deep growl rising out of my chest.

I took a step toward it.

Then I heard my father's voice. It was clear, not blurred with booze or grass.

No! Don't! I burned mine.

Burned! That word sent a quiver of fear down my back. That was when I woke up.

I listen. The Sardine Can is quiet aside from the determined humming of the crappy refrigerator in the hallway kitchenette.

Dad's not up yet. That is also as usual. I've slept with my jeans on, so all I have to do to get dressed is swing my feet onto the floor and slip them into the New Balance runners I leave side by side next to my bed, then pull on the cleanest of the T-shirts I keep in the one drawer attached to the headboard. I'll do laundry later this week. I don't sweat, so my clothes don't really smell bad when I wear them day after day, unlike those of most of the guys at school.

I wish there was someone I could tell about my dream. Not Dad, though. It's not that he wouldn't listen—if he was sober. But if he's not, then trying to talk with him will just make things worse. I don't even want to look at him when he's like that.

For the hundredth time I wish Uncle Cal was here and for the hundredth time I feel that pang of loss in my gut.

My room is so small that I don't have to stand up to reach my backpack and jam the stuff I need for the school day into it. I make as little noise as possible even though I know my father can probably hear me—drunk or stoned. His hearing is as good as mine, even when it's been damped down by a night of drinking or smoking or whatever he's chosen to do to turn off the world around him. Or maybe it's the world inside him. Whatever happened on his last assignment must have been horrific. And our losing Mom right after he got back just made it worse.

When Mom was alive, Dad sometimes would talk to me about

what it was like over there. That was especially true when Uncle Cal was visiting.

As I drive to school and walk down the hallways, I can't help but continue to think of Uncle Cal. Cal Sanchez was his name. Even though we weren't related at all in terms of blood, he'd meant it when he told me to call him Uncle Cal. Dad and Mom and I were his family. His original kinfolk were all gone.

He was one of those people who looked like he could be any one of a dozen different ethnicities. Black, Mexican American, Arab, South Asian. Which came in handy for the work he did. To us he always referred to himself—with a broad, teeth-baring smile—as being Indio, the Spanish word for someone who is Native American. He had been in Dad's squad or cadre or whatever for years. It was never totally clear what they did. I guess it fell into the realm of what movie soldiers call black ops. Out of uniform, blending in. Infiltration, information gathering, and more.

I'll never forget the first time Dad brought Uncle Cal home with him. It was one of the years when we were renting a really nice house and not squatting in a used tin can. I was twelve then. I noticed right away that with Cal around Dad was finding it easier to talk about things. So I started asking a lot of questions and they answered them.

They told me how the desert smelled in Kuwait, what Saddam's palaces looked like now, how it felt to walk through the Khyber Pass with a hundred eyes watching from every mountain crag. They also shared what it felt like to see an RPG streaking at your convoy, knowing there's nothing you can do but hope it doesn't hit your vehicle. They laughed about how camel spiders can jump six feet high to bite you and how people's ears would fall off after they got bit by sand flies and then got infected with Baghdad boil.

It was like that from then on every time Uncle Cal came home with Dad. They told story after story. My favorite tales were the ones that took place in the forests of Borneo and Brazil. The things that my father and Cal did there were volunteer jobs, not on any government payroll. They lived with indigenous peoples, tribes who followed the old ways. Uncle Cal and Dad were trying to protect the people and the forests from loggers and greedy outsiders. Some of them were armed mercenaries hired to wipe out the natives so that others could build roads, clear-cut the land, mine for gold, or build dams. The exact details about what Dad and Uncle Cal did and precisely where they were always stayed vague. Mostly they just talked about the beauty of the rainforests and how the people and the land and the animals were one, like it was in ancient times.

Those were the coolest stories I'd ever heard. Cal and Dad would keep it up until it got so late that Mom would finally tell them to stop.

"Time out," she'd say. "You two may not need to sleep at night, but Lucas has school tomorrow."

She smiled when she said that, but Dad knew she meant it and he always listened to her.

Cal always reminded me of someone, but I could never figure out who until one day when Mom and I went to the zoo and I saw a jaguar for the first time. It walked right up to the edge of its moat. Its lazy, muscular gait was so familiar it made the hair stand up on the back of my neck.

I couldn't wait to see Uncle Cal. I knew that whenever he showed up he would have something cool for me, like the long Afghan knife he'd given me for my thirteenth birthday, handcrafted by a blacksmith he knew in Kabul. It had my initials engraved in the steel. Yet it didn't have to be anything material. It might be a story or a new move in self-defense. Or it might just be that feeling of warmth and safety I got whenever he was around, the way his presence brought a smile to my father's face.

But that was not how it was the last time when Dad came home. He walked into the house alone, dropped his bag on the floor, and just stood there, looking at Mom and me as if we were strangers.

"Where's Uncle Cal?" I asked.

"Gone," Dad said. "One more star."

His lips were tight and he looked away as he said it. I knew enough not to ask again. I didn't intrude while he and Mom went off into another room together. I threw on my running shoes and my shorts and went outside. I was trying not to listen, but as I started to run through the woods, I could still hear them talking softly. And just before I went over the first hill I started to hear someone weeping as if their heart was broken.

I'm at school now. Here I am walking down the hallway toward my first class of the day and I'm still thinking of Uncle Cal. Maybe it was walking past the Sunglass Mafia that brought him to mind again this morning. As usual, they studied me like a lab specimen with their hidden eyes. Usually they do that quietly. But not today. Today they looked up from the book that the tallest of the girls— Marina, I think—was showing to them. Then they made remarks to each other in Russian. And the sarcastic comments they made were about me.

I wasn't doing that paranoid thing of assuming that people speaking another language are talking about you. I was taught a good bit of conversational Russian. Now that I think of it, Uncle Cal was the one who taught the language to me. And once I learn something I don't forget it. That's why I know that the "pathetic mongrel" they were referring to is me. What I don't understand is why they're on my case. I'm further down the social ladder from them than a worm is from an eagle. They're wearing designer jeans and mine are from Walmart. One of their Rolex watches is worth a hundred times more than my entire wardrobe. They are so painfully cool that just about everyone wants to be like them and people jump to do their bidding just to be able to tell their friends that they are, like, "in" with the SGMs.

Not that they ever really let anyone else into their inner circle. Why are they even noticing I'm alive?

And what does *bodark* mean? That's a Russian word Uncle Cal never taught me.

The only person who makes me feel more uncomfortable than they do is Dr. Kesselring. Despite the fact that he has a round Santa Claus face and everyone acts like he's the patron saint or the savior of our community because he's bringing in new jobs, he creeps me out. He smells wrong and there's a kind of cold calculation in his eyes. When he spoke to the school at the start of the year, those owlish eyes of his searched me out in the audience. Originally, it was supposed to be a joint appearance with Rogan Machescou, the other main player in Maxico, but an unexpected illness—"a bit of, ah, flu," as Kesselring put it at the start of his talk—prevented his attendance. The rumor, though, is that Machescou is dying of cancer.

"*Opportunity,*" the doctor declaimed in a high, self-satisfied voice, adjusting his glasses with his left hand and not taking his gaze off me for a second. "You young people must learn to always *seize* the opportunity." Then this little smile twitched the corner of his mouth and he nodded. Way weird. Needless to say I was not one of the eager teenagers who made their way up to shake his hand when he was done.

Renzo's waiting for me at the first turn in the hallway. He's always at school first. Not just before me, but before anyone else. He has a perfect attendance record—not just this year, but every year he's been to school since kindergarten. He's more than proud of that fact. It was one of the first things he told me about himself after we became buddies.

"I am going to be in the Hall of Fame of Perfect Attendance," he'd said. "There's only two other people in the whole history of the school district who've done that. Behold the one who will soon be number three!"

Renzo's two arms are raised in his usual ironic morning salute to me. *It's about time you got here.*

"Yo, dog," he says, poking out a fist for me to bump it with my own knuckles. "Whassup?"

"Nothing much," I reply. I wish I was right, but this feeling in my gut tells me that's wishful thinking. Dad used to talk about having a danger barometer in his belly. Whenever something bad was coming his way, he knew about it long ahead of time—the way a storm gauge registers the drop in pressure before most people sense even the hint of a storm. A storm is coming. And I have no idea what it will be or why.

We round the next corridor in the labyrinth that is RHS. Meena's there. Her smile is like the sun chasing away storm clouds.

"Good morning, gentlemen. Hey Renzo, hey Luke."

"Hey," I reply. And for the first time today I remember that today is the day I was going to ask her if she'd ever think about going out with me. Like on a date. Take a deep breath, Luke.

"Hey," I say again, eloquent silver-tongued devil that I am.

"My lady," Renzo makes a low sweeping bow and takes her arm as she reaches out to link her other elbow with mine. We go down the hall like that, arm in arm like the Tin Man, the Scarecrow, and Dorothy setting off to see the Wizard.

Three friends with not a care in the world.

I wish.

DOGS

"Dude, where are you?" Renzo's voice, muffled through a double mouthful of burrito, brings me out of my daydream in which I actually did ask Meena to take that ride with me and we're roaring down the highway together. But I didn't and it is now 6:00 P.M.—six hours past missing my chance.

I look up at him across the table that is garishly decorated with images of crowned knights on cowback using French fries as lances.

"What?"

I'm not eating. It's not just that the grease-saturated air and the tasteless faux medieval setting of this fast-food joint kill my appetite. I prefer my meat red and fresh—not the ground-up frozen cow residue served here. But I enjoy keeping him company during his dinner break. Taco Prince is where Renzo puts in three hours a day after school and all day Saturday. The pay is low, the food is lousy and, best of all, employees can eat as much of it as they want.

"Bro," Renzo says, "I know what you are thinking about."

"Huh?"

"Or should I say who?"

I look down at my hands. He's my best friend, probably knows me better than anyone my own age has ever known me. I guess I shouldn't be surprised that he's figured out how much Meena means to me.

"Why don't you ask her out?"

I don't even try to pretend I don't know what he's talking about. I just keep looking at the palms of my hands as if I'd written the answers to a quiz on them. But there's no answers there, just like there's no chance there could ever be anything but friendship between Meena and me.

"Earth to Luke," Renzo pushes his paper plate aside and leans forward. "Am I getting through? Ask Meena out."

I look up at him.

"Afraid she'll say no? She likes you. I can tell. You two would be perfect together."

I shake my head. "It's just not possible," I say. "Can we drop it?"

"Like this?"

Renzo picks up an imaginary object from the tabletop, holds it out over the nearby waste bin and splays open his fingers.

"Nope," he says. "And you can't either. You gotta do something, bro."

I shake my head. Just like that, he's shown me why I value his friendship so much. Normally he'd change the subject. But this time I know it's no use. Once Renzo gets an idea—especially when it comes to helping a buddy—it is harder to get him to let go of it than to pull a bone out of the mouth of a pit bull.

He sits there, staring at me and chewing, waiting.

"All right," I admit. "You're right. But what can I do?"

Renzo looks up at the ceiling, as if the answer was written

somewhere on the multicolored rafters.

"What if I were to tell you that a certain person whose initials are M-E-E-N-A just might have happened to confide in me how much she'd like to ride on a motorcycle?" he says.

"Really?"

He crosses his heart with his index finger, smearing some of Taco Prince's special sauce on his white apron as he does so. "Hope to die," he mumbles, then swallows. "So."

I hold my hands out, palms up. "Okay, Cupid, you win. I promise I will ask her to take a ride with me."

Renzo wipes his fingers on the grinning face of a crowned clown painted on a napkin. "When?" he says.

"Soon, but not tomorrow."

"Skipping tomorrow?" he asks.

"Safety Day," I reply. "What do you think?"

Renzo nods as he takes a big bite out of another supposedly edible burrito. Of course he already knew why I'm not coming to school tomorrow. He knew it as soon as we heard the announcement over the loudspeaker.

Safety Day means the usual boring crap. Lectures on what to do in case of a school emergency: fire, flood, terrorists, brain-warped burnouts sneaking their fathers' assault rifles in to school to even the score with the world in general.

I know, by the way, who some of the latter might be. I can smell it in their sweat, detect their fear and frustration. But it doesn't worry me. I'd know a long way ahead of time if they ever did try to bring something deadly in to Rangerville High School.

If I close my eyes and take a deep breath I can tell you the location of every person in a room, even if there's a hundred people. I can pick up the scent of Meena's delicately applied Shalimar perfume from even farther away than that. A little smile comes to my mouth in spite of myself at that thought.

I look over at Renzo. He missed that smile. Too deep into fishing out the last deceased French fry from its greasy paper shroud. Everything they serve here smells rancid and dead, but I don't tell Renzo that.

Scent is why I stay away from Safety Day. Not mine, though. There's a strict Zero Tolerance Policy at RHS. Thus, Safety Day always includes a lecture on drug safety and an extended visit from Chief Frank—who Renzo refers to as "Chief Hot Dog"—and his police dog, Wonder, the Substance-sniffing Shepherd.

No, I do not use drugs. Ever. One look at my semi somnambulant sire should be enough for any pothead to rethink his habit. Nor do I avoid Safety Day because there's sometimes so much ganja smoke in the Sardine Can, that rusted wreck in which we reside, that my clothes reek of it. When it gets too bad, I unroll my sleeping bag and spend my nights outside to avoid the contact high.

The smell of Dad's dope, of course, is what Renzo assumes is my reason for blowing off classes tomorrow. He's one of the few people who's ever come by my trailer, seen my father, and knowingly sniffed the air.

But that's not it. It's my own scent that worries me. You should see what it does to a dog—any dog, all dogs. As soon as any canine catches wind of me it does one of two things. It either whines frantically and tries desperately to escape or it whimpers and rolls over on its back to bare its throat in submission.

If Wonder the Weed Hound behaved that way when it encountered yours truly, it would blow my Zero-Tolerance-for-Drawing-Attention-to-Myself policy. Big time.

Renzo balls up the paper plate, shoves it into the grease-stained bag, and then uses both hands to dunk the trash into the bin like a basketball.

"Two points, LeBron," I say, tossing him another much-needed napkin.

As he wipes his face, he nods knowingly at me. "Buckaroo Luke," he cracks, laughing at his own joke.

"Bucking" means missing school without an excuse. The way learning is done in school just doesn't make sense to me. You're stuck in the same routine, locked up hour after endless hour in an airless building. Slow torture.

My finger traces the outlines of the cow-cum-steed on the sticky tabletop.

If I could, I'd enlist right now in the Rangers like Dad did when he was seventeen. But I can't do it yet without a guardian's permission. Dad says no go. So for now I stay.

Renzo scrapes back his chair.

"Back to the grease pit," he says. "Later, bro."

He holds out his fist and I bump it.

"Later."

Later, I think as I go out the door. I wish it was a lot later.

Ten months from now. My birthday. Then I will really be out of here.

At least there's no school tomorrow for me. Which means a day spent in the woods with my backpack, hoping that I can just lose myself for a time in the trees and not feel the weight of everything that makes me feel like I'm stuck in a bus going a hundred miles an hour down a dead-end street.

FIRE

Another day. I'm on my way to school.

I wonder if Dr. Kesselring has called to tell the school that I wasn't really sick—as my carefully forged excuse claims.

I shake my head at the thought of my brief run-in with him yesterday. If he hadn't been in a car I would have smelled him and ducked out of sight. But by the time the black sedan stopped next to me in the parking lot, it was too late.

It was nine in the morning. I was in the parking lot at the head of my favorite trail into the Cowasuck Preserve, miles away from the school. I'd just gotten off the Commando and was zipping the key into my backpack when I heard the car—which I assumed was just going to cruise by—stop. The power window rolled down.

And I caught his scent, an odor of too much cologne and something else that I couldn't define, something that made me think of decay.

"Young man?"

I tried to pretend I hadn't heard him.

"Lucas King, is it not?"

The hair on the back of my neck stood up. It wasn't just his knowing my name that freaked me out, but the glib self-satisfied tone of his voice. It made me think of an owl holding a mouse in its talons.

Out of the corner of my eye I could see him staring at me, a smug smile on his face as he reached up to adjust his glasses lower on his nose.

"Should I ask why you are not in school today? Education is so important, you know."

I didn't turn around. I didn't say anything. Nor did I snarl, which is what I really felt like doing. *If I ignore him*, I thought, *he'll go away.* But he didn't. He kept on as if we were having something other than a one-sided conversation.

"Ah, yes, of course. Now I wonder if your father knows you are not in school as you should be. In fact I wonder what your father knows in general. Your *interesting* father."

If I had clenched my fists any tighter, I would have driven my nails into my palms and blood would have started dripping from my hands. *He wants me to turn around*, I thought. *But I won't.*

So I stood there, all the muscles in my body as taut as bowstrings. I was ready to run or, if necessary, do something else.

Then the sound of a musical ring tone came from the car. It was so incongruous that it almost made me laugh because I recognized the song. It was an old country number by one of my father's favorite singers, Patsy Cline. "Crazy" is its title. Which probably means that song was chosen to reflect how Kesselring felt about the person making the call.

"Rogan," Kesselring said. His hands were cupped around the phone and his voice was a whisper that anyone with normal hearing—unlike mine—would not pick up. "What is it now? No, I do not think you should continue the treatment. I know what your condition is. But you know that there are . . . risks in going too fast. *Ja, ja. Ach,* at least wait until I get there, *mein freund. Bitte?*"

I heard what sounded like a snarl from the other end of that conversation and then the connection was broken. Kesselring took a deep breath. He wasn't pleased about the mysterious conversation that just ensued. What treatment? Plus I wondered why the good doctor, who has presented himself as an American, lapsed into colloquial German at the end of that stressed tête-à-tête. But he quickly regained his composure.

"So," Kesselring's mellow voice crooned, "do have a nice day, Lucas King. I am certain we shall meet again."

Then the window rolled up, the car's wheels crunched on the gravel, and it was over. Except it wasn't over. I knew that then and I know that now. I just don't know what's next.

PEACE

Halfway to school, and the pistons of the Norton are softly chugging. Background music for the mantra that has started going through my head again.

What? What? What?

What, if anything, should I do about Meena? Despite what I promised Renzo.

What was going on with Kesselring?

Why was the Sunglass Mafia paying so much attention to me?

That strange meeting with Dr. Kesselring keeps replaying itself in my mind again. What was happening?

There was a smile on my face as I roared out of the driveway, my tires throwing gravel. Before the good doctor came to mind, my thoughts were about Meena.

But now, as I turn the corner and see the school a hundred yards ahead of me, the buses pulling in, I start to feel like a balloon with a slow leak. I park the bike, slip the keys into my back jeans pocket, hook my arm into my backpack. What's waiting for me?

Meena and Renzo are standing by the main door. My heart thumps as Meena smiles at me. Then she turns her smile into a theatrical frown.

"Lucas King, where were you?" Meena shapes her full lips into a pout that looks so kissable, I miss a step and have to catch myself to keep from falling. She grabs my lapel and shakes me. "You are a bad, bad person. I thought you would be able to look at my paper yesterday. Now, without you to proofread my awful English, I am surely going to get a lower grade on my essay."

What I want to do now is put both arms around her. What I do instead is force an ironic look onto my face. "What?" I manage to say. "Only an A minus?"

Meena punches me in the shoulder with her small fist. *"Très mal!"* she laughs.

Renzo holds up his hand and I high five him. "Yo, dog," he says, "missed you yesterday, man. But now the three musketeers are back together."

I look at my two best friends and then up at the big sign with red letters posted prominently next to the entrance door. It's only one of a bunch of signs just like it all over RHS.

NED, the letters read.

The picture under those letters is of an ancient cell phone, vintage 2000, with a red slash across it.

No Electronic Devices. That includes every kind of handheld, earplug-connected, personal communication apparatus you can name. No cell phones. No Blackberries. No iPods. *Nada.*

I am grateful for that sign.

It's not just because it is a necessary restriction. You can bet that every teenager here would be expending every bit of time they could get away with engrossed in whatever form of instant messaging they can access. But I also like the electronic device restriction because my own inability to use them goes less noticed.

Meena and Renzo are totally clued in to all of that. They are talking about it right now. A foreign tongue as far as I'm concerned.

"You like that YouTube clip I forwarded?" Renzo asks. "Got that song from this Bosnian girl I friended at MySpace."

"It was very funny. But MySpace is so over," Meena says with a tragic sigh. "It is all Facebook now."

"Maybe, but Craig's List is still the place to go for musicians," Renzo insists.

"Yes, and for male prostitutes," Meena adds, raising one eyebrow as she says it.

Renzo is so shocked for a minute that he is speechless.

Meena's remark was so quick—and so outrageous—that it surprised us both. If her father ever heard her make a remark like that she'd probably be on the first plane back to Karachi.

I hold up my hand. "Girl, you didn't just say that?"

Meena lowers her head and turns her eyes up to look at me. It makes my heart throb when she does that.

"Just kidding," she says in a soft voice.

"Okay," I reply. I'm still feeling off balance. Moments like this, when Meena is so darn American, so at ease and sure of herself, make me forget that her future life is all planned for her. It's as if she has no thought of the future that's in store for her. It makes me want to be with her—to, yeah, rescue her like some hero in a corny film, pick her up and carry her out of the restricted role ahead of her while the crowd cheers.

Renzo, who is totally unaware of the self-indulgent flight of cinematic fancy I've been experiencing, still looks hurt. Meena puts a hand on his forearm.

"Lorenzo"—she's totally sincere—"I am so sorry. Sometime,

truly, I would really love to hear one of the songs you are writing."

Renzo's face brightens like a hillside touched by the morning sun.

Did I mention that my best buddy spends much of his spare time in school in the music room? He is super tight with Mr. Redbetter, the band director. Renzo plays bass, stand-up, and electric. He's been writing songs that are a blend of emo, new country, and Seattle grunge. He has serious aspirations about putting together a band.

He wants me to be part of it.

In an unguarded moment last spring I told him that my Dad loved music and even used to play folk guitar.

Mistake number one.

"You play?" he asked. The tone in his voice was so eager that I had to tell the truth.

"A little," I admitted.

Mistake number two.

Mistake number three had been letting him steer me into the band room.

Renzo had then carefully lifted Mr. Redbetter's Hummingbird out of its case. A measure of how much he was trusted. That guitar was at least twice as old as both of us put together. No one but the most serious music students were allowed to even touch it.

"Sit," Renzo said.

I sat.

Then he lowered the guitar into my hands.

"Show me."

It was a very good guitar. I felt it speak to me as I tuned it, the light echo of the harmonics reverberated deep in my bones. With my first fingertip strum across its strings I closed my eyes.

Ahh.

I leaned into it, not playing it so much as listening to what it had to say, letting the music take me wherever it wanted to go. And as it sometimes happens, I lost track of time and space.

When I stopped and opened my eyes, Renzo was sitting on the ground in front of me. His right hand was cupping his chin and his mouth was open.

"A little?" he said. "Are you kidding me?"

"Thanks," I said, handing him back the guitar.

I'd waited as he reverently put it back into the hardshell case, snapping shut the middle latch then each of the other two in turn. I hoped that would be the end to it. But it wasn't.

He took a deep breath.

"Dude, if you don't agree to be my lead guitarist I am going to kill myself."

"Thanks," I said again.

But I hadn't been agreeing to anything. And every time since then when he's brought it up all I've said in reply is that one, polite, noncommittal word.

Thanks.

Why?

Because it is not at all me. Totally not.

It goes back to what I said at the beginning about not being able to wear a watch. To why out of every kid in RHS, probably every teenager in the world, I am the only one who never uses any of those twenty-first century electronic communication tools. I can't. If I pick one up, not only does it feel like I'm holding a red-hot rock, it just plain doesn't work.

Which is why I can never go into the school computer lab. If I need something off the Internet, I rely on Renzo or Meena to get it for me. Put my hands on any computer, screen goes dead. No e-mail, IMs, or online porn for Lucas.

No big loss.

Music, though. That's one thing I regret.

I tried once to play an electric guitar in a big box store. It was plugged in so that anyone could try it. Smoke came out of the pickup and it probably would have burst into flame if I hadn't put it down right away. My hand over my pulsing left wrist, I walked away without looking back.

And that is why I can never be the plugged-in lead guitarist in Renzo's mythical band. Also why when he made that comment about my being the top dog now at our school, I could only mentally shake my head.

I am everything that is not cool. I am so unwith it that the best thing I can be is invisible. I am antipodal to being top dog. It is so not me.

Meena and Renzo wait outside as I go into the attendance office. I hand over the note I have perfectly forged in my father's handwriting. "Luke was suffering from a migraine." It's accepted, no questions asked. Apparently I was wrong about Dr. Kesselring contacting the school.

As we start down the hall toward our lockers, Renzo turns to me. "Luke," he says, "we got ten minutes before the bell. Could I get you to back me up on my new song?" There's a mischievous sparkle in his eyes as he asks. The creep knows that I've never let on to Meena about my guitar playing.

"Lucas," Meena says, "you play guitar? Why have you never told me?" There's a look on her face that is almost worshipful. "I love the instrument."

"I'm not that good," I lie.

"Busted." Renzo chuckles. "He's that good and better."

Both of them are looking at me. Meena taps a locker with the knuckles of both of her hands. "You show me now, right?"

I look up at the hall clock. As Renzo pointed out, there's still ten minutes to go before the bell rings. I can't use that as an excuse. The music room is just down the hall. I lift up my hands in a gesture of surrender.

Meena grabs my sleeve. "We go, now!"

I let her pull me, Renzo following behind with a grin on his face as wide as a crocodile's jaws.

Ask her now, he mouths at me, then holds his hands out as if holding a motorcycle's handlebars.

Do I want to hit him right now or hug him? Meena links her arm in mine, drawing me even closer to her. I can't feel my feet touching the floor as I walk. Her presence so close is making me dizzy. I'm not sure I'll even be able to play a C chord.

It's as if time and space don't exist. I don't remember Renzo handing me the Hummingbird or even sitting down. But the guitar is in my hands and I'm playing it, Renzo's bass keeping a beat as solid as that being added by the drums. I'm being careful not to touch his amp, so there's no interference.

And who is playing the drums? Another one of the surprises this day had in store for me. Meena! She's not a pro on percussion, the way Renzo is with his easy, even weave of notes. But she's not bad and she has a feel for the new song that Renzo handed us and is now singing.

> *Got up today*
> *going to take a chance*
> *walk up to that girl*
> *and ask her to dance . . .*

Meena actually has her own drum set at home. A present from

her father, she told us as she sat down, picked up the drumsticks, gave them a little twirl, and then played paradiddles on the snare. So much for my preconceptions about Muslim households. Her foot thuds the bass pedal in a solid double beat. She lifts her head and tosses back her hair.

"Go for it, boy," she shouts.

Renzo reaches the bridge, nods at me.

> *It's my day, it's my day*
> *Let my dreams carry us away*

My own deep voice isn't much, nowhere near what I can do with my fingers on the strings, but I join in. And so does Meena. Her voice is a sweet, pure soprano that weaves in with my bass and Renzo's tenor lead.

> *It's my day, it's my day*
> *Let my dreams carry us away*

There's a whole different smile on her face now as her breath and mine and that of my best friend join together and I'm lifted up out of all my usual gloom and despair like a hawk rising on wide wings. For a moment my dreams really do carry us away.

7

THE SUNGLASS MAFIA

I drift out of the music room not sure how I feel. Did I really finally ask Meena to take a ride on my motorcycle with me today? Did she really agree, her face lighting up like a spotlight? My arm still feels warm from her squeezing it as she leaned forward to whisper, "It is going to be such fun!"

This day has already been more confusing than any other day I've ever spent in school and it's just started. Big as I am, I've always managed to pretty much go unnoticed before today. Making myself anonymous has been my main modus operandi.

Then something happens that really unsettles me. I turn a corner and almost run head-on into a six-foot-nine roadblock who makes the football team's all-state tight end look little. I'm shaken not just because I didn't smell or even hear him, meaning he has taken me totally by surprise. It is also what he says—which makes me realize he was listening outside the music room while I was jamming with Renzo and Meena (who, it being a B day, have both headed off in opposite directions to classes we don't share). His name, if I overheard it right, is Vlad.

"*Klassni bend*," Vlad intones.

His voice is so deep it sounds as if it is coming from a well. "Like Kino," he says. Then he walks past me, his face so expressionless behind his shades that I almost wonder if I actually did hear him just say that our band was *klassni*, cool. No, I did hear it. After all, he compared us with Kino with that parting remark. Kino was a legendary rock group in Russia. Part of the Leningrad music scene, where the late great king of angst-filled music was Viktor Tsoi, Kino's lead singer and writer. Russia's Kurt Cobain.

I'm probably the only non-Russian kid in this school who would understand that reference—or the Russian Vlad just spoke. Which makes me wonder how much Vlad knows about me and if that remark was not just meant as a compliment but something else. Kind of a veiled threat. *We know who you really are.*

"We" being that tight clique of kids I mentioned before, the seven Russian juniors and seniors known as the Sunglass Mafia. Their "Sunglass Mafia" nickname—a moniker that no one ever speaks to their faces—comes from that rumor about their family connections and the indisputable fact that they all wear wraparound sunglasses, even in school. For some reason, the teachers never make them take them off, even though sunglasses are generally not tolerated.

Vlad and his *patsans*, his homeys, are all upper class, in more ways than one. Their parents—though no one has ever seen them—came here at the same time as everyone else in the flood of overseas corporate vultures who'd been informed that our county was ripe for the taking. The business the Russians took over, on the opposite side of town from the giant Maxico complex, used to be a small manufacturing plant that made pickup parts for GM. Now it's been retooled to produce some kind of green technology having to do with solar power. Boring, and not at all top-secret like Maxico, which has been described in the press releases as doing cutting edge research in the field of gene-splicing and nano-biotech, whatever that is. Aside from those who work there, only Dr. Kesselring and his closest cronies, such as Chief Frank and the rent-a-cops, are allowed inside the high-fenced Maxico compound. Kesselring even has an office there and is the public face of the company, what with the real CEO Rogan Machescou's lack of public appearances.

At any rate, the Russians are here and they are not about to uninvade. Business, especially from the looks of the Sunglass Mafia teens, is too good! They've got the best clothes. Every label they wear is the most expensive. Top of the line. Casual High Couture. And they wear those threads with super style. They're not built square and blocky like I am. They're all tall, slender, pale-skinned. Their sharp-featured faces are positively classic—like those of runway models. Any one of them would be right at home on the fashion pages.

They all have eastern European names and speak perfect English with a slight accent. Yuri. Boris. Ekaterina. Marina. Igor. Natasha. And vulturelike Vlad, the music-lover. They arrive at school every day in two oversized Land Rovers with tinted windows. I've heard it whispered that the factory where their parents work is not actually green at all, but that's just a front. It's actually involved with black market dealings in things like new designer drugs. Of course that's the kind of rumor you'd expect in a high school, where more imagination is expended in fantasizing than you'll ever find applied to any assignment from a teacher.

The real explanation is probably less fantastic. Since the end of the Soviet Union, there's a whole class of cutthroat entrepreneurs that have risen in Russia like the old robber barons of nineteenth century America. Fabulous sums of wealth have been accumulated from oil and gas and control of various aspects of the so-called new democracy. And now Putin, who is Russia's new czar in everything but name, is engaged in a power struggle between his political aims and those new merchant princes to the point where some of them, rightly or wrongly, have been jailed for corruption. So getting out of Dodge, taking their wealth, and moving to America, where the dollar is worth less than the ruble these days, may seem like a smart move for some of those new billionaires.

How do I know all this about Russia, including pop music trivia? It's because even when I seem to be just staring out the window at the distant woods where I'd rather be, I can't help listening to what the history teacher is saying about current geopolitical events. Whenever I do watch TV, it's always the History Channel that keeps me glued to the screen. And whenever I hear something, as you may recall, I don't forget it. Even when it's something I'd rather forget. And I remember the facts in every book my father or Uncle Cal ever gave me to read, and every conversation they had with me—conversations that got even more detailed as I got older and they realized what an information sponge I am. Like they were training me for something.

Vlad's not the only member of the Sunglass Mafia who seems to be lurking around me today. Every time I look up, or turn my head because I think someone is watching me, it's always one of them. As I'm going into world history class it's Boris, casually leaning with his back against the wall in the hallway. In the lunch room it's Ekaterina, pretending to drink from the water fountain. In the library it's Marina, looking over the top of the book she can't seem to stop reading, even though I'm sure that she's been assigned surveillance on me. The poems of Anna Ahkmatova, whose work was banned in Stalinist Russia, but who refused to emigrate, staying as a witness to all the awful things that happened then.

Ahkmatova was my mom's favorite Russian poet. She would sometimes recite from memory lines like those that come now to my mind. They're from a poem written after Ahkmatova's husband was shot for his supposed role in an antigovernment conspiracy:

> *Terror touches all things in darkness,*
> *Leads those lit by the moon to the axe.*
> *An ominous knock comes from behind the wall:*
> *Is it ghost, a thief, a rat . . .*

Ahkmatova. I'm feeling a weird sort of kinship with Marina because she's reading that book, clearly engrossed by it. I almost get up and walk over. But then she does what every member of her clique has done all day. When they see me catching sight of them, they don't turn away. No—smiles come over their faces. Interested smiles. The kind of smiles you see on the faces of cats when they notice an unsuspecting mouse. Arched eyebrows. Ah?

That smile on Marina's face is so cold, so uninviting it sends a shiver down my back. It makes the hair rise up on the nape of my neck and a low growl start deep in my chest. When the bell rings I go out the door farthest from where she's still sitting, her face buried again in the book of poetry.

Thinking of poetry, I'm pretty sure I know what classical English poem Uncle Cal would have started reciting if he'd seen Marina. *"La Belle Dame Sans Merci."*

I don't like being watched. No, more than that. I hate being watched. It goes against everything I've been taught by my dad about evading surveillance, and every instinctive feeling within me.

This has got to stop!

The day drags on like it's never going to end. I'm so nervous it is wearing me out. I manage to keep up a facade of normalcy with Meena and Renzo, pretend to pay attention in class. But everywhere I go, I catch sight of one of the Russians keeping watch on me.

The only time that I see one of them who's not watching me freaks me out as much as being the object of their attention because of what happens. As I start to leave the library, I can see through the window one of the Sunglass Mafia standing with his back to me across the hall.

It's Yuri. He's just outside the doorway of a classroom, staring into it. It's the classroom where Mr. Gretz, the football coach, teaches American history. I've never taken a class from him. I make it a point to avoid classes taught by coaches, who have a tendency to try to recruit athletic-looking students for their teams. But I know a little about Gretz because he's an American Indian nut. His whole room is filled with Native artifacts and art and none of it is cheap tourist junk. He has a good eye and every item—from the Zuni kachinas and Iroquois baskets on the shelves to his prize possession that hangs on the wall, a Navajo Two Hills rug—is a real collector's item.

The rug is what Yuri is looking at.

It's between periods and Mr. Gretz is alone in the classroom, writing at his desk. Yuri snaps his fingers. Mr. Gretz looks up.

"Can I help you, young man?" Gretz says.

Yuri points at the rug, lazily hooks his index finger.

There's a moment of hesitation. Then Mr. Gretz puts down his pen, stands up, and walks over to the wall. He unhooks the rug, rolls it up, and carries it to the doorway. As if nothing unusual has just happened, Mr. Gretz returns to his desk, picks up his pen, and resumes his writing.

The rug over his shoulder, Yuri turns and sees me watching.

He pats the rug with one hand. *"Klass,"* he says. Cool. Then he walks away with it.

When the last bell of the day rings, I've made up my mind.

I see Meena coming down the hall toward me. She's all excited. And I would be now, too, if it wasn't for the way the hairs on the back of my neck have been standing up every time I catch sight of one of the Sunglass Mafia surveilling me like Igor is doing right now from the door of the computer lab.

"Luke—" Meena starts to say, her hand held out as if to take mine.

I hold up both my hands in front of me, maybe a little too quick.

She stops short, reading my face as much as that gesture.

"I'm sorry," I say, talking faster than I mean to. "Something has come up. Can you take a rain check on that ride? Tomorrow, maybe."

She just looks at me, the disappointment so clear in her expression that I feel lower than a worm's belly.

"Sorry," I say again. I turn and dive into the tidal wave of kids jostling toward the doors to the parking lots and buses. Two quick turns and I'm in a deserted hallway, then at the door onto the empty athletic field. My Commando stays parked in the front end of the lot by the school. I'll pick it up later—after dark when the safety of the night is spread over me like a comforting blanket. But for now it will be a decoy for anyone waiting for me, friend or possible foe. But not Meena.

Meena. I can't stop to think about her right now. I need to stay focused on my escape plan.

It's half an hour before any coaches or athletes will be working out. No one is around to see me cross the field. So I sprint—fast enough to break a few school track records, no doubt. It only takes the space of a few heartbeats for me to reach the safety of the narrow strip of forest that connect to the larger woods edging the town park. My breath becomes calmer, though my speed is no slower as I reach the safety of the old spreading oaks, the tall beeches, and friendly maples. Maybe some circling bird sees me, like that broadwing hawk up in the sky, but I doubt any human eyes follow my progress.

I don't go home. The thought of finding Dad drunk or stoned is more than I can bear right now. I sit down with my back against one of my favorite trees in the park, an old oak tree, and wait until dark. Then I wait longer. Finally, when I hear the distant bell of the Protestant church in town chime eleven, I figure it is late enough and I run the two miles back to the school. The Sunglass Mafia seems to have split. Their vehicles are gone. Aside from my bike and a school bus, the lot is empty. For a moment, as I start my bike, I think I see something moving over in the direction of the unfinished swimming and diving complex at the far end of the school. I look and listen, lift up my head to smell the air. No new sounds. No fresh scents. Just my imagination.

Dad's door is shut—as it often is at the end of the day, even when it is hours before midnight as it is now. He sleeps a lot. I guess it's a sign of depression. But at least there's still no smell of booze or pot in the air.

Sleep. That has to be the major thing on my mind right now. I need rest.

I go into my room, kick off my shoes, and sprawl on my side, half-curled up like a big dog. The moon is shining in on me through my one small window. As I listen to the steady sound of Dad's breathing from the other side of the thin wall, I think of the other things about the members of the Sunglass Mafia that bother me.

There's the fact that despite my unusually keen hearing, I've never overheard them have any substantive conversations with each other. They aren't mute. They talk in classes, voice a cursory "excuse me" on the rare occasions when someone bumps into them in the crowded halls. They utter polite, perfectly phrased greetings to any teachers or other adults they may encounter. Model student citizens of RHS. That's how the clueless adults all see them.

But when the members of the Sunglass Mafia are together they don't usually say much to each other the way most kids our age do. In Russian or English. I've picked up on their slang, which isn't that hard to understand if you know Russian well enough. But their most significant intergroup communications seem to consist of just looking at each other. And what was it that just happened today between Yuri and Mr. Gretz? The hackles rise on the back of my neck as I think back on it.

Another thing about them is the one that really bothers me. The girls wear what I know have to be the most expensive perfumes. The guys use high-class cologne. Aside from not sensing Vlad earlier today, I can usually smell them all a mile away. Literally. But underneath those masking odors, my sensitive nose doesn't pick up the usual perspiration and natural skin oils that give every individual a unique smell. Aside from signature artificial fragrances, the dozen members of the Sunglass Mafia all smell the same. It's an ancient, almost musty scent.

Like what? It comes to me just as I close my eyes and drift off to sleep. It was like the odor coming off an Egyptian mummy I saw once in a museum. Like old, dry death.

THE DRAKE HOUSE

The same moon that shone down on me as I lay on my bed illuminates the old abandoned building at the base of the hill. It's the Drake House. The Drake House is on the other side of the woods, a good five miles from our trailer. I've never gone into it. I'm not even certain what it was that drew me out of my bed to come here tonight. Restlessness? The need to do something, even if it was only to run through the night? Was it just that the woods called to me and I couldn't resist? It's strange. I can't even recall how long it took me to get here. But I'm back now, wondering what led me to this abandoned mansion.

You know how you instinctively avoid something that smells rotten? You may not even know you're doing it, but you shy away. It was like that the only other time I came close to it. It was three months ago. I was chasing a deer. Wherever it ran, I'd stayed close behind, across the lowland cedar swamp and then uphill through the tall hemlocks. My feet striking the earth in rhythm with my heartbeat, the link between myself and that graceful game animal was as ancient as that of the first hunter and his prey. The deer was tiring, but I wasn't. I was almost close enough to touch its flank. I'm not sure what I would have done if I'd actually caught up to it. I never found out.

The deer leaped high and dived through a thicket of honeysuckle. I followed . . . and emerged at the edge of the field above the Drake House. The sight of it froze me. I'd heard about the place, the haunted mansion that people avoid. Even teenagers looking for somewhere to have beer parties stayed away from it. When I saw it I understood why. I was a hundred yards away and I didn't want to get any closer. It fascinated and repelled me at the same time. It wasn't the old building's smell. It was something other than odor. Something that alerted a sense other than smell or taste or touch. *Stay away.*

The big house looms up like some stereotypical haunted mansion out of Transylvania or an old horror movie. It's not all falling down, like you might expect an old uninhabited place out in the middle of nowhere to be, but it is totally disused. I know that because something about it made me so curious that I did some research in the archive room of the local library. The Drakes, it seems, were a strange standoffish clan who first came to the country and built the mansion over a century ago. No one knew where their money came from. They never bothered anyone, but they also never made friends. They all died or moved away before I was born. Aside from the fields being cut for hay on a regular basis by a farmer who lives several miles away, no one has worked the property there since then. It's still owned by someone who pays the taxes on the property. But no one at the county clerk's office could say for sure who that was because the checks come from an out-of-state lawyer. That same lawyer is the one who pays the farmer for the mowing as well as a handyman who comes here now and then to see if anything needs repairing like a broken window. The road leading up to the Drake House is the most visible sign of how avoided this place is by the locals. Its pavement is cracked by neglect, pierced by grass and sumac and fire cherry saplings that protrude like spears thrust into the body of a dying giant snake.

In a way, there's nothing unusual about the Drake House being unoccupied. There's a lot of empty farms around here now, as well as stripped storefronts and abandoned houses in the town itself. Over the last few years, jobs in this part of the state have melted away like snow struck by the rising sun. No more making anything in America—unless it is money or stock derivatives or bad loans. I don't understand it all that well and I know I'm digressing, but I find myself thinking about all that right now. It's probably because before Mom died, Dad used to gripe about that stuff.

"All we export now is bad debt, weapons, war, and fantasy," he'd say. "A million ways to die."

"To-mas," she'd say to him, speaking his name gently.

To-mas is the Abenaki way of saying Thomas. I loved the way she did that—softly saying his name or mine the Indian way. To-mas. Loo-kas. Just our names—but something in her tone always made me feel as if things were going to be all right.

"But look at me," Dad would say, his fists clenched. "I'm part of it. Letting them use my . . . abilities. Like an attack dog."

When Dad got like that she'd have to say his name a second time, "To-mas" even softer than before. That would usually do it. He'd lower his arms, let his shoulders relax, sit back down as she rested her hand on his back, kind of like a horse trainer calming a high-strung stallion.

I study the house from behind this big old broken-trunked skeleton of an elm tree. It's a last remnant of the giant trees that I've been told used to grow all around here. Killed by Dutch elm, yet another disease brought from Europe. I've never seen a healthy full-grown elm, but Dad said they looked like green fountains of life.

It's night, but the light of the moon overhead is bright. I can see the countless grooves cut into the wood of the tree. Circles and swirls, crossing lines, intricate curlicues where beetle grubs bored under the bark that finally flaked away, leaving the ruined tree standing like an obelisk placed by some vanished culture. The beetles' bore marks look like Mayan hieroglyphs. Which is how my life seems to me lately—written in an indecipherable script, a purposeless tale told in a tongue I can't understand.

I didn't enter the Drake House before. But tonight I have to go inside. There's something in there that I need. Desperately. If I can just find it, it can help me make sense of it all.

It takes no more than a few heartbeats for me to lope up the abandoned driveway to the front door. It's locked, but I don't pause. I sense that all it will take is a quick shove of my shoulder. I thrust against it. The frame cracks, then splits with a loud *thwack!* The door flies open, splinters of wood spinning through the air as I stagger into the room. Dust swirls up from my feet. Weak moonlight streams in through a huge round window at the head of the stairs at the back of this big, cavernous entrance hall.

The shapes of furniture covered with dusty blankets look like robed figures, witches or warlocks bent over in some eldritch ritual. But aside from me and the swirling dust, nothing else is moving in the dead air.

Why am I being so reckless? Breaking and entering like this? I don't know. I don't care. There's no logic to what I'm doing. I just knew that I had to get inside.

I stand here, panting, panting. It's not because I'm tired. It's the adrenaline surging through me. I feel as if there's a red-hot poker being held against my left wrist, where my birthmark is now glowing as if it was made of burning coals.

"Where is it?" I growl those words as much as I shout them. My head is lifted up toward the ceiling, my eyes are closed. My fists are clenched so hard that my long fingernails are digging into my palms and drawing blood.

"Where," I howl again.

A breathless voice answers me. Breathless as in there's no breath, no real life it in. The voice is cold as the stone of a dead star. It hurts, deep in my bones, to hear it, to feel it. I feel the way a glass must feel before it bursts into a shower of splinters.

NO.

That is, more or less, what that voice just said. More . . . or less. It's not the normal *no* you'd get when you ask a question. It's deeper, more antediluvian. It is a total negation of everything—of possibility, of success, of life itself.

I can go no farther.

A thing I've never seen or imagined before materializes in front of me. It's shaped itself from the dust, risen and gathered from the darkness itself. It looms over me. Twice my height, it's hunch-shouldered with muscle like a bull or a giant bear. But it's not covered with hair like one of those creatures. Its skin is bare, corpselike in its paleness. Though its shape is like that of a large man—with incredibly long arms and short squat legs that seem built more for leaping than walking—it is far from human. Its eyes are unblinking as it looks down. It doesn't stare at me. It stares into me. Those huge round eyes are as green as foxfire, aglow with malevolent light. It opens its mouth, baring sharp teeth that can only serve one purpose.

Grue, I think, somehow knowing its name.

I know, too, that there has to be some way to fight it.

But I cannot move. I'm as rooted to the floor as that old dead elm was to the soil. Its eyes have hypnotized me like a bird being stared down by a snake. One long reptilian arm reaches out. A single grooved talon on the end of its little finger flicks the center of my forehead and then withdraws. I feel blood begin to flow down between my eyes from the small cut it made. I watch helplessly as it lifts its talon, allows a drop of my blood to fall on its outstretched tongue. The grin on the creature's face broadens.

First taste good.

It leans closer. Its fetid breath is on my cheek. I have to do something. Now. I summon up every bit of internal strength I can find. I close my eyes, freeing myself from its mesmeric gaze. Then I try to hurl myself backward to escape.

Too late.

A powerful hand has just wrapped itself in an iron grip around my pulsing left wrist.

SAFE FOR NOW

The grip is too strong for me to break. I strike out with my right fist. It, too, is caught by a powerful hand. I snarl, twist my body, the blankets wrapping around my legs.

"Luke. Luke!"

I open my eyes. My father is leaning over me, holding me down.

"Son," he says. "You're safe for now."

Safe for now. Even in the confusion of waking up from what has to have been the worst nightmare I've ever had, I know there's something strange about his choice of words and how he just said them.

He didn't say, "Wake up, it was just a dream."

He said, "You're safe for now."

For now.

He lets go of my arms, steps back, and sits on the edge of my bed. I sit up, untangle the blankets, and swing my legs to the floor so that I'm sitting next to him. I look around. The nightstand next to my bed is in splinters. My chair is broken. The clock radio has been hurled against the wall and is nothing but a pathetic pile of fractured plastic, wires, and circuit boards. I've torn my sheets into shreds and there's a line of holes in the wall next to my bed where I must have thrown my knees or elbows. The only place I seem to not have touched is the ceiling.

"Holy crap," I whisper.

"Holy crap, indeed," Dad says. "If I hadn't grabbed you, you'd've reduced this trailer to a pile of rubbish. More of a pile of rubbish than it already is."

Then my father smiles. It's been a long time since I've seen him smile like that. I smile back. The fact that he's here for me like this and not lost in his usual mist of sorrow and loss makes me smile even broader.

"I'm sorry I wrecked the room, Dad."

He puts his hand on my head like he used to do when I was a little kid. He strokes my hair back.

God, I love it when he does that. If I had a tail, I'd wag it.

"It's okay, Son. Nothing here we can't replace for a buck ninety-nine at Walmarts—except for you."

We sit there without saying a word. His arm is around my shoulders and I'm leaning against him. I can hear the steady, slow beat of his heart. When I was a kid I thought that my father was the strongest person in the world. Nothing could beat him. I'd always be safe when he was with me and Mom. That is almost how I'm feeling now.

Almost.

I sigh.

"Want to talk about it?" Dad says.

"The dream I just had?"

"Whatever."

Whatever.

Dad's always been a man of few words, words always carefully chosen. Anything I want to share with him, he's going to listen to it. Really listen. He's ready to help in whatever way he can.

It's the kind of opening he hadn't given me even once since Mom's death. Should I tell him everything that's bugging me?

Where would I start? With being hopelessly in love with a girl whose parents and their culture are light years farther away than the Capulets were from the Montagues? With this strange feeling that there's something terribly wrong with me, something missing from my life that keeps me from ever being whole? With the fact that lately—and the realization hits me like a rock striking the middle of my forehead—lately I've been afraid of myself. Afraid of what I might do.

I've read some about the meaning of dreams. Freud and Adler and Jung. Those guys. Was that bloodthirsty, drooling monster a virtual manifestation of my own out-of-control animal nature? Or an archetype? Not a creature threatening me from outside but the beast within?

Dad might be ready to listen to me. But am I ready to share, especially when I can't understand it? Any of it.

I sit there without saying anything. Dad feels how I've stiffened up. He takes his arm from around my shoulders, leans back. He pulls up his legs into a lotus position and turns so he's sitting on the bed and looking at me. He's comfortable like that. I used to see him stay in that pose for an hour or more, meditating. He used to spend a lot of time in South Asia and some of it was spent studying yoga with real masters. Having had that training, having learned that sort of discipline, how could he have fallen into such self-pity? How could he have decided to self-medicate with drugs and alcohol like he's been doing? But now, just like that, it's as if he's come back to himself.

I wonder if it's real. But I find myself relaxing again, seeing him like that. Some of what I've been going through lately has been about his being here but not here, present in body but markedly AWOL in spirit.

"So, my dear son, what can you tell your father about what has just happened?"

I couldn't help laughing. His intonation and accent are a caricature of those of a person from India. It's the phony guru voice he always used to use to make Mom and me break out in giggles. He is good at it, so good that he once called up one of those right-wing radio shows when the host was raving about how Indian and Pakistani immigrants were a danger to the nation. Dad had a ten-minute argument with the man—all in that sing-song accent—before finally dropping back into his own voice and making the man sound like even more of a fool than usual.

"What is wrong, my dear boy? I am only talking in my normal fashion, that of a true American Indian."

I can't help but laugh. I hold my hand up. "I surrender," I say. "Part of it is about a girl at school. I like her, but I'm just not sure what to do."

"What's her name?"

"Her name is Meena. Meena Kureshi."

"Kureshi?" Dad says. Then he pauses. I think I can guess what he might have been about to tell me. It's not just that he and I need to keep a low profile and getting involved with any girl could interfere with that. With all of his knowledge of Southeast Asia, Dad has to understand how hard it would be to get involved with a girl from a Muslim culture. But then he surprises me.

"It's not easy with girls, knowing what to do or say," Dad says.

"Sometimes you just have to do what you think is right. But that dream of yours wasn't about Meena, was it?"

I shake my head. But I don't say anything. That dream was all too real. I'm still not ready to talk about it.

Dad looks out the window. Just far enough away from my bed that I didn't break it.

"Sun's going to be up soon," he says. "Let's hit the deck."

I locate my sweatshirt and jeans—thrown into the next room when I kicked the chair into its constituent parts—pull on my shoes, and follow Dad out to the minuscule plywood platform tacked to the back of the trailer. It's barely big enough for the two of us to sit with our legs hanging off it. Dad hands me one of the two glasses of orange juice he's poured. We sit, facing the east as the sun slowly shows its face, first as a faint promise of light above the trees, then as a great glowing ball of life.

"There's always a new day," Dad says.

"You really think that?" I ask.

Dad looks at me.

"My turn to say I'm sorry," he says. "It's just been hard."

"Okay."

We sit a little longer. I'm going to have to get ready to head off to RHS. Maybe it'll be better today. Then again, maybe I should just blow off school today and spend the time with Dad. The mood he's in now, I think he'd be cool with it.

Dad's looking at my face. There's something more he wants to say.

"What?"

He hesitates. I can see from the subtle change to the set of his jaw that whatever it was, he's decided this is not the time to tell me about it. There's the same reticence in him to reveal something that I was just experiencing back in the trailer.

"That was some . . . dream, eh?" he says.

"Uh-huh."

"So what did the grue look like?"

"What?" I haven't said one word yet about my dream, or even mentioned that there was a monster in it.

Dad realizes he's made a mistake. He drops the hand that he was just lifting toward my forehead and looks off to the side.

"Wasn't that what you said before you woke up? You were talking in your sleep about it. I'm pretty certain that I think you said 'grue' or something like that. Or maybe I was wrong."

Now I know Dad isn't being straight with me. That's about three times as many words as he'd normally use. The lump in my stomach is back.

I gulp the last of my juice. "Gotta get ready for school," I say. "English test today."

"Okay," Dad says. Dropping the subject like nothing just happened.

He takes my empty glass, gets up, and goes into the trailer, trying to act normal.

I follow him in, playing a similar part. I can sense that no matter what I might say, I'm not going to get anything meaningful out of him now.

"Have a good day," he says, not looking at me, busy with washing the two tumblers.

"Right."

I turn sideways to get past him through the mini-kitchen and squeeze into the bathroom. Gotta get rid of the stubble before I split. RHS has a strict policy about facial hair on guys. No 'staches or beards, not even a soul patch. I have more facial hair than most guys in their teens and need to shave every morning. If I laid off the Norelco for a week I'd have a full Prince Albert.

I close the door, lean toward the mirror. And freeze. Just above my eyes, a line of dark dried blood has caked over the razor-thin slash in my forehead.

LATE

I'm only five minutes late when I rumble onto the school lot, but it might as well be an hour. I toss my head and then push my hair back out of my eyes. As usual, going forty has tangled my hair up some. But my thatch is so thick that all I ever need to do is run my fingers back through it to get it to fall back into place. There's no helmet law in this state. I wear one if I'm on a long ride, but I always skip it for the few miles between the trailer and RHS. Yeah, I know most accidents happen near home. But you can't carry a helmet into school and the first time I left my helmet strapped to the Norton someone ripped it off and I had to buy a new bonnet.

The buses are all empty and parked in the big lot to the left of the school. No one is outside. All of the doors of RHS are already closed and locked—the usual routine since all the school invasions and shootings that have taken place around the country over the last decade.

I wonder for a moment what it must have been like when my

dad and mom went to school. No metal detectors, no uniformed policemen in the hallways, no worrying about whether or not one of your classmates is going to go postal and try to blow up the place. It has to have been a better time.

I trudge up to the main entrance, study my reflection for a moment in the opaque glass. Now that I've washed away the blood, the thin cut in the center of my forehead is almost invisible. I heal fast. Maybe no one will notice.

Maybe I can forget about it all, about the dream that was more real than any dream I've ever had before. Maybe pigs will grow wings and fly.

I press the button to the right of the door and lean toward the weather-beaten plastic intercom.

"Yes?" a bored, unfriendly voice asks. It's not only the same kind of speaker system, it's pretty much the same voice and tone you hear when you drive up to the outdoor menu board at Taco Prince.

I resist the impulse to tell the disembodied presence that I'd like two large burritos and chips.

"Late student," I say. "Overslept," I add, as if they cared.

"Name?"

"King. Lucas." I recite the number and location of my homeroom and my homeroom teacher's name. Then I wait, counting under my breath. This time I get to five before . . .

BRRRRRP.

I obey the buzzer's implicit order to push against the briefly unlocked door. Mr. Murry, one of the school's burly uniformed guards is waiting for me. As expected. I've seen him often enough before that I'm sure he recognizes me, but the blank expression on his broad face doesn't change. I hand my backpack to him before he can ask me for it. He doesn't change his expression, just passes it back to the adult hall monitor standing behind him with the same economy of motion as a pro quarterback handing off the ball on an end around.

"Arms out."

"Yes, sir."

No irony in my voice, even though I'm sighing internally about having to go through this little charade yet again. If I was emotionally damaged enough and mentally desperate enough to want to do serious harm to the people and property of RHS, I'd sure as hell have a better plan than arriving late and going through this solo scrutiny.

He wands me as I execute a slow pirouette.

"Machine."

"Yes, sir."

I pass through the red-lit metal detection unit at the required measured pace of a condemned man accepting his fate.

Mr. Murry hands me my thoroughly inspected unzipped backpack.

"Thank you, sir."

"Office," he says.

"I know."

The expression on Mr. Murry's face changes a little and he surprises me.

"King," he says, "You're a good kid. Always polite. Never mouth off. Why put yourself through this?"

I meet his eyes for just a moment. I'm not only surprised at what I see there but also shocked that there's a similar expression on the face of the adult hall monitor standing behind him. Real concern. As if for some reason they actually like me.

It moves me and worries me at the same time. Part of me wants to start blabbing about how confused things are now, how my life is in the spin cycle and I don't know what I'm doing or feeling most of the time. But a bigger part of me is close to panic. I don't want to attract attention by being either liked or disliked. I want to stay under the radar. I don't know why, but somehow I do know it's the only way I can survive.

I stay inside my shell.

"Thank you, sir," I say. "I'll try to do better."

I turn, take four quick steps down the hall, and escape through the door into the main office. There, at least, no one makes a big deal about me. I sign the late sheet, get assigned detention. Only the fourth time this month, so I don't have to have a "little talk" with the AP yet. Just being tardy is no big deal here in the larger scheme of things. The school's official "three strikes and you're out" policy is for more serious offenses—like fighting or insubordination. And fighting or talking back to teachers are two things as far from my mind as the earth is from the moon.

It's an A day, so English is my first class. When I land there, Ms. Nye doesn't do anything more than nod in the direction of my desk. Even though I'm fifteen minutes late, she knows that I'm one of the three or four students who can be counted on to do the required reading and answer her questions with complete, logical sentences.

Renzo, whose seat is to my left, raises an eyebrow, but says nothing.

Meena, though, looks daggers at me. "What?" she mouths as I take my seat next to her. Her perfect lips thrust out as she does that.

If I just leaned over I could kiss her.

Control. Got to stop thinking that.

I flash her a thumbs-up. No problem.

She shakes her head and sighs. Hopeless! Then she smiles. A warm flush runs through my whole body. Her smile has enough light in it to kindle a forest fire. She's not upset with me for putting off our motorcycle ride yesterday. It makes me want to burst into blossom or cry or both.

Of course I do neither. Just nod and open to page 48 in *Of Mice and Men*.

By the way, as you may have already guessed, there's no English test today. I lied about that to my father. So sue me.

But I still feel crappy about it. I'm not used to lying to Dad, despite the fact that lying has always come easy to our family.

Prevarication is, you see, an occupational requirement when your father has one of *those* jobs. Lying, from the top down, is the rule. There's a memorial wall in a building in Langley, Virginia. It has over a hundred stars on it now—with plenty of room for more. Each star is for a man or woman who died. A black book bound in Moroccan goatskin sits in a steel frame under the stars. Topped by a thick plate of glass, it shows those same stars, arranged by the year of death. But the names next to those stars and dates are far, far fewer than one hundred. Some of the spaces remain forever empty. What they did for this country was so secret that even after death they could never be acknowledged for doing what they did for their country.

Dad told us a story about a friend of his. Of course he didn't mention his name, even to me and Mom. After his friend died—in circumstances that could not be described and in a country that could not be named—they sent a letter to his wife. The letter was hand-carried by a special messenger who let her hold it long enough to read it. Then he handed her a medal and let her hold it for about the same amount of time. When she'd finished crying, she did what she knew she had to do. She handed the messenger back the letter and the medal. He took them both, expressed his condolences again, and left, knowing she would never tell anyone about the letter or the medal, both of which would be kept in the man's confidential file. All she could share was the cover story that he had been killed overseas in an accident while working as an advisor.

An advisor. That's also how they described the job that Dad used to do. Just "an advisor." That's all Mom or I could even say to anyone whenever we were asked about what Dad did.

"He's an advisor overseas. Doing work as a contract employee. Nothing much. Boring stuff."

How many times have I said something like that to outsiders? Lying by telling a partial truth.

But the rule between me and Dad is one that neither of us ever broke before. Be straight with me and I'll be straight with you. Our golden rule.

Then he lied.

And I lied back.

The English class is still going on. Ms. Nye is talking about compassion, about people taking care of each other. About the final sacrifice made at the end of the book. Was it made out of fear or love?

Can we protect those we love without destroying them?

The knot in my stomach has grown the size of a couple of clenched fists. Why did my father lie to me?

Why won't he help me understand what's happening?

SUMMONS

The simultaneous sound of the bell and the speaker in the class-room pull me out of my pity party.

"Luga Ging board my gnosis."

That's not what it actually said, just what it sounded like. Learning to decipher the esoteric language of the public address system is one of the non-credit requirements of life in any school, juvenile detention center, or prison. That's a highly applicable quote from my dad, who has experienced all three on four different conti-nents. (In telling you that I may be saying too much.)

"Lucas King, report to the main office!"

That's how I interpreted the message blatted over the hall speaker.

As we rise from our seats, Meena pokes me in the side.

"What for?" she asks.

"Capital punishment, most likely," I crack.

Renzo nods sympathetically. "See ya in the next lifetime, bro."

I'm not worried. Aside from this morning's tardiness, my conscience is clear. Like I said before, avoiding trouble has generally been my middle name.

We exchange fist bumps in the hall before I peel off for my rendezvous with destiny as they head down the corridor to the Barf Bar.

Due to the weirdness of school schedules, the lunch period the three of us usually share is about the time that leisurely human beings eat a late breakfast. Depending on how long it takes in the office, I may miss today's luncheon delight—"Sloppy John Does." (What the student body calls the semi hamburger slop on a bun concoction the cooks ladle out to us. The rationale is that Joe was so embarrassed to be associated with it that he sued for the name change.) Alas.

The office of the Crash Helmet (AKA Assistant Principal Nash) is at the far end of the school. But I know a fast way to get there.

RHS is shaped like a snake having convulsions. There was an economic boom in Cumin County several years ago. Banking, high-tech, service industries. RHS being a central school, the nonstop growth meant that it had to absorb more and more students. Rather than build an entire new school complex, RHS began adding one wing and then another . . . and another.

A two-story classroom block, a science wing, a new gym, a larger library. Blueprints drawn up, ground broken for another auditorium. Each unit clicked onto the main building like Lego blocks manipulated by a clueless kid with no particular end in mind. Maybe a house. Maybe a maze for giant rats?

It looked like the boom would go on forever. But it didn't. Turned out there actually was an end to the economic growth. Actually less of an end than a cliff that everything fell off. The nonstop stopped dead.

RHS has over 900 students, but that's a third less than projected. And with the economic woes of the county (problems Doctor Kesselring's corporate-friendly policy has yet to solve) there weren't enough funds to finish the half-completed projects. The Bush Performing Arts Wing and the Reagan Swimming and Diving Center look great from the outside, but they're like Ukrainian painted eggs. Empty painted shells.

I know all of this stuff and more, statistics that would numb you into a coma, because I spent two weeks last spring helping Meena with her research paper, "Our Own Gormenghast: The Building of Our Buildings." Yes, the title was my idea. If you're not a fantasy fiction fan then I need to explain that Gormenghast is an enormous castle, as big as an entire kingdom.

No one knows the ins and outs of the whole of the complex convolutions of Gormenghast. There are forgotten wings, vast secret rooms, dark hidden passageways that even those who know seldom dare to enter. You can accuse me of hyperbole in my comparison. But the point that our high school is big and confusing is valid. Every new student is given a map and still ends up getting lost.

Unless they have a sense of direction like mine. I know all the shortcuts from one place to another—including this one that leads me across the half-constructed stage of the empty performing arts wing, through the back of the music department, across this roof, down a trapdoor into the half-completed auditorium, then emerges in the hallway across from the biology lab.

This particular route entails my going through a few doors meant to stay locked. But I sniffed out the places where the janitors hid their spare keys during my first week at RHS two years ago. It also means going through a few dark places—the wiring never having been installed—that most couldn't navigate without a flashlight. Such as where I'm heading now. But I've always been able to see in the dark—like a cat, I guess.

I'm halfway across the slightly dusty concrete floor of the darkened diving area, next to the deep end of the empty pool where the bolts and bars that would have held the boards and the platform jut up from the floor. I stop. I've heard something. Seen something. Smelled something.

The faint mark of a footprint in the concrete dust ahead of me. Recent feet. A muted laugh. A scent like that of dry parchment.

"Privyetiki!"

The accented voice that just whispered that sardonic, cutesy howdy-do in slangy Russian came from the deeper duskiness behind the partially-built bleachers at the far end of the room.

A tall shape rises, seeming to form itself from the shadows like darkness made visible. His wide smile discloses teeth that glint so white I'd almost think there was a light inside his mouth.

It's the leader of the Sunglass Mafia.

"Come," he says in English. False pleasantness in his voice.

I don't come.

He raises a hand, gestures.

Sorry. Still not moving.

Displeasure in the way he shakes his head—like a stage hypnotist who just failed to mesmerize someone he assumed would be easy to entrance.

He raises one hand toward his omnipresent sunglasses, pauses, seems to come to some decision. He lowers his hand, leaves the sunglasses in place. Then he glides more than walks toward me.

I should be afraid. I'm not.

He stops a deliberately uncomfortable foot away from me.

"You know me?" he asks.

I do. At least as far as his name goes. And his scent. "Yuri."

"*Klassno*. Cool. You are a listener, not so?"

I don't answer. I don't ask what they want.

I say "they" because Yuri's not alone. Very much not alone. My eyes don't move from his face, but my peripheral vision takes in the similarly pale, perfect faces that have drifted into range behind him. Natasha, Boris, Ekaterina, Igor, and Vlad, the music lover.

I don't see Marina because she is behind me. But my other senses are very much aware of her. She's breathing on the back of my neck.

Marina. Who was reading Ahkmatova. The one girl in their group who's looked sort of attractive to me. Not to the point of making her the object of elaborate erotic daydreams. I've kept that exclusively to you-know-who. But I have, more than once, taken note of the exotic shape of her face, the sinuous grace of her body . . . and I'm starting to sound like the intro to a badly written romance novel.

Yuri is still staring at me like a bug he's considering turning into a stain on the concrete.

Why am I not more worried?

Maybe they're wondering the same thing.

"*Da ti chto,*" Yuri says to himself. You've gotta be kidding.

I keep my mouth shut, my breathing regular.

How much damage could I do if I picked up that piece of rebar, a thumb-thick span of steel, lying on the concrete two steps away? That broken six-foot length of two-by-four over there might be better. Especially since it is splintered and sharp at one end.

"*Khakhalya,*" Marina whispers by the side of my face, "Boy toy, want to play?" Then she puts her tongue in my left ear. That does make it a little more difficult to stay still. I feel her hand on my hip, sliding along my thigh. Much more difficult.

"*Nyet!*" Yuri snaps.

Marina nyets. I feel her move back from me.

"Are you a problem?" Yuri asks. No one else in the Sunglass Mafia, aside from Marina, has said a word yet. He's clearly the leader of the pack, or flock, or whatever the right word might be for them.

"Define 'problem,'" I reply.

Yuri smiles. It is not an encouraging sight.

"I know your kind," he spits.

I wish I did. But I have the feeling that asking for an explanation is neither the smartest nor the most fruitful approach right now. So I take a stab at what I hope will be viewed as peacemaking.

"Live and let live."

Yuri's smile broadens, but not exactly into anything approaching pleasure.

"You think you are funny, *druzhok*?"

But he does take a step—or a glide—backward. He touches his index finger to his forehead then points it toward the spot on my forehead where the cut I woke up with is beginning to throb. I heal fast and it had already scabbed over. But now I can feel that it is beginning to bleed. Not the best time for that. No way that Yuri had anything to do with making that cut. But it seems as if he . . . what? Recognizes something about it?

Yuri plucks up the four-foot piece of rebar I'd been surreptitiously eyeing. Without looking back he hands it to the tall, vulture-shouldered hulk leering over his left shoulder.

"Vlad," he says.

Vladimir takes the bar in his two hands, grasps it by both ends and then, with a slow exhalation of breath, bends it into a half circle.

Impressive.

He nods at me, then hands it back to Yuri.

Yuri drops it to clang on the concrete between us.

Luckily it misses my toes. I don't move.

"Dosvstryech," Yuri says. See ya later.

Marina steps in front of me. If it wasn't for that old, cold scent about her she really would be a candidate for at least a second-string spot in any testosterone-stoked dreams I might have. Now, though? Not. Nightmares, maybe. She reaches a finger out to touch my forehead, brings it back, puts it in her mouth.

Her pleased smile exposes pointy canine teeth.

"Maybe we play later," she says. *"Doggi."*

12 CALL HOME

I'm halfway to my next class before I remember what started this late morning odyssey. Ironically apt classical allusion—seeing as how the old Greek wrestler's journey was sidetracked by encounters with monsters. (Yes, when I'm feeling upset I get all wordy and referential. Google "Odysseus," or be like me and open a dictionary.)

I'm not going to attempt another shortcut. This time I'm sticking to the hallways, illuminated by an abundance of daylight. Stay where I can be seen by the crowd. Probably an even better idea considering what I did after the Sunglass Mafia made their dramatic exit.

I have no doubt they'll be back in the disused aquatic complex before the end of the day. The smell of the place told me it's their regular hangout. I almost smile at the thought of how Yuri will react when he finds that rebar Vlad bent is now twisted into the pretzel shape of an Olympic ring. Or when he sees the letters USA scratched into the concrete next to it. Stupid, I know. But their attempt to bully me raised my hackles.

By the time I reach the main office I've taken twice as long to reach my destination as following the normal hallways.

Mrs. Carruth, the spiffy administrative assistant whose actual title should be "She Who Really Handles the Everyday Running of the School" is at the front desk.

"Lucas King."

She efficiently plucks a Post-it note from her phone and presents it to me with a roll of her wrist.

"Call home," is printed on the small yellow square of paper.

"Want privacy?" she says, not unkindly.

I nod.

She jerks her head toward the stripped cubicle office that belonged to a secretary before last fall's downsizing. "In there."

It's a land line, not a cell phone. For some reasons, land lines work for me, though the new cell phones don't. My hands are as clumsy as paws as I try to punch in our home number. Three tries so far and each time at least one wrong digit appears on the digital display and I have to hit Cancel. Half of me is praying that this won't be like the call he made to school two months ago. So drunk that our conversation consisted of his slurred voice saying, "I'm sorry, Son," again and again and my answering him a dozen times with "It's all right, Dad," and then finally, "I've got to go."

The other half of me is praying even harder that it won't be the conversation he told me might happen someday. Just in case of that, I have to be ready with the right words to say.

The right numbers come up on the tiny screen. I press Talk.

Connecting.

It buzzes once.

Answer it, Dad.

Bzzz.

Answer it.

Bzzz.

Answer it now. But don't let it be on the fourth . . .

Bzzz.

"Hello."

His voice is clear. He mechanically hits each of the two syllables of the word exactly the same.

Crap!

"Hello," I reply. Not my usual *Hi, Dad.*

"Hello, Lucas."

My father never calls me Lucas. Just Luke. We've only said four words between the two of us, but we've already passed on enough information for each to know what's going on.

"What's up, Pop?" I keep my tone breezy, a little hint of annoyance at having my happy school day interrupted. Do I need to mention that I never call Dad "Pop"?

"I am glad I reached you, Son."

My heart sinks. Worst case scenario.

"Just wanted to let you know I've been called out of town."

Taken, he means.

I keep my voice calm, level. It has to be a speakerphone at his end.

"Does that mean you're going to miss the soccer game?" I demand.

Me, who has never willingly played or watched a soccer match in his life.

"That's right. I'm really sorry. Really, really, really sorry."

But not half as sorry as I feel right now. He said "really" four times. My heart is thudding in my chest so loud that I'm afraid the four armed men in the room with him can hear it on the other end.

"What about dinner?" I ask in the petulant voice of a

disappointed adolescent whose father has let him down yet again.

"Lucas, there's no need to worry."

That means it could hardly be worse. I hear him take a breath and the small shudder in his breath tells me they've already done something to hurt him. Broken ribs, maybe.

"There's groceries in the fridge and money in the coffee can," he continues.

Whatever happens, I am not, repeat, *not* to go home. Someone, maybe more than one, will be waiting for me. Threatening harm to the one surviving member of a man's family is more efficient leverage than torture. "Coffee can" has told me where to go instead.

"Now I have to go," he concludes.

"Okay, Dad." He's delivered as much of the message as he can. I've remembered the meaning of every practiced phrase that he's used. It's a risk, but I have to drop character for a second. I have to say it.

"I love you, Dad."

"Love you too. Bye."

Click.

PLAY THE PART

Mrs. Carruth looks a question at me as I emerge from the cubicle. She's great at reading body language. I don't try to smile. Play the part of the scowling adolescent male so deep into himself there's no room for anyone else.

"Well?" she asks.

I shake my head. "The usual. Going away on business for a couple days. I'm on my own."

"Anything I can do to help?" she asks.

Aside from calling in an air strike?

I put a disgusted look on my face. "No."

"It's not easy being a single parent," she says. Urging me toward the empathy she suspects I'm lacking.

"I guess so." I accept the hard plastic hall pass from her that gives me permission to make my way to my next period between bells.

Yeah, I think as I leave the office, *it's not easy being a single parent.*

Even harder being one who's just been taken prisoner.

Why have I accepted that to be the situation so quickly? Because of two things, I guess. The first is that ever since I've been a small child I've known that my family seems to be marked for trouble. Maybe it's because my father chose a way of life that always ends up putting him in danger. Maybe it wasn't a choice, but fate. Whichever it is, trouble always finds us.

The second is the way I was raised by my parents. Even though neither of them ever talked directly about what Dad did, my parents began teaching me the things I needed to know (in case "something" happened) as soon as I started to walk. By the age of five I knew how to find the darkest, most hidden place in any room, curl up small, and not move no matter what—even if there was the sound of screaming and things breaking—until Dad or Mom spoke the safe word that told me I could come out.

King is not really our last name. Despite what it says on all the documents we have, our social security cards, our driver's licenses, Dad's one credit card, the records from the schools I supposedly attended before RHS.

I'm not saying that any of our records are forgeries. Every document we have is legal. It's all solid, checkable. Every record regarding the two of us that can be found in the multitude of databases that track every American citizen will withstand a thorough background check.

But none of it is real, aside from two things. My father is my dad. And when I was born somewhere other than Wolf Lake, Michigan, the first name given to me was Lucas. That's about all that stayed the same when we resurfaced here after Dad sold our old house and just about everything in it and then took us by a circuitous route through three-quarters of the country to get here. We also changed vehicles along the way. The nondescript car pulling the unmarked trailer loaded with our stuff (including the Norton) was the third one we used over a full month of migration.

I've read about what it was like for kids who grew up in the 1950s when it looked like the world was going to be destroyed in a thermonuclear war. There were regular drills in school teaching them to "duck and cover," get under the desks. As if that would protect them from a hydrogen bomb. Houses all over America had backyard fallout shelters. The closest thing to that in modern times was the hysteria about the year 2000 bringing some sort of apocalypse. I remember people all over were out stocking up on food and water and ammunition, all set for the Armageddon that never arrived. But not my dad and mom. They were already prepared—for more real, more personal, more probable threats.

I was not raised with hysteria or paranoia. Just the absolute certainty that our family had to be ready. One day something, an undefined but nonetheless real something, could occur. I had to be prepared for that day.

Learning self-defense was part of it. And not just from Dad. Mom ran self-defense classes at the Y for women. She'd been a marine herself before marrying Dad and settling down. I also was taught to keep my head down. Try to blend in. Practice self-control.

"Breathe slow and deep, Luke," Mom would say. "Especially when you feel anger coming on."

Like when the whole world is turning red all around me? When the birthmark on my wrist is starting to throb?

Yes, like that. Like now.

I stop growling as I stalk down the hall toward Spanish. Because of my unusual aptitude for languages and because I've fulfilled so many of my other requirements, RHS is allowing me to take both Spanish and French this semester.

Breathe deep. That's what I have to do. Slow down the heartbeat that will sound like the lead in a drum line if I lose control.

Part of me wants to start running, leap through that window there, and race across through the woods to the trailer. It doesn't care if someone, a whole gang of someones, is waiting. The more the better for me. More enemies for me to get my hands on, tear apart, sink my teeth into.

Stop it!

I place a trembling hand against the wall. Lucky it's still between classes. I'm alone in the hall. The clock on the wall indicates five minutes till the bell.

A full three hours until the end of the school day. I can't leave until then. Much as I want to. Whatever happened, whoever took my father, they did it in a way not meant to draw attention. There's no likelihood that they'd risk coming directly to the school. Not after setting me up with Dad's phone call. Stay in school for now, surrounded by students and teachers. Safety in numbers.

They're expecting me to come home at the normal time. Expecting me to be unaware of anything out of the usual.

Do they not know I could smell a trap? Catch the scent a hundred yards away from the house of any unfamiliar person there?

As I turn one of the fifty-four corners in the maze that is RHS, I reach the door to my Spanish class just as the bell rings. I lean back against the wall, surfing the waves of kids going in all directions at once, a chaos that sorts itself out into little rivulets flowing as they're supposed to into each designated pool of learning called a classroom.

Even though I'm the first one by the door, I wait until everyone else is in before I make my own entrance. There's a smell of sweat and fear in the classroom. But it's almost comforting to me because I can tell it's coming from the half of the class who don't know what real anxiety is. All they're worked up about is that they aren't ready for the test our teacher is about to administer. For me it'll be a mental break to be able to turn my churning brain to the mechanical task of answering questions on a test I can ace. I need this kind of momentary distraction.

I slip into my seat as Señora comes down the aisle.

"*Hola*, Lucas," she says as she hands me the test paper with a dramatic flourish.

"*Gracias*, Profesora Vega," I reply. "*Bueno.*"

"*Mi pequeno lobo*," she smiles, patting me on the shoulder and then moving on.

Her little wolf.

LATER

Last period is finally over. I'm trying to decide whether to get my motorcycle or try to make my escape leaving it behind in case I'm being watched. I probably am. It's a safe bet that at least two cars are somewhere waiting outside the school.

Meena comes up to me. There's an unfamiliar look on her face. I'm feeling torn apart inside at the thought of what might be happening to my father, but I still can't help but notice how perfect she is. Even if she doesn't seem to know it. It's not just that she's pretty. There's her intelligence and this inner strength that I feel in her. Whenever I'm around her there's a connection I've never felt with anyone else. There's a very old Greek story about how the first humans were double beings, a man and woman always joined together. They had so much power, though, that the gods of Olympus grew jealous. So those first beings were cut apart, made into separate men and women. Ever since then every human being is always looking for his or her other half.

My lost other half? Is that what Meena could be for me if things were different? That's what my heart wants right now. Even though it is impossible, especially now.

Meena leans close to me, so close that I can feel the warmth of her body. She's holding her backpack tight to her chest with both hands, looking down at the floor.

"Luke?" she whispers.

"Yeah?"

"I have been thinking, really thinking."

Long pause. That is not usual for Meena. Words flow from her like the waters of a clear mountain brook. She turns her eyes up at me. My knees grow weak.

"You like me, don't you?"

My throat is tight. I force words out. "Sure. Absolutely. I mean, you are one of my two best friends."

Meena shakes her head, a determined set to her small, perfect jaw. "No," she declares. "You will not do this. Not after I've come this far." Her eyes reach further into mine. "I mean that you like me more than as a friend. Be truthful."

My throat is dry as the Sahara Desert. "Yes," I manage to croak.

Her hand reaches out and grasps mine. In public!

"Luke, I am tired of always having to be a good little Pakistani girl, having to do everything that my father expects me to do. So you understand?"

"I do," I whisper.

"Good." She smiles. "You know, I told Renzo I was going to say all this to you. I asked him first if what I thought about you liking me was the truth and he said to me 'Hello? Girl, have you been that blind? He is head over the heels. You go for it!' Then I rehearsed what I would say in front of the mirror in the girls' room and . . ."

Meena is her old self. But as she chatters on, the momentary bliss I felt is being replaced by a sick feeling. Of all the times for the chance to hook up with the girl of my dreams, for true love to come into my life, this has to be the worst.

Though I've momentarily lost track of her words, Meena is still talking. "So," she continues, "am I finally going to get that ride on the back of your motorcycle today?"

"Yes," I say. "I mean no."

Meena looks confused.

"No?"

I squeeze her hand. Thank God for detention, I think. The one legit excuse I can use. I don't let go of her hand, which is in both of mine now. I motion with my chin toward the big study hall.

"Detention. Remember?"

"Oh," she says, disappointed but certain it's only a momentary glitch. God, I wish it was.

"After detention?" she says.

"I . . . I wish I could," I stammer. "But I just got a call from home. Something has come up and I may be tied up all weekend." Like tied up and being tortured. "It's . . . it's my dad."

A sympathetic look is on Meena's face now. I haven't confided in her as much as I have Renzo, but she knows a little about my home situation.

"Oh," she says. "I understand."

I wish I did.

Then the smile comes back on her face. "Monday," she says. "As soon as school is over. Would that be good?"

"It'd be wonderful." Even if it is impossible.

She gives my hands a squeeze. "I'll see you later, then."

"Later," I agree.

Meena puts her hands on my shoulders and stands up on her toes to kiss me on the cheek. "Not too much later," she breathes into my ear.

She turns and waves before she goes around the corner. I wave back, forced smile on my face.

Detention. Of all days to have to stay after school for an hour and pretend to study, this is the worst. It was hard enough to keep my emotions under control after Dad's phone call. But then to have the impossible opportunity to be with Meena added on top of it? And now too much time to think and not be able to act? My head is throbbing. I can't stop clenching and unclenching my hands in my lap.

A minute ago I was grasping the sides of the top of this desk so hard that the plywood or plastic or whatever it's fashioned from made a loud cracking sound. People turned around to look. I had to shove my hands under the desk before I accidentally broke it in half.

I know what I have to do.

I can't do it here.

I keep thinking that again and again. Dad always taught me to focus, to do one thing at a time and not think too far ahead. But when it's not possible for me to even get to that one thing, what am I supposed to do?

This is driving me crazy. If I were capable of sweating I'd have a river of it pouring down my face. Another minute of this and I swear I'm going to start howling.

GREEN LIGHT

"Mr. King?"

My head is buried in my arms, my eyes shut as tightly as possible. But I know the concerned voice as well as I know Coach Wrangell's clean Mennen-scented odor. He's today's detention room monitor. He's been trying for two years to coax me into coming out for his wrestling squad—having seen something in me that I've managed to hide from most adults.

Although I've given him every lame excuse in the book, he still seems to actually like me. I can always count on a little smile from him when we pass in the halls—like it's our little secret that my carefully mild exterior hides what could be a sectional heavyweight wrestling champion. Somehow just seeing him has always made me feel like maybe I'm a better person than I think I am.

I lift my head up to look at him.

"Yes, sir," I say.

He shakes his head. "Always polite," he says, more to himself than to me. "Even when he's hurting."

"Sir?"

He puts a hand on my shoulder. "You doing okay?"

I can't lie to him. "Not so good." As monumental an understatement as admitting there's actually some water in the ocean.

He drops down on one knee as smoothly as if he was going in for a takedown.

"What have they got you in here for this time? Burning churches like Thomas Malory? Insubordination? Purloining the Crash Helmet's favorite pocket protector?"

A smile cracks the edge of my tight lips. Everyone knows that Assistant Principal Nash has a thing about his pocket protectors. He'd sooner go out in public in his boxer shorts than not have one of those little white plastic envelopes tucked into his shirt stocked with three different colored pens and two pencils. What makes my smile a little broader is knowing that Coach Wrangell, who minored in English at Ithaca, knows I'll catch his literary reference in that first item. Sir Thomas Malory, the long-ago English author of *Morte d'Arthur*, was once accused of burning churches.

"None of the above," I answer. "Just the usual. Late for school again."

"Bull!" Coach Wrangell hisses. A little louder than he intended. He takes a quick look around to see if any of the other semicomatose detainees noticed. Nope. It would take a tidal wave to wash some of the burnouts in here back up onto the shores of awareness.

"Tardiness? You're in detention for that?"

"Yes, sir."

"Don't those . . ." he stops himself before saying something he knows will be both unkind and accurate. "Don't those . . . people in the school office know what you've been dealing with?"

Do you? I think.

He means Dad's problems with substance abuse. My father's name has been in the papers twice in the last two months for public intoxication—drunk and weeping and baying at the full moon.

Coach Wrangell realizes he may have said too much. He stands back up, makes a sweeping motion with his hand as if wiping a blackboard.

"Mr. King," he says, "consider your sentence commuted. Green light. Go. Head on out of here."

"Thanks, sir."

"*No problema.* And if you ever have the time after school, you know where the wrestling room is?"

"Yes, sir."

I walk slowly and deliberately out of the detention room, stop in the hallway, and take a breath. I'm forcing myself to think logically about what I have to do and how I need to do it. I could try sneaking out the back of the school again, cutting through the woods. But I'd probably be observed and followed. Fast as I might be able to move, I can't outrun a motor vehicle. Plus, as anyone with any knowledge of animal—and human—behavior knows, once you start running, something is going to start chasing you.

Act like nothing is wrong.

Get my stuff out of my locker.

All of my stuff.

Put my backpack over my shoulder.

Walk casually out the front door, down the steps.

One step at a time.

Remember, I'm a clueless bored teenager. Don't look around like a deer on the lookout for a hidden mountain lion. Peripheral vision can handle that better. Don't lift my head to sniff the air, but pick out any unfamiliar scents that the wind may be carrying. Let my eyes and ears and nose do their work.

And they do. What I catch out of the corners of my eyes are three strange cars. Black ones with tinted windshields. One in the trees at the west end of the big lot. A second is parked in among the maintenance trucks. The third car is back behind the main school building with just its front end showing. All three have their engines idling. I can hear them. V-8s.

I smell cigarette smoke from not far away. There's no smoking anywhere on campus. When kids light up it's never until they've exited the school grounds and are on the other side of Divide Street or Hoover Avenue. Inside those cars, keyed-up men are smoking. Men so poised and ready to spring into action that there's a rush of adrenaline going through them.

Swing my leg over the Commando.

Reach down with my right hand to insert the key.

Feel farther down onto the bike's frame with my left to see if I can find what I think may have been placed there.

Yup. My fingers quickly locate a small semicylinder magnetically attached—just where Dad said they like to put such things. No question I'm under close surveillance. As if the three ominous cars I've identified aren't proof enough that I'm about to be followed and ambushed.

I quickly pry the object off. I don't drop it. I palm it. Then I turn the key, kick it over, feel the throb of the 750 ccs of its engine. It's a bike ten times better than the Combat model introduced in 1972, the one that was so overpowered it broke crankshafts like toothpicks.

Don't look around.

Chug out toward Divide Street.

Slow and steady toward the intersection.

The stoplight is green now, but I've learned it has the fastest transition from green to yellow to red of any traffic signal in the city. The first of the black sedans is two cars behind me. Its driver thinks I'm unaware of him. He's clueless about what I'm planning.

I pull over and pause while the light is still green, button up my jacket, wait. Then I cruise toward the light at the exact speed to catch the two seconds of yellow between Go and Stop. The result is that two cars back, black sedan number one gets stuck at the light. Divide's a narrow street. With a steady flow of traffic turning into the opposite lane toward him, he's blocked from trying to run the red light.

I don't speed up, but as I take a quick right, I open my left hand and let the tracking device that had been planted on my motorcycle fall to the pavement. It bounces once before being crunched into its constituent parts by the wheels of a passing truck.

16 THE PRESERVE

I ease the bike up to the point where the arrow is just tickling twenty-nine. It's a thirty mile per hour zone here. There's usually one of Chief Hot Dog's five-ohs lurking in a police cruiser just around the next corner. There're more tickets and less warnings now that the state is in such a big fiscal mess. The fifty bucks they collect from every ticket does a nice job of augmenting salaries. Teens with first licenses and heavy feet are a major cash crop for cops.

By now the people on my tail must have noticed that their tracking device has stopped functioning. I'm hoping they'll just curse and chalk it up to equipment failure. I check the mirror on my right handlebar. No sign of the car that got stuck. That light stays red there for a long time. I cross the next intersection, where Hammond joins Divide.

Just as I expected, there's a city police cruiser parked twenty feet back, its radar gun trained on the traffic. But even in economic hard times it's too much trouble to put down the jelly donut and give chase if someone's not doing at least ten miles over the posted limit. I'm still only hitting a modest thirty-two and I'm ignored.

With any luck that first chase car behind me will speed up enough after the light finally changes, trying to make up the distance between us, that he'll hear the *whoop-whoop* of a siren behind him after whizzing past Hammond.

The outskirts here on the west side of the city are laid out in a grid. From the air it looks like a checkerboard. None of the streets and avenues near RHS are one way, so what happens next is just what I've been expecting. Rather than follow Chase Car Number One, Numbers Two and Three have boxed the grid, turned left instead of right, then left and left again and gotten ahead of me. First one, and then the next of the two remaining black sedans pulls in behind me at Mill Avenue, just before I reach the intersection where Creek Street crosses.

I pay no attention to them. La, la, la, I'm just motoring along with not a care in the world. Like the world's most careful and law-abiding novice motorcyclist, I diligently signal with my arm and my blinker. I turn onto Creek like a kid on a trike with training wheels and keep dawdling along. They're staying back in traffic, keeping one or two cars between me and each other. Classic technique. I'm betting they are thinking of me as a callow kid—despite who my father is. Deploying three teams in cars is overkill enough. This is U.S. soil and not Waziristan. So I'm assuming that there's no aerial surveillance in place. I haven't see a sign of a helicopter and seriously doubt that they'd use any high-tech assets like high-flying drones or a satellite to keep me in sight.

Creek Street is well-named. The little stream, its waters rippling like liquid silver, flows along it, crossing back and forth under three bridges. At bridge number two, I slow down to a crawl, signal again, and carefully put down my feet for stability as I turn onto the unpaved pathway that passes under the bridge here. Technically speaking, motorized vehicles of any kind are not allowed. But it's not at all out of the ordinary for motorcycles to use the narrow trail, which leads left into the five hundred or so acres that are all that's left of the Cowasuck Preserve, which was meant to stay forever wild. I'm on the west side of the preserve, directly opposite the parking lot where I ran into Dr. Kesselring on Tuesday.

Kesselring. Because of him, the preserve is no longer as big as it used to be. Last year Dr. Kesselring used his political pull to rezone a third of it as residential. Like a butcher slicing flesh from the living body of an animal, he cut off dozens of ten-acre parcels that were sold at bargain prices to his cronies for building lots. But the preserve is still sizeable enough for what I have in mind.

I chug calmly down the slope, turn left onto the path that is heavily overgrown with maples and cedars. Brakes screech from the road I've left behind. Car doors slam. I reach out idly to pluck a leaf from one of the overhanging maple branches as I go by. Its complex pattern of veins is less complicated than the maze of roads and trails ahead of me that weave through the preserve.

Just before I go out of sight, I hear the harsh sounds of two men cursing at each other from the bridge. I don't look back. But I do smile.

17 THE MESSAGE

Despite the narrowness of the trail, I speed up once I'm out of sight. But I stay on the hard-packed parts of the trail, keep my turns gradual so as not to throw up soil and leaves that would mark my passage. Others on motorcycles—dirt bikers mostly—have been here recently and my tracks are not that visible among theirs.

I weave my way from one trail to the next until I'm half a mile from the main road in the part of the preserve that's mostly evergreens. Cedars, hemlocks, and, as the land rises, pines. I stop under the shelter of the Five Nations Pine. It's the biggest and most ancient tree in the preserve. Its five main branches, each one as big as a large tree itself, rise to spread overhead like huge green umbrellas. I've climbed it a hundred times. Its name comes from the Five Nations, the Iroquois people who founded a league of peace under a great white pine about a thousand years ago.

White pine needles come in bundles of five, just like the five Iroquois nations of Mohawk, Oneida, Onondaga, Cayuga, and

Seneca. The roots of an old pine reach out far to all the directions. Anyone seeking peace could trace those roots back to the trunk and find shelter under the branches of that symbolic evergreen. I've always felt some of that peace whenever I've come here. True, my own Abenaki ancestors were often at war with the Iroquois, but we were just as often their friends. We all knew the value of peace back then.

In the past I've always come to the tree on foot though. It feels like kind of a sacrilege to have brought a motorcycle here, but I'm hoping the old tree will forgive me. I walk back along the trail kicking needles over the tracks my wheels have left behind.

Then, just to be sure, I methodically go over the Commando with my hands and eyes. Where there was one tracking device there might be another. But it seems as if the first one was the only one. That's slightly reassuring. They're assuming I wouldn't have been expecting something like that.

It also means none of them were raised by someone like my Dad.

Never assume anything. One of the first laws of survival.

I wish I could assume that I'm safe. I wish I could just lay back on the soft earth carpeted with generations of needles, looking up at the old tree overhead. I wish Meena was here with me. I feel an ache in my heart as I think that. I think of chances lost forever like the needles that have fallen from the old tree—brown and yellowing on the ground, never to be green again. This quiet, sort of sacred spot is the first place I wanted to take her on my bike. But wanting doesn't make it so.

I may have lost them for now, but not for good. Chances are that someone, maybe even a halfway decent tracker, is following me right now through the preserve. Maybe they've hijacked a dirt bike to speed up their pursuit. So, after checking yet again to eliminate the possibility of another tracking device, I get on the Commando and head out. If I turn right, cross the boardwalk, and follow the Marsh Trail, I'll come out in the woods just behind our trailer.

I turn left. It brings me up to the state highway within ten minutes. I walk the bike up to the road, not wanting to leave any skid marks in the earth to show where I came out of the woods. Then I get on, slowly picking up speed until I'm doing seventy. Ten miles to go before I reach the place Dad's coded message has directed me.

The old oak tree lifts its spreading branches high on the tallest hill in the middle of Youth Haven, the deserted Boy Scout campground that's only used in the summer. Little chance anyone else will be here this time of year. A perfect drop spot. I look up toward the hidden hollow that Dad showed me last fall, twenty feet up the huge tree's rough trunk. I climb it as easily as a spider scaling a brick wall.

Climbing trees came as naturally to me when I was a little kid as walking does to most four-year-olds. By the time I was seven, I could swing my way to the top of the tallest tree, scramble or shinny up just about anything from the side of a building to a flagpole.

I reach down in and find something smooth and metallic. I pull it out. It's a can stamped with a familiar logo. *World's Best Lemon Drops*. In spite of my anxiety, it makes me smile. Dad has this thing for lemon drops, the only candy he ever eats. Though long empty of its original contents, it still holds the odor of those lemon drops—and my Dad's scent. It must have been placed here only a few days ago. So my father was already aware then that something might go wrong and it worried him. Worried enough for him to sober up . . . and leave this fail-safe message.

I pop open the can, take out the message he's left for me. It's only six words. They're in plain English, not code. But no one other than me would understand what the message means. No one other than me would feel this frisson of cold, like chilled fingers, run down his spine while reading it.

GO WHERE YOU SAW THE GRUE

Whether I want to or not, this is my only option. If I leave now, I'll get to the Drake House just at twilight.

THE STAIRS

A mist is sweeping in, a diaphanous curtain being pulled up from the marshes behind the house. The light from the setting sun is as faint as a flickering oil lamp. The outline of the abandoned mansion fifty yards away is blurred by fog and twilight to the point where it seems like nothing more than a corny outdoor stage set for a low-budget Roger Corman film.

I don't have a flashlight or even a match to light my way. If I were someone else, that would be a major roadblock. If it weren't for my ability to see almost as well as a cat in such semidarkness, I probably wouldn't be able to move through this spooky atmosphere up to the door.

But I can. Lucky me.

I swing my leg over the Norton, push it back out of sight behind the gatehouse that's just as uninhabited as the deserted mansion it once guarded. At least I am hoping it's deserted.

I zip my key into the deep inside right pocket of my jacket

where I would be carrying a wooden stake and a cross if I really were in one of those old gothic epics. But the only weapon I have is the certainty that my father would never have sent me here to walk into a trap. Whatever it is that I'm supposed to do or find here, Dad has trusted that I can succeed on my own.

Still, I stand in the shadow of the gatehouse watching and waiting, listening and smelling the air for a good long time. I need to be sure that no one has followed me here, lurking at my back and waiting for me to expose myself.

The oil lamp of the sun burns out. The blanket of mist has now fully shrouded everything. Although it has yet to rise, even the moon, which will be at its fullest tonight, would not be visible in this cloud-occluded sky.

Time to do whatever.

A quick crouching run brings me to the door. It's solid, made of heavy oak, and inscribed with curlicue designs and fitted with an old-fashioned, heavy door handle. It looks just as it did in my dream. This time, though, it's not locked. As soon as I put my hand on the latch, there's a *click*. It swings inward. Smoothly. No creepy creaking sound. No half-heard echo of mocking ghoulish laughter as I step inside.

My steps are soundless as I cross the hardwood floor. Walking quietly has always come naturally to me. I can pause in mid step and wait with one foot raised, looking and listening—the way a heron does when it's wading through the shallows looking for prey. My hands are held up in front of my chest, my fingers slightly curled, my shoulders hunched as I stalk forward. No sound other than my soft breathing, my own heartbeat, and the faint whisper of a wind starting to rise outside. No strange odors other than those of mold and decay, rodent droppings, and dusty moth wings.

I slowly cross the space between the door and the bottom of

the wide flight of stairs. Up there. That's where I have to go.

There's a big window at the top of the stairs. The wind outside has picked up. Mist swirls across the cracked panes of glass, thinning as I go up a step at a time, staying to the side near the wall. I'm not really scared, but I do wish I'd never seen *Psycho*. Three times— the remake once and Hitchcock's elegant original twice.

I count the steps as I climb them, trying to shake the image of a knife-wielding homicidal maniac in drag.

Nine.

Ten.

Eleven.

Twelve.

It's not working. I'm becoming even more intensely aware of the fact that being well-read and having a lifetime fascination with horror flicks is not terribly useful or reassuring while you're in the midst of reconnoitering a potentially haunted dwelling. The hair on the back of my neck is standing up. A random line of poetry from Coleridge flickers like heat lightning across my cerebral cortex: "a fearful fiend doth close behind him tread."

I lean back, look down the stairs. All I see below me is the deserted hallway and a few items of furniture shrouded by dusty blankets. But the wolf mark on my left wrist suddenly throbs—as if it's been seared by a hot iron.

I slowly turn my gaze back up.

There it is, backlit by the full moon that seems to have leaped up into the sky like a ghoulish jack-in-the-box.

The grue.

It looms over me. Its huge shoulders are broader and more grotesquely muscled than I remember. Its pale skin seems even more corpselike than before. Its voracious, unblinking stare pierces into me just as it did in my dream.

I know with terrible certainty that malevolence, violence, and hunger are all this beast knows.

Its fanged mouth drips venom.

Its clawed hands reach for me.

FIGHT OR FLIGHT

The fight or flight response: a term that refers to the most basic, instinctive survival reactions of any sentient organism, whether a rabbit or a human, to imminent peril. (Of course that leaves out possible reaction number three, which is to freeze in terror. But that is not really a survival mechanism—for the prey animal, at least. Although it is just peachy for any hungry predator with no need to expend further energy in pursuit of dinner.)

Fight or flight. Attack or attempt escape. Conditioned reflexes. Built into the DNA after millions of years of adaptation. Triggered by the sense organs: eyes, ears, and nose of that threatened being—let's say, seventeen-year-old male *Homo sapiens* halfway up a flight of dark stairs. A desperate signal is sent to the brain.

The brain then, in an equally swift lightning flash of neurons and synapses, triggers the adrenal glands. Those two complex endocrine organs, located near the anterior medial border of the kidneys, release a flood of fluid into the blood. Adrenaline, also known as epinephrine. It raises the blood pressure, stimulates the heart, heightens awareness. In short, it's a sudden injection of strength.

Even a small, usually weak person can show superhuman power when an adrenaline rush kicks in. The hundred-pound mother who lifts the front end of a car off her trapped child.

All of that scientific gobbledygook has just swooshed across my thoughts, in concert with the tidal surge of chemical stimuli through my arteries. I am a living example of logical cognition linked hand in hand with primitive and mindless somatic response. I know all that thanks to that physiology book I was perusing several days ago in the school library.

Thinking and feeling all this has taken me no longer than the time to draw in a single quick breath. But no matter how little time has elapsed, the essential question remains—like the giant claw-handed embodiment of doom hulking over me.

Advance or retreat?

A growl is building in my chest. I'm clenching my hands into fists, lowering my head like the beast that appears poised for imminent attack.

My body knows what it wants to do, whether it is capable of it or not. My genetically inherited instinctive behavior is not that of the rabbit. It's more akin to the modus operandi of *Gulo luscus*, the wolverine, a forty-pound furred demon that thinks nothing of taking on a grizzly bear twenty times its size.

Yet a voice speaks from someplace in the back of my head. A deep voice that I know as well as my own.

Dad's voice. Repeating the word that he always says to me when he suspects I'm about to do something rash. Not "don't." I never knew my grandparents, but my father told me that they raised him to realize that "don't do that" is one of the least effective things to say to a young person. Tell your child not to do something and sooner or later, when you're not around, you can bet that kid is going to do it. Instead, Dad's parents always encouraged him to use his best judgment. Consider the consequences of any action.

Dad boiled it down to just one word.

"Think."

Think.

Run away? No. I'm not going to run. Maybe I'd be fast enough to get away—or maybe not. But running from danger is not part of my makeup. Trying to avoid trouble before it gets to me is one thing. But playing the part of a coward is another. This creature is between me and something I need to do—for my father and myself.

Fight? No. Attacking this nightmare apparition head-on might be brave, but it would certainly also be desperate and fool-hardy.

The grue is not attacking. It's swaying back and forth, studying me. It's looking at me in the same way I'm looking at it. Its motions are . . . yes . . . mirroring my own. I lean right. It leans right. I lower my clenched fists a little. It does the same. I bare my teeth and so does it. An exaggerated reflection of every angry, violent urge I've ever felt?

That is when I notice it. On the creature's right wrist is a familiar mark, red and swollen as an infected tattoo. I relax, raise myself up out of the defensive posture I'd taken. The gruesome being does the same. I breathe in and out slowly, calming my racing heartbeat.

The grue's mouth is closed now. Its eyes have grown dull. Its arms are hanging limply by its sides. It's still big, but not as massive as it seemed before.

I open my left hand, step slowly forward and gently grasp the monster's huge wrist. It doesn't resist as I pull it toward me. It seems solid at first and then, like a handful of sand, begins to become less substantial. The grue's shape wavers, becomes amorphous, sifts into nothingness.

Part of an ancient prayer comes into my mind.

Creator, grant me the strength to recognize that my greatest enemy is myself.

I wipe the dust of what I must never allow myself to become from my palms. Then I continue up the stairs toward whatever destiny awaits me.

20 DOWN THE HALL

The moon seems bigger, fuller than I've ever seen it before. I stand at the top of the stairs in front of the large round window that seems to have been placed for just such a purpose as this.

Moon viewing.

It's almost unreal the way the earth's lunar companion hangs suspended above the trees tonight. I have a perfect view of it now that the wind has dissipated the mist like an eraser wiping chalk from a blackboard. A great luminous ball, the mountains and seas of its surface are as visible as if I was peering through a ten power scope. Perhaps it's something in the atmosphere tonight. Maybe the glass of the window is creating this effect. Or it might just be the angle I'm seeing it from. Or perhaps it's me. For whatever reason, I feel as if I could just stand here for hours, staring at it.

I shake myself like a Labrador retriever ridding its coat of water after emerging from a lake. I've always felt that tie to the moon, but this is not the time to lose myself in contemplation.

Wake up. Do what you came here to do.

And what is it I'm supposed to be trying to do? And how can I be sure I'll be able to do it?

My internal voices have been engaged in this kind of duet ever since my father's coded message to come here.

Do it!

Do what?

I've never felt so indecisive before.

Even though, for whatever reason, I wasn't terrified by the monster on the stairs, I truly am apprehensive about what I might find at the end of the hallway behind me. Part of me wants to delay things as long as possible. That's at least part of the reason I am allowing myself to be so entranced by my favorite heavenly body.

My favorite heavenly body.

No. I can't let myself start thinking again about Meena right now. Focus.

I close my eyes to block the lambent light streaming out of the night sky from what the Iroquois nations call the oldest grandmother's face. I turn around, open my eyes again. I study the long moonlit passageway. It sort of resembles one of those halls in that massive old mountain hotel in *The Shining*. Minus the mocking voices of the murdered twins.

"Honey," I whisper, just to prove to myself I haven't lost my sardonic sense of humor, "I'm home."

I'm still stalling. There's really no doubt about where I'm supposed to go. The faint footprints in the dust of the hallway lead straight to the closed door at the end. Another set of the same prints lead back out again. I know they were made by my Dad's favorite shoes. I recognize not only the tread patterns of his size eleven New Balance 990s, but also the groove on the back of the left heel where a small wedge of rubber is missing. It got chunked out when Dad tried to stomp the bent edge of our trailer's superannuated aluminum steps back into shape last month.

As if placed there to dispel any lingering doubts I might have, there's also an arrow drawn in the dust pointing right at that door. I can almost hear Dad chuckling as he bent to do that, knowing how superfluous that marker would be for his well-trained son. No doubts that I'd get this far.

I'm pretty sure, too, that Dad was well aware I'd react just as I am reacting now. It's as if he was saying "Yooo-hooo!" in a falsetto voice. I'm actually feeling the ghost of a smile like his on my lips.

That dust-drawn direction marker is a combination of an inside joke and a morale booster. It takes me back to the lessons he'd give me in the woods about the right and wrong ways to leave a trail for someone to follow you. Making a big-ass arrow out of sticks or carving something in the side of a tree is the dumbest way to do it when you want to make sure that the only ones who can follow your track are your friends. When you are one with the forest you know other, subtler ways.

I stalk silently down the hall, placing my feet exactly in the almost invisible footprints made by my father, pausing only to brush that little arrow into obscurity. I put my palm against the door—and yank it back. I've felt something as nerve-tingling as a jolt of electricity. I put my hand back again. Or allow it to be pulled back. It's as if I'm being drawn like a piece of iron to a magnet—or one of two magnets feeling the irresistible force when the opposite poles are aligned.

It's not the door that is attracting me. It's whatever is waiting on the other side.

Whatever it is, it wants me.

THE CHEST

I take a deep breath, filling my chest with air, as if I'm about to dive into deep water. Then I push the door open and enter the room. I take two steps forward. The door closes silently behind me as if pushed shut by an invisible hand, though it's probably just that it's hung on its hinges in such a way that no force more mysterious than gravity is the cause.

Nothing attacks. No ominous ectoplasmic shape rises up to engulf me. No sudden knife or razor claws pierce my back. It's as quiet as the grave—aside from the thudding of my own heartbeat.

It's easy to see the nothingness in here. There's a round window high on the wall to my right, a smaller cousin of that big round pane that seemed to magnify the reassuring moonlight. This portal, too, lets in a similar effulgence of radiant night light, so much that I can see my shadow.

It's disturbing just how empty this room is. Once probably someone's chamber, but no bed or table or chairs here now. No

107

sofas, no dressers, not even a throw rug on the plank floor. None of the familiar furniture of human habitation. Aside from the accumulation of dust motes floating in the air, illuminated by the bright moonlight like tiny nebulae, this room is about as bare as it must have been when the Drake House was first built a hundred fifty years ago. Unnaturally empty. There's not even the buzz of a fly or the latticed span of a spider web in any of the corners.

I didn't know ghosts had such good house cleaners.

Though I may be the only breathing being in this old abandoned bedchamber, I can sense that I'm not alone. I feel that magnetic attraction. It draws me, breath by breath, across the room to the oak-paneled wall covered by built-in bookcases long devoid of a single volume.

My hands reach toward that bookcase, almost of their own volition. I'm not thinking now, just letting it happen. My right hand places itself flat against the wall where I can sense that another hand was recently placed. My father's hand. My left hand touches the bookcase where the dust was recently disturbed, slides under the shelf. My fingertips find an indentation. I press in.

Click.

The sound of a latch being released. The section of wall and bookcases in front of me swings back. It discloses a secret room. The moonlight from behind me is bright enough for me to see inside. It's not big at all, perhaps six feet deep and eight feet wide, just a bit roomier than a walk-in closet. I step through the opening.

Unlike the bigger room, this one is not empty. It holds two things. The first seems fitting for this setting. A big coffer, like one of those sea chests from *Captain Blood* or *Pirates of the Caribbean*. Massive enough to hold a sizeable treasure . . . or several skeletons. What's out of place is that the hasp of the chest is secured not by some ancient iron padlock but an efficient, quite modern combination lock.

The other object in the hidden room has been placed on top of the sea chest and is also incongruous. It's a foot-tall battery-powered storm lantern with fluorescent bulbs, the kind of emergency light you keep on hand for power outages. It's also familiar as hell. The last time I saw it, it was on the bureau in Dad's room.

I lift the lantern and find an envelope beneath it. My name written in my father's handwriting, along with these underlined words:

Read Before Opening Chest

Good thing he wrote that and I read it. I was about to grab that lock and twist it open with my bare hands. Something, something inside the old sea chest, is calling me. The hair is standing up on the back of my neck and on my arms. The wolf mark is throbbing.

Breathe.

Breathe.

Breathe.

A shiver goes down my spine. I turn on the hurricane lamp. I push the secret door shut, after having made sure that I know the location of the inside release so that I can open it again without having to break through the wall to eventually get out of here.

I sit down with my back against the chest. It's as if there's an electric current prickling its way across my back where I'm in contact with the wood and metal of the box. The light of the hurricane lamp over my shoulder casts the elongated, deformed shadow of my head and shoulders across the floor. Almost like the shadow the grue cast.

My hands are trembling. It takes two tries for me to open the flap of the envelope. I slide out the folded note and begin to read.

22 MY FATHER'S LETTER

LUKE,

IF YOU'RE READING THIS, THEN IT MEANS THAT
THINGS HAVE GOTTEN VERY BAD, VERY FAST. SO I'M
TRYING TO MAKE THIS LETTER AS SIMPLE AS POSSIBLE.
I'M JUST GOING TO GIVE YOU THE FACTS YOU NEED
TO KNOW. SIMPLE AND CLEAR, EVEN IF THEY SOUND
UNBELIEVABLE. BUT THERE'S NOT ENOUGH TIME FOR
EVERYTHING. IF I'M LUCKY AND YOU'RE LUCKY, THERE'LL
BE TIME IN THE FUTURE FOR US TO BE TOGETHER AND
FOR ME TO TELL YOU. IF NOT, THEN . . .

THIS IS MY THIRD TRY TO WRITE THIS. I'LL NEVER
GET IT EXACTLY RIGHT.

FIRST OF ALL, IF YOU GOT THIS FAR—AND I'M SURE
YOU DID—IT MEANS THAT YOU MANAGED TO OVERCOME

THE GRUE. JUST REMEMBER THAT YOU DIDN'T GET RID OF IT. IT'S STILL THERE AND THE NEXT TIME YOU SEE IT MIGHT BE WHEN YOU LOOK IN A MIRROR. REMEMBER, YOU CONTROLLED IT ONCE AND YOU CAN DO IT AGAIN.

I'M PROUD OF YOU FOR GETTING THIS FAR. I'VE ALWAYS BEEN DAMN PROUD OF YOU, SON. I DON'T HAVE TIME TO TELL YOU HOW PROUD BECAUSE I HAVE TO FINISH THIS NOTE AND THEN GET IT THERE.

OKAY, SO HERE'S THE HARD PART OF WHAT I NEED TO TELL YOU. I AM IN BIG TROUBLE. MY JOB MADE ME A LOT OF ENEMIES. I THOUGHT I WAS OUT OF IT. THE WAY I TRIED TO GET OUT OF IT WAS STUPID. I BLAMED MYSELF FOR YOUR MOTHER'S DEATH. BUT WHAT I DID, IT DIDN'T WORK THE WAY I THOUGHT IT WOULD. IT MADE ME SICK AT HEART AND SICK IN SPIRIT AND I BECAME WEAK, SO MUCH LESS THAN I'D BEEN. HELL, IT MADE ME LESS THAN I SHOULD HAVE BEEN FOR YOU, SON.

I'M ASHAMED OF WHAT I BECAME AND HOW I WASN'T THERE FOR YOU. I'LL NEVER FORGIVE MYSELF FOR THAT DECEPTION.

BUT I DID WHAT I DID OUT OF ANGER AND GRIEF. I THOUGHT IT WAS THE ONLY WAY. I BURNED IT. I THOUGHT THAT WOULD HELP ME GET OUT AND GET AWAY. I THOUGHT THEY WOULDN'T BE INTERESTED IN ME ANYMORE. I THOUGHT I WAS OFF THE RADAR.

BUT IT SEEMS I WASN'T. I BEGAN TO REALIZE THAT WHEN I STARTED SEEING PEOPLE WHO DIDN'T LOOK

RIGHT, DIDN'T SMELL RIGHT. I REALIZED THAT I HADN'T BEEN ABLE TO GET OUT OF THE GAME AFTER ALL, NO MATTER HOW DAMN CLEVER I THOUGHT I'D BEEN. I GUESS NO ONE EVER DOES. THEY CONTACTED ME AND I KNEW I COULDN'T SAY NO. ESPECIALLY WHEN THEY TOLD ME THE PART ABOUT YOUR MOM.

THAT'S WHY WE MOVED HERE, BECAUSE IT'S HERE. THAT'S WHY I STARTED . . . PLAYING A PART, PRETENDING TO BE A DRUNK. IT KILLED ME TO SEE HOW THAT HURT YOU. BUT I HAD TO STAY IN CHARACTER. THAT WORKED FOR A WHILE.

SO NOW YOU GOT A PHONE CALL FROM ME, RIGHT? AND YOU UNDERSTOOD WHAT I WAS TELLING YOU BECAUSE YOU'RE HERE. THAT MEANS THAT MY ENEMIES MUST HAVE ME NOW. OTHERWISE WE COULD'VE WAITED ANOTHER YEAR. BUT I THINK YOU'RE ALREADY STRONG ENOUGH TO BEAR THE WEIGHT. SO THOSE ENEMIES OF MINE, CALL THEM AGENTS, THEY'VE GOT ME. DON'T EXPECT THEM TO BE BEARDED MUSLIM TERRORISTS OR FOREIGNERS. THEY MIGHT BE, BUT THEY ALSO MIGHT BE PEOPLE BORN AND RAISED IN THIS COUNTRY AND WORKING FOR A PART OF WHAT THEY BELIEVE IS OUR OWN GOVERNMENT. OR THEY MAY JUST BE GREEDY BASTARDS. I HAVEN'T GOTTEN ENOUGH EVIDENCE YET TO FIGURE OUT WHO'S BEHIND THIS.

WHOEVER THEY ARE, THEY GOT ME. NOW THEY WANT TO GET YOU BECAUSE THEY KNOW THE ONLY WAY

THEY CAN FORCE ME TO DO WHAT THEY WANT ME TO
DO IS TO THREATEN YOUR LIFE.

SON, I'D DO MOST ANYTHING TO KEEP YOU SAFE,
TO PROTECT YOU. BUT NOW YOU ARE GOING TO HAVE
TO GO TO ANOTHER LEVEL ON YOUR OWN. EVERYTHING
I TAUGHT YOU IN THE PAST IS GOING TO MEAN MORE
TO YOU FROM HERE ON IN . . . AND I ALREADY WROTE
THAT ONCE. I CAN'T TELL YOU EXACTLY WHAT TO DO OR
WHERE TO GO. BUT YOU'LL BE SAFER AND STRONGER AND
MORE READY FOR WHATEVER COMES AT YOU. MAYBE
YOU'LL FIND A WAY.

THERE'S SOME VERY BAD PEOPLE AROUND HERE. I
DON'T KNOW WHO ALL OF THEM ARE YET, BUT I DO
KNOW THIS MUCH: DON'T TRUST THE POLICE. WATCH OUT
FOR KESSELRING.

LUKE, THERE IS SO MUCH STRANGE STUFF IN THE
WORLD THAT MOST PEOPLE NEVER SEE, NEVER KNOW
ABOUT. YOU'VE ALREADY SENSED SOME OF THAT. I KNOW
THAT. YOU KNOW YOU'RE DIFFERENT. YOU JUST DON'T
KNOW HOW DIFFERENT YOU ARE OR WHY.

AT THE END OF THIS LETTER WILL BE THE
COMBINATION FOR THE LOCK. YOU'RE GOING TO OPEN
THAT LOCK, LIFT THE LID OF THE TRUNK. BUT FIRST,
READ THE LAST PAGE THAT FOLLOWS THIS ONE. I KNOW
YOU'LL REMEMBER IT. YOU HAVE THAT SAME KIND OF
MEMORY THAT I HAVE. BUT MORE THAN REMEMBERING
IT, YOU HAVE TO LIVE IT. UNDERSTAND, SON? LIVE IT.

I LOVE YOU, SON. NO MATTER WHAT YOU DO, NO MATTER WHAT YOU HAVE TO DO. AND WHEN I NEXT SEE YOU, WHETHER IT IS HERE ON EARTH OR AT THE END OF THE ROAD OF STARS OUR ANCESTORS TOLD US ABOUT, KNOW THAT THERE'LL BE NOTHING BUT PRIDE IN MY EYES AND THAT MY ARMS WILL BE OPEN FOR YOU.

YOUR MOM AND I WERE ALWAYS SO PROUD OF YOU.

DAD

I'm holding the letter in my hand as I press the back of my wrist against my forehead. I've read it twice, even though reading it once carved every word my father wrote into my memory as firmly as letters cut into a block of granite.

I've also read the last page that came after his letter to me. Just as he said, the combination of the lock was at the bottom . . . below what filled the rest of the page. Part of it was that simple, clear information he mentioned at the start of his letter.

Simple.

Clear.

I wish it was unbelievable, but it's not. It makes sense, terrible sense. After what I am about to do next, my life will never be the same again.

The rest of the page was a list.

It was also like an instruction manual. Or an abbreviated Ten Commandments.

However, I'm fairly certain that God never gave Moses a tablet engraved with the words "Thou Shalt Not Eat Thy Neighbor."

23
THE LOCK

I have to do some deep breath control exercises that my dad taught me—Black Tiger Way—right now before I go any further. It's not just that I'm angry and confused and frustrated. I'm also not at all sure that I'm worthy of my father's faith in me. I have to regain control of my mind before everything spins away. There's too many things happening all at once. The Sunglass Mafia, Meena actually wanting to be more than just a friend at a time when any kind of relationship in my life is probably going to be impossible—even if I survive. And then there's Dr. Kesselring. I don't know why, but I have the feeling that somehow he figures into all of this. I don't have a clue what I can do about anything, including the very immediate problems of those shadowy presences who've taken my Dad and are now after me.

I feel like a guppy who's been dropped into a shark tank. A white rat in a python cage. A goat who's stumbled into a lion's den.

After a few deep breaths I don't feel that much better. But I can't keep putting off the inevitable. Despite my doubts, I turn to the box. I lift the combination lock with my left hand, the steel cold against my palm.

How come they always name locks Stanley? I think. *Why not call one Brenda or Wolfgang?*

A weak attempt at humor. I start to spin the dial with my right hand.

Thinking of weak humor, I'm pretty sure that my father indulged in some of that when he picked out this lock with its memorable combination. It's 6-6-6. The number of the Beast in the book of Revelation. Chapter thirteen. Verse eighteen.

A final *click* and I pull the lock open and remove it from the hasp. I shrug off my backpack, put it down next to me. I unzip one of the side pouches. Slip the lock inside.

You'll need a sharp knife. You'll find one in the chest.

Still stalling. Open the seventh seal.

I flip back the latch.

Lift up the lid.

24
SECOND SKIN

It doesn't look like much. It's small, barely bigger than a bath towel. It's a dull, lifeless gray. It looks stiff and dirty and fragile as a garment left for centuries in a tomb. You'd think it would fall apart in my hands if I tried to pick it up. But I know it's more than what it looks like. I can feel how much more it is.

What I feel is an invisible tide of pulsing energy. It's like being in front of a huge open blaze, standing close to a burning building. My skin, every part of my skin, even under my clothes, is absorbing that heat.

Take off all your clothes.

I quickly shed the backpack, untie my sneakers, yank off my socks. Even the bottoms of my feet feel hot, as if the wood floor would burst into flame at their touch. I strip off my Territory Ahead shirt—the one that Meena said I looked smoking in. If I left it on any longer it might be incinerated. I unbutton and shrug off my Levis, step out of my boxers. I quickly fold the clothes, stuff the socks into the sneakers, stow it all inside my backpack. For later.

It needs your blood.

I don't have my own knife with me. I came here straight from school and it's still at home. But I don't need it. Dad thought ahead about this too. In the bottom of the chest is the razor-edged Afghan blade that he always carries. I pick it up, feeling its weight.

I take the knife in my right hand. I hold my left wrist over the open trunk. I press the edge where I've been told, just at the front of the wolf's head birthmark. Where the mouth is open. Not too deep. I don't want to sever a tendon or hit an artery. The blood rises as soon as I pull the blade away, welling up like water from a hidden spring tapped by a drill.

Yes! A voiceless whisper.

I toss the knife to the side, hear its tip *chunk* as it sticks into the wall. I pay no attention to it. I just hold my wrist out and let the blood fall.

More!

Drip.

Drip.

Drip.

Drip.

The first blood that lands on the gray skin spreads as if it were a drop of oil falling onto the surface of water. Its sheen is like that of a rainbow.

The second drop falls and the skin ripples, as if there were muscles moving beneath its surface.

With the third drop the skin grows larger, twice then four times as big as before.

With the fourth drop . . .

How can I express what happens then? All I can say is that I feel something from it, something from within me that I can only describe as a feeling of the deepest kinship. Maybe like meeting an identical twin separated from you at birth?

It's mine. It was born with me. I belong to it as much as it belongs to me.

There's no going back now.

I lift the wolf skin from the trunk. Or do I? Does it rise up of its own accord to meet my grasp? It doesn't matter. We're together. It's time for us to be together.

The light of the full moon through the round window high in the wall feels warmer than sunlight ever has. As I hold the skin I see the beauty of its shining fur, feel the strength it wants to share with me. It's perfect, complete from head to tail. I caress the head with my right hand. The dark openings for the eyes, the ears, the nose are not empty. My wolf skin senses me as much as I sense it. I press my face against it. A scent as sweet as the breath of a wolf cub. Fur as soft as a mother's caress.

This is not a pelt that was torn from the body of a lifeless creature. I know now that it was birthed with me, carefully set aside for the time when I was ready to accept my birthright. That, my father's brief instructions told me, has long been the way of our people. You must learn to be human first before you can accept the power and not be lost in it. Otherwise, you become a creature out of nightmares with no compassion for any being, no urge other than to hunt and kill.

I hope I really am ready. There's no turning back now.

But I have to stay methodical.

Always think ahead.

I fold the wolf skin over my left arm.

Not yet. Soon. Soon.

I turn off the hurricane lamp, place it inside the chest, shut the lid. I pry Dad's Afghan knife out of the wall, close its blade, stow it in my backpack. My father's letter, carefully folded and placed back into its envelope, I slide between the cover and the front page of my literature textbook.

A momentary pang at that. Will I ever open that book in a classroom again? Will I ever be able to sit and listen to a high school teacher droning on at the front of the class while Renzo pretends to shoot himself with his index finger? Will I ever walk the halls of RHS like a normal teenager again with no major worry other than my thwarted dreams of romance with Meena?

Meena. I want this last thought of a normal human life to be about her. But it's not. For some reason the faces of the members of the Sunglass Mafia suddenly come to mind. The way they looked at me, the things they said—as if they recognized something in me I hadn't yet seen in myself.

At the edge of my mind there's an answer to those questions. It's there along with a certainty that if I ever do get back to RHS, there's going to be another meeting—or confrontation.

The skin I'm carrying over my arm, my second skin, pulses, sends a wave of heat, of hunger through me. I feel as if my stomach is being hit by a pile driver and squeezed in a vice at the same time. It bends me double. Damn!

My hands are shaking, but I manage to shoulder my pack and straighten up. I open the secret door, step out into the larger room, close the door behind me. Nothing but empty bookcase and wall to be seen. I scuff the dust with my bare feet so that although someone might notice it's been disturbed there's no clear trail leading across the room toward the wall.

Go out the door.

Close it behind me.

Walk down the stairs—with nothing on and too much on my mind.

Open the front door of the Drake House.

Step outside.

The sweet free smell of the night air and the feel of it on my bare chest are too damn intoxicating.

Do it now!

Complete yourself. Now! Then run, run with the wind as if there was no tomorrow. Run as if the great light of the moon in the sky will always be shining on me.

Stop.

Breathe.

Everything I've done since taking the skin in my hands has required an act of will greater than anything I've ever tried before. Not just my hands, but my whole body is trembling. This must be what it feels like when you're a drug addict and in need of a fix.

Put it on! Now! Put it on!

Not yet. Think ahead.

Walk down the walkway, reach the place where I parked the Commando behind the shed. Secure the backpack onto the bike with the bungee cords.

Now?

Yes, now.

This is the place. I can make my way back here without having to open any doors. I'm not sure that opening doors in any fashion other than smashing them down is going to be possible afterward. Will I have hands or just paws? And how will I take it off once I've put it on?

I . . . can't . . . wait . . . any . . . longer.

I lift it up with both trembling hands, slide on my second skin.

RUN

Yes!

I don't just say that word. Every part of my being howls out that assertion. Yes.

It's not like putting on a coat. The skin, my second skin, flows around me, embraces me, molds itself to me, melts into me. It fits to every contour of my body, to every pore of my skin. I feel myself changing as it happens.

Remember those scenes in *An American Werewolf in London* where the poor victim of the curse falls to the ground in agony? He twists and moans. His face elongates into a Halloween horror mask. The bones of his hands crackle like corn being popped as they become paws. It's worse than being stretched on a torture rack.

In the movies, that's the way it happens. But this is not like that at all. No pain. No agony. Not that I don't change. But there's nothing violent about it. It's as natural as a butterfly emerging from its chrysalis. And I'm not changed into some mindless beast. I'm still who I was before, I'm just . . . more. I'm both wolf and man.

Before, I could hear and smell better than most humans. Now those senses are magnified to the level of a wolf, especially my sense of smell.

Canines experience the world as much through their noses as through their eyes. Sometimes more. The olfactory nerves and the part of the brain that processes scent is as developed in them as the optic nerve and its processing components are in humans. Imagine "seeing" a scent on the wind, a trail that you can pick out from a hundred thousand other trails twining in the air around you. Each scent trail has its own, what? Color, maybe. That might be the easiest way to describe it.

I'm still standing erect on two legs. I haven't fallen down to all fours, though I know I'd be perfectly comfortable if I did. I was wrong about what might happen to my hands. They're not exactly like the feet of a wolf, paws that wouldn't be able to do things like pick up a tool or turn a door knob. Not like that at all. I wiggle my fingers. Five in all. I haven't lost my opposable thumb, though my fingers are larger and slightly less flexible than before. There's thick fur all the way down to my nails—which are much more clawlike. There are heavy pads at the base of each digit and my palms are broader, equally cushioned with tough skin. To run as a wolf all I'll have to do is curl my fingers back a little.

I don't have a mirror, but when I lift my hands up to my face I can feel how drastic this metamorphosis has been. My human body inside the second skin has shaped itself to fill out the muzzle, the longer head of a wolf. My canine teeth are fangs, my incisors shaped to cut and tear meat.

It's all good.

No, way better than good. I take a deep breath. An indescribable feeling hits me. It's a wave of elation like nothing I've felt before. I almost lose myself in the pure joy of it, the surge of power.

But I feel more than just joy. Excitement, impatience, then anger. Like giant tsunami waves those emotions come surging in, one after another. I feel like a tree being buffeted by hurricane winds from every direction.

It's so hard to control myself. In the past, if I felt upset, I had to hold myself back from punching my fist through a wall. Now, now I can feel that I would do far more if I give myself up to the emotions I'm feeling. Despair at having my father taken, unhealed bitterness about my mother's death still tearing at my heart.

Arrghhh!

Something's happening to my vision. The whole world is washed with crimson, soaked with blood. I could tear an entire building apart right now. I would do it in this red rage—regardless of what might happen to those inside, guilty or innocent.

When you put on the skin, you have to run.

That was what my father's instructions told me. He didn't mean I should flee from accepting my wolf-marked destiny. He meant that I literally had to start running. Expend as much energy as possible right away.

Release enough of the long pent-up power held in my second skin to maintain control. My human body has needed to be one with it, but it can't allow my reason to be overcome by it. I can't lose my heart, my human compassion. If I do, I really will become a monster.

What happens now between me and my new skin has to be a partnership, a symbiosis.

To reach that point, I need to run.

Run to keep from hurting myself—or anyone else.

Run to understand what I have become.

Run to gain balance.

Run, Lucas!

Run!

AWAKE

I'm panting as I lean back against the trunk of the old oak tree on the hill in the deserted scout campgrounds where I found my dad's message. I'm not panting because I'm tired, even though I have been running long enough for the moon to move the distance of three hands—or paws—higher into the sky. Panting is just the way that members of the canine family, who lack skin glands like those of the apes and hominids, cool themselves down when their bodies are overheated. My panting is the lupine equivalent of breaking a sweat.

It's so late now that most people will be asleep. But not me.

Thoreau, the famous nineteenth-century American transcendentalist, once said he had never met a man who was fully awake.

He never met me. I'm the opposite of tired. I'm alive and energized like never before.

I didn't come back here straightaway. If I had, I would have covered the twelve miles between the oak and the Drake House in less than twenty minutes. It's too beautiful a night to be making a beeline anywhere. I ran for the joy of running, letting my feet and my nose lead me wherever they wanted. And I ran because I needed to run.

I stayed off the roads after the first few miles. I didn't like the hard feel of blacktop or concrete under my feet, the sickening smells of asphalt and oil and gasoline. I needed to find a cleaner place, one less soiled by this modern world that poisons and paves over our Mother Earth.

I also didn't want to attract attention from any late-driving trucker or from the houses close to those roads with their halogen-lit light poles. Pathetic—like frightened children clutching flashlights and clinging to their mother's legs. Fearing the dark and whatever nightmare creature might come out of the forest at night. Like me. Poor little humans.

Whoa! That was an arrogant thought. These are people, not prey. I have to keep Dad's advice in mind. *Beware of arrogance.* That's what my father's instructions told me.

Anyhow, none of the . . . people . . . in those houses saw me. But their dogs sensed me. Each house I passed where a dog resided, my passage was answered by a long terrified howl.

There was also a pack of wild dogs in these woods. Every now and then they kill a deer like the wolf ancestors they still remember in their blood. They might even be dangerous to a solitary hiker here in the preserve. But not to me. I caught their scent at about the same time they caught mine. And what I smelled was their fear as they ran from me and kept running

So I turned back to the forest. I followed the animal trails sewn like countless threads through the forest preserve lands that cover the hills and small mountains of the county.

I ran so fast that I felt as if I was flying, leaping over streams, pounding along trails deep in beech leaves and pine needles, racing through meadows as the tall grass whipped past. Not even the heady scent of the herd of deer that stampeded in panic as I neared them tempted me enough to follow another instinct, a predatory one.

True, the image was tantalizing. Leaping high to bring down one of those fat four-legged meals on hooves—my teeth crushing its windpipe, ripping through the hide, tearing off strips of meat, my muzzle bathed in the hot blood, then chewing a leg bone till it cracked and I could lick out the sweet marrow. That thought did slow me down a bit.

As did the rabbit that bolted out in front of me, zigzagging in panic. I smelled its fear, tasted what it would be like to just snap it up, shake my head once to break its neck, and then squat down with it between my paws and finish it off in a few quick bites, the little bones crunching in my teeth.

But my hunger wasn't as powerful as the other urgency that I felt in my body and knew in my mind. It was not time to eat. Not yet. That could come later. Maybe go to Taco Prince. Convince Renzo to give me a few pounds of raw hamburger. Hah. Even in the shape of a man-wolf I still had my corny sense of humor.

No, I had to keep running. Stretch my legs, suck more of the night air into my lungs. Touch, smell, see, feel. Fully experience what I had become. I was like a race driver getting in a new machine for the first time and taking it around the track. Or maybe more like someone climbing behind the wheel of a car for the first time after having only walked before that. Or maybe there's just no simile to match this experience.

I've finally run enough to adjust to this new self. I'm pretty sure I've reached the point where my cognitive faculties won't be submerged by the waves of ferocity that have subsided now like the calm surface of a very deep ocean.

So, here I am back where I started. Just above my head is the hollow where I found the empty lemon drop can that held his note. The thought of how far I've come since then makes me feel dizzy.

Half the night lies ahead of me before I can take off the skin. Although it would be so easy, so satisfying to remain embraced by a skin of power, fuller and more complete than any weak little human being can ever feel.

Oops. Another arrogant thought! I have got to keep remembering Dad's advice. It's not that I can only wear the skin at night, but—as my father's instructions explained—night is the safest time. People are less likely to see those like us in the dark, though we can still see them. And there's only so long that one can stay a wolf without starting to forget what it is to be something else. It's a delicate balance.

Take it off before dawn.

However, I still have four or five hours.

How much can I do before then?

Where shall I start?

A thought strikes me.

I stretch my mouth in a wide wolfish grin. Where else?

27
WATCHERS

The clouds have shrouded the face of the moon. Dark now, too dark for ordinary humans to see much farther than a few yards without the aid of a light or night vision equipment. I miss the moon's comforting presence, but this darkness is working in my favor. It helped hide me from the two men I saw watching our trailer. But I could see them as well as I can smell them.

I've already located the car they came in. I'm standing next to it now. It's parked down the highway from our trailer, next to a maple behind the old barn at the edge of what once was a hay field but is now grown up with grass, locust saplings, fire cherry, and sumac. Even the sign fastened on the barn's side announcing the availability of NEW HOMES BUILT TO ORDER is faded. That sign, once a statement of promise, is now the sign of a failed state. A single sumac three feet tall lifts like an exclamation point out of the center of the weed patch—formerly a flower bed—at the sign's base.

It's a familiar sight all around this county. The housing market is now in the same sad shape that the local agriculture industry was back when half the area's dairy farmers sold off their land to real estate speculators.

"Burning Down The Housing Market" was the title that Renzo came up with for his research paper on the subject for a Civics project. That clever, if only slightly apropos, reference to the classic David Byrne song was my friend's major contribution to the research end of his assignment. Guess who proofread and rewrote it for him and now has all the history and statistics permanently lodged in his burglar-proof memory bank?

It seems that even as a wolf I still have all these irrelevant thoughts buzzing through my brain. As well as a few urges that have never seemed quite that important to me as they do now. All of them involving chasing, leaping, attacking, biting, tearing . . .

Think. Don't stop thinking.

The car is a black Mercedes. It's the first one of the three that tailed me from school. I recognize the license plate that I read backward in my handlebar rearview mirror. But there's just one car here and only two people staked out back at our trailer. That suggests a couple of things.

One is that they didn't figure out that I gave them the slip on purpose. They think I escaped their tail through dumb luck. (My not coming home yet is likely chalked up to a teenager taking advantage of the lack of parental supervision to stay out all night.)

The second is that though they're still on my trail, they don't think I'm that dangerous. Not with just two men expecting to grab me. They haven't even left anyone to watch the car.

A disgusted growl escapes my throat. Only two men. It's insulting. A dozen wouldn't be enough. This is no challenge at all. The satisfying image of their bodies sprawled on the ground, their throats torn out and blood soaking the earth around them almost overwhelms me. The urge to make that image a reality ripples through my body like an invisible riptide, pulling me down toward the deep fierce water that could drown everything human and rational.

I turn my head toward one of the low-hanging arm-thick maple branches. My back teeth sink into it and I taste the bittersweet bark. I twist my head and even though its wood is more resistant than the radius and ulna bones of a human forearm I easily bite through the entire branch. *Crunch, crunch.*

No.

Think.

I realize that I'm not feeling any revulsion at the thought of tearing those two men limb from limb. It's not just that they deserve it because they've taken my father captive. It's not anger or a desire for revenge. It's more like a wolf might view its prey. No fellow feeling. No viewing the potential victim as a person who had a mother and a father, someone who has known joy and pain, who has laughed and cried as you do.

Nope. No empathy.

Just sort of . . . so what? No big deal.

Interesting. Part of myself couldn't care less and just wants to, as Jean-Luc Picard on *Star Trek* always put it, "make it so." However, somewhere inside me, another section of my psyche is appalled. It's wondering with some trepidation if I will still be experiencing this kind of detached, serial killer, sociopathic point of view about causing death and human suffering after I take off my second skin.

This is not the time for carnage. Not yet.

A plan has already been forming in the back of my head. That's why I just sniff at their concealed car but don't flatten its tires, smash its windshield into tiny beads of shatterproof glass, rip its doors off the hinges, pull open the hood and reduce its engine to broken rubble. I want to, but for my plan to succeed I need to leave them an avenue of escape. I lope back to the hilltop and check out the watchers. Still there, right where I saw them before.

I descend the hill as slowly, as silently as dark water down the face of a smooth stone. I reach the back of the trailer, pause hidden in the tall grass.

The first one, whose light, thinning hair has been sprayed in place in a Donald Trump comb-over, is sitting in the less sturdy of our two dilapidated metal lawn chairs—relics we inherited from the trailer's former owner. He's placed the chair next to the little wooden shed out back of the Sardine Can. The shed is too small for a garage, but just big enough to store my Dad's tools and my Norton.

I'm only twenty feet away from him. Comb-over Man's fingers are twitching as he sits there. He reeks of cigarettes. I can smell the sweat seep from his pores as he fights his addiction, trying to control the urge to light up. Like a shop clerk with an hour to go before he can bolt out into the parking lot to contribute an equal amount of pollution to his lungs and the air.

Unlike a shop clerk, he's packing more than Camels. A semi-automatic pistol, a Glock 17, rests in his lap. His legs are crossed. His right pants leg is hiked up just enough for me to see the lower part of his thickly muscled calf and the handle of the stiletto in an ankle sheath. Well-armed with weapons that have probably been put to deadly use more than once.

I flex my clawed hands. With one swipe I could take off his entire face, just leave a mask of red subcutaneous tissue and white, bloody bone. Just the thought of that will have to be enough for now.

What else might I do?

Take two quiet steps and I'd be behind him. It would take no longer than a heartbeat for me to reach over to snatch the Glock from his lap, slip the knife from its sheath, lean close to his ear, and growl the word "Run!"

I shake my head. Not a good plan. I don't want anyone to even suspect that there's something more dangerous here than a vapid potential teenage hostage. Plus, fight rather than flight might be his impulse.

His last impulse.

I fade back farther into the dark, circle the trailer. The man next to the fuel tank to the left of our front steps is much like the Comb-over Man. Six feet at most. But the width of his shoulders, the thickness of his neck, and the narrowness of his waist indicate that he's a gym rat. Everyday activities are not desk work. This is a man who looks dangerous—and knows how dangerous he is.

The front door watcher is also similarly attired to the one in back. Basic black. Well-tailored suit, black turtleneck under it. No white in sight. Dark socks and jet-black, thick rubber-soled shoes. His hair is dark and thick. No need for the Rogaine I smelled on the other man's scalp. Eyebrows so thick they form a single shaggy ridge across his forehead.

Like his cohort out back, he's not clean shaven. That three-day growth of beard makes me suspect that these two are not in the regular employ of any arm of our government. He's sitting in the better of our set of inherited lawn chairs, an indication that Comb-over Man out back is Number Two in this hierarchy.

The front door watcher's body language, as well as his better armament—a Mossberg shotgun resting across his lap in addition to the mandatory Glock in the holster under his arm—also show he's in charge. He's more alert. Scanning the darkness around him with night vision goggles like the ones his buddy out back left sitting on the rusty drink stand next to the lawn chair. Better at sentry duty than his nicotine-deprived pal. Still, his scent—no adrenaline odor, no sweat—tells me that he's keeping watch without much expectation of actually seeing something. His scan of the driveway ahead of him, but not the bushes next to him where I'm crouched on all fours, is followed by a yawn.

Poor sleepyhead. Wouldn't take but a moment for me to rock him to sleep. Permanently.

I hold back the deep-throated growl I feel building in my chest. That's not my plan.

And I do have a plan.

28
TO GET AWAY

It's pretty basic. Get them to run without realizing they're being chased. What makes it possible—easy in fact—is that this place is my home, not theirs. Well, calling the elongated tin box we've been living in a home is stretching it. So let me put it another way. This is my turf, my territory. My hunting grounds.

I prowl back around the Sardine Can. Comb-over Man is as blind, deaf, and dumb to my presence as he was before. Perfect.

The crawl space under the trailer isn't that visible from the front or the back because there's a skirting of plywood. But on the side closest to the woods, there's a loose piece of three-quarter inch that can be slid to the side to get under the trailer. Our trailer is set up on a triple course of concrete blocks. The space is large enough, the floor high enough, for a good-sized man to crawl in and move under it in a crouch. There's more than enough room for me to enter comfortably on all fours, turn, slide the plywood panel back in place. I do it all as quiet as a mouse, invisible as a mole burrowing underfoot.

But not as stealthy as a rat. I hate rats, so there's no way I am ever going to compare myself to one in any way, shape, or form. I hate their sneakiness, their viciousness. I've got some grudging admiration for their toughness. Everywhere people go, you find rats, and they're almost impossible to get rid of. If there was a nuclear war, Uncle Cal once said, you can bet that the two creatures who'd survive would be the rats and the cockroaches. It was rats that spread the bubonic plague. And rats can chew through anything, from solid metal to two feet of concrete. One of the first things I did when we moved here was to check the place for any signs of rats. It's kind of a phobia with me. If I smell a rat—and believe me, that is something I can do from a long way away—I start growling to myself.

The fact that there were no rats in the trailer was about the only good thing about it. It had been through a couple of owners before us and it was here long before my father and I arrived in town. Dad bought it at a bargain price. Who else would have wanted a cramped, rusted aluminum packing case? Smaller than a railway car. Only four rooms, no closet space, and set back half a mile from the highway with no other people within a mile.

Perfect for what I assumed Dad wanted. To get away. Away from anything that reminded him of Mom, of the life he'd lived, the responsibilities he'd shouldered, the burdens that woke him up in the middle of the night—unless he had self-medicated himself to the point of a stupor. To hide from something that I thought was all in his head.

That's what I thought. But I was wrong on two counts. The dangers we were hiding away from were not imaginary. And, in fact, Dad was not hiding but carrying out some kind of plan he'd kept even from me. While we were both keeping our real selves hidden—including this new self I never realized I had to hide.

Few as our remaining material goods were when we moved here, the tin can still wasn't big enough to hold many of them. Dad rented a storage shed. Most everything went there, including the two boxes of favorite books I'd accumulated. No bookshelves in the trailer and no room for any. That's why I never brought any books home from school. I always left everything I needed, including a couple of changes of clothing, in my locker. That stuff, of course, is now in my backpack. The only book in my room is one of photos called *In Wilderness is the Protection of the World*.

The one thing Dad added to the trailer is what I'm about to use. A trapdoor cut into the floor of his bedroom and concealed under a ratty throw rug. I lift it up. The only sound is the soft slide of the rug across the trapdoor. Less noise than a zipper being opened.

Not much in Dad's room. As usual. One chair, the bed, a minuscule dresser. His bag, though, is gone, along with his spare shoes, his sweats, and most of his clothes. Undoubtedly packed by his captors to preserve the fiction that he had been called away on a trip. His few remaining clothes hang in the midget closet, his spare boots on the closet floor. His empty duffel bag is in there too. I lift myself up on my hind legs to unhook it with one dexterous paw. I drop down to all fours, turn, and open the drawer in the minuscule dresser by his bed. His checkbook seems to be gone, but I do find his extra wallet. Dad made a point of showing me where it was. It's an exact duplicate—IDs, credit cards, and all—of the one he carries. The thing under the wallet surprises me. Dad's map of national parks and forests. He kept it after all. Maybe there was dust on it because my eyes get misty as I look at it. There's also a black zipper bag, the kind you might put documents into. I don't know what it is, but I'd better take it. I flip it all into the duffel.

I pick the canvas bag up between my teeth and pad down the

hall into my room. Time to pack. It doesn't take long. Everything here that I own or care to keep fits into the bag with room to spare. I wrap the T-shirt with the words One Love and a picture of Wyclef Jean—when he had his dreads—around the framed photo of my mother. The clothing and other stuff is useful, but that photo is the one thing in the Sardine Can I'm not ready to sacrifice. Maybe one thing more. I pick up the wilderness book. Not that heavy and the map of the national parks fits neatly between its covers.

I pause by the bathroom to stick a few things into a zipper container that fits in the top of the duffel bag. I also use the toilet, which is not that easy to do when you have to lift a leg to aim. I almost forget myself and automatically flush it. That would be a big mistake!

I pick the bag up in my teeth, carry it back into Dad's room, drop it through the open trapdoor.

I go back into the bathroom, which is at the farthest end of the trailer. There's one small ugly window in the bathroom. It rusted shut years before we took possession of the Sardine Can. The heavy towel hung over it is as much to avoid looking at it as to ensure privacy. But it does mean that a faint light in the bathroom will not be noticed from the outside.

I take the box of matches from the lower shelf of the decrepit vanity that long ago lost all its vanity and barely holds up the sink. Although my paw hands are dexterous, I have a little trouble with the matches—opening the box and then striking them. It's not because I'm incapable of doing it. I'm hesitant. A part of my brain shrinks from the thought of fire. It takes a surprising amount of self-control for me to light a match and hold it. The sharp odor of the sulfur and the flare of the flame makes me drop the first match as soon as it lights.

Control. Concentrate.

On my third try I manage to hold onto the burning match, though I keep it out at arm's (should I say leg's?) length. I use it to light the two hurricane candles I've placed on a plate inside the shower stall. The thick candles are guaranteed to burn for twenty-four hours. I can guarantee that they won't.

I look out the window. Number One is in place. I turn to look out the window in the back door. Comb-over Man is still twitching for a ciggie.

That gives me another idea. I go back into Dad's room and pull out the bottom drawer of his dresser, all the way out. There's a baggie taped to the back of it. My father's stash. There's only a few flakes of weed left in it, along with some rolling papers, a partly smoked marijuana cigarette, and a Bic lighter. The musky odor of the grass is almost too much for me to take with my enhanced sense of smell, but I take it back to my room. I place the rolling papers, the baggie, the lighter, and the half-toked joint in the bathroom next to the burning candle. With luck, the shower stall will protect them from being totally destroyed.

Then I go back into the kitchen area.

I lift myself up over the gas stove. It's a little hard to aim my breath with this long muzzle, but I eventually manage to blow out the pilot light. I glance at the statement from the gas company that I tacked just above the foot-wide shelf next to the stove. The writing is faint, the lighting poor, but with my enhanced night vision I have no trouble reading it. A little growl of satisfaction escapes my mouth. Just as I remembered, propane was delivered two days ago. Not a big tank, but it's plenty big enough.

I turn on all of the gas stove burners. Two steps and I'm in Dad's bedroom. I drop down through the trapdoor, reach up to lower it slowly so it makes no noise. I pick up the duffel bag and lug it, swinging from my mouth, to the opening at the far end of the trailer. I lean out to look around. The coast is clear.

With the bag in my teeth, I hightail it (literally) for the woods. I've done all of this and I'm fifty yards up the hill in less time than it has taken to describe my exit from the Sardine Can—which is about to undergo a serious metamorphosis as dramatic as the one I recently went through.

I drop the bag at my side, sit back on my haunches with my tongue hanging out, and wait.

SHOW TIME

I have the equivalent of a grandstand view. I can observe not only the whole trailer, but also both the front and the back and the two men in black keeping desultory watch. The main feature is about to start. And it will be in full 3-D. All I need now is some popcorn.

It won't be long. Even though I made sure that all the windows were tightly shut, the trailer is so poorly insulated that the scent of the faint traces of escaping propane is already reaching my hypersensitive nostrils.

Watcher Number One notices something too. He has his head raised. Something is out of the ordinary but he doesn't fully realize yet what it is, even though his cerebral cortex is registering the warning signal from his olfactory nerves. He stands up, the shotgun held loosely in his right hand, walks back a few paces away from the trailer.

Comb-over Man is oblivious, though no longer sitting down. He's moved back from the trailer to unzip and relieve himself

142

against the side of our storage shed. How lucky for him.

"Hey, Nick, " Number One calls out, kindly informing me of Comb-over Man's first name, "Do you smell . . ."

Gas, of course. But he doesn't complete his question. It is interrupted by a faint, but ominous sound. A sort of gentle *thwummp* as the gas catches and then a much louder *WHOMP!*

Show time!

It's not quite as spectacular as a Hollywood explosion, but it's impressive nonetheless. I don't leap back, though instinct urges me to do so. But I do blink and I pant a bit harder as the windows and doors of the Sardine Can are blown out by billowing tongues of flame. It's hard to keep from howling in triumph.

The whole structure of the trailer doesn't burst apart, but it's immediately an inferno—like a blowtorch consuming itself. Few things are better designed to be fiery death traps than the older generation of house trailers from which the Sardine Can was birthed.

Number One and Nick are slowly getting back to their feet, limping toward each other. They could have been killed by the explosion. Not my plan, but it wouldn't have bothered me at all—in a moral sense. If I have any feelings right now that could be described as moral.

Intellectually, though, I'm pleased they survived. Necessary for my plan to keep working. They're alive, but they are not happy campers. The shockwave from the blast knocked them sprawling, as if swatted by the invisible hand of an irritated giant. They're madly slapping the burning patches on their clothing ignited by that sudden sunburst of heat. If smoking was what Nick wanted to do before, he should be happy now.

"Christ, Eddie!" Nick yells as he extinguishes the last flame on his sleeve. He limps forward, holding his crotch with one hand and waving his pistol with the other. "Christ, Eddie!"

And now I know Number One's moniker too. Eddie. Assuming that Nick's mentioning the cognomen of the savior of all mankind was mere blasphemy and not Eddie's first name.

Eddie no longer has any eyebrows. His face is as charcoaled as a vaudevillian in one of those old racist blackface skits from the twentieth century. Nick's hair, what's left of it, is standing up straight in front and completely singed off in back. He's still clutching the area between his legs as he hobbles forward with a pained look on his face.

The dialogue that ensues between the two of them is as colorful and X-rated as you might imagine. To save time, I'll just sum it up with the two questions that it eventually boils down to.

"Whuh happened?"

That one, I can answer. But I won't.

"Whadda we do now?"

That, I believe I can guess.

Eddie puts the shotgun down by his feet. He reaches into his pocket and pulls out a small phone. He fiddles with it for a minute without, apparently, any luck. He landed heavily on that side when the blast sent him sprawling. He lets loose another inventively long string of curses. His vocabulary is impressive. He throws the dead phone into the still-blazing mass of burning wood, metal, glass, and plastic rubble that no longer resembles a can, box, or container of any sort. Eddie stares at the blaze for a minute as if expecting his cell phone to rise regenerated from the pyre like the mythical phoenix of old.

Nope.

Then he turns roughly to Nick, who's placed his pistol in his belt and is trying to free something—oh my—from his zipper, his teeth clenched in concentration.

"Gimme yours."

Meaningful pause, as Nick stares at him in disbelief.

"Your phone, you effing idiot."

Nick's phone, unlike the uncertain state of some of his other apparatuses, proves workable. Despite the roar and crackle of the flames, I can hear Eddie's end of the conversation.

"It just goddamn blew up. Boom! No, I don't know why. What? No, the kid's not here. You want us to go keep an eye on the other guy? No? The other team's watching Kureshi? Okay, okay."

Did I hear him just say the name of Meena's father? Or did I just imagine it because I can't keep her out of my mind, even now in the midst of all this? But if I did hear it, what does it mean? Is her Dad in danger? And if so, why? And why is it that everything that is happening always leads to more questions I can't answer?

Eddie folds the phone shut and places it in his own pocket rather than into Nick's outstretched hand.

"We're going in."

"There?" Nick stares at the raging inferno.

Eddie rolls his eyes.

"Jesus, Nickie. Lemme ask you a question. When they were handing out brains, were you one of the guys who thought they said 'bran' and told them you didn't want cereal?"

Nick makes one final adjustment to his pants and shakes his head. "I don't think so," he says.

Eddie shakes his head and picks up the shotgun. Clearly controlling the urge to put his partner out of his misery with the Mossberg, he points toward the road and gestures for Nick to follow him.

"We gotta go back to the house."

And I'll be following them.

MAXICO

Eddie and Nick reach their car without incident. They climb in, Nick a bit gingerly, and then roar off spraying a rooster tail of gravel as they pull onto the highway. They're doing at least seventy by the time they disappear around the curve half a mile down the highway.

Now all I have to do is stay on their tail. And how am I going to do that? Even though I've discovered that I can now run for miles at a time without tiring, I am still way slower than even a Smart Car, one of those new mini-autos that look like a freezer on wheels, much less a powerful Mercedes. I don't have superhuman speed.

But I do have other superhuman—or perhaps just average wolfish—powers. Before I donned my second skin I was able to pick up more with my nose than other humans. Now, as a skin-walker, following the scent trail of that car and its two slightly parboiled passengers is as easy as using a GPS—and much less likely to direct me onto a dead-end road a mile from my destination.

This late at night, there's little traffic, but I still stay off the road, cutting across fields and woodlots now and then to intersect and pick up the scent trail once more. I'm not wearing a watch, of course. For the usual reason plus one. But from the motion across the sky of my friend, the moon, I estimate that it takes me about an hour to reach the place where they left the state road.

A newly-paved access road leads off the main highway to cross a vast expanse of dried-up rolling lawns before disappearing a mile farther back into hills and trees. I read the new sign raised up on steel posts. MAXICO BIOPARK, the bold words standing out in relief.

Maxico. The wealthiest of the multinational corporations recently settled here, the one where Meena's father works. And that is what makes it likely that I wasn't wrong in thinking Eddie mentioned him being under surveillance. The factory that was here before used to employ over four hundred people before it became another icon of twenty-first-century America, when outsourcing our progress to South Asia became our most important product. It was thought that when the place was resurrected that some of those jobs would come back to the locals. Wrong. The kind of biotech research that is being carried on behind the fences and walls that guard it is so secret the company brought in all its own people. It's so hush-hush that Meena doesn't know anything about what her father does. And he doesn't even have the highest clearance level, which means he works in one of the buildings in the outer ring of the place, not deep inside. She's been aching to visit him at work, but even the closest family members are not allowed inside the fence I'm now looking at. And those who are in the inner ring, it seems, aren't allowed out.

The inner ring of Maxico, it seems, is like its own little separate country. They have their own housing, their own commissary. Their workers were all brought here on buses and they stay sequestered on the compound all the time. As I've mentioned before, the only locals I've ever heard of who actually have been inside the Maxico compound since that ceremony are Dr. Kesselring and his pet policemen.

There's about two hundred acres in the Maxico grounds that surround the high security ring, including the sixty acres that was the short-lived Wild Wonders Safari Park. Its lions, tigers, bears, and other exotic animals failed to attract enough tourists to stay in business. I wonder if any of the cages still exist. Maybe they're now being used to house the company's serfs. The animal park's fencing along the road (which failed to prevent the brief escape of one tiger and two leopards) was replaced as soon as Maxico moved in. They put up the long, long fence I'm studying. Not only does it rise ten feet high, it's also said to be buried six feet into the ground. Topped with double rolls of prison-style razor wire, the erection of this formidable barrier was the only job that briefly employed local contractors.

I can see one of the distant outer buildings of Maxico through trees beyond the chain-link fence. It's well designed to keep most intruders out—or whatever is inside safely within. The closed steel gate across the entrance, monitored by cameras, requires a keycard to open. Nick and Eddie have one, of course. Eddie leans out, swipes it. The gate opens, they pass through, it closes.

And me without one of those little plastic passes.

Not to worry. I choose a shadowy section of fence a hundred yards from the gate. It's dark enough that any security cameras won't pick up anything more than a flicker in the night. A quick run, a leap, and I clear the fence with a foot to spare. The brown lawn is wider and much more open than I'd like. There may be more hidden cameras monitoring the area. But it's been a long time since a mower has been used here. The two-foot-tall brown grass and weeds have made the rolling terrain into more of a hay field than a golf course. I stay low, move fast, barely rippling the grass. No more than the shadow of the wind on any screen that may be monitoring the area.

Soon the grass and weeds turn into forest. It looks like some kind of tree plantation of evenly-spaced forty-foot-tall pines. Within the trees, I still stay low but I move more slowly. I'm not picking up any nearby threat, but I am smelling something that is disquieting. Something I can't quite identify. Once again, the rumble of a low growl builds within me. I swallow it back. I need to be silent.

The forest edge is now just ahead of me. The land beyond the trees is overgrown with ferns and rises slightly. I drop to my belly and crawl forward until I reach the top of the hill. Then I peer down through the curtaining ferns. Below me, and on the other side is yet another wall—ten feet tall and made of concrete. It stretches as far as I can see in either direction. I'm high enough to look over the wall and see a really big building on the other side. It has to be the inner sanctum of Maxico, the place where only a select few are allowed to enter. Six black cars are parked on this side of the wall near a big entrance door.

Figure two men to each car. That means there are at least a dozen enemies down there. I visualize myself leaping, a lethal blur, ripping their throats out one after another, standing over their torn bodies growling, my muzzle and teeth dripping with blood. It's a pleasant, reassuring image, especially because of another scent I've just detected. My father's scent, still in the air hours after he was brought here. Kill them all, then rescue him. Do it now. Attack!

No. That thought is very, very real in my mind, but not realistic.

It can't be that easy. Although Nick and Eddie were unaware of me, the higher-ups can't be as clueless as they were. Who knows what's on the other side of that wall and in that giant building. I don't know what effect bullets would have on me, but I doubt that I'm totally invulnerable to them, despite my newfound power.

That first, strange scent is stronger now. I can't figure out what it is, though it raises my hackles. It's not human, but it is something living. Maybe more than one something.

A ripple runs down the muscles along my back. My shoulders are hunched, tense. I dig my nails into the soft earth, crushing the roots of the ferns. Every muscle in my body aches to race down the hill and take action. That's where my father is being held. I want to rescue him. Now! But I can't allow myself to just rush in. It would probably be suicidal. I need time to plan. And that means I have to wait. I don't have that much time now.

This night is almost over. Dawn will be here before long. All I have time to do is pick up the duffel bag of possessions I left near the ruins of our trailer and make my way back to the Drake House. That's all I can do now.

I've actually accomplished a lot since finding my second skin. I've avoided my own potential kidnappers. I've followed them back to this place where I know my father is being held. I have to be content with this for now.

Damn it.

I want to raise my head and let out a long angry despairing howl. But I control myself. I inch back into the trees, turn, and begin to make my way back toward the road.

Tomorrow, I think. *Tomorrow.*

COMPANY

Well before I reach the ruins of the trailer I can see that there's company. The glare of lights is visible almost before I catch the scents of strangers and their vehicles. It's not Nick and Eddie making a return visit, but two fire trucks, an ambulance, a dozen cars, and a TV news van.

The fire must have been visible from some distance. Maybe a passing motorist saw it. Then again, the sound of the propane going off like a bomb was probably heard a mile away. The first responders have been here long enough for the tanker trucks to have dowsed the blaze. The spotlights on their fire engines are trained on the smoldering, twisted bonfire that was my more-or-less home for a while. Two rescue workers are probing with long poles—undoubtedly looking for bodies.

I'm not about to reassure them that there were no fatalities. I sit back on my haunches in the darkest area behind the bushes. I should trot up the hill, retrieve my duffel bag, get back to the Drake House before the sun comes up. But for some reason I'm fascinated by the chubby newsman with the mike who's positioned himself so that both the smoldering remains and the rescue workers are just behind him. I think they call it an establishing shot.

"We're here at the scene of what appears to have been a terrible tragedy . . ." he's saying. His cheeks quiver as he talks.

Why do I keep looking at him? Soft neck. Round, piggy limbs. Nice and fat, he is. Why am I hoping that he'll just step away from the cameras and walk over here into the shadows? Why am I drooling?

Oh.

I suddenly recognize what I'm feeling right now. It may be due to all of the exercise I've had over the last five or six hours. I haven't put anything at all into my belly since I gulped down lunch at RHS. Or maybe my second skin was without sustenance for so long that its need is desperate. I'm hungrier than I've ever felt before. I feel the hunger not just in my stomach but in every part of my being.

Eat now, eat.

Don't eat people.

Another of my father's carefully printed rules. I snort. Easy for him to say. Try running thirty or forty miles on an empty stomach and then stick to a low cholesterol diet.

I force myself to turn my gaze away from the two hundred fifty pounds of gray-suited meat who's still babbling inanities for the camera. I trot up the hill, find the duffel bag, pick it up in my teeth, and start at an easy lope toward the Drake mansion.

I've managed to control that almost overpowering urge to hunt and feed. But as I enter the preserve and pad along its trails, part of me is hoping that I'll meet some solitary hiker out for a walk in the moonlight. It's quiet all around except for the rippling of the stream.

One way to kill hunger is by drinking. I put down the duffel bag and wade into the stream. I lower my head and lap up water. Drink. Drink. I'm thirstier than I thought. But when I leave the stream and pick up the bag in my teeth, another spasm of hunger hits me so hard that I almost bite through the strap.

Then I realize I'm not alone here. I catch the scent. Company. I lift my gaze.

I see her. She's alone. She was walking the path on the other side of the stream. Her steps were so quiet on the needle-cushioned path that I didn't hear them. Perhaps she's been called from sleep by the dreaminess of the full moon and the warm night. Her head is turned toward me. The moonlight outlines her graceful shape. A growl escapes my throat as I drop the bag. She hears it, sees me, tenses to flee.

Too late.

I don't think. There's no room for thought when a predator makes a decision like this. One leap and I'm in the stream. Another and I explode out of it in a silver spray of water like one of those crocodiles in that Planet Earth series launching at a migrating wildebeest.

She's too frozen with fear to move. Her liquid eyes are wide and wild. I snarl as I knock her to the ground. As my gaping jaws close around her throat, I bite so hard that I hear the crunch of a windpipe breaking. Warm blood fills my mouth. Her feet kick at the leaves, then her struggling stops.

God help me.

But I'm too hungry to let the shock of my own ferocity stop me. This meat tastes too good.

I feed.

DAWN

A wolf can eat more than twenty pounds of raw meat when it's hungry. Maybe more than that if it's a large lobo. Then, gorged to the point of something like drunkenness, it may roll over on its back and sleep close enough to guard the torn remains of its prey. That way, when you wake up you don't have to go out for breakfast.

I hear the start of the dawn chorus of twittering birds before I open my eyes. The message they're tweeting me is that it's time to wake. The first light of dawn is seeping through the branches overhead.

Branches in my bedroom? Am I still dreaming?

I'm stupid groggy as I wipe my face with one hand. My hand, not a paw. My face, not a wolf muzzle like in my super realistic dream.

But my fingers and palm feel sticky. I hold them out to look at them. They're stained with dark, dried blood. I hear the rippling, tinkling music of water over stones. I don't have to turn my head to look for the source of that sound. It's the stream I lapped water from and then exploded across to take down . . .

This time I do turn my head. Her body is there next to me. A young one.

"Sorry," I say. "But I was really hungry."

I place my hand on her flank, run my fingers through the cold, thick hair on down to her left hoof. She's a little undersized, though she is probably more than two years old. She was part of the deer herd whose expanding population has been a problem since there are no two-legged hunters allowed in the town preserve. No hunting allowed here. No four-legged predators. Not till now.

What were the words my Dad told me that our Indian ancestors spoke whenever an animal gave itself to them?

I lift the deer's head, lean down, and breathe once into its mouth. Giving it some of my breath to thank it for allowing me to take its breath. I lower its head to the earth but keep my right palm on its forehead, put my left palm against my own chest.

"Thank you for feeding me," I say aloud, "I thank your spirit for allowing me to use your body."

Her ribs are exposed on her right side. The heart and liver are gone, as well as the best meat from her flanks that would be referred to as prime roasts and steaks if we were talking about a butchered cow. I can't help but crack a brief smile. She tasted good.

I look down at what was covering me like a blanket. My second skin. I don't recall shrugging it off, but I must have done so automatically before I slipped into a groggy sleep. Some instinct told me that although being discovered naked with a wolf pelt over me and a disemboweled deer by my side might be bad, being found still in the shape of a wolfman would be infinitely worse.

The second skin is no longer the nearly petrified, pathetic, shriveled scrap of flesh it was when I first saw it. It has grown to the dimensions of a good-sized cape. No longer stiff, it's now soft and pliable, the hair thick and lustrous. It shines as if with an inner light.

Amazing what a good meal can do for you.

It feels warm to my touch, the warmth of kinship. It's like the connection someone might experience when putting a hand on the shoulder of a beloved twin.

Then I use the water of the stream to quickly wash the blood from my face and hands and chest. Early as it is, this is a popular trail. A morning jogger might come by at any minute. I don't want to be discovered bloody . . . or nude. I open the duffel bag, thankful that I've packed everything I need. Underclothes, T-shirts and jeans, socks, and my second-best New Balance runners.

My wolf skin folds down into a surprisingly small bundle and fits easily into the top of the bag. I shoulder it and then look back one more time at the doe. Nope, I can't take it with me. A teenager lugging a duffel bag will likely be ignored, but not one with a stiffening carcass over his shoulder.

If this deer's body is found, its death will likely be chalked up to a pack of dogs. Though no dog would have come within a mile of the woods last night while I was there.

Next stop, the Drake House.

ON THE HIGHWAY

Everything is as I left it. There's no sign or scent of anyone or anything around my motorcycle and my neatly folded clothes. I put my hand on its seat, run it back down and along the isoclastic frame.

The feel of its leather and metal beneath my palm is reassuring. Those few seconds of thinking about it were a brief release from the other thoughts bombarding my brain. I no longer feel the ironic self-confidence that I was experiencing last night while sheathed in that second skin like a hand in a gauntlet of steel. Even my awareness of not being actually invulnerable was tempered by an arrogant sort of fearlessness. I was cautious, but it was the watchfulness of a leopard eyeing a goat and waiting for the right moment to pounce. This morning I'm feeling more like the goat.

I swing my leg over the bike, lean forward, and press my cheek against the gas tank. I am so glad this is a motorcycle and not a car. I couldn't get into a car right now. Not after what I was dreaming before I woke up next to the deer I killed.

I didn't dream about running through the forest, fighting enemies, eating so much raw venison that my stomach still bulged with it. My dream seemed to have nothing to do to the events that occurred after putting on my second skin. Instead, I was driving in a car. It was not a black Mercedes. It was my mom's car.

I was on a highway that looked familiar and also like no road I'd ever seen before. I was alone in the car, going somewhere to pick Mom up. She was still alive in my dream. She was waiting for me. I had to pick her up or something awful would happen.

Houses and trees whipped past in a blur. Too fast. I needed to slow down.

I took my foot off the gas, pushed down on the brake. Nothing. I tried the emergency brake. The car kept barreling along, going faster and faster. I could steer it, but I couldn't stop it. If some innocent pedestrian were to step in front of me, I wouldn't be able to keep from hitting them. I had to figure out how to slow down my headlong rush to nowhere. But I couldn't. I couldn't stop.

I wish I could get that dream out of my head. It disturbs me far more than anything that really happened over the last crazy twenty-four hours. Even though I'm wide awake I'm still trying to figure out ways to stop that damn car. Maybe turn the wheel so the red car—that's right, I remember now that it was red, even though we never owned a red car. Crank the wheel far to the right and tie it in place with my belt so that it just keeps going in a big circle until it runs out of gas. But that would take too long. Maybe drive it into a muddy field where the wheels would bog down. Or into deep water. Even into a tree before it hurts anybody other than me. Anything to make it stop.

But if I do any of those things I can't get to my mother. Mom's waiting for me. But I can never get to her. Not ever again.

I hate that dream. If I were to close my eyes I'd find myself stuck back in it again like a dragonfly caught in the center of an orb-weaver spider's web.

I've read Sigmund Freud. But I don't need an uptight upper middle-class Austrian shrink to analyze the meaning of that dream. The message was being screamed, not whispered, to me by my sub-conscious. I straighten up and sigh.

Enough self-pity.

Accept it.

I put my feet down and step backward off the Commando, letting my hands slide back along its seat as if I was grooming a favorite horse.

A song comes into my mind. It's an oldie but baddie that was blasting from the ear buds of some kid's iPod as he passed me yesterday morning outside the school. Even someone without ex-ceptionally keen hearing like mine could hear it if they got within twenty feet of him. He was smiling and bobbing his head to the beat, in delighted agreement with his plan to achieve premature deafness. Even more irritatingly, he was singing along—off-key, of course. "Highway to Hell," he sang, "I'm on a highway to hell."

I guess that's my soundtrack right now. It stays with me as I shoulder the duffel bag and walk up the path to the front door.

DOCUMENTS

The inside of the Drake House doesn't feel the way it did the first time I entered. It's still a deserted mansion, but there's no longer anything here that stirs a sense of foreboding in me like I felt just yesterday evening. Twelve hours and a lifetime ago.

There's nothing here for me to be afraid of anymore.

Yea, though I walk through the valley of the shadow of death I will fear no evil . . .

And why is that?

Because I am the meanest SOB in the entire valley.

I pull the sheet off one of the chairs. It reveals not some medieval carved wooden antique but a leather padded recliner like one that might still be on the showroom floor in Furniture Warehouse. I sit down in it, my duffel bag in my lap, pull the recliner handle and lean back into the chair's embrace. As soon as I do so I realize how tired I am. I could close my eyes and nod off before the count of three.

I lever the chair back up, stand. No sleeping now, even if I have become a seminocturnal prowler of the night. No time for even a cat nap (or a dog nap). Things to do.

No sign of the grue as I trudge up the stairs. And why should there be? For the monster is me.

Instead of the welcoming moon shining through the circular window at the head of the stairs I am greeted by the rays of a sun that is just a finger's width above the horizon. I'm up early enough to make it to RHS without being late again. I burp and then pat my stomach. Grim ironic smile at that. I don't have to worry about making breakfast before heading to school.

As if I could ever go back to school again. Whatever I've gained, a huge part of my life, any hope of a normal life is lost to me forever. My ironic smile turns upside down. My heart hurts as I think of the good mornings, when I'd get up and Dad would be sober. Then I'd make pancakes and fry bacon for both of us. Neither of us would say much, other than "Pass the syrup" or "Take more of these." But what we felt together on those mornings went deeper than words.

There's nothing I won't do to save him.

I put my hand on the window and look out at the friendly forest. I wish it was evening, already turning toward night. Then I could be strong and silent and deadly again. I could be loping through the twilight, on my way back to the place where he's being held.

I lower my hand from the window. I have to wait. And I also have to have a better plan than just going there and powering my way through whatever defenses they have. The disquiet I felt last night at that strange scent I picked up while I was scouting Maxico returns to me. What was it? I don't know who the enemy is. I don't know precisely why they've taken Dad. And why was Meena's father mentioned by whoever is running the operation? Should I tell Meena her father is in some kind of danger? Or is he? I don't know a bloody thing.

I unclench my fist before I drive it through the window.

One step at a time, I tell myself. One step at a time.

First step is putting my second skin safely away. Lugging it around in a military duffel bag is not practical. No way I could store it in my school locker. If I am going back to school again after this weird weekend is over.

Go down the hall.

Open the door.

Cross the room.

Release the latch.

Swing back the section of bookcase.

Each mechanical step gives me a small sense of satisfaction. Like a condemned man taking comfort in the small things he can still do—comb hair, wash face, brush teeth, make bed—while there's a lethal injection waiting just around the corner.

I sit on my knees in front of the trunk. As I gently pull my second skin from the duffel bag, the black, zippered document bag I took from my father's bedside table comes out with it. I start to put it back into the duffel, then think twice and lay the black zipper bag down to the side.

The skin is light in my hands, but it pulses with energy. Its silvery sheen is so bright it's as if there's a light bulb glowing from within. It hasn't shrunk back to the small shriveled size it was when I first found it. It's as large and filled with life and breathless awareness as it was when I draped it around my shoulders for the first time.

I place my second skin across my lap. I stroke it slowly with my palms from the head back to the tail.

"Venison taste good last night, buddy?" I ask.

I'm almost surprised when the head doesn't nod in response to my question and growl, "You bet!"

I lift my second skin carefully, put it back into the trunk.

"See you later," I promise. Then I close the lid.

And what do I do now? Can I leave it here? Will it be safe? What if someone else comes to the Drake House? I know this place is deserted, but that doesn't mean no one will ever come here. It would be my dumb luck if the long-vanished owners or their heirs should show up just now. Maybe with a demolition order because they're going to build a housing development on the grounds or run a connecting spur from one highway to another through here.

My eyes catch the black bag to my left, the one I found in my dad's drawer with his spare wallet. I just put it there a minute or two ago, but I'd already half forgotten it. What does it hold? No time like the present to find out. Better to occupy my mind with something rather than torturing myself with further effing fruitless fretting.

I unzip the bag. Shake the contents into my lap. Two United States passports fall out first. I open one, then the other. My dad's face looks up at me from each of them. In one he's wearing a beard and there's a prominent scar down the side of his face. And in the other he has a crew cut, and his jet-black hair is blonde. His brown eyes are now blue and there's no scar. You can do wonders with contacts and makeup. And, of course, the names on the two different passports do not match each other. Nor are either of them Thomas King.

As surprises go, the passports are no biggie after the events of the past day and night. But the next document that I pull from the bag and unfold is totally unexpected.

A DEED

I read the several pages twice to make sure I understand. Then I look around the room I'm sitting in with new eyes. Now I know who owns the Drake House.

I do.

Or we do. The document in my hand is a deed made out in my father's name—which is neither the name I used to think was really ours or one of the names on the passports. Thomas King. Does that mean our supposedly assumed name is actually our real family name? Maybe a name that even the government agency that employed him all those years never knew?

What's more, the Drake House is not a property that Dad recently obtained. It was conveyed to him by his father and to his father by his father's father before that. It's our ancestral home. There's a final page paper-clipped to the deed. My father's will, naming me as his sole heir.

When we came to this town, this wasn't a place Dad just chose at random after all. He was bringing us back to our roots.

A feeling is growing in me as I sit in this hidden room furnished with nothing more than the closed trunk holding my second skin. Now that I've gotten past the fear and foreboding, the indefinable sense of uncertainty that first overwhelmed me when I entered this house, I can feel it embracing me. I was born here.

That's why my wolf skin was in this trunk, why my father's directions led me here. I've found more than just my second half. I've found home. I'm not going to have to worry about some anonymous owner showing up. I have met the landlord and he is me.

I'm overwhelmed by a flood of emotion, perhaps because I'm so dead tired. I feel like laughing and crying at the same time. I'm even angrier than before at the people who've forced their way into our lives, taken my father captive for some reason I still don't fully understand, and made me into a fugitive. I've found my home and now I have to hide or run away or find some way to fight them? It's not fair.

For a moment I wonder why Dad and I didn't come here first rather than moving into the Sardine Can, that rattletrap of a trailer, that heap of molten metal, blackened two-by-fours, and scorched aluminum, whose value was only slightly diminished by its destruction. But I do know why. Dad didn't feel I was ready to confront my destiny, even though he knew that sooner or later I'd have to. So we moved close enough for it to happen, even if an emergency meant that I had to do it on my own and sooner than he'd planned.

Thinking of planning, Dad clearly planned that I'd find this bag and read its contents. And there's more inside. I put down the deed and pull out an envelope sealed with a metal clasp. *Family Genealogy* is written on it in my father's hand. Interesting. I set that aside without opening it, saving it for later.

The next thing I pull out is my father's checkbook. So that's where it was. I haven't much thought about it till now, but I am going to need some money. I have exactly four dollars in my wallet, not counting the two dollar bill I keep there for luck and never spend. The weekend—which is now—is when I'd usually do the shopping. Dad would leave a signed check with the amount blank for me on the table. Dad never got a PIN and has never used an ATM. There's the whole technology-zaps-when-I-touch-it thing, but also part of it is that most ATMs have cameras focused on whoever uses them. True, there are surveillance cameras everywhere. They're on street corners, in every store. But Dad told me that special attention is paid to the ones at the automated tellers. Just as he told me to always make sure that whenever I did locate a surveillance camera, to never look right straight up at it. Keep your head down. Wear a hat.

Once I had that signed check from Dad, I'd go to the Big Express Market, pick up whatever we needed and then write fifty bucks over the purchase total so I'd have some pocket money. I'd use that extra to buy gas for the Commando, as well as a PowerAde, a bag of corn chips, four or five candy bars, an ice cream sandwich.

As I think of it I realize just how comforting that familiar routine was to me, something stable and certain that I could count on in my life. Predictable and regular and normal, not like the emotional chaos of losing a mother and having only half a father left, stuck in a home that wasn't a home, a life that seemed as incomplete as a book left half-finished by a dead writer.

A chill runs down my back at that thought. My story is not the last novel of Charles Dickens, even if it seems as weird a mystery as the death of Edwin Drood. I may not know the eventual ending, the denouement. But I am sure of this—I can't leave my task unfinished. Otherwise neither my dad nor I will survive.

Mysteries. I look at the thick brown envelope with the metal clasp. Maybe there will be some answers in there. I open it and pull out the contents. It's a family tree that follows my father's side of our family. Some of the sheets of paper have become discolored with age. Maybe they are as old as the dates written on them, all the way back into the early seventeenth century. Some of the names of ancestors back then are clearly people who just walked out of the forest, for there's no last name for them, no dates of birth or names of parents. Anna, wife of Peter. Francis, husband of Marie.

All of the oldest ones, except for some with Dutch names such as Van Antwerp and Van Slyke, look to have been Indians. Some are even listed that way. Peter, the King's Indian. Indian Marie. They're all from the part of the country that my Abenaki ancestors called *Ndakinna*, "Our Land," before it was cut into pieces and renamed New York, New England, New Amsterdam. It makes me wonder what my oldest ancestor, Peter, the King's Indian, was *really* named. And I see now where our last name came from. Peter's son—who, if I count the generations right, is my great-great-great-great-great-great grandfather—is listed as Thomas King.

None of that is a big surprise. I've always known our family was mostly Indian with some Dutch and English married in. But what is new to me is not just the actual names of people whose blood I inherited. It's the knowledge of what that blood has carried and the roles they have apparently played.

Next to the name of one of those first native ancestors, Peter, the King's Indian (who died in 1653 in New Amsterdam, the year after it became a self-governing colony) is one word followed by two letters printed in red. The word is "Spy." The two letters are WM.

I leaf through the documents, which are arranged in chrono- logical order, with the oldest ones on top, the rough right or left edges of those yellowed oldest pages showing they were torn out of a book. This genealogy is not a copy, but an original that has clearly been handed down for generations. The letters WM appear regularly, but no more than once every generation. Every name with WM next to it has at least one other brief notation, written in different hands and different inks over the years. Some of those notations are as intriguing as "Spy" or "Envoy of the Crown," or "Agent for the colonie." But others are chilling. "Hung as witch." "Killed by gunshots." "Lost, presumed drowned in Hudson." "Disappeared, fate unknown."

Despite that family history of violence, it's an unbroken line of descent all the way down to the present day. None of them appear to have lived long lives, but all of them had at least one child who reached adulthood and had a child of his or her own. To my name with that same WM in red ink. I recognize the handwriting of the person who wrote in my name and printed the WM next to it. It's my father's hand.

I know that as well as I understand what must be the meaning of those two letters—WM—printed next to so many names over the centuries. Wolf Mark. Like me, from Peter, the King's Indian on down, my direct male ancestors wore a second skin. It means that although I may be a monster, I am not an anomaly. There were others—like my father—who carried the wolf mark before me. And, also like Dad, my forebears who could put on a second skin found ways to be of service. How nice to know that I come from a long line of useful monsters.

I fold the genealogy up and slip it back into the envelope. Then I pick up the checkbook again.

Dad taught me how to forge his signature so well that even a pro couldn't tell the difference. This checkbook solves the minor dilemma of getting such necessities as food and gas. Maybe a sleeping bag to curl up in, since I'm not about to either sleep on the cold floor or invest in a new bedroom set. Although I could sleep in that recliner, which fit my big body so well that I'm pretty sure it was one of Dad's favorite chairs at one time or another—the two of us sharing the same mesomorphic build.

Dad's credit card is tucked into the plastic fold in the back of the checkbook. I already have the duplicate. I could use a credit card for gas. But would that be wise? Credit card accounts can be monitored. "Always avoid using credit cards as much as possible" was another of Dad's rules. That is especially true for me now that I'm being hunted. More than one fugitive has been tracked down by following a trail of credit card purchases across the country.

I slip the card back into the plastic fold. As I do so, my finger finds something metal. I pull it out. It's a key with a cardboard card attached to it by a piece of string.

There's a number on the card and two names. The top name is a familiar one, RANGERVILLE HOME SAVINGS, the local bank where Dad has his account. The name below it is even more familiar.

LUCAS KING.

REASONS

I'm either brilliant or totally insane. You decide. I can't. I've just pulled into the parking lot of RHS, five minutes ahead of the buses. Yup, I am going back to school.

Why? you ask.

Here's my reasons, in no particular order of importance.

First, by going back to school, as if I don't have a clue that anyone is after me, the people who have my father are going to chalk up last night's failure to pure bad luck, not any effort on my part to thwart them. That may mean they'll be less likely to be super vigilant tonight when I do whatever it is that I'm going to do. Okay, I do not have a clue about what I am going to do. But something is going to come to me.

Second, I do not want to have the local authorities out looking for a missing, possibly endangered teenager. Which I am, more or less. Though on the other hand I could be more of a danger to the authorities than anything they might imagine as a threat to me.

My cover story when the authorities finally do catch up with me? And you know they will. I decided to stay out all night since my dad was away. And like a typical rebel without a cause (they think) I'm not about to say where that was and what I was doing. If anyone knows where Dad and I live (oops, used to live—RIP Sardine Can), they'll be even more understanding about my not wanting to spend the night there. Even the kids at RHS from the big mobile home park by the creek would look pityingly at me if they knew where I've been domiciling.

Third, I'm not sure what else to do with my day aside from hiding fretfully and restlessly inside the Drake House. I'd be climbing the walls if I did that. Or more likely punching holes in them. There's nothing like the mind-killing routine of going to classes and hearing bored, tenured teachers drone on to dampen my thoughts. Like a wet towel dropped on a hot rock.

Fourth, and this is not number four in actual importance to me, I get to see Meena. Maybe for the last time.

Meena. I've got to tell her, somehow, what I heard. But how do I do that without telling her everything? Will she think I'm nuts or just turn and run?

I lock the bike, pocket the key, stroll from the lot toward the main door. So far, so good. No one either looks shocked to see me or recoils in fright at my presence. I feel like someone attending his own funeral. A ghost being allowed to walk through the life that might have been.

No sign yet of Renzo. But I've caught his scent, so I know he's already gone in ahead of me. After all, as I said before, Renzo is an attendance superfreak. No one gets a bigger kick out of being able to state in a loud voice, "Here!" whenever a teacher calls out his name. Even being tardy is anathema to him. He's probably already sitting in his seat eagerly waiting for attendance to be taken.

As I enter the hallway I catch another even more welcome scent. Meena. And here she comes around the corner. Despite my trepidation about what I should say to her, I start to smile when she's still fifty feet away. She sees me, but she doesn't smile back. And she's not alone.

I may have neglected to tell you that she is not the only South Asian kid in RHS. There's a dozen other kids of people who are working with her father—actually for him—in the outer complex at Maxico. All their parents are engineers or scientists of some sort.

Although they're a tight clique, they're not distant or vaguely threatening like the Sunglass Mafia. They act a little clannish when they're together, but they also take part in school activities and some, like Meena, are really outgoing. Maybe it's that our little town never got caught up in the anti-Muslim fervor that's been stirred up around the country by opportunistic politicians. (My dad has his own word for people like that: vultures.) Also, all the disasters Pakistan has had to deal with created some sympathy around here for that country and its people. RHS had a fund drive last fall to raise money for the flood victims.

So usually when you see one of the kids in the Pakistani crowd, you get at least a polite nod from them.

I nod at Meena's friends and then raise my hand in my usual wave to her. Meena doesn't return it. She looks down and away from me. The eleven other Pakistani students form a phalanx around her and sweep her past me. Her eyes are red as if she's been crying.

What the hell is happening?

"Meena?"

I start to follow.

One of the girls in the group peels off, turns back, and places herself determinedly in front of me. Fala Muhammed.

She stares at my chest.

"You must stay away from our dear friend and stop the troubling," Fala says, her words so fast it takes me a moment to understand them.

"What?"

"Stay away from our friend. You do not understand."

"Understand what?"

Fala takes a quick step backward with an alarmed look on her face. My voice has come out as a growl. I soften it to a whisper.

"Listen," I repeat, "Whatever I did, can you tell Meena I apologize?"

Fala looks down. "You truly do not understand, do you?"

Before I can answer, she continues. "But how could you? You are so free here, so American, so carefree and free."

I almost let out a loud *hah!* at that. Free? As free as any skin-walker about to be kidnapped or terminated by unidentified enemies can be.

I bite my lip. Fala is still talking. I've almost missed what she's saying.

". . . honor killing," she continues, shaking her head. "Just a week ago a Pakistani girl in Europe was burned to death by her own father for going on Facebook and friending men. Mr. Kureshi is too modern for that, but he is still very religious. If he knew our Meena was thinking of doing something like riding on a motorcycle with an American boy, she would be on the first airplane to Karachi. So we are stepping in and helping her return to her senses."

Fala's words trail off. For a painful moment, we both stand there. I'm clenching my fists so hard my nails are drawing blood. I want to scream, cry, howl. But I can't. I can't show how I feel any more than I can ever have a chance to be more than a casual friend with the girl who makes my heart ache. I can't even be a casual friend anymore.

Meena.

I speak two of the hardest words I've ever had to force from my mouth.

"I understand," I say.

Fala lifts her hand and gently touches my sleeve. "I am sorry. You are a very nice boy."

She turns and quickly walks away.

FIRST CLASS

My first period of the day is English literature, the class I share with Renzo and Meena. I walk into it with a black cloud over my head.

I said I would go along with Fala so as not to make waves. But I still have to talk to Meena, if only to warn her that there's something hinky going on that has to do with her dad.

I'm one of the top four in this class, just behind Meena and Renzo and a girl named Brita. Brita's not rich enough to hang with the Barbies, but she dresses like them, as best she can. Even if her clothing is from Target and not designer chic, she tries to look down on me and Renzo and the rest of the class. As if we cared.

Renzo's nickname for her is the WF girl. WF for water filter. Get it? Ever seen one of those commercials for a Brita water filter?

I take my seat, right next to Renzo.

He looks over at me and nods.

"What's up, dog?"

Not dog, wolf, I think.

But I nod back. "Not much."

No, not much. More than much is up, so much more my head's about to explode. I've got to talk to somebody. He's my best friend. But what could I tell him? This is all so crazy, so frightening. He'll probably think I'm trying to mess with him, or, worse, that I've gone off the deep end. But what if I do tell him everything and he believes me? Then how will he react? If he has any sense it'll be by beating a rapid retreat, getting as far away from doomed Lucas King as humanly possible.

I sense Meena slipping into her usual seat to my right. I smell her, hear her, feel the warmth of her body. It sends a shiver down my back. I'm more sensitive than I've ever been before and also more confused. She softly clears her throat. But I don't look her way. I open my book and pretend to study its pages, even though the words written on it make about as much sense as lines of little black ants right now.

The class is calmly going on around us. No one knows the inner turmoil that is raging in my head like a force ten gale. I'm an old pro at not showing my emotions, keeping my face as calm as the surface of deep water, despite the sharks and other assorted sea monsters in those dark depths. I'm on autopilot. I raise my eyes to focus them on Ms. Nye as she speaks my name.

"So, Mr. King, do you agree with Steinbeck's ending? What would you have chosen to do if Lenny was your friend?"

"Well," I reply, my voice so calm and level it surprises me, "there wasn't any other choice. The characters were caught, like in a tragedy. There couldn't be a happy ending."

Ms. Nye nods, not realizing that what I've said is about myself as much as it is about Steinbeck's story. "Thank you, Mr. King."

Ms. Nye is writing something on the board as she continues to talk, waving her hands for emphasis. She's dressed in what she calls her flag outfit. She always comes to school wearing it when she is about to address a topic that has something to do with American literature as social commentary. White blouse, red scarf, blue skirt and black pumps with stars on them. She's moved from *Of Mice and Men* to *The Grapes of Wrath*.

Ms. Nye is really into this lecture. Her green eyes are glowing like a light has just been turned on behind them. She's been writing so furiously that she has chalk on her hands and two smears of chalk across her cheek where she accidentally brushed her fingers. This happens to her a lot. But it doesn't make her look goofy—at least not to me. It looks sort of like a deliberate marking, like the way tribal warriors apply face paint before going off to defend their people.

"A powerful idea," she's saying, "is hard to stop. Even people who never read Steinbeck's book were affected by it, especially when it was made into a movie. Take note of the fact that Woody Guthrie, the folk singer, saw the movie without ever reading the book. Then he went out and wrote 'The Ballad of Tom Joad' with the express purpose of what some would call rabble rousing. He wanted to share the story with people like the Okies in the film, poor out-of-work men and women who couldn't afford the twenty-five cents to go to a movie back then. Joad, of course"—she looks at me and I nod—"was Steinbeck's main character in the novel. Portrayed by Henry Fonda in the film. And now," nodding, "a full eighty years later, when we're suffering economic hardships that parallel those of the 1930s, we have the Boss performing a new song about looking for the ghost of old Tom Joad . . ."

I'm hearing what she is saying without really hearing it—even though my retentive mind is taking it in, recording it for later playback. It's the sort of lecture that I'd usually love. History, music, social commentary, and literature all rolled up in one. Normally I'd be in seventh heaven. I'd be listening as avidly as a lion in a zoo does when it hears the footsteps of its keeper approaching at feeding time with a bucket of raw meat. Growling in happy expectation.

But not this morning. The clouds are down around my head. I'm looking through the dark distorting lenses of anguish and uncertainty.

The class continues on around me, like a play in which I don't have any meaningful part. It is taking an eternity for the class to be over. My mind is racing in so many directions at once that I can't believe how slowly the minutes are ticking away. I notice the redheaded kid with a wedge cut two rows ahead of me—whose name is Woodrow (Renzo refers to him as WW, Woody Woodpecker)—looking down at his watch and then up at the clock on the wall. If I was wearing a watch I'd probably be looking at it, too, wondering if the wall clock was right. Of course all I have on my wrist is my birthmark. I glance down at it.

Wait a minute!

My left wrist is empty. There's no longer anything there to notice. The red mark in the shape of a wolf has vanished from my skin. Was it only there because I hadn't yet reunited with that other part of myself that is now locked safely in that trunk back in the Drake House? Another question with no answer.

The bell rings for the end of the class before I can delve any deeper into the bottomless morass of speculation about past, present and future enigmas. I put my books and notebook into my backpack, sling it over my shoulder. Meena didn't say a word the whole class. She must really be upset because she always talks in class—and whatever she says is always worth hearing. She has a first-class mind that matches her beauty. She has both sense and common sense and is one of the most intuitive and smartest people I've ever met. If she was anyone else's daughter she'd be on the RHS list of top ten potential academic recruits for the best American colleges.

But I guess that American college is not in the cards for her. She won't remain here in the States after her senior year at RHS and her graduation. That was one of my biggest worries and heart-aches before real heart-rending troubles knocked down the door of my psyche. Her father's contract with Maxico, from what she told me, will expire this coming June. She and her father will be heading back to Pakistan as soon as he finishes whatever he is doing at Maxico.

And then the Kureshis will leave.

And Meena will be out of my life forever.

However, there's no longer any need for me to wistfully wait for that day of departure several months from now. That eventual, inexorable loss of the girl who owns my heart has been rescheduled, moved up to the present moment. There already were more obstacles between us than jumps in the high hurdles. Now there's a wall taller than the one the Israelis built to keep out the Palestinians. So much bad luck has piled on that I feel like a hundred-pound quarterback who's just been sacked in the end zone by the entire defense of the opposing team. All that Romeo and Juliet had between them were feuding families. Try adding skinwalking on top of religion and different home continents. It's so ironically comical that a bitter smile comes to my lips.

Get real, Lucas. Anything more than friendship between her and you never could have been, despite the fact that she said she liked me, held my hand . . .

Plus there's that one other little minor roadblock between the two of us: That my father is being held by unidentified men in black who—unless they are planning to take me on a surprise birthday trip to Disneyland—undoubtedly seek to also do me harm.

Let go, Lucas, Let go.

But although all of my romantic fantasies about Meena and me ever being together, even in the most innocent way, have been dashed, I'm still firm in my decision that I have to talk to her. I need to warn her that her father may be in trouble—no, almost certainly is in danger.

Unless every star and planet in the galaxy is aligned against me, I have to find a way to talk with the one who's been the major light in my soul for the past year. Maybe in the three minutes between this class and French.

But Meena is up and out of her seat before I can say a word to her. All of a sudden there's a dozen bodies between her and me as she slips out the door. I have to catch up to her. I stand up, almost knocking my desk over. A hand grabs my right arm.

I turn so fast, a snarl on my lips, that Renzo snatches his hand back as if he's just touched a hot stove.

"Whoa!" he says, "Bro, I just wanted to ask you what's the matter?"

"Nothing," I say. There's no way I'm going to catch up to Meena now without making a scene in the hall. I almost smile at the thought of what that would have been like—me tossing kids aside as easily as if they were paper dolls caught in a gust of wind, leaving a path of destruction in my wake and scaring the life out of Meena while doing it.

I should be grateful to Renzo. That is pretty much what I was just about to do.

Renzo reaches out a hand again, a little more tentatively this time, places it on my shoulder.

"Luke," he says, "I'm your best buddy. Right? I can see something is really wrong. Want to tell me about it?"

I do, but can I? I sigh, let my tense muscles loosen.

"You don't know how wrong it is," I say.

"So tell me. Maybe I can help."

I look around. Aside from the two of us, the room is empty. Even Ms. Nye has left. The expression on my best friend's face is genuine concern. Maybe I can talk to him, share at least an edited version of what is going on. In fact, I suddenly realize, there is a way that he actually can help me.

"Okay," I say, keeping my voice low. "But you have to promise me two things."

"Done," he says, crossing his heart and holding up his hand like a Boy Scout. It might seem like an ironic gesture, but the look in his eyes tells me that he is dead serious.

We go out into the hall and step out of the flow of bodies into a little alcove that used to hold a bank of lockers.

"First, you have to believe everything I'm telling you, crazy as it may sound."

Renzo nods.

"Second, you can never mention this to anyone. Ever."

"Sealed," he says, tapping his mouth with his index finger.

I take a breath. There's no going back. "Okay," I say. "First of all, my dad has been kidnapped by some really bad people. I can't tell you much about it now, but it is the truth. And we can't go to the police. Understand?"

Renzo's eyes get a little wider, but there's no look of disbelief on his face as he nods again and then bites his lower lip with his teeth . . .

"So what can I do, bro?" he asks.

38
SECOND CLASS

It is going to be a long break between classes.

Getting to my second class has just become the equivalent of making it through a minefield or traveling on one of those roads in Afghanistan that Dad and Uncle Cal used to tell me about with an improvised explosive device waiting around every corner.

Not only has my whacked plan about coming to school as a way of taking my mind off my troubles gone further awry than Columbus aiming for the East Indies and ending up in the Caribbean, I can't stop the voices in my head that keep asking more questions without answers, more riddles with no clues.

All I was hoping for was a chance to warn Meena before second period. Something as simple as that would be possible. Now it seems as if no matter which way I turn there's another roadblock.

As Renzo heads off down the hall to the left toward the computer lab, full of purpose after our quick conversation, I look to the right—the direction of the French classroom two corridors away that Meena has probably already entered.

Ranged across the far end, not really looking my way but fully aware of my presence, are several members of the Sunglass Mafia: Vlad, Natasha, Boris, Ekaterina. They are effectively blocking my way. It's no surprise to me. I caught their musty, perfume-shrouded odors well before my eyes registered their presence. I'm still a hundred feet from them, but I sense what they're up to. Encircle me, cut me out of the crowd, and then whisk me down one of the disused corridors just ahead that lead into the abandoned pool complex they've set up as their little fiefdom within RHS. Like the Borg in *Star Trek*, they're certain my resistance will be futile.

None of them are built like weightlifters, but I know that power doesn't just come from bulky muscles. I'm lean and lanky myself. I can feel every one of those sinister eastern European kids pulsing with a freaky kind of strength. They think that compared to them, everyone else is no more than a second-class citizen. They have the lazy self-confidence of cats waiting for a mouse to get close enough to them to pounce.

And then what? What will they do if they do grab me and spirit me off?

Frankly, I don't think they can do it. They may imagine that they can handle me, but I beg to disagree. A growl builds in the back of my throat and I flex my fingers.

Let them try, a voice inside me snarls. The world begins to get red around me as I take a deep breath.

No.

No way am I about to go that route. The open corridors of the school are not the place for me to get all Terminator on them. Innocent people might get hurt.

I spin on my heel, whip around so fast that my motions are a blur. I hear gasps around me from the few other kids who noticed me virtually vanish in front of them. Most just move on in blissful unawareness of anything other than their own daily adolescent soap operas. I move low, slipping between people, heading for the end of the hall.

I don't pause until I have reached the intersection with the next long, equally jammed corridor. Just before I turn right again I take a quick look back over my shoulder. Vlad's tall vulture-shouldered shape appears around the corner, then Natasha, Ekaterina, and Boris. Igor and Marina have also now joined them. They're all in pursuit now. No more lying in wait for me to blunder into their trap.

Unfortunately for them, there was a moment of hesitation before they realized I'd caught on. I'm ahead of them and staying ahead. They're grimly making their way toward me, but their progress is impeded. They have to turn sideways, push past people. They could probably just plow through the crowd like scythes through grass. However, I can see that they are holding themselves back from that sort of mayhem.

Normal they are not, but they clearly do not want to call attention to just how abnormal they are. They're moving fast, but not fast enough. I can't read what's in their eyes behind those sunglasses, but I am pretty sure it isn't glee. No eyebrows raised in amused disdain above their dark glasses. Their lips are tight, drawn back over their teeth. They're hissing in displeasure at my little evasive maneuver.

T.S. dudes, as Renzo would say.

T.S., which might stand for terrific stuff, but doesn't.

I lift my left hand and waggle my fingers at them. A childish gesture, but it still feels good.

Another right turn and I've rounded the big block of classrooms at the center of the school. I'm back at the intersection where the members of the Sunglass Mafia were originally waiting and blocking the hall. I am also now just fifty feet from the entrance to French class. I've made it with time to spare. From what the hall clock says, I have an entire minute before the bell rings. The corridor around me is starting to drain of congestion as students flow into their respective classrooms.

Just a few more steps and I'll be through the door and home free. I pause at the entrance, holding my breath, hardly daring to go inside. I lean forward to look in, my right hand grasping the doorframe. My heart starts to pound like the bass drum in a rock band.

Meena is there.

She's in her usual seat, right next to the empty one that's mine. Her head is down, her long dark hair falling across her face so that she doesn't see me. It looks as if she's writing something.

A hand with fingers as strong as steel bands encircles my left wrist to pull me back from the door.

"*Ya po tebye seoskuchilsya*," Yuri's sarcastic voice snake-hisses in my ear. "I've missed you."

NYET, BRATAN

Yuri's tight grip is like a handcuff around my wrist, but his fingers feel as cold as a Siberian winter. It makes me wonder what his body temperature is. Minus ten degrees?

I look straight at his face, not at the hand that's applying even more pressure now. Powerful as his hand may be, it is constructed just like any other human hand. The same principles of body mechanics and leverage that make every martial art in the world effective apply to it too.

I drop my fingers, circle my hand down and around Yuri's wrist in the ancient, graceful technique guaranteed to break any wristlock. The student offers the master a cup of tea.

I hold my palm up in front of Yuri's face.

"Nyet, bratan." No way, brother.

There's a startled look on Yuri's face. Is it from my breaking his wrist grip with such ease or from my answering him in his own language?

According to Uncle Cal, my Russian is pretty good. I don't have that giveaway drawling American accent. Of course I'm nowhere near as fluent as Cal or Dad. My father speaks the language like a native, usually with the flair of an urbane Muscovite.

"Although," Cal added, "if your father needs to, he can for sure lay on a Georgian accent." Cal chuckled. "To an educated Russian that's the equivalent of talking like an uneducated hick . . . or a certain dead Soviet dictator."

Did you know that Josef Stalin, who brutally took over the vast empire that was the Soviet Union after the Russian Revolution, was a Georgian? The fact that the USSR's Supreme Leader was well aware of the fact that he was from a group low on the intellectual pecking order may have been one reason why he had so many of his supposed betters slaughtered. Before, during, and after World War II, Stalin killed more of his own countrymen than all the foreign armies put together. Uncle Joe holds the twentieth century record for mass murder, far surpassing Pol Pot, or Mao, or Hitler.

Not that knowing foreign history is about to get me out of this impasse.

Yuri stares at me.

I stare back.

We're stiff-legged as two pit bulls about to lunge at each other's throats. But he's the first to relax his stance. One of his eyebrows rises above the dark shades. He lifts the hand that had grabbed my wrist, two fingers held out like the barrel of a gun. Then he taps his own chest with those two fingers and rapidly says something in Russian.

I carefully keep my face impassive. The last three words are the most important ones. Three words that I understand. Real well.

". . . *Sluzhba Vneshney Razvedk.*"

"SVR?"

Yuri nods. *"Da, SVR."* He looks back over his shoulder at the other members of the Sunglass Mafia, who have now silently appeared behind him. "SVR," he says again, indicating the rest of the six with an inclusive gesture. All six of them smile at me. Lots of sharp canine teeth.

Yuri turns his hand so that the outside of his wrist, encircled by a gold Rolex, is facing me. He puts one finger on the face of the watch, pointing at the number twelve. Then holds that finger up toward me.

I nod.

He jerks his thumb back over his shoulder, dips his hand down in a diving motion. It's clear enough that he means the disused aquatic complex, their own little secret spot, is where we'll be meeting.

I nod again.

Yuri grins, his two long upper canine teeth reflecting the light.

"Klassno," he says. Cool. *"Da skorovo."* See ya soon.

He pivots as effortlessly as a skater turning on ice and glides down the hall followed by his entourage.

Great. As if I didn't have enough difficulty in my life, I now have a lunch date in their lair with a mob of teenage Russian secret agents.

The entire confrontation used less time than it took me to describe it. No more than a minute has passed. I manage to step inside the classroom just as the bell rings.

The French teacher cocks her head at me.

"Très mal, Monsieur King," she says, but it's in mock disapproval because I know I'm one of her favorites and her words are followed by a little smile.

"Pardon," I reply, smiling back as if I didn't have a care in the world. As if my gut was not doing cartwheels around my heart

which has just sunk lower than my stomach.

I slide into my seat, glance to my left. Meena's hair is a dark screen between us. Is she ever going to look into my eyes again?

Call me shallow or foolish, but that bothers me more than anything else right now.

NOTES

Class has been going on now for half an hour. Meena is still acting as if I don't exist.

I look over at her.

Silent, her eyes hidden behind the dark barrier of her long tresses.

How can you listen to someone when they're not talking?

I take a piece of paper from my notebook.

ARE YOU OK? I write.

Then I slip it onto Meena's desk.

Her right hand reaches over and slides it under her curtain of hair. I hold my breath, wondering if she is just going to crumple it up or tear it into pieces along with my heart.

I can hold my breath a long time.

Dad and I used to have contests when we lived in west Texas near this spring-fed lake that was crystal clear and cool, even when it was 100 degrees in the shade. We'd both jump in feetfirst off a pier that ran out into the lake. As soon as we hit the bottom together we'd grab hold of the legs of the pier and stay there, facing each other underwater. The idea was to see who would let go and swim to the surface first for air.

First we'd just hold on, looking at each other through that water that was almost as clear as the air. Then, eventually, Dad would hold out one of his long index fingers, slowly point up, and nod. That was especially dramatic because his index fingers, unlike those of most people, are the longest fingers on his hands.

Ready to give up?

Then I'd shake my head, stick out one of my equally long index fingers, and point down.

No way!

What usually happened was that neither of us would really win. We'd lean toward each other looking for signs of weakness. Poking or tickling wasn't allowed, but anything short of touching was fair game. Eventually we would start making wacky faces at each other. Both of us would try not to laugh until finally it got to be too much to bear and one of us would swallow some water, then the other would lose it and do the same. At that point we'd just grab each other's hands and kick up to the surface together, coughing and choking and laughing fit to burst. Mom was always there waiting on the end of the pier, looking down with this half-anxious, half-amused look on her face.

"You men!" she'd say. "I thought you were going to stay down there all morning!"

All morning. It feels as if that is about how long I've been holding my breath since I passed my note to Meena. She's still not looking over at me.

I shake my head and turn toward the front of the classroom.

Something bumps my elbow. I almost let out a yelp and jump

out of my skin—a metaphor that's especially appropriate for me, isn't it? Somehow, though, I maintain control. I stay facing forward, but I turn my eyes just in time to see Meena's hand retreating back toward her desk. She's still not looking my way, but she's passed me a note.

I let out my breath in a long sigh. Then I lift up my notebook, prop it open so that it forms a barrier between my desktop and anyone else's line of vision, and read Meena's note.

Seven words, printed in bold block letters.

I WANT TO RUN AWAY WITH YOU!

KNOWING

I look over toward Meena. She's pushed her hair back over one ear, which is perfectly shaped as a little golden shell. She's looking at me with this mischievous twinkle in her eyes. I know, and I know that she knows, that actually running away together isn't in the cards for us. (In my case, it seems as likely as the Chicago Cubs winning the World Series—though maybe nothing is really that hopeless.)

In smaller print underneath those seven words, she's drawn a smiley face and written "Just Kidding." But what she's telling me is not just that she hasn't lost her sense of humor. Despite what her friends and family might think, she's not turning her back on me. There's a bond between us that hasn't been broken. That is just about the best I can hope for under the crazy circumstances buzzing around me like a nest of riled-up ground bees.

Her right hand is resting on the top of her desk. She raises it thumbs-up. I do the same with my left hand. I'm about to write something on the note and hand it back to her. Maybe something as silly as "Our chariot awaits," or just a simple, sincere "Thank you."

Then I remember everything that Meena's note briefly drove out of my mind. I look into her eyes. They're the eyes of someone who is not just beautiful, but also one of the smartest people I know. I can see her read the seriousness of the expression on my face. She furrows her brow and her lips shape a word.

What?

She deserves to know, just as much if not more than Renzo did. And in that one moment I make my decision. I print four words on the note and hand it back to her. She reads them, looks back at me. She doesn't ask why I've written those words: I NEED YOUR HELP. She nods.

Music room.

She nods again.

We don't walk out of the French class together when the bell rings. That would be too obvious. Instead we take different routes to reach the music room where Renzo has been for the whole of the last period. He's in the back, inside one of the practice rooms and bent over the computer that Mr. Redbetter lets him use—usually to get downloads of songs he's working on.

But that's not what he's been working on. He's been doing research on the Maxico Corporation, trying to find out something, anything that might help me.

Renzo looks up at me and then Meena as we enter and close the door behind us.

"She know?"

"Not yet." I turn toward Meena. Instead of asking what we're talking about, she sits on one of the chairs and cocks her head, ready to listen.

I suck air in over my teeth, trying to find the right words. "Meena," I begin, "there's a lot you don't know about me." Now there is an understatement! I look back at Renzo. He makes a rolling motion with both hands.

Keep going, he's telling me. But where?

I've done this once with Renzo. Not lying exactly, but telling just enough of the truth.

"This may sound crazy, but my dad has been doing secret work for the government for years. So secret that I could never talk about it, even with the two of you, my best friends." I pause again, bite my lip.

"Go on," Meena says.

"Okay. Well, he tried to quit after my mother's death. Or that's what I thought. But he was still involved and then yesterday it happened. What I have to tell you about."

I did a lot better at this with Renzo. The earnest look on Meena's face is making me want to tell her everything. But I can't do that. I have to be careful.

"What happened, Luke?" Meena asks.

"My dad got . . . taken. Kidnapped. He called me, but he used code words in the call to let me know that he was in trouble and to warn me not to go home."

"Which is why our friend here disappeared right after school yesterday, without saying a word to either of us," Renzo adds.

I glare at him. "Let me finish this," I say.

He doesn't deserve my anger, but he holds up both hands in a gesture of appeasement.

"Just trying to help, bro."

I shake my head. I've got to control myself.

Breathe, Luke. Stay calm.

I put my hand over my mouth, shake my head. "I know. I'm sorry. It's just hard to explain this."

Renzo nods and Meena just keeps listening. They're better

friends than I deserve.

"So last night I went home anyway. But I didn't go into the trailer. I sneaked up through the woods and saw that there were two guys there, waiting for me. They were going to use me as a hostage to make my dad tell what he knew about something. I'm not sure what. I got close enough to listen. They're working for Maxico. Something really bad is being done inside there. And what I heard next has to do with you, Meena. They said that another team of men was keeping an eye on Professor Kureshi, your father."

I close my mouth and bite my lip again. This is when Meena is probably going to either tell me I'm crazy and tell me that the Maxico Corporation couldn't possibly be doing anything wrong. Or maybe freak out at the thought of her father possibly being in trouble.

But she does none of these things. Instead, the look on her face becomes more thoughtful. "Luke," she says, "I believe you."

I almost ask why. My story sounds like some wild fantasy or the plot for a second-rate spy movie. But then Meena reaches out and takes my hand.

"Something has been bothering my father," she says. "I was not certain what it was and wondered if in some way I was displeasing him by becoming too American, though he has hardly said a critical word to me since we've been here in this country. So much of his time has been spent at his work, his research. So it would make sense if there was something being done at the corporation that is wrong. That would bother him greatly and he would be thinking of doing something about it. My father is a very moral man. He would never stand for anything that was illegal."

"Thank you." My words come out as a hoarse whisper. My throat is choked with emotions I can't describe. On the one hand, I'm relieved, my two friends are here trying to help me. On the other hand, this may be putting them in danger. And then there's the fact that Meena is still holding my hand and her palm is so warm against mine that it's making my whole body feel like a match about to burst into flame.

"Want to see what I got so far?" Renzo says.

His words bring me out of the semitrance I've fallen into.

"Yes." Meena says it at the same moment I do. She stands up and, still holding my hand, pulls me over so that we're both standing behind Renzo where we can see the screen. Looking at a computer is no problem for me as long as I don't touch it or get within about six inches of it—which always results in the screen going black as everything shuts down.

Renzo slides his fingers across the touch pad, presses a key.

"*Voilà*," he says. (That, by the way, is about the only word in French he knows.)

The screen displays the Maxico website. As it scrolls down, the text and photos tell the innocuous story of a benevolent corporation using the latest advances in biotechnology to do such things as improve the yield of food crops, produce more drought-resistant cotton, make domestic animals healthier, find new weapons in the fight against disease, etc.

"Boring," Renzo says.

Maybe deliberately so.

"So far this is all I've been able to access. This and more of the same. Nothing but PR. Sure, there's other stuff. But I just can't find a way to get into it."

"Can I try?" Meena asks.

She lets go of my hand and takes Renzo's seat as he moves aside.

Five minutes later all she's found is two things. The first is a corporate video—with none other than Dr. Kesselring droning on in a self-satisfied voice about the great good Maxico is bringing to the world. The second is that the company has been accepting a full truckload of beef cattle every other week. Since they're not involved in ranching within the compound, the only conclusion is that those bovines are meant to be used as meat. But why so many?

"Did you try Google Earth?" Meena asks, still working the touch pad. "Maybe the satellite view could tell us something more? Oh darn!"

Image unavailable.

"Same thing happened to me," Renzo says. "It's blocked out from space the way the vice-presidential compound in D.C. was when Cheney was in office."

"I help," a deep voice says.

The door had opened silently behind us, but I'd felt the approaching presence that has just joined us. So I don't jump like Meena or say "*Yeep!*" as Renzo does. I don't even have to turn around to know who it is.

I guess I shouldn't be surprised that he's here. After all, Vlad does appreciate music.

Vlad doesn't even bother to ask if he can sit down. Ignoring the displeased looks on my two friend's faces, he edges Renzo aside, leans over Meena's shoulders, stretches out his long arms. His fingers blur as they move across the touch pad, depress one key after another.

"*Zaprosto,*" Vlad intones. Easy-peasy.

The screen comes to life with an image that gradually grows larger as the camera, miles above the planet, zooms in. It's the Maxico compound. Concentric rings. First the perimeter fence with watch towers at regular intervals. Then the encircling forest. And last of all the concrete rampart that protects the hidden kingdom from barbarian incursions. I take in all of the details, as eager as a Mongol warrior who's just found a breach in the Great Wall of China. Within it, for the first time, I can see the inner building. Bigger than I'd imagined. Flat roof. That's good.

There's something else in that image that also catches my eye. Behind the central compound, at the back of the property are small buildings and enclosures. It's hard to read them at first from above and then I realize what I'm looking at. It's the former animal park. Its fences intact, it is not deserted at all. And the moving figures within those enclosures are not human beings.

Lions and tigers and bears, oh my.

Vlad straightens up, looks down at me, raises one eyebrow.

"*Blagodariu*," I say. I thank you.

"*Da Eto fignya*," he replies. Nothing to it.

Then, as easily as a breeze slipping through the pines, he's out the door and gone. Renzo's mouth is open, amazed at what just happened and probably that someone that big could move so quickly.

Meena puts one finger to her lips, then points it at the door where Vlad just exited. "Is he your friend now?" she asks, her brow furrowed.

"Maybe," I say. "Or maybe not."

Meena and Renzo look at me, waiting.

I turn and look up at the clock on the wall. No answers there, just seven minutes before the next bell. Not much time for me to say what else I need to say, to act as if I actually have a plan. Which I actually do not. Should I tell them about my dealings with the Sunglass Mafia? No, it'll just make matters more complicated. And it's not like I understand what Yuri and his crew want from me. I shake my head to myself.

"Luke?" Meena says.

I turn back to face my two friends. "There's not much more we can do now, I guess. But there's one other thing I didn't mention.

Those guys who were waiting for me at my trailer . . . well, they set fire to it."

"Luke," Meena says, "I'm sorry."

"It's okay," I say. "There wasn't anything left in there that I care about. It's just that sooner or later the news is going to get out about it and I wanted you guys to know. Also, I don't have any place to stay tonight."

"No problem, dog," Renzo says. "You can bunk at my place." He pulls out his cell phone. "I'll call my mom and let her know."

"Great. And Meena, maybe you need to talk to your father."

She nods. "You're right. He needs to know that there may be some kind of trouble." She reaches out for my hand again. "Thank you, Luke," she says. She leans closer and looks up into my eyes. I think she's going to kiss me.

LATER STILL

The speaker on the wall emits a static buzz. It's raucous and annoying enough to make your fillings rattle. Then the disembodied voice speaks.

"Lucas King, report to the main office. Lucas King. To the main office."

The happy sensation of getting punched hard in the stomach is getting to be such a regular thing that I'm almost used to it. I spare a split second to turn and look down at Meena's face. I want to remember the expression on it right now, hold it in my mind because I may never see her again. I wish this could be one of those corny movie moments, like in that old film *An Officer and Gentleman* where Richard Gere strides in and lifts up the love of his life and carries her off in his arms.

Meena looks up into my eyes. "Later?" she asks.

I nod, but what I'm thinking is that right now the Lucas King Unabridged Dictionary definition of the word "later" is "never."

Renzo holds out a fist for me to bump, then splays his fingers like an explosion and holds his hand up to his ear with the thumb and little finger held out as if it was a phone.

I nod.

They stay in the music room. I start down the empty hall alone. No one in sight. Five minutes till the next bell. My head is up as I sniff the air. No one lying in wait for me that I can smell.

What now? Should I be strolling along? Stepping as hesitantly as someone picking his way through a minefield? Sprinting in panic? I settle on a fast, nervous walk. Probably what a normal seventeen-year-old would be doing in a situation like this.

What will be waiting for me in the office? The only question I don't have to ask is whether it might be something good. If it wasn't for bad luck, I wouldn't have no luck at all.

How bad?

I gradually realize that I've been feeling a familiar pulsing from my wrist. I look down at it. The wolf mark has reappeared, red as blood.

That bad, eh?

I could make a run for it. If I turn left here, the corridor leads to that same back door on the side of the school near the woods that I used to make my getaway day before yesterday.

But then what?

If it's not the worst-case scenario in the office—involving, let's say, tranquilizer darts, handcuffs, and a straitjacket—then the last thing I ought to do right now is head for the woods. Instead, I'm hoping that my guess about who has asked for me to be called to the office is right. I keep walking as I look up at the wall. The hall clock shows that it is 10:05 A.M. I'm a little surprised it's taken them this long. Then again, they probably needed time for their coffee and donuts.

202

So, I tell myself, if the ones waiting for me are the ones I expect, flight would be the height of foolishness. That would be the equivalent of an admission of guilt. And I am guilty. It would result in them coming after me like one of those pitchfork-waving mobs in a 1930s monster film.

Looking too calm, though, would be stupid and could be a giveaway. Serial killers specialize in being unflappable, inhumanly so. I'm not one of them—at least not yet. I need to look concerned, but not shifty. Uncertain, but not panicky.

I think of the lessons that Uncle Cal and Dad were always subtly teaching me, sometimes just through the stories they told me about stuff that happened to "people they heard about." By the time I was eleven I'd copped to the fact that all those stories, like the one about "these two guys we heard about who were under deep cover in Karbala and were stopped for questioning by Saddam's police . . ." were actually about them.

Stay in character. That was one of their lessons. Don't break cover, especially when you know or suspect that you may be suspected. Live as if you do not think anyone is aware of you even though you know that you are always being watched.

Imagine that all the walls have ears. Which they do in a lot of places. Uncle Cal once showed me something he'd been given in 1990 when he was an eighteen-year-old marine embassy guard and in Moscow for the first time." It was a neatly printed index card that he was handed when he first arrived at the front entrance of the American ambassador's residence. It read:

"Every room is monitored by the KGB and all of the staff are employees of the KGB. We believe the garden also may be monitored. Your luggage may be searched two or three times a day. Nothing is ever stolen and they hardly ever disturb things."

"Why," I asked Uncle Cal, "didn't they just sweep for bugs and get rid of them and then hire a whole new staff?"

Dumb question. But Uncle Cal, as always, was patient with me.

"Well, Luke, they'd just put in new electronic surveillance that for sure would be harder to find." A long pause to let that sink in. Then he leaned back with one of those big yawning grins that showed his large white teeth. "And who were you going to hire in Moscow back then who didn't work for the KGB?"

"I see," I nodded.

Uncle Cal raised one of his long fingers—as long as Dad's and mine now that I think back on it. He placed it next to his nose.

"Just remember," he drawled, "wide-eyed innocence is sometimes the best defense. Especially if you've got something to hide. It's always—always—better if the enemy doesn't know that you know what they know. Even when they suspect it."

I have an idea what they might suspect. But I keep going straight. The one thing I do know right now is that the shortest distance between me and whatever destiny awaits me is this condemned man walk to the main office.

The outer office is empty except for Mrs. Carruth, who looks up. She touches a key on her phone.

"He's here," she says to the unseen listener.

Then she looks over the top of her glasses at me, lifts her pen, and points at the door to Aiken's office.

LYING

The expression on Mrs. Carruth's face as she said "He's here," on the intercom and the fact that Mr. Murry, the security guard, is standing just inside the office door waiting for my arrival—or maybe about to go and get me if I didn't show up in the next five minutes— tells me what to expect.

Mr. Murry tries to look professional and uninvolved, but I can read his mind. He's worried about me. He likes me because I'm always polite. He thinks I'm a good kid.

Wrong on both counts.

Mr. Murry actually pats me on the shoulder as I walk past him. Then he walks out and shuts the door behind him. What is happening right now is way beyond his pay grade. He's done his job.

Ushered the lamb in for slaughter.

What he does not know is that I'm not the hapless innocent kid he believes I am. Well, hapless maybe, but not clueless. And the opposite of a lamb.

Don't growl, I tell myself as two people I've never met before stand up to face me. I didn't expect one of them to be a woman, but I doubt that's going to change the equation.

Look surprised, Luke.

The third person in the room is Principal Aiken.

Aiken for a Breakin'. That's what he's called behind his back. It's because he always puts on a scowl—like one of those pro wrestlers who plays a bad guy—whenever a kid gets ushered into his inner sanctum. There's a big American flag hanging on his wall. A snow globe with the Statue of Liberty is proudly displayed on his desk. He's the one who recites the Pledge of Allegiance over the school loudspeaker every morning.

Being one of the proud and the few was the big event of his life. He keeps his thinning gray hair cut as short as it was when he was a sergeant twenty years ago. That and his straight posture is all that's left of the appearance of being a marine. His face, aside from his bulbous cratered nose, is as gray as his hair, classic sign of poor blood flow from a lack of exercise. He has three chins under his round face and they quiver when he acts like he is getting angry. What was once bulky about his body is now just plain fat, about forty pounds too much of it for his narrow-shouldered six-foot frame and his surprisingly small feet.

He keeps a bottle of Old Crow in his desk drawer next to a roll of breath mints. I know that because I can smell them both on his breath. I always feel a little sorry for him when I see him. He's a perfect candidate for a heart attack. Being a high school principal is no easy job.

He uses anger—feigned anger—as a tool. He tried it on me once when I got called in to the office because somebody in the school was dealing dope and as a new kid living in a trailer I was a suspect. Of course I knew who was doing it—not that I was about to tell. The real dealer was a burnout kid who reeked of weed so much it didn't take a canine sense of smell to nose him out.

"What the hell," he'd yelled that first time as soon as I stepped through his door, "are you up to, Mr. . . ." (the fact that he paused then to look at the paper on his desk to make sure he got my name right was the first sign that it was all an act) ". . . King?"

"Nothing, sir," I'd replied, looking down at the floor. Believe it or not, avoiding someone's eyes is not a sign that you're lying. Making direct eye contact and not breaking it is more of a tell.

Nothing came of that first meeting with Aiken for a Breakin'. I didn't break and he told me to get my ass back to class.

I hadn't been worried. I'd known I hadn't done anything wrong just as well as I was aware of the fact that Principal Aiken was faking his anger. His body language and his scent told me that. No adrenaline, no unusual body odor aside from the Old Crow—which I knew all too well from my father's empty bottles in our trash.

Now, though, is way different. My personal inventory of things done wrong over the last two days is only matched by the things I'm still likely to do. I'm on the wrong side of the law. And it's the law that's facing me. The only reason Principal Aiken is here is because I'm legally a minor. Without any parent present—which as you and I know is a total impossibility right now for me—he has to be the one who plays the role of being *in loco parentis*.

The two officers who are here are not part of Rangerville's force. Our local five-person police department, headed by Chief Roger Frank, mostly confines itself to acting as Dr. Kesselring's personal bodyguards. Lately they've spent even more of their time at the Maxico complex. They also all have new, extremely expensive trucks. Working for Maxico pays well. The two who are now looking me up and down are state police, better-trained and undoubtedly much more honest than our town popos.

The policewoman is the one who speaks first. She looks Latina. Thick, tight curled black hair, freckles on her square brown face. Even features. No distinguishing scars or birthmarks. Just a small black mole, a beauty mark, to the side of her left eyebrow. Medium height. Sunglasses tucked in her shirt pocket bulge out a little from the swell of her chest. Not because she's big-breasted. She has a strong muscular build. Probably a weight lifter, does judo or karate from the way she balances herself on her feet. Mom had that same way of rocking back a little just before demonstrating a self-defense move.

She's the tougher one in this team. As a state policewoman you have to be tough to stay on the job, especially when you are good-looking like her. Uncle Cal was a policeman for a few years after he left the Marines. He shook his head as he told me what it was like for the first woman who joined the department.

"Name was Lucy Alonso, little Eye-talian girl. Second day on the job she opened her locker and found a pair of bull testicles hanging there with a sign that read YOU NEED THESE, HONEY. They thought for sure they were going to get her to either cry or quit."

Uncle Cal threw back his head in a laugh. "Didn't work with little Lucy, for sure. She stuck that bloody mess into a baggie, said 'thanks for the Rocky Mountain oysters, boys,' took 'em home and cooked 'em. Took her only two years to make sergeant."

Lady Popo pierces me with an all-business stare.

"Lucas King?" as if she didn't know.

I nod. "Yes, ma'am."

"Officer Ortega." I already know that too. It being written on her name tag.

Her voice is throaty and deep, but not in a sexy way. A nice tone to it, probably a good singing voice.

She jerks her thumb toward her partner without looking at him. "Officer Clark."

I nod to him. "Sir."

Officer Clark almost nods back. Sincere politeness usually gets them. However, he manages to keep a straight face.

He's about 5' 10". Fair skin color, northern European ancestry. Blue eyes. Short brown hair with a little wave to it, creased where his cap pressed it down. His long nose looks like it was broken once. No facial hair. Distinguishing marks a brown quarter-sized skin blotch on his left cheek, two small black moles below his right eye. Long-armed and fairly broad-shouldered, fingers like a basketball player. The middle knuckle on his little finger of the left hand bulges. Broken and poorly set at one time. Big feet for his height. Size twelves. A little too skinny for his uniform, which looks newer than Ortega's. She wears her uniform like a second skin. He wears his like a costume. Ten to one he has less than a year on the job.

Clark folds his arms to make himself look more serious, leans back against Aiken's desk. When he stands up, unless he's careful, his holster is going to hook on that pile of papers and spill them on the floor.

"We need to ask you some questions, young man," Ortega continues. Her voice is polite but stern.

Time for me to ask the right question. Another "yes, ma'am" might seem a little too compliant, as if I was expecting this.

Which I was.

"Is something wrong? Is it my Dad?" I speed my voice up as I blurt out the questions. "Has he had an accident?"

Officer Clark lifts a hand toward me. "It's okay, son. Calm down. Nobody got hurt."

It's clear why he's number two here. He's not even doing a good job at playing good cop. That third sentence of his gave too much away. He already really is sympathizing with me.

Officer Ortega momentarily looks disgusted. She makes a quick gesture back toward Clark who bites his lip and shuts up. She studies me like a surveyor assessing the terrain.

"Ma'am, please?" I say. "What's wrong? Why am I here?"

I can see her mental process at work. She's going to try to play both parts.

She points to one of the chairs in front of the desk.

"Sit down, Mr. King." Still no nonsense, but her tone is softer.

I sit, keeping my eyes on her. My body language says that I'm nervous, uncertain, a little scared. Officer Clark pulls a pen and pad from his back pocket. As he leans to the side to do so his holster rides a little farther up onto the desk.

I turn back toward Principal Aiken as if I'm hoping he'll be my ally.

"Sir?" I ask him and then swallow hard.

"Just answer their questions, Mr. King," he says, holding up both hands and gesturing toward Ortega.

I return my querulous gaze to her.

"Please, ma'am, can you tell me what this is about?"

"In a minute, if you'll just cooperate."

"I'm sorry. I'll try." I lean forward, my hands clasped in my lap.

"Where were you last night?"

Time to hesitate again, act a little guilty here. I turn slightly to the side, a sign of being evasive. "Last night?"

"Last night. Were you at home?"

There's a curfew for minors in our area. If you're not over eighteen, you are supposed to be in before 11:00 P.M. unless you are with a parent or a guardian.

I cover my mouth with my hand. That's another tell. Covering your mouth with a hand, however briefly, usually means someone is lying or thinking about not telling the truth.

Then I shake my head and drop my hand back in my lap.

"No, ma'am. I wasn't at home."

I can see Officer Clark nodding, a little smile on his lips. He's glad I'm being straight with them. Way too much empathy to be a cop.

Officer Ortega raises an eyebrow toward him. He tightens his lips.

"Where were you last night, then?" she asks, her voice edging toward sternness.

"Am I in trouble? I know there's a curfew. But I didn't think it would make any difference."

"Just answer my question!" A little more edge of steel in her voice.

"My dad's away. And I just didn't want to be in the trailer alone. So after school I just grabbed some food and my sleeping bag and took my bike and went and camped out in the woods. We used to do it all the time, my mom and my dad and me back before . . ."

I choke up then as I've been planning to do. It's easier than I expected. I cough, regain my composure.

"I just wanted to feel like it used to be, to pretend they were there with me, camping out like we used to do."

I put my head down and lift up one hand to pretend to wipe away a tear. Turns out I don't have to pretend about that at all. I really am crying.

Officer Ortega doesn't let up, even though she leans toward me slightly and her voice softens.

"Have you been home at all since last night, son?" she asks.

"No, ma'am."

That, at least, is the simple truth. All I have to do now is act properly shocked when they let me know about the fire, how they'd expected to find my body and my dad's in the ruins of the Sardine Can. How they found no corpses at all. How someone finally figured out they should call the school and see if I was there. Which I was. How they found out that my father was out of town and I had been left home alone. Which made me a suspect in possible arson.

I've established myself as a clueless, transparent kid in their eyes. It's time for them to break it to me about the fire and the loss of my home and see how I react.

Which means I am home free in more ways than one.

What makes it easier is that this is when Officer Clark decides to stand up and take a step forward. Not only the entire pile of papers on the principal's desk is dragged with him by his holster, but also the globe with the star-spangled Statue of Liberty inside it that shatters in a spray of glass, water, and artificial snow on the floor.

TAKING NOTES

There's nothing to be heard in this room other than the ticking of the clock on the wall and the sound of stressed breathing. Neither Officer Ortega or Officer Clark are saying anything and I'm keeping my mouth shut.

Both of them are so royally ticked off at each other that I'm feeling like a fifth wheel—attached maybe, but unneeded. The scene that followed Clark's inadvertent shattering of the globe and the scattering of Principal Aiken's papers was as chaotic as the running of the bulls in Pamplona. Imagine three flustered adults attempting to act like they are still in control while trying simultaneously to gather up soaked papers, avoid slitting their wrists on the innumerable slivers of glass carpeting the floor and glittering like tiny razors, and control the twin impulses to burst into profanity and strangle one another.

The only way they could still exert their authority was by telling me to keep back to avoid cutting myself. Only one of the school custodians coming in with dust pan, mop, and broom had restored any semblance of order. He'd been summoned, of course, by the ever-efficient Mrs. Carruth. At the sound of the crash she'd poked her head in, taken note of the situation, and disappeared as quickly as a prairie dog popping back into its hole at the sight of a hawk.

Officer Ortega seems to be regaining her composure. She looks around, her lips pressed together, her breathing softer. We've been relocated to the small interview room next to the principal's office. Only three of us. Principal Aiken has stayed behind. The question of protecting my rights ranks second to his primary bureaucratic imperative—save the paperwork.

Ortega looks over at Clark, who has his pad and pen out again and is avoiding her gaze. She sighs, nods to herself, and gets right to it.

"Mr. King, did you cook anything when you went back home last night—before you left to camp out?"

I put an appropriately confused look on my face. "Why are you asking me that?"

"Just answer the question," Clark says, starting to stand up. Forget about being good cop. He's too embarrassed now for that. He's also sweating like crazy. Sour flop sweat. I'm wishing he'd used a better deodorant this morning.

Ortega raises her eyebrows at him—two thunderheads lifting above a ridge. Clark quickly subsides.

I look at first one of them and then the other. "No. I just grabbed some bread and some lunch meat out of the fridge and a can of soda." I pause, as if taking a further mental inventory. "I didn't use the stove at all. I almost never use it, in fact. It's such a piece of junk, that it's like, you know, a fire hazard."

Officer Ortega doesn't intend to, but she gives a little nod at that piece of information I've fed her as carefully as a zoo-goer slipping a piece of fruit through the bars to a sharp-beaked bird. She takes a breath.

"I'm sorry to have to tell you this, Mr. King," she says in a carefully measured tone, "but there was a fire in your trailer last night."

"Huh?" Disbelieving, gradually becoming shocked at the realization. I'm definitely going for the Oscar with this performance. "No, no!"

She has her hand on my shoulder. "Yes," she says.

"How bad was it?"

Clark has to say something to remind me he's still there. "Total loss, kid."

I lower my head. "My dad is going to kill me. If I hadn't gone out camping I could've been there." I pound my fist against my thigh. "I could've put the fire out."

"Or you could be dead," Ortega says. "I've seen how fast trailer fires burn. Once they start, it's like an oven in a matter of minutes. In fact, the first responders thought you and your father had been caught in there. They spent an hour looking for your bodies after it had cooled down enough."

"Oh," I say, keeping my voice weak. "Was everything lost? I mean, we didn't have much. But couldn't they save anything?"

"You can see for yourself, kid," Clark puts in. "We'll be taking you out there next." He looks at Ortega. "Right?" he asks, realizing he's overstepped again.

Ortega resists the impulse to rip his head off. "Right," she agrees. "You ready?"

Officer Ortega is in front of me and Clark is trailing close behind as we make our way the short distance to the front exit of the school. Short it might be, but not short enough. The bell rang as we left the interview room, signaling the start of the migration of us teenage lemmings from one period to the next. The timing couldn't have been worse if Ortega and Clark expected to slip me quietly out of school without anyone noticing.

Leaving a high school while being escorted by two blue-clad peace officers is, to say the least, one way to get people's attention. The RHS rumor mill is going to be grinding out grist for the rest of the day—if not the year. I'm not in handcuffs, but after the story has been told half a dozen times I'll probably be described as having chains fastened around my ankles and my waist and a Hannibal Lector mask clamped over my face.

I'm looking around, hoping to catch a glimpse of Meena or Renzo, give them the high sign to let them know I'm okay. The one familiar face I do see, though, is one I'd rather not. Yuri.

He's managed to position himself by the door. He's staring at me, his eyes unblinking as those of a cobra.

Sorry, buddy. No way I'm going to make our little lunch date. As you can see, I'm going to be tied up for a while—if not thrown in the slammer.

Yuri nods slowly, as if reading my mind. He turns sideways to let us pass through the crowded doorway and I feel his hand slide down into my pocket, leave something there. It's been done so quickly, so effortlessly that only he and I know what's happened.

Though I won't be able to rendezvous with the Sunglass Mafia as they'd expected, I'm not off the hook with them. As soon as I have enough privacy to read the note Yuri passed me, I'll know what they have planned.

Oh boy.

I can't wait.

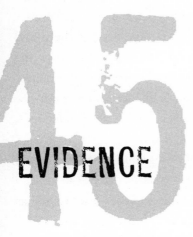

EVIDENCE

I sit back against the Commando with my arms crossed, biting my lower lip, an anxious look on my face that is only half-faked. The smoking remains of the Sardine Can look sadder in the sunlight than they did in the night. They smell a lot worse. At one point when the two cops and I were close to the blackened wood and metal I started coughing so much that they had to get me a drink of water.

Aside from the stench of plastic and paint, charred wood and half-melted metal, there's also still a little heat rising here and there, despite the heavy soaking from the hoses. The air ripples as if invisible butterflies were hovering there.

It was, I discovered, a well-attended blaze. Rigs from three different stations responded. (Not because it was that bad. The lives of small-town firemen can get pretty boring without a good blaze or two and once a party starts, the more the merrier. Nothing a fireman likes more than a good fire. I guess that's why last year two firemen in a nearby village got arrested for arson.) There's half a dozen tank trucks, about a hundred firemen and first responders, and more pickups than you'd find at a beer party.

Now all that's left are lots of car tracks, so many that (I'm happy to see) they obliterated the tread marks of the black Mercedes.

Things are cordoned off, the yellow tape sagging here and there. One end of it is tied to a board that sticks out from the back of our garage shed, which miraculously survived untouched. That means I at least still have the tools and spare parts for the Commando. But there's no way I can use a shed as my residence. A problem I may have to deal with soon. Or not.

I was a little surprised at first that Ortega and Clark let me ride my motorcycle here, closely followed by their cruiser. On second thought, it made sense. Ortega looked like a kettle about to boil as we left the school. Whenever I looked back in my handlebar mirror I could see her head turned toward her partner, her jaws going. My not being in the car made it possible for her to go up one side and down the other on him.

Once we reached the site of our trailer, which looked like something from a bombed-out neighborhood in Baghdad, I was subjected to more questions. Then they told me to go over to my bike and wait.

And here I sit.

Two fire investigators, a state trooper, and someone from some state agency I'd never heard of are having a conference along with Ortega. (Officer Clark has been reduced to a "wait in the car" role.) I answered all their questions—in the semiautomatic tone of someone in the first stages of shock, not forgetting to sprinkle in lots of yessirs and no-ma'ams, but I'm not done. I know there's still more to come.

I'm hoping that enough of the evidence I planted survived

the blast. I've got my fingers crossed that their investigator is smart enough, but not too smart.

Ortega approaches. She has a bag in her hand that she holds down to her opposite side to keep me from seeing it. I can already smell the paraffin and the herbal scent though. Luck, it seems, is with me. A lanky middle-aged man in a well-worn brownish-yellow suit strolls along beside her, a clipboard in his hand and half a dozen pens in a pocket protector. He's still wearing boots but has stripped off the rest of the uniform, mask included, that he was wearing as he prodded his way through the ruins. His suit coat is slung over his shoulder. There's sweat on his brow, the combination of the sunlight and the heat from the wreckage he's been studying. His straw-colored hair sticks out in all directions.

I stand up from the motorcycle, a nervous look on my face.

"Mr. King," Ortega says, her voice clipped and serious, "Lieutenant Sonneborn and I have some more questions for you."

"Ma'am?"

The two of them escort me over to the fire investigator's car. They wait long enough to calculate they've made me sufficiently nervous.

"Young man," Sonneborn begins, his voice nasal with a Midwestern twang, "what were you doin' last night?"

"I camped out," I answer.

Sonneborn nods. Just what he expected me to say.

"No, son. I mean before you went off in the woods. What were you doing back here, all by yourself, in there?" He hooks a finger back toward the ruins, keeping his eye on me all the time.

I reach up and run my hand through my hair. "Nothing, sir," I say, looking off to the left. A double tell, true, but I want to make sure they have plenty of body language to read.

"Young man," Sonneborn says, a little note of triumph in his suddenly sterner voice. He taps me on the chest with his finger. "You look at me. They tell me you're a good kid, planning to enter the service. Is that right?"

If the recruiters are looking for wolves, I think. But I look him straight in the eye and nod. "Yes, sir," I say, a little military snap in my voice.

Ortega holds the bag in front of my face. "Then you don't want this on your record, do you?"

"Oh crap!" I blurt, staring at the contents visible through the clear plastic. It's the Bic lighter, miraculously unmelted, the singed pack of rolling papers, the burned plate with what's left of one of the candles and the remains of the joint stuck to it.

"Are these yours?" Sonneborn asks, tapping the bag with the same finger.

"Tell the truth," Ortega says, all good cop now.

"No sir . . . ma'am. They're not mine. I mean the candle is, was ours, but not the . . ." I let my sentence trail off into nervous uncertainty.

"Then whose were they?"

"The truth," Ortega urges. "Just tell the whole truth and you won't get in trouble."

No, ma'am, I think. Telling the whole truth will get me in more trouble than you can imagine. But part of the truth is not a bad idea. I hesitate for effect.

Sonneborn steps in. "There's not hardly even enough of a controlled substance here for a misdemeanor. Is there, Officer Ortega?"

Ortega studies my face. "No, there's not."

I give a heavy sigh. "All right. It was my dad's. I found the . . . cigarette while I was here alone last night. I tried smoking it, but I didn't finish it. I turned out the lights and lit the candle because I'd heard that's what people do. But it just made me more lonely. All I wanted to do was just get out of there."

"You just left the candle burning?"

"I guess I did. But it was on that saucer and in the shower." I pause.

Ortega speaks a single word. "Gas."

I let my legs go a little loose, as if I've just been hit in the head and I'm trying not to fall. "Do you mean . . . ?"

Ortega and Sonneborn look at each other.

"Just wait here," Sonneborn says. The two of them walk back to the other assembled investigators. As they do so, Ortega looks back over her shoulder to give me a friendly nod.

I'm already pretty sure it worked. As I listen to the conversation that follows, beyond the earshot of any normal person, but easy enough for me to hear, I'm certain.

The gist of it is that they've concluded that the fire was caused by a faulty stove leaking gas inside the trailer. The point of ignition was my still-burning candle. The whole thing was an unfortunate accident, not arson.

More time passes. Finally Ortega and Sonneborn come back to me.

"This young lady," Sonneborn says, hooking a finger at Ortega, who can't keep from knitting her brows at his description of her, "tells me that the local police department informed her that your father has been using illegal substances. So we're all willing to not make any mention about you smoking dope. Losing your home is punishment enough. You understand what I'm saying?"

"Yes sir, thank you, sir."

"Seein' as how you are almost eighteen, we also figger there's no need to get child services involved until your father gets back. Plus the budget's so tight right now—what with the loss of federal funds—there's not likely to be a bed for you anywhere. You have a place you can stay for a few days?"

An entire mansion, I think.

I just nod, thankful that the national deficit has just disposed of one more awkward problem—having to explain to the authorities where I'll be staying after losing my home.

"All right," Ortega says. She holds out her hand to take mine in a firm grip. "You stay out of trouble, right?"

Not likely, I think.

"Right, ma'am," I say.

PHONE HOME

I look at Ortega's watch as she grasps my hand. It reads 2:00 P.M. No point in going back to school from here. Even if I could leave now, by the time I got there the day would be over.

Renzo will probably be in the band room though. But I'm not sure what more I can say to him now. And I'm sure that Meena's first thought will be to get home as fast as she can to talk with her father. But will he believe what she tells him? The wild story that she heard from her classmate Luke about his overhearing men talking about keeping watch on a Professor Kureshi? And what if he does believe it? What then? I have no idea.

Just like I don't know where I'm going now.

Thinking of going, I'm not going to be able to do even that until this policewoman releases her grip.

"You really do have a place to stay? Like you told Sonneborn?" She jerks her head back toward the fire inspector.

It's what I was afraid she was going to say. But I have an answer.

"Yes, ma'am. I'm going to stay with my friend Renzo. You want his number?"

Ortega nods and loosens her hold enough for me to take my hand back. She takes out a pad. "Go ahead."

I repeat it twice, once a little too fast for her to catch it, then a second time, number by number, along with his address.

"Now give me your number."

I look over at the ruins of the trailer. "Uh . . ." I hold my palms up.

Ortega almost smiles at that. "Your cell."

"I don't have a cell phone." A true statement. Like watches, cell phones do not like whatever electric or molecular field I have emanating from my body. All I get is static when I try to use one.

Ortega looks at me like I just told her I'm from Mars.

"A teenager with no cell phone? You lose it in the fire too?"

"No, I never had one."

"No Blackberry? Don't you text? No tweeting?"

I shake my head each time.

"So what's your father's cell? No, don't tell me. He doesn't have one either?"

Another shake of my head.

"Why?"

I pause, as if trying to come up with an answer to a question I never thought to ask myself before. "I guess," I say slowly, "we never felt like we needed them. My mom was the one who used a cell phone. She used hers all the time. But after she died . . ." I sigh. "Maybe it was because Mom . . . I don't know."

Ortega finally looks as if I've said something that makes sense. As a policewoman she's probably dealt with plenty of grief and observed the sometimes illogical ways that people deal with loss.

But she is also a cop and, it appears, a thorough one.

She takes a phone out of her pocket, flips it open, and dials the number I just gave her. She turns slightly away as I step back a foot. Not just to give her privacy. If I'm too close, all she's going to hear is a crackling sound like someone crumpling paper.

However, a private conversation is not what she's about to get. Although I can't hold a cell phone in my hand or expect one to work when it is anywhere too close to me, my hearing is so keen that when someone else is on a handheld device I can overhear the other person's voice even from a long way away.

Renzo's mother answers on the third ring.

"Hello? Baggio residence."

"Mrs. Baggio?" Ortega asks. If she'd asked me, I could have told her it was Renzo's mother. Her voice still holds a little hint of the accent of southern Italy where she was born.

"Yes."

"This is Officer Ortega." Ortega is talking quickly but clearly now, forestalling any of the worried questions a mother is sure to ask when her kid's not home and the cops have called. "Nothing's wrong. I'm calling about a friend of your son's."

"You mean Lucas?"

"Yes, Mrs. Baggio. There was a fire at his residence. His father is out of town and he needs a place to stay. He told me that he could stay there."

"Is Lucas all right?"

"He's fine, but could he stay there for a night or two until he manages to contact his father?"

"Of course. Lucas is always welcome. My boy Lorenzo, he called already and told me Lucas would be coming over tonight. Of course Lorenzo will be at the band today until four. But you tell Lucas he's welcome to come earlier if he wants. Any time. We're happy to have him."

"Thank you, Mrs. Baggio."

Ortega turns back toward me as she flips the phone shut. I'm relieved she hasn't asked me to talk on it.

"Looks as if you're set for tonight," Ortega says. She looks at her watch, realizing they've kept me here way past lunchtime, given me nothing other than a cup of water. She looks over at the car where Clark is waiting.

"Want something to eat?" she asks.

Her question makes my stomach rumble. Five pounds of raw meat? The deer carcass comes to mind with the satisfying image of me bending over its body and ripping out mouthfuls of warm, bloody flesh.

I shake my head. "No," I growl.

Ortega takes a quick step back.

I quickly clear my throat. "I'm okay," I say quickly, managing to restore some semblance of a human tone to my voice. "I'll grab something at Taco Prince."

Ortega studies me for a minute. That atavistic growl of mine set off some warning signal deep in the cortex of her brain. The deep rumble of a nearby predator stirring her ancient ancestors out of sleep as they huddled around a fire. Fight or flee! But modern logic takes back over again and she relaxes.

I'm a cop. Why be scared of a skinny teenager?

"Okay," she says. Then she smiles as she delivers the standard line all TV and movie police use. "Just don't leave town."

I start the Norton, steer it down the driveway, turn toward town.

Too many thoughts, as usual.

By the time I reach the main road I've decided at least one thing. I'm not going to be going to Renzo's house now, despite Mrs. Baggio's invitation. Nor is it likely I'll be staying there tonight.

There's too much to do. I have a couple of other destinations in the darkness.

A mile later I pass Taco Prince, but I don't stop. Overcooked beef laden with chemicals is not what I want to fill my stomach with.

I need to feed. I also need to take a nap. It's been a long time since I've had much sleep. But both of those things can wait, for a little while at least. There's another errand I need to run. I pull into the parking lot of Rangerville Home Savings, the bank whose name is printed on the cardboard card tied to the safety deposit box key that I have in my jean jacket.

47
TAKE THE MONEY AND RUN

I wait my turn in the line for the teller. He's a young guy, black, wears a bow tie, seems friendly and efficient. Just before it's my turn at the window, I reach into my pocket for the key and find a tightly folded piece of paper.

Yuri's note. It slipped my mind or, more accurately, had been fluttering at the edge of my consciousness like a bat hovering in one of the darkest corners of a room. Not the time and place to pull it out and read. Matter of fact, a handwritten note is not the wisest thing to have in your fingers as you approach a bank teller. Like Woody Allen's "I have a gub" in the ancient film *Take the Money and Run*.

"Next."

I leave the note, dig farther and pull out the key as the woman in front of me steps to the side to put her bank book back in her purse.

"Good morning, sir. May I help you?" The cultured Oxford

accent of a well-educated West African. Mr. Okigbo, the name plate in front of him reads.

"Yes, thank you." I hold up the key. "I need to get into a safety deposit box."

Mr. Okigbo takes it, looks at the key and its wooden tag, hands it back to me, gestures to my left. "Mr. Jackson over there at the desk will help you. Next."

Mr. Jackson is an older man. His desk is located just in front of the bank vault under A PENNY SAVED IS A PENNY EARNED, the motto inscribed on the marble wall. He's just as efficient and unsuspicious as Mr. Okigbo, the teller.

Placing the key by his computer, Mr. Jackson opens a program, scrolls down, nods, and holds his hand out, palm up.

"Photo identification?"

I've already removed my driver's license from my wallet. He glances at the license, at my face, again at the license, nods a second time. Then he takes a leather-bound ledger, opens it, turns it toward me and hands me a pen.

"Sign here, next to your name."

I've never seen the ledger before, but there's my signature. A perfect replica. I'm not sure when it was done, but I know my father did it. He can sign my name as well as I can sign his. I take the pen and successfully reproduce my own signature.

We walk back into the open vault where there's at least a thousand small metal doors on two sides. Mr. Jackson walks unerringly to the one bearing the number of my key, inserts my key in one of the two slots, a key of his own in the other, turns them both.

"Take out your box," he says.

I slide the long metal box with a hinged lid on it from its place. It's too heavy to have just a few papers in it. Whatever is in there, it's packed in solidly.

Do I open it now?

Mr. Jackson taps my arm, indicates one of a series of closed doors just outside the vault.

"You can use that room for privacy. Just return to my desk when you want to put the box back."

I enter the room, close the door. I put the box on the one small table, just a little bigger than a school desk. I sit at one of the two clunky, uncomfortable wooden chairs. Clearly not a place where people want to spend much time.

I lift the lid. My first thought is that it's a good thing I brought my backpack with me and left my school books—which I doubt I'll ever see again—in my locker at RHS. I'm going to need all the space I have in it to fit all of these wrapped stacks of used bills that jam the eight-inch-deep, twelve-inch-wide, and two-foot-long box.

Used bills are the safest. People get suspicious if you start throwing around stacks of stiff, shiny currency. Twenties and above are the most often counterfeited. Denominations lower than that are too cumbersome if you want to have a lot of cash on hand. The stacks of cash are divided between twenties, fifties, and hundreds. More twenties than anything else because people are used to seeing lots of them. A lot of places still are reticent to give change for a bigger bill, though most no longer look twice at you if you just have one or two fifties or a single C note. Although some places if you give them a hundred, they immediately hold it up to the light to check the watermark, run a marker pen across its face, or use a special light.

I remember my dad and Uncle Cal laughing as they described to me how people try to identify a phony bill.

"What they don't know," Dad said, "is that the best counterfeiters use the same papers, the same inks, the same methods as the U.S. Mint, especially when they're not just freelancers but doing it with the blessings and all the resources of a foreign country. That's true all over the world. Forget the yen, the Euro, or the deutsche mark. The only really safe currency is gold. People have been trying for thousands of years and no one's ever found any way to make gold other than digging it out of the ground."

"True enough for sure," Uncle Cal grinned back. "But seeing as that pretty yellow metal is so heavy, we might as well just stick with the good old United States greenback."

Unlikely I'll ever be coming back to this bank. All of the money goes into my bag. I stop counting after thirty thousand dollars and just load it in. My pack filled, I'm ready to take the money and run.

Wait. There's something else in the bottom of the box. An envelope. I undo its clasp, shake it over the table.

Two things fall out. The first is another safety deposit key. I read its label. A bank in the next town over. It makes me wonder if that safety deposit box will be similar—packed with easy-to-use dough and yet another key for a third bank.

I put down the key and look at the second thing. I lift it up to the light and study it. What does it mean?

48
THROUGH THE DOOR

There's a zipper pocket on the inside of my backpack. Although the stacks of bills fill the pack to the top, I can still open that pocket. I slip the new safety deposit box key into it, along with the second thing that fell out of the envelope. Then I zip the pocket tightly shut.

A nagging question floats back up to the surface of my mind like wreckage from a torpedoed ship. What now?

There's a good five hours left before the rise of the sweet full moon into the sky. It'll take me less than half an hour to get from here to the Drake House. Not only is it my best place of refuge, it's the safest spot to stash all this money. But then what? The prospect of waiting and anxiously twiddling my thumbs until darkness descends is not appealing. Could I take that nap I was just considering? No way. I'm too keyed up to just curl up in the secret room and sleep like a contented canine until night.

What now, indeed?

Is someone surveilling the outside of the bank right now and waiting for me to come out? Was I followed when I had my police escort to the burned out trailer? Is my father okay?

Is there anything I can do other than ask myself more questions?

My hand brushes a lump in my pocket. Yuri's note. I haven't looked at it yet.

I take it out, unfold it, and read. A snarl escapes my lips. I hope it wasn't loud enough to be heard through the thin door to this private room. I count slowly to ten. No armed security guards burst in. Maybe no one noticed. Maybe they're just used to emotional outbursts when someone opens a family safety deposit box and finds something in it they don't like.

I fight the impulse to tear Yuri's note into shreds as if it were his throat.

I read it again.

Brief, but it says a lot.

Far too much.

And it answers one of my questions.

What now?

Go straight back to school.

The clock on the facade above the main entrance reads 4:10. The buses have all departed. There's no activity around the gym. It's an away game tonight. But the school is still open because of after-school activities, like the band practice that I now know Renzo is missing. I growl and bare my teeth at the thought of that.

Stay calm, Luke.

The only sign of life outside is a large tractor trailer backing up at the distant far side of the school where the main loading dock is located. A little late for deliveries. Then again, it's probably better now than when the driveways are packed with buses.

Something about that trailer nags at me, but I've got too much else on my mind to waste time thinking about it.

I walk up the steps. The door starts buzzing like a giant hornet's nest before I even have a chance to lean over to speak into the intercom. Someone's been monitoring me through the closed-circuit camera aimed at the front entrance.

Mr. Murry is still at the desk. His shift doesn't end till 5:00 P.M. He seems to be engrossed in today's *Rangerville Herald*. I'm hoping I can just stroll past him now that he's identified me on the TV monitor in front of his desk and buzzed me in. But he lowers the paper.

"Luke," he says. "Hold up a minute." He lifts one of his beefy hands that are big enough to palm—and maybe pop—a basketball, turns the paper so I can see the photo on the cover. The smoldering rubble that was the Sardine Can. "You okay?"

"Thanks," I say. "I think I am."

He nods, an understanding look on his face. "My sister and her family lost their trailer in a fire like this five years ago. Anything I can do? Need anything?"

I shake my head, anxious to get past him but not wanting to brush off his concern and waken any suspicion on his part.

"It's okay," I say. I reach over my shoulder to pat my backpack. "I've got enough in here to get by." Understatement on the order of describing an earthquake as a speed bump.

"Where are you . . . ?" he asks.

"My dad will be back in a couple of days." I hope. "I'm staying with a friend."

Hah!

"Oh," Mr. Murry says. "Right. The Baggio kid?"

"Uh-huh. Meeting him now."

I hope.

He looks at his watch. "Well, the band has another hour of practice. Might as well go down there. No need to sign in." He smiles. "You're no visitor here."

Nope, but I am feeling like a stranger in a strange land that just keeps getting weirder.

I walk down the empty hall. I round the corner and then, instead of going right toward the band room, I take a sinister turn.

My feet are silent, but they know I'm here. I can feel them waiting. The hair is standing up on the back of my neck. The wolf mark on my wrist feels so hot it should be sizzling like bacon on a griddle.

I've heard the expression that someone can be of two minds. That usually means a person is undecided about which alternative to take. But in my case being of two minds describes my current condition a little too accurately.

There's my logical mind, the human mind. I've been thinking with that all of my life—until recently. But now there's another wholly different consciousness. It's not separate. It's linked to every part of me. But it's also . . . what? Parallel. It's like I'm living on two levels at the same time. And that second level is trembling right now with the eager potential, the absolute lust, for violence.

Stop.

Stand still.

Breathe, Lucas.

Think.

Get it together.

Old stories from Europe tell how a man or woman could sell his soul to Satan for power. In return, that soul-stripped human would be given a belt made of wolf skin. Put on that belt and be transformed into a wolf, a ravening beast that sees humans as prey, tears their throats out, eats their flesh.

Our DNA carries links to every ancestor that came before us.

My family's not just American Indian. That genealogy of my dad's also listed those lines. Some of my ancestry goes back to a part of Germany I'd read about without realizing I had any connection to it. Griefswalsd. There strange stories were told of were-creatures that stalked the nightmares of the townsfolk. In 1640, old records say that the city lived in dread of not just one werewolf, but a whole colony of them that took up residence on Rokover Street. Anyone who ventured out in the night might be caught and killed and devoured by them.

Finally, though, a group of students from the university decided to fight back. They melted down all of the silver they could gather—their buttons, their belt buckles, their drinking cups—and molded them into bullets. And in a great battle they managed to kill every one of those monsters. Or so the story goes.

One of those students was a great-grandfather of mine many times removed. But was he also one who wore a wolf belt? One who hid the curse?

That history runs through my mind as I stand here, trying to calm myself down.

No, even though part of me feels different, I'm sure that Satan has nothing to do with what I am. Dad wouldn't lie to me, and he told me that I could control my wolf nature.

I think about the American Indian side of my blood. True, darkness does sometimes enter our native traditions about men or women taking on animal shapes. There are stories of witches, those whose minds are twisted and who sacrifice a family member to gain that power. There are Abenaki stories of such twisted-minds who put on the wolf skin. *Galugalu* is what we call them. That name, though, is borrowed from French. It hearkens back to the werewolf stories our French allies told us of the loup garou.

That genealogy of Dad's suggests that my Abenaki ancestors

knew another way to be skinwalkers. It seems as if they were not overcome by blood lust. Instead, they were able to use their abilities to serve the state as good soldiers—or spies. *Nopaosad.* That is another of the Abenaki names for a person such as my father . . . or me. It means one who walks far, one who is on the war trail, a scout.

Nopaosad. I like that name. What I am, what I have is not something I bargained for. It's something that I was born with. It's a gift, not a devil's curse. And among our Indian people, a wolf is not an animal to fear. Wolves, our old stories tell us, have always been teachers to the human beings. In a wolf pack every adult cares for the cubs. So they show us the way we should treat our children. At night, wolves gather on the hilltops to sing. They look up at the Wolf Road, the path of stars that leads to the place we go after death, where the hunting is always good. They say that trail was made by an old wolf who walked into the sky after he died and left his tracks behind so that his people could find their way to the Good Hunting Grounds.

Wolves are not evil. I'm not evil. I do not believe that and I never will believe that of my father. Different, though, that I can believe.

Accept it, Luke.

My breathing is slower now. I feel . . . together.

Time to open another door and walk through.

MOVED IN

I pause with my hand on the doorknob. I can sense the presence of those who are waiting on the other side.

Is this the best way to proceed?

It would help if I knew why.

Not just one why. I'm surrounded by whys.

Why was my father taken?

Why are Yuri and his pack so interested in me? I don't think they're allied with the people who took Dad. It's a gut feeling, nothing logical. Not that there's been much logic in my life lately.

But even though they may not have been agents in my father's abduction, I also find it hard to think of the Sunglass Mafia being innocent players in this game, the rules and goals of which are foreign to me. Why have Yuri and his friends moved in here at RHS?

Another why: Why, assuming that the note from Yuri was telling the truth—and there's no reason to doubt it—do they want me so much that they've just taken my best friend as a hostage?

That, by the way, is what Yuri's little note said.

BAGGIO BOY WITH US.
WE WAIT FOR YOU.

Why did Renzo, a total innocent, have to get dragged up in this? But I know the answer to that. It's my fault. Vlad saw me with him and Meena when we were looking for intel on Maxico. No, Vlad is not my friend. I stifle a snarl as my hand tightens on the door handle so hard that my knuckles grow white.

The answers to all my questions may not be pleasant. They may even be fatal. But some of them may be found on the other side of this door. I sigh and push through.

A lanky dark shadow detaches itself from the wall where it was indolently leaning. It glides toward me.

Yuri, of course. There's enough of a smile on his face to show his canine teeth. They look a little longer and sharper right now. It's enough to send a chill down a person's back. Unless that person knows his own eyeteeth will be just as sharp—and twice as long—a few hours from now.

He nods and I nod back. It's like boxers touching gloves—or maybe two predators from different species who are observing a temporary truce because they have to share one waterhole. Yuri steps to the side and makes a sweeping "after you" gesture.

My table must be ready. With me, maybe, as the main course?

The hair on the back of my neck prickles as I walk with him close behind me, but I'm not afraid. What I need to keep under control right now is not panic but rage. The world around me flickers, flows crimson at the edges of my vision. I breathe slowly, deeply, trying to hold down the urges that could overwhelm me in a heartbeat.

The whole crew is waiting, as before. This time, though, they're not standing but sitting. Boris and Ekaterina are lying back in chairs that look too comfortable to have been designed for students. There are tables and lamps around them. And of course, rugs. There's Mr. Gretz's prized Navajo carpet. There's also a Persian rug just beyond it. That one used to be in the principal's office. They've made this corner of the no longer deserted aquatic complex seem creepily homey.

I imagine them walking around from room to room throughout the school, picking out their furnishings like newly married couples shopping in department stores for their first homes.

Ah, I like that, have it brought to me.

One mesmeric gaze of the sort Yuri used on Mr. Gretz and then . . .

Yes, master.

Did they have the janitors bring the furniture in here, walking like hypnotized automatons? Probably.

It seems as if the Sunglass Mafia can do anything that they want with anyone except me. They've really moved into this space now. But why here?

I look further around the room to the left. Marina and Vlad are over there sitting at workstations with computer monitors in front of them. The top shelf of Marina's station is lined with books. Pushkin, Yevtushenko, more of Ahkmatova's poetry. Vlad snaps his fingers and gives me a thumbs-up—as if we're old buds.

Then I notice, in the far corner beyond them, Igor and Natasha lounging on a couch. They're on either side of a still figure perched stiffly between them.

Renzo looks like a wax dummy. No expression on his face. His hands are resting in his lap as he sits there with Igor's hand on his right shoulder, Natasha's on his left. A deep growl escapes my mouth.

I take three quick steps toward him. Faster than they'd expected. Boris just manages to get between me and the couch, where Igor and Natasha actually look a little alarmed. I look down at what Boris is holding in his hand, pointed at my chest. How did they get that past the metal detector? A foolish question, I suppose. As foolish as wondering how many other weapons they have stored in here.

"Budyem druzyami!" Yuri says. "Let's be friends." He slides up next to me and pushes Boris's hand and the gun in it to the side.

One of my favorite Russian phrases immediately comes to my lips, a slangy response for when someone is trying to play you. *"Nye nado mnye lap-shu na ushi vye-shat,"* I snarl. Don't try to hang noodles from my ears.

A deep laugh comes from behind me. Vlad, I think. But I do not turn around. I keep my eyes on Yuri, who holds up both of his hands in a pacifying gesture.

"Druzhok."

"I . . . am . . . not . . . your . . . buddy. Let . . . him . . . go." I force the words out of my throat, which is constricted with rage.

"Of course," Yuri says, dropping the slang and speaking in cultured Muscovite Russian. "He is unharmed. We only invited him here to be sure you would honor our invitation. When we send him out of here, he will forget us, forget your problem, hold nothing of this in his mind. Marina?"

Marina gets up from behind the desk, walks over to the couch, and holds out a hand to Renzo.

"Come, *moi pupsik*," she says.

He smiles as he rises and takes her hand. She turns him toward the door, with surprising gentleness. "Now go to your band practice, my sweetie, and then go home. Go to bed and sleep with no dreams. You will not remember."

Renzo walks toward me, unseeing. As I step aside to let him pass, I look at him closely. No visible bruises or wounds. As he approaches the door, he begins to walk less stiffly, more like the old Lorenzo. He opens it, goes out. By the time he gets into the outer hall and arrives late for band practice, I have no doubt that all of the problems I laid on my best friend will be gone from his mind. And that's a good thing. I breathe a small sigh of relief.

Marina shakes her head. "So sorry to see him go," she says. "*Ya golodna kak volk.*" She smiles as me. "I'm as hungry as a wolf. And I love Italian food."

It would almost be funny if it was a joke.

WE TALK

There's a long silence as I stand there, my finger half-curled, my shoulders tense, my head down. My stance is like a sprinter about to drop into his blocks. My mind has already jumped the gun.

Sluzhba Vneshney Razvedk. Those three words that Yuri spoke to me earlier today, as if by way of an explanation, both explained things and made them more confusing.

It used to be called the KGB. It's the Russian secret service, the equivalent of America's CIA. They dropped the old name and reorganized under Putin. FSB is another name for the domestic security agency that was Cheka, NKVD, and KGB in the Soviet era. Espionage, counterintelligence, counterterrorism.

In the old USSR anybody might be a spy, from your school teacher to your neighbor, to a hawker on the street selling imitation American jeans. It's not all that different in modern-day Russia. Spies don't just walk around in black cloaks and look like the villains in James Bond films. They might even be teenage foreign exchange students. In fact, Dad told me, it's a good bet that more than a few teenage foreign exchange students sent from one country to another end up being used as "assets" in one way or another by their home nations—whether they know it or not.

These teenagers know it, far more than you'd expect any teenage student to know. Are they even actually teenagers, now that I think of it?

Yuri is looking at me, a half-amused smirk on his too-perfect face. As if he's thinking they've got me cornered.

That makes me even angrier. I want to rip my teeth through his throat. If I was wearing my second skin now, I'd tear them all apart.

Putting on the wolf skin last night changed me in more ways than I'd realized. Not only do I feel stronger and faster now—even when I don't have it on—I also feel this tendency toward violence, like a powerful riptide threatening to pull me under. The warning in my father's letter comes back to me.

Fight the beast, hold it back.

Stay at least partly human or I'll lose myself completely.

I roll my shoulders, straighten my back.

"Who are you?" I ask. My voice sounds calmer than I feel.

Yuri raises an eyebrow. So, it can speak? He presses his lips together in a why not expression.

"We are," he says, "just what you see." Emphasis on the word *you*.

And what do I see? A gang of elitist, spoiled foreign teenagers from families with Russian mafia connections? A group of undercover agents? Or—and this comes to me as I take closer notice of their pallor, their longer than normal canine teeth—something else? A band of vampires?

Yuri nods, as if he's been reading my mind. All of the above is correct?

This is truly crazy. But it's not so crazy when I consider who and what I am. If I'm living proof of the existence of werewolves, then why can't vampires also be possible? Do I ask him now if he's really seventeen or if he only looks that way? Was he born in Transylvania five hundred years ago before he became one of the undead?

"No," he says, "I am not that old."

This mind-reading trick of his bugs me. *Can you hear all of my thoughts?*

He shakes his head. "Only when you direct them toward me as if you are asking a question," he says. "You are not so easy to read, not like the others here in this silly little school. And unlike the rest of the . . . cattle, you seem impossible for us to control."

I've taken a half step toward him. That dismissive word "cattle" really got my goat (to use another hoofed metaphor).

Yuri holds up a hand, fingers forked in a peace sign. "We talk, *da*?" Yuri asks,

"*Da.*"

"You speak good Russian?"

"*Nyet, kamerad.* Just a little."

Yuri shrugs. "So we stay in English." He points at a table with two chairs that used to be in Mrs. Carruth's office. "We sit."

I sit across from him, which puts Marina behind me. She glides forward, leans, puts her lips close to my left ear.

"Ask me how old I am, *lyubov moya*," she whispers. My love.

"Old enough to stop playing games," Yuri says in a stern voice. Marina laughs, then takes her hands off my shoulders and steps back.

He looks at me. "It troubles you when I call them cattle, not so?"

"Yes."

"But you feel hunger toward them yourself? More now than you did yesterday, eh?"

"Yes."

"You and me, all of us here in this room, we are different. We are stronger, better. That is how we have been . . . made. So why should we care about them? Why not do as we wish and the hell with them?"

Yes or no isn't enough of an answer now. I think of my father, my mother, of the few people who are my friends.

"Because, even if I am different, I am not going to give up being human."

Yuri smiles. It's the first real smile I've seen on his face and it makes him look both more likeable and a lot younger. Maybe he really isn't centuries old. Maybe just eighty or ninety.

"Good!" He pounds his fist on the table. "It is good that we talk. We can work together, my friend. You pass the test." He slaps me hard on the shoulder with the palm of his other hand. A friendly slap that would have broken bones on an ordinary person.

But I'm not ready to get all huggy and kissy-face with him and his blood-sucking mates.

"And if I had not passed your test?" I ask.

Yuri lifts both hands palm up. "*Byez problyem.* No problem. You would not have left here alive."

51

QUESTIONS

Herr Wulf. That was Adolf Hitler's pseudonym when he began making the transition from unsuccessful painter (he sucked at drawing people) to politician—before burning a path of genocide and conquest across three continents. Translate his given name, Adolf, into English. It means Father Wolf.

Wolves occupied the Führer's every thought. But his were not the real animals that care for their young, play like dogs, and hunt only for food. Real wolves do not exist with the single-minded purpose of killing and eliminating those weaker than themselves. Hitler's idealized wolves were the stuff of myth and racist archetype. They were perfect and merciless killing machines. A blend of human and animal. He called them his werewolves.

He wanted his people to become werewolves—if not in fact then in bloody metaphor. His aim when he oversaw the creation of his fanatical corps of young people, the Hitler Youth, was "to eradicate thousands of years of human domestication" so that he could "see once more in the eyes of pitiless youth the gleam of pride and independence of the beast of prey."

Like wolves attacking a herd, they could cull out the weaker animals. Gypsies, communists, political rivals, the old and the ill, and especially the Jews would vanish down the jaws of the ravening beast. Like the wolf Fenris in Norse myths who swallows the sun, the old world would end and the Reich's new one last a thousand years.

The name of Hitler's headquarters in the Ukraine was Werewolf. His French base of operations was called Wolf's Gulch. He had the Volkswagen factory named Wulfsburg. His favorite Disney cartoon (and this is so goofy that you might think I'm making it up, but I'm not) was *The Three Little Pigs*. However, he never watched it all the way through because he imagined a way different ending. People close to him remembered the favorite tune he used to whistle all the time, "Who's Afraid of the Big Bad Wolf."

Though he may not have been a true lycanthrope, that madman who transformed his nation into a merciless power was more sanguinary in his deeds than any shape-shifter in the pages of a novel or on the silver screen.

How do I know all this historical trivia? It's not just stuff I've read that's stuck to my brain like superglue. Uncle Cal and Dad told me a lot of it. We were watching a DVD of *Raiders of the Lost Ark* one evening while Mom was off at an exercise class.

Dad had kicked it off, during one of the rare lulls in the action, "Half this film is pure fantasy."

"But only half," Cal added.

"Half?" I asked.

Cal hit the Pause button and looked at my father.

"There are people out there who'd gladly trade their souls for power," Dad said. "They'll twist anything, even the most sacred, to their uses. That swastika is an old Pueblo Indian sign for the power of the four directions, the cleansing strength of the sacred whirl-winds that sweep across the land."

Before long the movie paled next to the facts that filled my mind.

The Third Reich was all tied up in mysticism with its twisted cross and lightning bolts and propaganda about German destiny as the master race. Hitler really did believe in the occult, in magic and witchcraft, in shape-shifting and vampires. He had agents all over the world, not just in Europe, but also in Asia and America and Africa. They were just collecting every supposedly powerful object they could find.

Cal paused. "They were also looking for people," he said. "Special people."

"What kind of special people?" I asked, even though I suspected.

Uncle Cal looked at Dad and Dad looked back at him. It was like a nod passed between them. Like, I realize now, they were agreeing that it wasn't yet the time. Just give me a subtle hint, plant another seed that would grow with time.

Cal laughed. "People that for sure do not exist," he said. "People who could work magic, witches, warlocks, mind-readers, folks who could predict the future. Most of all, though, he was after men and women who really were shape-shifters, who could transform them-selves into wolves."

"Or leopards," Dad added.

"Riiigght," Cal said in a slow drawl as he stared a little harder at Dad—who turned his head away like he was trying not to laugh.

"The idea was that if they did find any people like that, they could recruit them . . ."

"Or abduct them," Dad said.

"Find out what made them tick, try to breed more like them, have his scientists do little experiments on them."

"Like kids in a science lab dissecting frogs," my father added.

For some reason the joking tone had gone out of his voice and Uncle Cal's. They both had what Mom called the "Bite Your Head Off" look on their faces.

"So did they actually find any of those special people?" I asked, expecting them to just say no. But Dad's answer surprised me a little then. It wouldn't now, not at all.

"Let's just say," my father replied, "that if the Nazis had ever gotten their hands on some real werewolves, they would have ended up getting their hands bitten off."

"Now let's get back to the movie," Cal said, taking the remote from the table and hitting Play. "Time to melt some Nazis!"

I've tried more than once since then to find written records of some of the stuff Uncle Cal and Dad shared with me. But those records were either destroyed or they're still so secret that I couldn't find them. Not in libraries, not even in the most whacked-out sites on the Internet I've had Renzo search out for me—me standing well back so I didn't short out the machine as he printed up articles to hand to me.

Why am I bringing this all up? Why are these memories coming to mind right now? I'm not entirely sure. But as I sit here looking across the table at Yuri, neither one of us saying a word, I have a suspicion. I'm being given what I can only describe as a mental nudge. I've seen how they can control normal people. I seem to be immune to being turned into a puppet. But it doesn't mean that they can't touch me in some other way, maybe give me some kind of mental suggestions that will make it easier for them to communicate—or manipulate.

You are not going to manipulate me!

Yuri raises an eyebrow at me. *"Nyet,"* he says. "No manipulate." I guess that last thought of mine came across. Then he surprises me.

"You like Russians?" he asks.

It's a question that might best be described as loaded like a gun with a hair trigger. Pick it up wrong and I'll shoot myself in the foot. I suspect that a simple yes or no won't work here. I decide to go with Yuri's sarcasm.

"Grilled or fried?" I ask.

Yuri keeps a straight face. But a deep snorting laugh from above and behind me tells me that my druzhok Vlad has appreciated that joke. That should be no surprise to me. After all, Russians have endured all the disasters of the century of revolution and perestroika—which Dad told me that they call *"Katastroika,"* catastrophe stroika—typical Russian graveyard humor. Not that humor has always done them much good. It's been estimated that as many as a quarter of a million people were sent to prison or executed by Stalin for making jokes. But people kept on making them. Back in the sixties in the USSR after the US beat the Russians to the moon, the Russian people had an easy answer to why their government never did send any cosmonauts to that airless, dead orb. They might refuse to come back because life is better there.

"So," Yuri says, "What is Russian business?"

He's deliberately playing straight man, giving me the lead-in to a joke that is well-known by everyone in modern Russia where things are, if not desperate, then truly difficult unless you are one of the new class of millionaires who are worse bloodsuckers than any monsters out of old stories.

"Russian business?" I answer. "You steal a crate of vodka, sell it on the black market, and then use all the money to get drunk."

More than one laugh comes from behind me this time,

including a throaty chuckle from Marina. Can she do anything without sounding like she's trying to seduce me?

"*Nicheyo sebye*," Boris nods, his voice dry. "Not bad."

Yuri nods too. There's a thin smile on his face now. I may not totally be a *kamerad*, but he knows now that I'm not just another clueless American teenager.

"Cooperate," Yuri says. He holds a hand out toward me. "We agree?"

"*Da*."

I accept his hand in a cool shake. I'll count my fingers later.

"Some answers now?" I ask.

Yuri leans back, folds his arms, tilts his chair up on two legs, and puts one foot on the table between us.

Body language expressing a feeling of superiority. Showing the bottom of your foot to another person is a sign of contempt in many cultures.

I lift my hand to my chin and look pointedly at the sole of Yuri's expensive designer boot. In one motion as slick as a seal ducking under the ice he drops the foot, leans forward, and spreads his hands in a gesture of ironic appeasement.

He looks around the room, jerks his head. Boris, Ekaterina, Igor, Marina, Vlad, and Natasha glide closer (the fact that they can move so silently still creeps me out) to range themselves in a semi-circle. A united front of bloodsuckers faces me.

"Ask us," he says.

So much to ask, so little time.

Don't try to arrange your questions in any order, Luke. Just ask them randomly. Dad told me that can sometimes be more effective. Being too methodical can let the person or persons you're interrogating guess what's coming next and get ahead of you.

"Have you killed anyone here?"

"Not yet," Ekaterina answers. It's the first time she's spoken. The matter-of-fact tone of her voice sends a shiver down my spine.

"You drink blood?"

"Is a big part of our . . . diet. But not all. I like the slushies," Vlad answers, then gives me another thumbs-up.

Slushies.

"Are you drinking people's blood here?"

"Not yet." Boris this time. "Just . . ." he shakes his head in the manner of a gourmand who's been told he has to settle for hot dogs instead of filet mignon, "cows."

And thus the riddle of the local cattle mutilations mentioned recently on the local news is solved.

"And the occasional large dog," Natasha adds, ironically helpful.

I shake my head. I feel as if they're managing to control my little Q&A too much. I'm being too methodical. Time to Monty Python it.

"What's your favorite color?"

"Red," they answer as one. It's like hearing a chorus of monks chanting—if those monks had voices with the wail of a night wind in them.

"Can you just answer one at a time?"

"Yes," they all chant. Really messing with me now.

Random, keep it random.

"Yuri," I look him in the eye, "would you take off your glasses?"

"Of course, *tovarisch*." That last word, the Russian word for comrade or friend is spoken with appropriate sarcasm to suggest he might mean just the opposite.

But he does as I've asked. He reaches up with both hands and lifts off his shades with a delicate, elegant motion. His eyes aren't as I expected. They're not black as night or red as blood. They're not sunk deep in their sockets. They're oval, an Asian epicanthic fold at the edge of each eye. They might even be called perfect eyes, like the eyes of a male model. The irises are green as jade. And they have the same ageless beauty as that precious stone.

The other thing that strikes me about Yuri's eyes is that they're not cold. In fact, there's a hint of warmth and humor in them. Even some vulnerability. Seeing his eyes like this makes me feel, and this is strange, as if this is a guy I could like or even trust. Maybe he senses that because the next thing I know those Ray-Bans are back firmly in place masking all emotion.

"Why do you all wear sunglasses?"

He sniffs and purses his lips. I've asked a foolish question. "Why you think?"

Because you want to hide that you're actually human, I think. But I don't say that.

"The light hurts them?"

"Close enough," he replies. "Next question?"

The big one now. "You're vampires, right?"

"Nyet," Marina breathes the word so close that her breath washes over my cheek.

It's the first answer that surprises me.

"Nyet means no," I say. Stupid me.

"Da." Yuri again. If his eyes were not hidden again by his shades, I know that I'd see amusement in them.

"Then what are you?"

"Upyr," Marina says.

"Huh?"

"Is a long story," Yuri adds.

And then, surprising me even more, he tells it. Leaving out all the details, it's both simpler and more complex than I expect. Some of the things we think of as myth or legend are real, just misunderstood. Such as a random genetic mutation that produces a human being with lower than usual body temperature, much greater than usual strength, and the ability—or need—to metabolize not just the normal food people eat, but the body fluid that carries oxygen to our cells and keeps us alive. Not undead, but born different. Aging slower because of their lower body temperature and slower heart rates. Also more than usually intuitive. Able to read people to the point of something like telepathy. Able to control normal people through a sort of hypnosis. Able to recognize each other. And thus, for centuries, banding together to keep their secret and avoid being identified by the unmutated humans who might seek to kill them. No overnight sojourns in coffins, no problems with crosses or silver or holy water.

"Although," Yuri adds, his lips twisting in an ironic smile, "we do tend to have an allergic reaction to, ah, certain woods."

"I would stake my life on that," Natasha adds, then looks a bit disappointed that I don't laugh at her pun.

Human beings, more or less. Maybe more than me. And for the last two decades—or maybe more—they've been known, and used, by at least one arm of the Russian security services. Trained in counterterrorism.

The Upyr Group.

"So you were all sent here to this school."

"*Da.*"

"Because I'm here."

"*Nyet.*"

That surprises me. Then why did they bring me to their lair?

"You are," Boris speaks up from behind Yuri's left shoulder, "what you call unexpected bonus."

"You mean you didn't know about me or my father?"

Forget about random questions. I need to know this.

"Not at first," Yuri says.

"So why were you sent here? What are you after?"

Yuri smiles that too-broad grin of his that makes him look much less human and much more predatory as it shows his canine teeth to their best advantage.

"Maxico," he answers.

WHAT'S AT STAKE

Maxico. Some things are starting to connect together, but not in a way that I can make sense of yet. All I know for sure is that this whole thing stinks.

Yuri's looking at me in a very "feline who swallowed your songbird" fashion. He's waiting for my next question, enjoying being the one who knows what's going on while I'm the clueless clod who's just started to smell a rat.

Why Maxico? But as I start to ask that question, I realize what my subconscious is telling me. Maxico was written on the side of that tractor trailer being backed up behind the school. I smell a rat.

That is not just a figure of speech. I've caught a strange scent, one I've smelled before. My wolf mark suddenly is burning as if someone touched my wrist with a hot poker.

Something moves in the back of the room, a dark figure near a large pile of construction materials wrapped in plastic.

"There!" I say.

Yuri spins in the direction I'm pointing. Vlad snatches up his gun so quickly that it seems to vanish from the table. Marina grabs the table with one hand—as easily as if she was picking up a feather pillow—to hold it in front of us.

I don't wonder why. My ears picked up the whistling of the projectiles flying toward us a split second before they thud into Marina's improvised shield.

Thwomp! Thwomp! Thwomp!

They hit so hard that the heavy table quivers from the impact. A few pierce partway though. One stopped only an inch away from my eye. The shaft of the arrow is blue, shining metal, but the sharp, three-inch-long tip is fire-hardened wood.

A gurgling scream is suddenly cut off. Boris is crouched over that dark figure I first saw, like a rescuer doing CPR—if that rescuer's bloodied mouth was at the victim's throat. The broken remains of a crossbow lies next to them.

But that downed attacker was not alone. There's a dozen more. Six of them look to be human. They're wearing outfits of midnight black with a silver emblem over their chests: an M surrounded by lightning bolts.

The other six are the ones whose rank odors I picked up. They're like huge black dogs, but they are not ordinary canines. It's not just that they're twice as big as any dog I've ever seen. There's a wrongness to them. The madness in their eyes tells me they've been made for only one thing. Death. White froth comes out of their mouths as they charge headlong toward us.

Three more wooden-tipped arrows come flying from another corner. They all hit Igor. He's turned by the force of the projectiles hitting him and falls to his side, curled around the arrow that pierced the left side of his chest.

What's at stake is not just their survival. Their enemies are effectively mine right now too.

Less than a second has passed. I'm seeing things as if in slow motion. Marina drops the table, leaping with Yuri to the attack. I grab one of the table's heavy oak legs and wrench it free before it hits the floor. The wood splinters as I do so. That makes me growl with pleasure. Gives me a nice sharp point.

I hear the popping sound of someone firing a gun with a suppression tube. Silencers, Uncle Cal once said, are never completely silent.

Something hits me in the shoulder. It's like an insect bite. I ignore it. I've got bigger problems.

Two of the black dogs are charging at me from either side. I club one on its skull with a bone-crushing blow, spin, drop into a low karate stance, and thrust the sharp-pointed table leg at the other in midleap. The tip drives into the creature's throat as its heavy body hits me, throwing me backward. As I fall, I roll to come up straddling it. Its paws scrabble at my chest as I thrust the sharp table leg harder into its throat. The cartilage of its windpipe crunches. It goes limp. It would have been even more satisfying to tear its throat out with my teeth. But sometimes you have to settle for second best.

I roll off it, come to my feet in a crouch, ready. But the battle is over. It's quiet around me. Well, not completely quiet. I hear strange sounds coming from six directions at once. The sound creeps me out because it reminds me of a baby nursing at its mother's breast.

Ekaterina looks up at me from where she's bent over behind the couch. She wipes her mouth, smiles, and raises one eyebrow.

No longer would her answer be "Not yet."

I look at the bodies of the two animals I've killed. Their scent is foul, like long-dead meat. Not the clean, wild odor of the doe I took down last night. Nothing appetizing about these creatures. I wouldn't eat their meat even if I was starving.

"Dogs, but not dogs," I say out loud.

"Men, but not men," Yuri says from behind me. "Even if the blood they were given is human."

I turn to look. He's holding up—with one hand—one of those black-clad bodies.

It's the size and shape of a large, tightly-muscled man. But it seems less human than a department store mannequin. Its features are too smooth, unblemished and poreless. It's dead, but its black eyes are still open. More like a power tool whose battery charge ran down than a corpse.

Then Yuri does something that might have shocked me if it had been the first brutal thing I'd seen up close. He makes a V of his index and middle finger, drives them into the face of the corpse, and plucks out its eyes. He drops the black orbs on the floor and then steps on them. They pop like large purple grapes. Similar sounds tell me that the other members of his little cabal are doing the same with the rest of these downed enemies.

"Dead," Yuri says, "but yet they transmit."

Yuri tosses the body carelessly aside, the way a shopper might discard a coat after deciding it's not the right style. He steps forward to bend over Igor, who's still on his side, curled around the arrow that seems to have pierced his heart.

To my surprise, he reaches up a hand and lets Yuri pull him to his feet. Igor reaches down and plucks one of the arrows from his calf as Yuri yanks the second shaft out of his hip. The arrow in his chest is still lodged there, but not that deeply. Yuri splays his left hand around the arrow, the shaft between his spread fingers. His right grabs the shaft and then he jerks back, pulling out the arrow. Igor's shirt tears as he does so. It reveals that what I thought was chest muscle is actually contoured body armor. The crossbow bolt barely pricked his skin.

Lucky thing Dracula never had Kevlar.

Apparently those wooden-tipped crossbow bolts that were shot at Yuri's crew came as no surprise. They know their adversary. Just as Maxico, whoever or whatever it is, is unsettlingly knowledgeable about them.

Which makes me wonder what Maxico knows about my father . . . and yours truly.

The blood-sucking seven are now gathered with their heads close together. They're speaking so softly that anyone with hearing less keen than mine would hardly hear a sound. They're talking colloquial Muscovite Russian, but I'm able to make out the general outline of what's being clinically discussed.

Igor, Natasha, and Ekaterina are being delegated the Hamletish job of "lugging the guts into the next room." Vlad is to go out to check on the Maxico truck that delivered the killing team. As Vlad leaves through a back entrance, Boris and Marina go to a closet and pull out mops and buckets. Cleaning the concrete floor is their job. There'll be no telltale stains when they're done. Neatness counts.

I step back out of everyone's way and stand by Yuri's side to watch. The body disposal trio is working just as quickly as Boris and Marina with their own grisly janitorial tasks. Double-wrapped in black plastic, the bodies of the more-than-dogs and less-than-humans are dumped into a wheeled cart and taken out the door to the loading dock.

A scratching sound comes from our left. They've missed one that was shot and fell down behind a pile of insulation. Badly wounded but stubbornly surviving, the inhuman thing is crawling toward us. Yuri stomps down to break its neck. As he efficiently pops out its eyes, he motions for Igor to come and get it.

"They have no speech," Yuri says. "Just, how you say it, one program? Kill the enemy. When their bodies have used up the blood they've been charged with, they die."

Yuri turns his gaze to my shoulder, and lazily raises an eyebrow.

"*Bratan*, you want to leave that there?" he asks.

What I felt as a bee sting was the impact of a crossbow bolt like the ones stopped by Igor's armor. What stopped this one was me. It's gone all the way through. The head of the bolt is sticking six inches out the back. It missed the bone or I would have noticed it sooner. Now that I've seen it, I feel a dull ache. I grab it to pull it out.

Yuri holds up a hand. "Wait."

He gestures to Natasha who brings him a small tool chest. Yuri opens it. Nods. Picks a pair of bolt cutters. He deftly snips off the arrowhead, which falls to the floor.

"Now," he says.

I pull out the shaft. There's a twinge in my wrist as the wolf mark pulses. I pull down my shirt to look. The wound in front is closing. I've healed fast before, but this? On a normal day I'd call it amazing. Right now it's low on the list of incredible things that seem to be part of my life.

Yuri picks up the wooden arrowhead. There are metal barbs just behind the tip meant to keep the bolt from being easily dislodged. Yuri studies it closer.

"Lucky," he says. "No poison, no explosive."

Vlad walks back in, carrying two Berettas. He's not alone. Two men dressed in gray coveralls and wearing ball caps walk behind him. Real humans, not simulacra, but their eyes are glazed. Their arms hang limp at their sides and they're walking as if their knee joints are half frozen. Whatever Vlad did, they're puppets.

"Only two," Vlad says, dropping the Berettas on the tabletop. "No trouble. I tell them, call in, say you have completed the clean-up.

They do it."

Yuri rights two of the chairs that were knocked over in the attack that was so brief it would be easy to imagine it never happened.

"We sit again?"

We sit.

Yuri pulls a small table between us. He puts his elbows on it and leans forward.

"More questions?"

Define the word *understatement*.

53

NO NICE PEOPLE

Genetic engineering. Gene-splicing. Stuff that seemed like science fiction a decade before the decoding of the human genome. Now the awareness of it is so common that we take it for granted that the crops we eat have been genetically modified. No one even blinks when scientists talk about adding a human gene to a frigging tomato to make it last longer on the store shelves. What might have been top secret or the province of some evil genius in his weird lab in one of those old low-budget B movies is now stuff that high school students like me read about in our biology textbooks.

Dr. Frankenstein, your castle is being converted into condos. Dr. Moreau, your island has been bulldozed by the twenty-first century. Who needs solitary mad scientists? Now we have corporations insanely devoted to profits and given the same rights as human beings by the courts.

"Maxico?"

"No nice people," Yuri says, *"Podonokni.* Scumbags." He shows his teeth, and looks off to the side.

Not a happy smile. Some memories connected to that.

"Who are they working for? Russia? China? The U.S.?"

A quick slash of Yuri's hand as if turning a page.

"None of them. All of them. Themselves. Multinational para-military. Sell whatever they can. Weapon systems, contract soldiers. Look at what they are doing here. *Padlani*. Bastards. Pah!"

Yuri turns his head to the side to spit.

I look over his shoulder toward the door where Igor and Natasha are about to disappear with the second of two heavily laden carts.

Yuri looks down at his long slender hands and perfectly mani-cured nails. "Super soldiers. That is what they have begun to make. Human and animal brutes. Insults to nature. Almost no mind at all, just programmed to attack. But they need to have the right DNA to make them come alive. That is why they want . . ."

He looks up.

"Me?" I say.

Yuri nods. "Ones such as you. Why they take your father. Why they want us. They catch us, they experiment with us. They use our blood, our genes."

He pauses, looks at me as if considering the consequences of going on. Then he decides, slaps both his palms down on the table-top.

"All right. I tell you everything. For a thousand years and more we keep ourselves secret, your people and mine. We let them tell their fanciful tales of the undead." He looks hard at me. "Stories of men who can turn themselves into wolves. Hah! We convince the world that those are just tales to frighten little ones. Our friends, allies, they explain us away as fiction, as imagination, as psychosis. Every movie, every television show makes it easier for people to see us as fantasy, as silly, scary entertainment. Can we fly like your Superman? No. Gravity works for us like everything with weight and mass. Crosses?"

He reaches to unbutton a breast pocket and pull out a small ornate Russian orthodox cross made of silver. He presses it to his lips. To my surprise, nothing happens. Yuri laughs.

"What you think? I burst into flame, scream? I take communion, accept the blessing of the priest. I dip my fingers in the holy water. I am a sinner, but I confess. I am Russian Orthodox. I follow Jesus Christ who died for all of us and came back to life. Ever wonder how he did that?"

Yuri carefully puts away the cross, buttons the pocket.

"Daylight? Too bright, gives me a headache. Our eyes are more sensitive to light. Garlic? Properly cooked is delicious. Can I cross running water? Are you joking? And I do not turn myself into a bat. But I am faster, stronger than they dream. I tell them not to see me and I vanish from their minds. And is hard to kill us with ordinary weapons—a few bullets do not hurt that much."

He doesn't mention the wooden-tipped arrows. Neither do I. Yuri holds up his hand, looks at it, studies the lines in his palm like a gypsy reading his own future.

"I am," he says, more slowly now, "like what you are. We are what we have inherited from those who lived before us. Genetic mutation, perhaps, sometime in the distant past. For us, the upyrs, it makes us seem like the weaker humans—until our first death. But that death—unless by fire—does not really kill us. We seem dead, but are in . . . incubation. And when we wake at last, we have become fully who we are."

He smiles grimly. "Once that meant breaking through a coffin lid, digging up through six feet of earth. Not pleasant task. No wonder we felt some . . . resentment . . . at those who buried us. But as years passed and our numbers grew, we learned to recognize, take care of each other. Then we live a long time, but not immortal. And though we can eat other food, what feeds us best, what our bodies need, is blood. Fresh blood. That much is true."

He pauses, licks his lips.

"So, Maxico? Immortality and power. That is what they try to make in there. They think they turn our blood into gold. So we are all in danger. They use us like they use the financial systems, the forests, the land, the oceans. All sacrificed for their profit."

"But you're working for the Russian government?"

Yuri raises both eyebrows at that.

"*Tovarich*," he explains, his cold hand on my shoulder. "My innocent young friend, in every government there are people engaged in warfare—not with other nations, but with each other. Those such as your father and me work in secret not just for my nation, for your nation. We want to keep this world alive, not drain it of life. Like the one who calls himself Dr. Kesselring."

"Kessel-rrring," the name escapes my mouth as a growl.

Yuri pauses to look at me. "What do you know of him?"

Aside from the fact that he's a major player in Maxico and that I caught him eyeing me like a fat kid looking at a candy bar? I don't say anything though. I can sense that Yuri is about to tell me whether I ask him to or not.

"His English, it is good now, no? You would not know he was born in East Germany with another name. He has made a great fortune, speculating in currencies, oil, rare earths, blood diamonds, timber, whatever makes the most money, whether legal or not. Many have died because of the things he has done or set into motion. Like in Zimbabwe where they find diamonds and poor people are digging them. The government sends in the army, kills all those poor people. Then Kesselring's network smuggles them out, mixes them in with legal diamonds. Big profit. Just one small example of all he does. But he has many enemies, some of them with great resources. Even a powerful man may be assassinated. So five years ago, he disappears. But our people finally track him here. Where his plans have become even bigger. Maybe too big to wait for more help. Too big to stop unless we act right now."

My lips have curled back from my teeth as Yuri has told his story. I'm trembling with anger. This man he's just described has my father. If I had my hands on Kesselring right now I'd rip out his throat.

Yuri pauses again and looks me up and down. "There are fewer like you. *Bodarki*, skin wearers. Your kind, they have a harder time controlling themselves—they even may attack those who want to be their friends when they get angry. Also too much arrogance and stupidity. Not so?"

Be calm, Luke.

Calm down. Calm down.

Don't react. Don't take the bait, even though you are wondering if his neck is strong enough to withstand your hands being wrapped around it.

I do stare at him though.

Yuri lowers his eyes. For all his strength, Yuri seems nervous. Over Yuri's shoulder my *bratan* Vlad is watching us. Vlad gives me the thumbs-up again. Then he mouths the words *Da, he is afraid of you.*

"Vlad," Yuri says. He doesn't turn around. Vlad looks up at the ceiling, a small smile on his face.

"He likes you," Yuri says. "He is the youngest of us, the most foolish. But we are glad he is among us. Just as there are those of us who serve, there are powerful men who value us and try to protect our secret. You guess who is Vlad's godfather, who he was named for, the judo-ka?"

I nod. It's not that hard to guess. How many people named Vladimir have been the head of the KGB, hold a black belt in judo, and a few other honors beyond that . . . like being Prime Minister of Russia?

"So, we work together for now?"

I take Yuri's cold hand as the wolf mark on my wrist pulses.

"For now," I agree.

54
DON'T GET ARROGANT

The feel of the motorcycle between my legs is calming. The wind in my face feels good. Soon the sweet dark will spread over the land. A small part of me wants to just keep going, riding into the sunset. A little voice whispers inside my head.

You could just keep going.

I have more than enough stashed in my backpack for anything I might need for a long time. And when this money runs out? Get more from the next bank where my father left a cash drop for me. Maybe there's a whole string of them all across the country. The map of the national parks and forests is in my backpack. Travel from one of those to another. Find the biggest untouched forest of all. Hide the bike. Walk into the green sanctuary of its depths. Run free as a wolf. Feed on the deer and the elk, never come back to so-called civilization.

I'm passing a field where cows are grazing. Fat cows. I've slowed my bike almost to a stop. My mouth is watering. Raw meat, hot with blood. I haven't eaten yet today. I'm hungry enough to eat a horse—no metaphor intended. I reluctantly twist the accelerator to speed up again.

Running away? Is that an option for me? Not really. Not at all. I can't leave my father. I can't leave Meena.

Quite frankly, would Yuri and the other upyrs even let me run away now that I've become part of their plans?

More than anything else, though, I know that I cannot run away from myself.

And part of myself, my second skin, is calling to me. I need to go where it's waiting, join myself with it again, wrap myself in its power.

The sun is far down in the sky. I'm supposed to rendezvous at midnight with Yuri and his crew. Before the security at Maxico starts wondering why their clean-up crew has not come back yet. As I think of that, I realize that I'm looking forward to that midnight meeting, ready to take on whatever is waiting for us at Maxico.

More than ready. That part of myself is eager to sink its teeth into the ones who took my father. They think they're safe in the Maxico complex behind their useless fence.

Let them try to stop me.

I feel . . . arrogant?

Remember, Luke, that was on the list Dad left.

Don't let yourself become arrogant.

Yuri, too, made mention of that being a main weakness of shape-shifters.

Now that I think of it, that was the Achilles' heel of most of the werewolves in the past that I've heard or read about. Drunk with power or blood lust, they believe that no one can hurt them.

My father told me lots of such stories, as well as others from our Indian side of the family, such as how Gluskabe, the greatest hero of our people, was brother to the wolves. A black wolf walked with him on one side and a white wolf on the other.

There were worse monsters than wolves in other old stories Dad told me. Like those of the Chenoos, who were once human. Greed and selfishness turned them into cannibals. They roamed the forests howling, looking for human prey. However, by staying calm and doing the right thing, even a child may be able to escape or overcome such monsters.

I know now that those Chenoo tales weren't just for the child I was then, but for the beast inside me. The monster I might become if I forget what it means to be human. But a man-wolf didn't have to be evil.

There were good werewolves, even in Europe. Around 400 B.C. a Greek werewolf from Arcadia named Demarchus took part in the Olympic games and won medals as a boxer. Seven centuries ago, the Viking Volsunga saga told of an outlawed father and son who were werewolves, but went on to establish their own kingdom. When St. Patrick arrived in Ireland in 435 he discovered that some of his best converts were werewolves.

But the stories most people remember are about the bad ones. Like the Beast of Le Gevaudan in eighteenth-century France, a ravening man-eater that roamed the hills and valleys of the Auvergne plateau in southern France. From 1765 through 1767, it attacked almost every day, usually women and children who it carried off and ate.

Finally, King Louis IX sent a group of hunters led by the Marquis d'Apcher. After long days of tracking they surrounded a grove of trees. Jean Chastel, the best shot among the men, had loaded his double-barreled musket with bullets made from a silver chalice blessed by a priest. Dusk fell and Jean Chastel was sitting, reading his prayer book in the last fading sunlight. He heard a sound and looked up. Walking on two legs, its eyes gleaming bloodred, the Beast of Le Gevaudan was coming toward him.

Chastel raised his musket and fired one barrel. The beast howled and charged, but Chastel did not falter. Taking careful aim, he discharged the second barrel of his gun and the beast fell dead.

Modern writers have argued that what the French marksman killed was just some sort of animal. Maybe a wild boar. One, I guess, that had learned to walk on two legs. In a French martial arts epic made a few years back called *Brotherhood of the Wolf*, a French Marquis and his faithful American Indian companion (portrayed, of course, by another Frenchman), both of whom appear to have studied Shaolin kung fu, defeat an army of evil Gypsies and kill the Beast, which turns out to be a giant African badger.

What was recorded by the historians of the time, however, was that the beast slain by Chastel was a loup-garou, a man-wolf that saw people as prey.

Hold onto your humanity, Luke.

I keep that thought foremost in my mind as I turn onto the road to the Drake House.

55

SON OF THE NIGHT

I take a deep breath as I step through the front door. The smell here is no longer that of a place that's abandoned. Something in the air vibrates, hums with life. An inhuman presence, true but it's also familiar. This dark house knows me. I feel it welcoming and accepting me. It knows me as its child, a son of the night.

Home.

That's how the Drake House seems to me now. How could I ever have seen it as foreboding or threatening? The only worry I'm feeling right now is that someone might have come here while I was gone.

Not possible. If there was danger I'd feel the pulsing of the wolf mark on my wrist.

What I feel is an urgency that cannot be denied.

I start running.

The moon has not yet risen, but I don't need its light to see as I bolt up the stairs, down the hall. I almost tear the door off the hinges.

I open the secret door, step inside.

I feel it sending me waves of warmth, even through the wooden walls of the closed sea chest. I take off the clothing that restricts my human body, drop to one knee in front of the chest, raise the lid. It's there, alive with my blood, shimmering with life.

My hands tremble as I lift it.

Time to become the wolf that I am.

Why do people fear the dark? Because it holds shapes they cannot see? Shapes that see them? Is there a memory in their simian minds of a time when people were the prey and other, stronger beings stalked them?

They fear the dark because they fear me.

I stand on the hilltop beyond the Drake House. I raise my head toward the sky and howl toward the stars, the Wolf Trail. As they swirl overhead, I run, run, run, fast as the wind at my back. I drink the cool air of the forest, every scent as clear to me as the words on the pages of a familiar book. A mother raccoon and four young ones scamper up a tree ahead of me. Their eyes reflect the moonlight from a branch twelve feet above my head as they watch me lope past. Tasty little morsels. I could bring them down with one swift leap, but I'm after larger prey. A rabbit bolts out from under a small cedar. Bigger than that. I keep going.

The forest ends as abruptly as a piece of cloth torn in half. There's a new house, three stories tall, built on five acres of former forest land now bulldozed flat. One of those opulent new mansions built on land taken by Dr. Kesselring. A year ago this was wild land and now, this . . . ugly thing, where no house should be. I feel rage at the sight of a human structure taking the rightful place of trees and forest soil. A swimming pool is gouged into the ground that was once meadow. A man in a business suit is parking his car in front of the garage. He thinks this land is his. As if pieces of paper give title to earth. The halogen light on his garage is bright. It blocks out the stars. It blinds him to me as I come close. I can take him down with a single leap.

I growl, deep enough, loud enough for him to feel that growl as much as hear it. A terrified cry bursts from his mouth—not loud though. More like the *peep* of a frog. His throat is constricted by fear. He takes a quick step back, stumbles and falls, drops the briefcase he'd been holding. He holds up one hand to fend off the attack that he knows will follow. His throat is undefended. One single, swift leap and it will be over.

I shake my head in disgust. I do not take pity on him. Contempt and pity do not go together. Instead, I let him live with his fear. He'll never spend a comfortable night here again with this dark memory in his mind. I growl again as he grovels. Then I leap back into the clean embrace of the dark forest.

Time to hunt.

By the time I reach the Maxico complex, I've fed. The deer carcass from the night before was gone, as I'd expected. Cleaned up by park employees who probably shook their heads about another deer being killed by wild dogs, not knowing that pack fled in panic from the scent of a true apex predator and are now far away. The deer herd, though, typical prey animals, were too much creatures of habit to leave their habitat. I found them not far from the stream where I made my first kill. The meat of the year-old buck downed was sweet, its blood hot and satisfying.

I lick my muzzle at the memory of that taste. The place the moon holds in the sky tells me that it is now near midnight. I've leaped the fence as before. I'm on the hill again, looking down on the main building behind its formidable wall. It's easy to see with my wolf-enhanced night vision. On a night such as this when the full moon makes objects cast a shadow it's as bright as day to me. Probably the same for my new *druzhoks*, my bloodthirsty buddies.

"Cujo," a mocking voice whispers from close behind me. "Good boy."

So Yuri has also read Stephen King—or seen the movie.

He and the others haven't surprised me or sneaked up without my knowing it. I smelled them when they were still half a mile away—a distance it took them a very short time to cover. They might not be able to fly, but they can cover ground four times as fast as any Jamaican sprinter.

We move back away from the hilltop, down into the trees where our voices are less likely to be heard.

"You're late," I snarl.

It's the first time I've tried releasing human words from my mouth since putting on my skin. Though my voice is an octave deeper and sounds as if it's been blended with a meat grinder, it's still recognizable—to me, at least—as my own.

I rise up on my hind legs and turn to face them.

Marina, who's standing by Yuri's right side, eyes me up and down . . . and then halfway up again ending just below my waist.

"Good boy, indeed," she says in a throaty voice. "*Kol-ba-si-nu.* Very impressive."

Yuri casts an annoyed glance her way, then turns his attention back to me.

"Are you ready?" he asks.

"For what?"

He shrugs. "We kill them all?"

"What if . . . innocent people there?"

Hmm, it seems hard for me to speak complex sentences, even

if I can still think them.

Yuri grins toothily. "We kill them all. Then we say sorry and let God sort out the innocent."

"Is that . . . all?"

Yuri studies me for a moment. Then he gestures for Boris to come forward.

"Show him."

Boris reaches in a pocket and pulls out something the size and shape of a cigarette lighter. He turns it from side to side and I see bubbles moving inside the liquid held in the plastic container. "Virus," Boris says in a smooth, self-satisfied voice.

"Boris is more than he appears," Yuri explains. "He is what you would call advanced biochemist."

Boris nods. "We inject this, it kills the medium. Total contamination of their whole system." He wiggles his fingers, then holds both hands out, palms up. "*O-pa! Koka!* Whoops! Bye!"

Yuri hooks a finger toward Vlad, who steps forward to loom over me like a giant vulture. Then he smiles, reaches out a big hand, and pats my head.

"Nice fur, *bratan*," he rumbles as he pets me.

It feels good—but I stifle the urge to drop to all fours and roll over so he can rub my stomach.

"Vlad!"

"*Izvinyayus*, my bad." Vlad pulls back up—but not before a quick, surreptitious thumbs-up to me.

"Show him."

Vlad opens his other briefcase-sized hand to disclose a device about the same size and shape as the one that Boris had. This one, however, is black and solid. I've never been able to use one of these—for obvious reasons—but I recognize it as a memory stick.

"*Virusom*," Vlad's voice sounds as if its coming from an echo chamber. If central casting ever needs a seven-foot-tall Dracula, this is their man. "Once this gets in: *prye-vyed myed-vyed!* Hey there, bear! It writes over everything, from mainframe to network connections. I am," he adds with a note of pride, "best hacker in Russia."

I'm impressed. They're not just interested in physically rubbing out their enemies. They've also embraced the twenty-first-century tools of digital and biochemical nihilism.

But that leads me to the next logical question. One that I should have asked back at the school.

"Why . . . need me if . . . that your plan?"

Yuri pauses. I'm guessing he assumed I was so eager to free my father that I'd just go along with whatever he suggested without wondering why I was being included in their plans.

"Well," he says slowly, "we try before to get in. Two nights ago. We did not do so good."

"Why?"

Yuri actually looks sheepish. "It turns out," he says, "we not so invisible to them as we expect. We get close," he gestures down the hill at the entrance port and the wall, "alarms go off."

"Electrochemical recognition system," Boris adds. "Too hard to explain to you. They also use it to track us."

"How . . . they find you . . . at school."

"Big embarrassment," Vlad adds with a grin.

Yuri glares at him. "Vlad!"

"*Sori,*" Vlad says. But he doesn't lose the grin.

Okay, I think. That makes sense. But another question comes to me right away.

"That . . . system." A hard word to growl out. "Pick me up too . . . I try get in?"

"Your body," Vlad says, leaning forward again, "it gives off electrical pulse. *Zzzz-zz-zz*. Something to do with how you join with your wolf skin. It jams circuits."

Which finally explains why I can't use a computer.

"So . . . they . . . not detect me?"

"Ah," Yuri says, spreading his hands palms up and shrugging. "Maybe, but also maybe not."

"Grrreat," I answer.

"Also," Marina adds, "there are more of them than we expect. Our intelligence . . ." she looks over at Yuri, "was flawed. They are much further along than was expected. We need more . . ." —another of those steamy looks at me—"how you say it?" She turns toward Natasha.

"Muscle," Natasha replies.

"Rrrr," I growl, nodding my head. It all makes sense now. I'm just what they need. Cannon fodder to clear the way for them. An expendable battering ram to get them in. Tall, dark, and stupid. But I don't mind. It's what I want too—not to be sacrificed, but to get my teeth into the people who've taken my dad.

TO GO INSIDE

Yuri holds up an iPhone.

"Those . . . not work . . . for me," I growl.

Yuri says nothing, he just runs his fingers across its lighted face. More apps for games there than you'd expect from a cold-blooded bloodsucker. He stops when it displays a set of seven numbers.

"Call this number from land line inside when you have control."

"Dial a . . . bloodsucker?" I'm even more amused. "Hrr, hrr hrr. You can invite . . . upyrs by phone?"

"*Da*," Yuri says, his tone that of an adult trying to explain simple math to an especially slow child. "We go back to truck and wait."

He's referring to the truck that carried the simulacra to the school. The two hypnotized men taken captive are sitting behind the wheel of that truck, concealed on a side road half a mile down from the outside gate.

"You call, we come."

"Phone tag," I chuckle.

They all look at me expressionlessly.

"Phone home?" I try. "Hrr, hrr, hrrr?"

Still no response. Maybe some undead people just have no sense of humor. Or else they haven't seen *ET*.

Then Vlad chuckles. *"Eto klassni* movie, *bratan,"* he says.

"Tsium-tsium," from Marina, of course. Kiss-kiss.

"Chau," Boris adds.

"Ne propadal," Ekaterina says. Don't be a stranger.

"Do sko-ro-vo, do-ro-goi," Natasha croons. See ya soon, dear.

Igor says nothing, but he does stiffen his back and click his heels together as he gives me a letter-perfect salute.

Okay, I take back what I said about their lacking a sense of humor.

Yuri looks daggers at his crew, then sighs. *"Druga dyebilih,"* he says, almost apologetically. My friends are morons. Then he lift two fingers to touch his forehead ironically. *"Do svidaniya."*

"Ya poshol," I reply, not to be outdone and also noting that Russian is easier to speak in a wolfish growl than English.

I'm off. In more ways than one, I suppose.

I drop to all fours, disappear into the tall ferns that don't even ripple as I start down the hill.

Few animals are as good at stalking as a wolf, and a wolf with a human mind is even better at the task of creeping up on those unaware of his presence. The first unaware ones are the two who stand guard on either side of the main gate through the wall. They're near the parked black limos that have been joined tonight by two other vehicles, a Lexus and a Spider. I don't have to wonder who those visitors are. The plates that read CHIEF and DOCTORONE are a giveaway.

The men patrolling the front are not Nick and Eddie, but they look enough like them to have been hired from the same "Rent-a-Bad-Guy" franchise. Their bored routine becomes apparent after only a few moments of watching them. They each stroll a hundred feet to the right or left of the floodlit entrance, lazily play their flashlight beams around the edge of shadow that they've reached, then saunter back, crossing each other's path to do the same on the opposite side.

I can take them one at a time.

Easy to kill. Harder to capture.

Knocking out a human being for more than a few seconds is not an easy thing to do. Too little force and they wake up almost immediately. Too much and the concussive injury to the brain is so severe that they're permanently impaired or never wake up. Hitting someone over the head is not the best option if you hope to avoid unintended fatalities.

I move so that my side is against the wall. Take a few breaths. Nothing. It seems that Boris was right. No alarms go off. The two entry guards remain unaware.

I wait in the shadows for the first one to turn and head back. One leap and I'm on top of him, riding him to the ground. I've barreled into him so hard that the wind is knocked out of him. He can't muster enough breath to scream.

"Hrrrrrr," I growl in his ear, "Quiet!"

That silences him even more. My paw hands are not as dexterous as when I'm in my human shape, but they work well enough, with the help of my teeth, to tear a long strip of cloth from his coat and use it to tie a gag across his mouth. The plastic handcuffs he'd obligingly fastened to his belt are enough to further secure him to a heating pipe that goes up the side of the building.

I crouch in front of him. It's dark here, but not so dark that he can't see me. I note, with some pleasure, the terror in his eyes. I lean close, drool on him, let him feel my hot breath.

"You want . . . live . . . stay quiet," I rumble. "Hrrrr?"

He nods and keeps nodding. He's still nodding hysterically as I slip away from him.

Watcher number two takes even less time. He's strayed from his usual routine to check out the Spider. When I leap on him, he hits his head against the bumper of Dr. Kesselring's vanity vehicle. Though he's out cold, his breathing is even. Likely to wake up with fewer nightmares than those his cohort will be having from now on in. I gag and bind him in similar fashion, pull the ring of keys from his belt.

Time to go inside and get ready to issue party invitations.

57
GETTING INSIDE

Taking out the two front gate sentries was only step one. Getting inside the wall is not going to be as direct as going through the door. From the place where I'm crouching, concealed by the parked cars, I can see that the gate has an intercom box next to it.

I can't ask whoever is inside to buzz me in. With my currently wolfish voice there's no way I can sound like one of the men I've just gagged and handcuffed. There's also another of those dandy little cameras mounted over the door. So forget entering that way—unless I can break down the door, which might not be that easy. It looks like reinforced metal.

I need to use another way to get inside. Yuri and the Night Stalkers (now there's a name for a punk rock group!) are waiting and time is a-wasting. And even though I'm being flippant—the only way I can stay sane in the midst of all this madness—I'm deeply worried about my dad's fate. Am I really up to this task? I may be a skinwalker, but I am still only seventeen years old. I'm not sure I know what the hell I'm doing.

No time now to play Hamlet.

Screw your courage to the sticking point, Luke.

Keeping to the shadows, I lope quickly back to one of the dark sides of the encircling wall. Tall for some. Not for me. One leap and I'm atop it and then another leap and I'm on the ground. The thirty feet between the wall and the side of the building is a grassy lawn, kept mowed short.

The moonlight is bright enough for my wolf eyes to pick out the trails left by creatures on four feet that have circled through this perimeter again and again. There's also the residue of a rank odor here that I recognize. Devil dogs. But there's no scent of anything near here now. I come up with a quick double deduction from observing this present lack of a pack of patrolling predators. First is that the ones formerly stationed here were those we killed back at the high school. Pulled away for a special search and destroy mission. And, secondly, seeing that none have been moved to take their place, that Maxico may not have an unlimited supply of genetically modified monsters. Not yet, at least.

I cross the empty lawn as swiftly as a wind gust. No human or animal presences here now, but there's always the danger of being picked up on infrared detectors or cameras. Speedy motion makes that less likely. I also hope that those who might be watching any screens inside will be as inattentive as the two men I've just neutralized. The kind of arrogant self-confidence I have to fight against in myself seems to characterize Maxico and its minions.

Now I'm at the wall of the large four-story building. I sit back on my haunches and lick my lips as I quickly study it. The bubble windows, though never designed to be opened, might provide access if I could pry one free.

No. Too much noise.

But the side of the building is rough stone. Small spaces between each stone. I reach up, my claws find the fissures. I start to pull myself up, hand over hand. Or should I say paw over paw?

Just like that I'm up to the flat roof in no time. I check it out before stepping onto its surface. No evidence of trip wires or monitors. Nothing more threatening than piles of pigeon scat. Maxico's security people appear not to be much worried about anything that might come at them from above.

I cross the roof in three swift leaps to the roof access door. I try the handle. Locked. Not quite as easy as I'd hoped. However, I don't see any alarm wires. I dig away some of the wooden frame around the lock with my claws, get a good hold on the edge. I heave. The door swings open with a small sharp *crack*. I pause, listen. No response to my breaking and entering.

There's a dusty, disused smell in the stairwell. No one has entered it in days—if not weeks. Another closed door at the bottom. Not locked, this time. I ease it open an inch, peer out at a deserted corridor. Peeling paint on the pink walls, old spider webs in the corners. Still no scent or sign of anything living or dead up here. Whatever Maxico is up to in this former factory complex, it's not up on the top floor.

I pad silently past doors left open to stripped and unused rooms. I reach the closed doors of an elevator. The lighted panel indicates it is still in working order and the car is presently on the second floor.

I continue down the hall. A hundred feet farther, at the corner of the building, is a closed stairwell. I push open the door and pause at the top of the stairs. Here, for the first time, my sensitive nose catches the odors of human activity. Hospital smells of blood and sweat, bodily wastes and disinfectant, alcohol and various medicines, as well as several sour, acidic, chemical smells I can't identify that make my nose crinkle. Lots of human scents, but none yet that are familiar. Also, and this makes me curl my lips back from my teeth, the rank animal odors that signal the presence of more of those mutated dogs.

I lean over the railing to look farther down. No movement, but I do hear the faint sound of disagreeing voices a floor or more below made indistinct by distance and closed doors. Slowly, silently, I begin to make my way down. I reach the next landing. Beyond the swinging door those voices are less faint now but still far down the corridor. I ease the door open a crack. No scents on this floor of any beings other than normal humans. My sensitive hearing picks up what is being said.

"Not much progress. Maybe his vitals are too weak to draw any further?"

"That's just your opinion."

"No, it's wrong to assume anything about one of these would be the same as a normal human."

That's all that I hear of their conversation. They exit through a door that's well-sealed and thick enough to cut off their voices.

I'm curious, but I can't follow them to satisfy my curiosity until I reach my first objective.

I close the door, turn, and glide down another flight. Open another door. This level looks antiseptic but empty. No voice. No recent scents.

The tile floors are clean here, the walls recently painted. A mop and a bucket still half filled with soapy water left along the near wall. The words OPERATING THEATER TWO on the wall opposite me. An arrow points toward the first of a dozen doors.

I raise myself up onto two legs to try the door I come to. The handle turns easily and the door swings in. I enter, close it behind me, and go down the corridor, leaving the hospital-like area behind.

From what Yuri told me, their first attempt at an incursion ended when Maxico's intruder alert system detected them. That launched a lockdown, making it impossible for them to get into the inner areas where their little devices could take effect. The Sunglass Mafia had immediately retreated without making contact with any of the facility's guards, but not before Maxico's minions got their scent and tracked them to RHS.

I pass through another room, one which looks like an employees' common room. No one in it now this late at night, though my nose tells me that it's fairly well populated during the daytime hours. There's an assortment of worn-out chairs and a NO SMOKING sign high on one wall. The lounge is stocked with the usual mundane assortment of currency or credit card operated food and drink dispensers. I almost laugh at the incongruity of it— sort of like finding drinking fountains in Dracula's castle or coffee machines in Dr. Frankenstein's laboratory.

I go down another corridor that is right where it was supposed to be, turn left, go down a short flight of stairs, a left again. I've done a good job of memorizing the schematic that Vlad showed me, obtained from Maxico's supposedly secure system by his expert hacking. And here's the door I'm looking for. It's not locked. And why should it be? Who would be able to find their way in here or know what was behind it other than their own tech people?

And there it is. Just that one switch is all that I have to throw. I'm tempted to do more, to smash this array of machines with red and green blinking lights and digital displays. But that kind of violent destruction, pleasing as it might be to me right now, would surely set off alarms. Turning off just one part of their system is my objective.

Click.

Done.

I back out of the room and close the door behind me.

I retrace my steps without running into anyone—though I surely would have done so had it not been for my keen senses. I've taken several turns to the right or left when going in the opposite direction would have resulted in an encounter with one of the six semialert security guards I've identified thus far working this graveyard shift. None of them were much more awake than the two men I've just found dozing in chairs in the formerly empty common room I passed through earlier. Good human help is so hard to find.

I slip past them and am in the hospital sector once again. I go into the room I'd taken note of when I was last here.

It's like a doctor's consulting room. There's a raised examination table by the window with a tall lamp positioned next to it. There are three chairs and a desk. And on that desk is a standard institution-type phone.

I lift it up and listen. The dial tone tells me that it's working. I read the instructions on the sheet next to it. Dial 7 for an outside line.

Beep. Beep-bee-beep, bee-bee-beep-beep.

"Hello."

"Yuri?"

"No, Boris Karloff."

Ho, ho, ho.

"I . . . here," I growl. Hard to keep up witty repartee with this lupine speech impediment.

"Is system off?"

"Maybe."

I sense the combination of eagerness and irritation from his side.

"Tell me. You found the switch. Yes?"

"Say . . . please, *solnishko.*"

Hrr, hrr, hrrr. Good one. *Solnishko* is a Russian term of endearment that means "sunshine." From the other end of the phone comes a low growl more like one of my own than something in Yuri's usually cultivated voice. I just wait. Finally I hear Yuri let loose one of his exasperated sighs.

"Please."

"*Da.*"

"*Alda,*" Yuri says on the other end of the line. Not to me, but to the six others gathered around him. Let's roll.

FAMILIAR

While they are coming, I need to get going. It's not that I don't trust my temporary allies—and I most certainly do not trust them. I just can't wait any longer. Every muscle in my body is tense. My throat wants to let loose a long, hunting howl. The voices in my mind have reached a fever pitch, although this time in total agreement.

I have to find my dad.

I have to find my dad.

I have to find my dad.

If I don't start doing something now I'm going to explode.

Actually, I may not have any choice. A split second after Yuri broke the connection on his end I heard a faint *click*. We may have been on the line a little too long. I might not have tripped any alarms elsewhere, but this time my presence may have been detected by someone else monitoring our conversation.

A soft *ding* sounds from down the hall. Less than a minute since hanging up. Could there be a response this fast? If so, then things are about to get interesting a little too fast.

I drop down to all fours, pad over to the door, listen. Soft, shuffling feet are coming from the direction of the elevator at the far end of the hall. I smell sweat, adrenaline . . . and gun oil. Two, no, three armed guards are cautiously approaching. Not the ones I avoided earlier. This is a serious bunch. Probably each in a shooter's crouch, pistols held out two-handed in front of them, ready to capture or kill whoever just made that call.

If I'm quick and ruthless, they'll all be dead before they can get off a shot. Part of me wants just that.

Yess . . . rrrhh, I growl. Yess . . . rrrhh.

But I need to avoid the way of the beast. My dad said that and I have to follow his advice.

The logic that I hold onto, the way a drowning man grasps a life preserver, reminds me that more will come. Do I want to end up stuck here on the second floor where there's no scent or sign of the one person I need to find and protect?

No way.

This office is on the second floor. The window by the examination table is not one of the sealed bubble portals on the bottom floor. It's a double-paned oblong window, three feet wide, that can be raised or lowered. I press the latch, lift the window, and slip through. Balancing on the narrow ledge outside, I close the window behind me and hear its latch click shut. Once again I scale the rough stone side of the building and back to where I started.

Up on the roof.

I run quickly to the broken access door, open it, slip down to the next floor, listen. No voices, no new scents, still abandoned. I open the door and once again I make my way cautiously to the stairwell that leads to the lower floors.

Listen, sniff the air. Then, quick as a gray trickle of water down the slanting face of a cliff, down to the first floor.

More human smells here. I listen for a few seconds to the sound of voices from the other side of the swinging door that opens onto this main floor. Someone is talking on a phone.

"Nothing there," he says. "Did you check the other rooms?"

His voice is efficient, professional, but there's no panic. Maybe whoever was on the other line didn't catch that much of my conversation or understand it. I imagine the SWAT crew upstairs shaking their heads at the empty room they've entered, then calling in that it was a false alarm.

What I want is not on this floor. I go to the end of the corridor in the direction of those three talkers whose partial conversation I overheard. The door here is a thick one, more hatch than door, designed to be airtight. I open it, pass through, close it behind me.

I'm on the middle landing of a stairwell. Poured concrete stairs with metal railings lead up and down. I lean and sniff the air. Malodorous scents—harsh chemicals and strange body odors drift up to me. Humans and beings other than human are down there. Then I catch another scent that pulls me up short.

What?

I must be wrong about it. It can't be. My memories must be confused. I growl softly, paw at my nose, and shake my head. Then I run down the stairs.

The basement is deep under the main complex. The long steel stairs turn once, twice, then again and again before ending at a large sealed metal door at least fifty feet below ground. There's a wheel lock on it, like a bank vault or the door of a submarine. Easy enough to open from this side. Like the lock outside a lion cage. Its purpose is to keep something dangerous within.

I press on the wheel and it turns smoothly. A well-oiled bolt draws back. The door opens. I fall to all fours, step forward. The door swings back shut behind me on automatic hinges. *Schwick!* The bolt slides back into place.

I'm locked in. Nowhere to go now but forward.

The corridor that stretches before me looks to be eight feet wide and eight feet high. For fifty paces it runs straight, then turns at an abrupt right angle. Recessed green lights in the ceiling reflect off the white walls, give everything an eerie underwater glow. As I stalk along, keeping tight to the wall, odors get stronger. They're so sharply foul that they make me want to gag. That other, familiar scent I caught a whiff of upstairs is getting stronger too. This is crazy, but I know whose it is. It's his! It's even harder now to choke back a howl.

Another turn, this time to the left. Still no sign of any living being. The corridor widens out into a vast high-ceilinged room. In the middle a platform is surrounded by an apparatus I can't identify. Chairs are placed back from it behind a glass partition. For spectators?

Closed doors lead off to all sides around the great room. One of them is an elevator for passengers. Next to it is a freight elevator meant for much heavier loads.

I am drawn to the third door to the left. There, the scent that I know is the strongest. It's painfully easy for me to pick it out among all the other odors and follow it the way a dolphin chases the single fish it has picked as prey, ignoring the school of others that it swims through.

I push through the door. It's like a hospital room. There's a bed, a body in it. God, no. Tubes lead down to that strapped-in body from bags filled with clear liquid. Other tubes lead down and away. There's the sound of a pump, like that of a respirator.

But this is not a hospital room. It's the opposite of that. A hospital room holds hope, provides care for someone with the chance of recovery. Not this place. The clear plastic lines, like those used to conduct the sap from tapped maple trees, runs from him to a metal cylinder whose pump keeps sucking, sucking. A hateful, metallic, chemical odor that sears my nose comes from it. All of my senses tell me that life is being slowly, inexorably taken from the one strapped to that bed.

I rise up on two legs to look down at him. His eyes are closed. His skin is gray, ancient and dry as that of an Egyptian mummy. Only the faint flutter of breath tells me that he's still alive. Not yet totally drained. Six feet away, just out of arm's reach of the bed, is a black plastic box the size of a suitcase, resting on a stainless steel table. There's just one thicker tube, also black, running from that box to his right arm.

His scent fills my nostrils. More than familiar. Family. My eyes blur with moisture. How long has he been here? I reach out my paw hand and place it on his sunken, once powerful chest.

His eyes flicker open and then focus on mine. His eyes hold the old strength I remember. There's immediate recognition. Even as a wolf, he knows me.

Though I can feel that it takes every ounce of strength to do it, he manages to pull back his lips and show his large white teeth in a grin.

"Luke," he says, his voice a harsh wheeze.

"Uncle Cal."

59
DOWN THE TUBES

It's been so long since I last saw him, thought him dead. I feel joy that he's alive, despair at his condition, red anger at what's been done to him. I gnash my teeth and close my eyes, trying to keep it together. The confusion of emotions pulsing through me express themselves in a long whine that almost turns into a howl.

"Luke." The calm in Uncle Cal's weak voice brings me back to myself.

My eyes meet his again. All that's left physically is the husk of the man he was. Yet every bit of his old strength and kindness remains in his eyes.

He turns his eyes to the right. "Water," he rasps.

There's a sink there, a dispenser of cone-shaped paper cups on the wall next to it.

"Raise me up first." His voice is rough as a file drawn across metal.

I crank the bed so that he's in something closer to a sitting position. Then I go to the sink. I'm clumsy in my haste. I can't manage to get one of the damn cups to come out. I swing my paw against the dispenser, cracking it open, cascading a small avalanche of paper cones into the sink. I push the handle of the faucet to the side, pick up one of the cups, and fill it.

"More," Uncle Cal gasps, after draining it in one gulp as I hold it to his mouth.

After the fourth cup he takes a deeper breath than he's managed before.

"Now," he says, looking with narrowed eyes toward the thumping gray cylinder, "pull the plug on that goddamn thing."

A hiss of released air comes from the cylinder as I jerk the plug from the wall. Then it goes silent.

"Thank God," Uncle Cal whispers in a voice weak but more like his own. "The sound of that pump's been driving me crazy for sure. You'd think if they was going to suck the guts out of a man they'd find some way to do it without making so much noise."

Whatever they've done to him, that ironic sense of humor still remains. Laughing in the face of death might not make any difference in what happens, but it's more satisfying than crying—for sure.

He looks at his ravaged body and actually chuckles. "Man, I have let myself go down the tubes, for sure."

I'm too angry to laugh with him.

"What have . . . they done . . . you?" I growl.

As soon as I say it I realize it's one of the stupider questions I've ever asked, but Uncle Cal is kind enough not to point that out.

"Pull out these damn tubes, will you, Luke?" he says.

I slip the tubes out one by one. His arms are so desiccated that not even a drop of blood appears on the wounds made by the sharp intravenous needles.

I pause at the IV that leads up to the plastic bag filled with the clear liquid nutrients they have been feeding him.

"Take that out too. Half of it's meds to keep me down."

Then I reach down for the thick black tube that leads from his right wrist to the plastic box.

"No!" he says quickly. "Leave that one in for now. Just get these frigging restraints off."

He's not held down by the typical straps used to secure a dangerous or delirious patient, but by bindings that are much more substantial. They're reinforced with thick steel thread woven into the leather. Instead of being connected to the bed frame, they lead to chains that are firmly anchored in the floor. Even King Kong would have a hard time breaking free. But they're held in place by a mechanism that can be easily released as long as one has two hands to do it.

As soon as I free his arms, Uncle Cal slowly begins to raise his left arm up toward his face. His teeth are clenched together, his lips drawn back. It's as much a strain for him to do that as it would be for a man of normal strength to bench press his own body weight.

He lifts his index finger, as if pointing at the ceiling, then lowers it to scratch the side of his nose.

"Thank the Lord," he sighs. "That's been bugging me for a week, for sure. Forget about waterboarding, Nephew. You want to torture a man, just give him an itch that he can't scratch."

"Uncle Cal," I growl. "Who . . . ?"

"Did this to me?" He looks down at his emaciated frame. "You might say I did it to myself. I got careless and they caught me when I was"—he looks at me pointedly—"like you."

Uncle Cal raises his left hand from his face and slowly reaches it across his chest to point at the black tube.

"Pull that out now. Then open that box."

I grasp the tube. It's warm, feels organic. More like a living exposed vein than rubber. I yank at it. Uncle Cal's arm moves, but the venous tube stays anchored. It's as if it's grown teeth and dug them in. It's not about to come out as easily as the others. A moan escapes from between Uncle Cal's teeth. He sits partway up, grasps his right arm with his left hand to brace himself.

"Pull harder!" he hisses between his teeth.

I pull harder. There's a tearing sensation, like thick cloth being rent apart. It rips it free. Uncle Cal falls back onto the bed.

"Quick! Dying."

I lift the box lid. Something that seems to be a combination of liquid and light flows out of it, dissipates in the air like smoke from dry ice.

I reach in and take out what rests in the bottom. It's black, mottled with lighter rosette patterns. No heavier now than a towel, but I feel the life that still pulses in it—delicate, fragile as the breath of a small bird.

I turn back toward Uncle Cal. He's holding out both of his skeletal arms, fingers spread wide.

I place the jaguar skin in his hands and he clutches it to his chest.

THOSE DAYS ARE GONE

I'm holding my breath. Like my dad and me, Uncle Cal is also a skinwalker, but one whose animal self is that of a great cat. I'm waiting for the skin to mold itself to his limbs, for his old power to return, for him to metamorphose as I do when my second skin comes in contact with my body—for a great man-beast to rise out of this bed of pain.

But nothing happens. Nothing dramatic, at least. Uncle Cal just lays there, his bony fingers holding the black jaguar pelt, his eyes closed. The days are gone when the boy I was thought his adopted uncle was strong enough to stand like Atlas holding up the world on his broad shoulders. He's dying.

His chest moves up and down, a vein pulses in his cheek. I'm trying to will the strength back into him. I'm not succeeding.

He opens his eyes.

"Too late," he says, shaking his head. "They sucked too much out of us, for sure. But at least I'll be able to take my last breaths whole." A look of resolve comes into his eyes as he focuses them on mine. "But I got a little strength from my twin skin here. Enough to tell you a few things. Listen close."

He begins to talk. His voice is low, but firm. He tells me how he was taken as a prisoner—betrayed by people he trusted who decided that money, lots of money, was more important than loyalty. Then he was listed as dead so that he could be used—like this. Though it's painful to hear, it's not that big a surprise to me after all I've learned recently. They began to use him. They kept him alive—barely alive—to extract his blood and what his blood (and mine and Dad's) contains, the genetic material that makes Maxico's evil work possible.

No one ever had the tools to do this before, but when some of the specialists working for the corporation made their break-through, all they needed was a test subject. With Uncle Cal's capture, they found one who turned out to be even more productive a source than they'd expected as they drained him dry.

"Give me another drink of water, will you?" Uncle Cal whispers. He drinks it greedily, coughs so hard that it sounds as if something is going to break loose inside his chest.

"It's . . . all right," I growl. "Rest."

"No. More you got to hear."

His eyes are bright and fevered as he talks. Softer now, but faster. Just as much as governments these days, multinationals like Maxico need soldiers, totally loyal expendables who'll do exactly as they are told without conscience or hesitation. Normal suicide bombers sometimes have second thoughts or are captured and give up those they served. But the humanlike simulacra beings created by Maxico—through the mixing of human and skinwalker DNA—have neither second thoughts nor real emotions. They are programmed to do as directed.

302

"Their war is against the earth for sure, Nephew," Uncle Cal's face is grim. "There's some in power now, way high up, who are ready to do things a better way. Not just here, but around the world. There's corporations and governments trying to do things different. Stop poisoning the ocean and the air, listen to those like us who care 'bout all the generations to come. All our relations. The other side, it knows that. So it's fighting back, using bribes and lies."

Uncle Cal takes a deep, painful breath. "And they're holdin' out the biggest bribe of all. Not dyin'. You know how you've changed, Nephew, taken a different shape? The cells in your body and mine, they're able to do something their scientists figure they can sort of tweak. You found out how fast you can heal?"

I nod my head.

"Uh-huh. Now they take that. Cellular self-regeneration. Make it so that what aging wears out, can be fixed. Not ever having to die. Living forever. Some men will do most anything to get that. This man named Kesselring, for one."

"I . . . know him," I say. The image of that hungry look on Kesselring's face as he first looked at me during that school assembly comes back to me. A growl builds deep in my chest.

Uncle Cal reaches up to wrap his long fingers around my hairy wrist. "We can't let them win!" His breathing is labored. He squeezed those urgent words out of himself like the last drops of juice from an orange.

I open my mouth to tell him to rest, not wear himself out. He holds up his hand.

"Listen. They got all they can from me. You ruined their last harvest." A grin that's like a rictus of pain briefly splits his face. "You done good, Nephew. You wearin' your skin strong. You keepin' the monster down. But you got to keep fightin' against it."

I nod.

"Maybe you too young for this. But you got no choice now. Now they got your dad."

He sees the look in my eyes, how my lips curl back to show my teeth.

"Now don't go getting foolish." His voice is just a harsh whisper now. "You *think* now about what you got to do. You fight, but keep thinking while you fighting."

I nod again.

"How . . . you know . . . Dad here?"

Uncle Cal lifts his hand slowly to touch his nose. "Smelled him first, Nephew. Then I saw him. They brought him by here."

"Where is . . . he?"

Uncle Cal tries to speak, but at first words won't come from his mouth. He raises his hand, points a finger down, coughs.

I fill the cup with water again, dribble a little of it into his mouth before he pushes it away.

"Down," he says. "Where they took me first. Level Seven. Big elevator out there." He wrinkles his nose in what looks like disgust at a bad odor. "How many?"

His question doesn't seem to make sense. "What?" I growl.

"I smell 'em on you. Bloodsuckers. They coming, right?"

Yuri and his crew. My upyr allies.

"Seven," I answer.

Uncle Cal sighs. "Worked with some of their kind before. Don't trust 'em."

As he takes a breath I think of arguing with him. He's never seen the sensitivity in those eyes that Yuri hides behind his opaque shades. Never heard Marina quietly reciting the verses of Anna Ahkmatova to herself. Hasn't seen that smile on Vlad's big face as he gives me a thumbs-up. Hasn't experienced their ironic sense of humor.

As I think that, I realize I am actually beginning to like Yuri and his crew. They're different, it's true. But they can't help who they are. They're at least as human as I am—maybe more. What we're fighting—together—is a worse evil.

Uncle Cal looks at me, as if he's been reading my thoughts. A hint of a smile comes to his face. "Maybe . . ."

He closes his eyes. His chest is barely moving, his breath shallow as a river in drought.

"Uncle Cal," I growl. My eyes are filling up. I don't deny the tears. They fall on the black jaguar skin that he has clutched to his chest, soak into it like rain into dry soil.

His eyes open again. He whispers something. I lean close to listen. Carried on the soft outflow of his breath, I don't understand at first. Then I realize it's poetry. I recognize the poem now. Wordsworth. "Intimations of Immortality." He's reciting lines that refer to the lost innocence of childhood.

"Those days," Uncle Cal breathes, "are gone."

Then he's gone too.

ATTACK

I clench my paw hands tight. My nails dig into my pads and draw blood. It drips onto the black jaguar skin, is absorbed as quickly as the tears that fell from my eyes.

Uncle Cal is dead. The only other adult in my life who meant almost as much to me as my parents. And this is the second time I have to grieve for him.

I fall down on all fours, turn in a circle growling. Emotions are swirling through me like tornado winds. Anger, regret, sorrow. I flop down on my belly, put my paws over my eyes.

It's quiet here in this room, aside from the breathless hissing of the air conditioning and the steady hum from the banks of fluorescent lights overhead. But this is the eye of a hurricane. All I have to do is step back out into the hall to meet its destructive force.

There's something else. It's pulsing at a level of sound higher than most humans can hear. I've been hearing it for some time now, since entering the room where Uncle Cal was strapped to that bed.

But I pushed it to the back of my mind as I concentrated on his whispered words.

I know what that sound is. Maybe I set it off when I entered his room. Or when I pulled out the tubes. It's an alarm. The hairs bristle on the back of my neck. Something is coming. Soon.

I lift myself up to open the door, slide out into the hall. My teeth are bared, I'm ready to fight. But no attack comes. Not yet.

The door closes behind me, cutting off my final view of Uncle Cal's body. Leaving him there seems wrong. But I have to. If I survive, I'll come back for him. I'll make sure his body is not dissected like a laboratory frog. I'll see that he's buried in the forest beneath a tree. If I survive.

I cross the wide expanse of floor to the door of the big elevator. That rank smell gets stronger as I approach it. It's been carrying things I'd rather not run into in a dark hallway, but it seems to be the only way. My father is somewhere down there. I stand up on two legs to press the button to call the elevator. Before I can touch it, however, I hear the faint sound of oiled wheels and steel pulleys swiftly bringing the elevator car up from below.

I leap back as the large doors open with a *whoosh*. A huge shape looms up from inside the car, hurls itself at me roaring.

"ARRRROOWWR!"

My own reflexes are too fast for it to hit me head-on. I move to the side and duck the huge clawed paw that is swung at me. One of the oldest lessons in martial arts is to not absorb an opponent's attack, but to let it go past you. I can't avoid a glancing blow from its bulky shoulder, though, enough to send me cartwheeling across the floor. The mental snapshot of my attacker recorded in that microsecond is of a hulking body, wide slathering jaws equipped with saber teeth, claws twice as long as those of a grizzly bear.

I hard roll into—and through—a table and several chairs,

through equipment that shatters, wires and cables that pull free and twist around me. The claws on my feet scrabble against the tile floor as I struggle to free myself from the debris.

"HAROWWRRR!"

Jaws fasten on my left shoulder, pierce my skin. I'm lifted up, shaken like a rat in the crushing jaws of a terrier. My blood and its slaver are splattering the floor. It hurls me to the side. I hit the wall like a ball of clay hurled against a rock. I slide down to the floor wondering if every bone in my body has been broken.

But despite the pain, what I'm filled with right now is not fear. It's rage. The wolf mark on my wrist throbs. I turn my head to lick my shoulder. There's warm blood there and torn flesh, but those jaws pierced no more than an inch despite the fact that the beast bit down with all its force. My skin is too strong, my muscles too tough.

I take a deep shuddering breath, refilling my lungs, reaching for that inner strength at the center which we call chi in karate. Then I let it out in a deep growl of my own, look up through my eyebrows at the creature twenty feet away. It lifts up on its hind legs, snarls. Its posture is like that of the grue. Except the monster that faces me this time is not a mental projection of my own aggression.

The creature that's just tried to kill me is clearly a product of Maxico's gene-blending scientists. Once, I'm guessing, it was an African lion. Remember that safari park that used to be here? Looks as if not all of its animals were taken away after all when it went out of business. But this beast is twice a normal lion's size now. Its huge teeth are like those of the ancient gape-jawed creatures that stalked the nights and the nightmares of ten thousand years ago. But it's far more than a saber-toothed cat. It's one of those things Boris called a recombinant. It blends feline and man in such a grotesque way that it looks as foul as it smells. Its eyes are mad and clever.

The worst thing about it is what I can see in those eyes. It's something that no one other than me or my father would notice. What I sense in this creature is something of the presence of my Uncle Cal. Here's where part of what they sucked from him went. They used his DNA to mold this. Some of his strength, his cunning is in this monster. But none of his soul. Or, it seems, his courage.

The lion creature's first attack has failed to destroy me. It seems surprised. It's no longer roaring. The deep rumbling sound from its throat is hesitant. It's not uncommon in the wild for a predator to back off when its prey fights back too successfully. Now, perhaps it is just thinking to try to keep me at bay until reinforcements arrive.

This is when the zebra or the wildebeest would go leaping back to the herd for safety.

Hrrnnnh!

I'm as far from a zebra as a guinea pig is from a rottweiler. I drop into a crouch and leap.

Not for safety.

For its throat.

DOWN

My front paws strike its chest. Although my claws are not hooked like those of a cat, they're sharp enough to dig into its skin and find purchase as I lunge for its throat.

It lurches backward, unbalanced by my weight. It rakes its scimitar claws across my back, searing lines of fire. I ignore the pain. I don't feel it as pain. My only thought, so strong that the word "thought" doesn't describe it, is to sink my teeth farther into its neck, rip through muscle and flesh.

It stumbles over something and falls. As it hits the floor with a great crash, it tries to roll on top of me. But I twist my body off to the side, keeping my jaws closed on its throat. Blood is filling my mouth, red as the mist in my vision. It's almost choking me. Only the length of my muzzle makes it possible for me to keep snarling, breathing in through the side of my mouth.

I brace my feet as I twist and pull back. The lion monster's windpipe crunches—a sound like that of crusted snow giving way under a heavy tread. It goes limp.

I've killed again. This time it is something closer to a person. That bothers the human part of me, the part that I have to hold onto no matter what.

The predator in me doesn't feel any elation from this victory. No depression, either—only disgust at the creature's bad taste. I back off, licking my lips. The taste of its blood is bitter, not sweet like that of the deer. No, on second thought, I'm not merely feeling disgust. There's also a sense of disappointment that there's not a meal to be had here after all this effort. After all, a wolfman needs to snack when he can if he's having a busy day.

Both parts of myself are in total agreement about one thing, however. No need to take a vote.

Go back to that elevator.

Get down to that lower level.

Get to my dad.

I shake myself like a retriever coming out of the water. A wide spray of blood comes off me, more the dead creature's than my own. There's a deep ache in my shoulder where I was bitten, but I can feel the wound healing itself.

The force of our brief battle left a larger and longer trail of broken equipment than I'd realized. I begin to pick my way through piles of debris to reach the elevator. Its doors are jammed open by a long piece of a table that was knocked back into it. It's a full hundred feet away, but aside from the wreckage left by my battle with the recombinant monster, there's nothing between me and this next step in seeking out my dad.

Something buzzes through the air like a hornet, strikes me in my lower back. I turn to bite at it. My teeth find the shaft of a wooden dart. I pull it out and throw it to the side as more whiz toward me. Some miss. But not many. I rear up onto two legs, use my paw hands to pluck them out, two at a time. None pierced more than skin deep. Wooden shafts. I almost laugh. Wrong load for a skinwalker.

Still, I'd rather not be hit by more. I leap sideways, dodge the next volley. A black-clad squad, all wearing the emblem of the large M surrounded by a golden circle and a series of lightning bolts, is advancing toward me from the other side of the hall. There's a dozen simulacra at the front. Behind them, more cautious than their expendable automatons, are four other figures with white epaulets on their black uniforms. From their looks—and smell—those four are real human beings.

The humans and simulacra in this security squad both mean business. They are not out to take prisoners but to wipe out the threat. I'm not sure how I'll do if they fire missiles with the explosive tips or poison that Yuri mentioned. Thinking of Yuri and his crew, there's a flicker of movement from behind the security force. Shapes approaching them from the shadows while I stand here being the big dumb decoy. Enough of that.

I crouch down and then leap, a leap long enough to make every existing broad jump record defunct by a dozen yards. I land at the elevator entrance, swing one paw to push back into the car the chunk of broken table keeping the doors open. I swat the Close button with my other paw. The doors slide swiftly shut with a soft thud—closely followed by a series of small sudden explosions as the crossbow bolts hit. The sounds of the explosions are muted by the heavy steel doors—as are a number of screams, quickly cut short.

Interesting. But no time to ponder or to reopen those doors.

Down, please.

I press my paw against the bottom button labeled L7. The speed of the drop and the length of time it takes, long enough for me to count to ten, tells me that this lower level is way down, far enough below ground to survive even a direct hit from a nuclear bomb.

Here I come.

Here we go.

Yo, yo, yo yo.

63 WORKSTATIONS

The doors open with a soft pneumatic *whoosh* as soon as the car reaches the lower level. I crouch in the corner to the left of the doors, make myself as small as possible. My arrival might be greeted by a welcoming committee eager to bestow such gifts upon me as a spray of bullets.

All I hear, though, is the repetitive dinging of alarm bells. It's reached the point where they want to alert human ears, as well.

I look out, keeping my head low to the floor. Eye level is where most humans look first, not down by their feet, when they scan a potentially dangerous room—or elevator. No motion at all, aside from the gentle rippling of the air vents that provide this underground zone with breathable atmosphere. It's an even vaster space than the level above. It's broken up into thousands of cubicles. Chairs, desks, monitor screens, headsets at each. A quick count tells me that the lines of these workstations are sixty across and a hundred deep, with six additional larger stations placed in a raised ring at the center of the oblong room, thirty feet above the others like an airport control tower.

Most of the cubicles look like they haven't yet been used. Only a dozen seem to have been recently manned. From the number of them, you'd think this place was designed to rival one of those annoying South Asian call centers. But no one is going to be contacting people from here to offer special rates for long distance and unlimited minutes. Although the workstation closest to me is deserted, it was recently in use. Printouts and sticky notes are scattered on the desk. The screen saver shows a school of piranhas washing across the computer screen. And taped to the wall of the cubicle is a paper.

"SERVO 411," reads the large print. It's followed by a list of steps and operating procedures. As my eyes run down those instructions, I grasp what these workstations are meant for. Like technicians manning predator drones, the people working here are the operators for the black simulacra. The humanlike automatons that attacked me and Yuri's crew at RHS and upstairs were being run from here by remote control.

Are the bells that continue to sound the reason that this cubicle and the others around it are empty? Was the alarm the signal for the operators to retreat to a more secure area? Or was it just the very recent destruction of the security force upstairs that sent them scurrying like rats? I can smell fear in the scents of every one of those who were working here and fled.

I do not have Vlad's little virus, but I do have another way to effectively render the dozen working terminals here ineffective— just in case there are more simulacra waiting to be put into service from here. Simple focused violence. In a few minutes I've reduced the control stations to heaps of rubble.

Beyond the cubicles I've just trashed and the hundreds of unfinished workstations is another area. The length of a football field away, there are rooms encased in walls of plastic or glass. As I approach them, I see that all of them are filled with instruments, computers, and banks of equipment. But if there's nothing my eyes see that suggests incipient danger, there's plenty reaching my nose that tells me to be wary. I'm not the only living presence on this level. Far from it. In addition to the decamped automaton operators, I'm picking up a profusion of other odors from living beings. Human smells, animal smells, other scents that blend both in ways nature never intended. Most are mixed in with the miasmas of stress. Adrenaline-laden sweat, vomit, excrement, blood. Too much blood.

Suddenly, one scent stands out for me above all others. It's a familiar one that makes my heart pound with hope. My father. There are also two other scents that I recognize—the two from the trailer, Nick and Eddie, probably reporting on my whereabouts. Or rather, that they still can't find a hapless teenager.

And then . . . but it can't be. Another odor. It's one that I can't possibly mistake. Meena's. It shouldn't be, mustn't be here. Have memory and longing fooled my brain into thinking that Meena is here? I shake my head and the scent is gone. I must have been imagining it. This would be too crazy, even for this subterranean world I've descended into.

Focus, Luke. Focus.

The faintness of my father's familiar scent tells me that some time has passed since he was brought through here. How long ago? Hours at least. But I can follow the trail with my nose as easily as a tracker uses his eyes to pick out paw prints in snow.

I look back at the elevators. The freight elevator I came down in and the one next to it are still stationary. The lion creature that attacked me was sent up from down here. That it wasn't followed by other similar savage guardians means either that such creatures are still few—not enough of Uncle Cal's blood and DNA yet to create more, perhaps—or that they're needed elsewhere in the Maxico compound. Maybe they're part of a force that has been sent up to try to repel Yuri and the others.

A grim smile crosses my muzzle. Be patient, Luke. Sooner or later there is sure to be another obstacle.

Whatever the reason is that I'm currently unopposed doesn't matter. It's about time that something was working in my favor. I'm getting tired of meeting new complications around every bend. There's nothing between me and the next sealed door other than fifty feet of open floor.

However, I'm not about to just stroll over there. Belly to the floor, I move cautiously, one slow step at a time. I stay low, below the normal line of sight. I've not forgotten those lessons in stalking that my father taught me.

Just for a second, I pause as I remember those days, the two of us in the forest behind our old house. That memory is so vivid that I can see it as clearly as if I was still there.

Dad is on one knee, pointing out a faint trail in the leaves. His other hand is on my shoulder, his touch light, reassuring. His voice is soft, trusting that I'll hear every word and drink it in the way the soil absorbs the rain.

I shake my head, blink moisture from my eyes. Something in the atmosphere, ammonia, maybe, is irritating them. I have to keep moving.

I reach up and turn the wheel. The door opens with a hiss. Before me I see another set of glass-walled enclosures. Three of them. The scent of blood is stronger and fresher here. As are those three other familiar scents.

The portal closes behind me as I make my way to the first of the airtight, glass enclosures. It's the size of a high school chemistry lab. One glance into it shows me all there is to see. Work's been going on here too. Work of a far bloodier kind than cutting up frogs. Stainless steel counters and tables, IV racks and lines, labeled bottles. Gleaming instruments, operating room–style lights to match the gloves, blue gowns, and masks hung on racks. All very neat and clean aside from the pools of blood in the clogged floor drains and the two dissected bodies next to each other on the tables.

I'd just recognized their scents but hadn't expected to find them like this. It's Nick and Eddie, the men who failed to retrieve me from our trailer. Grisly evidence that Maxico seems to have a one-strike-and-you're-out policy.

My hackles rise and I snarl as I back out and continue on to the next room, fifty feet farther on. Like the first room, the Plexiglas door is open. I go inside. More of the same. This time the body on the table is not human, but that of a very large bear. Its chest gaping wide, the heart has been pulled out and placed next to it on the table. Wires like jumper cables extend from the still-beating heart to a crash cart. Bloody footprints lead to the door of the sealed glass room and then out into the hall, past where I stand. The alarm bells sounded their retreat too.

I pick up the heart in my paw, lick some of blood that has leaked from it. I don't just do this for pleasure or hunger. It tastes good, salty and strong, the way the blood of a normal mammal should, tells me that they were at the start of the procedure to transform, infuse, and reanimate, to distort what was once a living being into one of their half-dead monsters.

"Give me some of your strength, brother," I growl.

Strength of body and strength of spirit, I think. Dreading what I may see next.

Then, I eat the bear's heart.

I hesitate before I pad over to that third glass cubicle. Unlike the other two, it is closed. I look through the clear wall and freeze. Then I rise up on two legs to strike my paws against the Plexiglas.

No!

The world around me grows red with my rage. I snarl and slam my head against the clear wall through which I've seen the last thing in the world I want to see. I bite at my own legs, shake my head.

I am going to kill them all.

Enough of caution.

No more skulking around.

I am going to kill them all.

I don't care who hears me. I want them to hear me.

I want them to know I am coming for them.

I am going to kill them all.

I raise my head and howl. My cry is louder than the alarm bells. It echoes off the walls of the immense room. It's made stranger by the anger and pain and grief I feel from what I see before me. Who I see before me.

It's my father.

His body is strapped in a standing position to an upright table. Wires run from his head and chest. Black tubes descend from both his wrists to a machine like the one I saw attached to Uncle Cal. Blood is pooled around his feet.

His head and arms hang limp and dead.

OPENING DOORS

I slam against the Plexiglas wall. It doesn't break. I hit it again and again. My mouth is open, my tongue hanging out. My heart is pounding like a drum and I'm panting.

Stop!

I have to force myself to think. Otherwise I'll just keep hurling myself against an obstacle that may break me before I smash it. There has to be a door.

I drop to all fours, circle the Plexiglas room. Though it almost looks like just another part of the wall, I find the entrance. It's a seven-foot-tall, three-foot-wide oblong of Plexiglas with thin ribbons of wire embedded around the edges. Printed circuits. There's a notebook-sized black keypad on the wall next to it with a yellow button in the center of its lower half. I rise up, reach out a paw, press the yellow button. There's a magnetic *click* and the door begins to move. As it slides to the side I leap through it, grab one of the chairs and wedge it into the frame before the door can close

320

again. Confused and clouded with emotion though my thoughts may be right now, I'm not going to take a chance on being trapped in this plastic killing box.

I hurl things aside as I thrust toward the table where my father is strapped up like a crucified god. I rise up to two legs, place my paws on his shoulders and lean close to his face. I'm praying that my fears are wrong.

Breath.

Breath is still coming from his mouth. It is faint and weak, but still breath. He's alive. I pull free the wires that spark as they make contact with each other. I swing my paw against the machine they connected to, smash it into pieces against one of the walls. Then I carefully pull out the black IV tubes inserted in the large veins of his wrists. His eyelids flicker. He tries to raise his head.

"Who . . ." he whispers. His voice is harsh with dryness.

"Luke," I growl, trying to make my voice as human as possible, "Me . . . Dad."

I support him with my shoulder as I reach up to tear free the arm and wrist restraints and then the heavier strap around his chest. His weight unbalances me for a moment and I almost fall. Though he's not as heavy as usual. His face looks drawn and he must be a good twenty pounds below his usual two hundred and sixty. But it adds hope that he's not drained as Uncle Cal was. I lower him as gently as I can to the floor, turn my gaze again to his face.

His eyes are open and aware. He's looking right at me.

"Luke . . . Son." He lifts up a hand, places it on my right arm, strokes the thick, glossy fur. It feels good as he does that, like when I was a little kid and he'd come into my room and push the hair back from my forehead.

"You . . . found . . . yourself," he whispers.

I nod.

"Sit," Dad rasps, then starts to cough. I lever him up so that his back is against the vertical table. The coughing gradually stops. He points with his lips behind me. I look around. There's a six-pack of sealed water bottles. I pull one free from the plastic collar, twist the lid off.

He takes the bottle in his hand and lifts it to his lips, swallows a little, coughs, then drinks more.

"You . . . all . . . right?" he asks me, a second before I can ask him the same question.

I nod again. My heart rate is back to normal. The world no longer is red as the blood I'd been planning to spill. Even though we're here in the center of a place that is as wrong and out of balance as anything can be in the world, I'm experiencing a feeling of peace for the first time in days. A dark door in my heart that was tightly shut has finally opened to let the sunshine in.

He smiles at me. "Me . . . too," he says, his voice a little stronger. He holds out his right fist and I tap my paw fist against it.

Maybe we don't have the kind of telepathy that Yuri and his crew seem to have, but my father and I are on the same wavelength. That thought of Yuri, though, reminds me that I am going to have to do some talking to explain everything that has been going on since I last saw Dad. I wonder how he'll feel about having Russian special (very special) agents as partners?

He looks over at the machine from which the black IVs emanate like malevolent tentacles. Takes a deep breath.

"See that?" he says.

I nod.

"They were about . . . to turn that on. Then the alarms started going off. They must have . . . hightailed it without even looking back. I blacked out for a while. Next thing I saw . . . was your hairy face. You know . . . I said it wouldn't bother me if you grew a beard.

But you seem to've took it a little far." He chuckles at his own joke.

"I guess . . . hrrrnh, hrrnhh, I'm having . . . a bad . . . hair day, Dad."

Dad matches the wide wolfish grin that shows all of my teeth with a big smile of his own. Then his face turns serious.

"They got your Uncle Cal, Luke."

"I know. I . . ." I can't continue. I shake my head, lift my left paw to my forehead, touch it to my chest and drop it toward the floor.

"Dead?" Dad asks.

I nod again.

The same anger I'd been feeling clouds his face. He tries to stand. His legs are still weak though. They shake from his effort and he can't manage to get up.

"Dizzy. Too many meds still in me," he says, shaking his head. He holds out his hand. I pull him up, wrap his arm over my shoulders. I start to move us toward the door.

"Wait."

Dad points with his chin at a padlocked metal locker at the far side of the room. "In there."

I help him sit in a chair, cross to the locker. I grab the padlock, take a breath and then snap it off. I rip open the door to reveal . . . just what I thought that cabinet might hold. I'd already smelled the gun oil.

The sight of its contents seems to restore more of Dad's strength. He limps over to stand by me, rests one hand on my shoulder, and leans to look inside the weapons locker.

A wide smile lights up my father's face as he reaches for an AK-47.

"Now we're talking!"

HARI'S JOB

He's recovered some of his strength, but as we move across the tiled floor, he still leans on me for support. Dad has always been taller than me. Six-eight to my mere six feet. I'm also more stooped in this wolf shape, even when walking on two legs, so Dad towers over me as we walk together.

The thought of how we look together brings a grin to my face. A drunk man being helped home by his improbably anthropomorphic dog? The grin is short-lived. How did it come to this? Having my father lean on me? I never imagined a day like this would ever arrive. Dad's been the rock on which my world stands—even when that rock seemed blurred with substance abuse, I knew there was still something solid under it all. I'd believed, I'd had to believe, that one day he'd snap out of it. My father always seemed powerful enough to eventually weather any storm. But not now.

I start to move in the direction of the elevator.

Dad pulls me in the opposite direction. "No. This way."

Deeper in?

I don't ask why. We move the way he's indicated. There's another door in the wall, one that was behind another bank of computers. Dad turns the wheel, pulls the door open. There's a hiss of air and with it a scent that brings a whine to my lips.

Perfume. But not just perfume. The best perfumes always create a new slightly different smell when combined with the natural odors of a human body. It's absolutely unmistakable and all too recent.

Dammit! She was just supposed to warn her father. Not this!

"It . . . can't be herrr," I snarl.

Dad sniffs the air and shakes his head. "No, it's Meena all right."

What? How does he know her scent? I've mentioned her name, but he's never met her.

"How'd you know?"

Dad squeezes my hairy shoulder. "I met her when she was little. Her dad is one of our people we had on the inside."

"What? Did Meena know that?"

Dad shakes his head. "Kind of like my . . . misdirecting you over the last year or so, I guess," he says. "Sometimes safer for the families not to know everything. Hari Kureshi is a good guy, one of the best. We trained together . . . after he went to Oxford."

"No . . . way," I growl.

"Way," Dad says, nodding. "After he figured out enough of what was going on here, we knew it had to be stopped." Dad looks into my eyes. "You've seen some of it, right? Those soulless automatons."

I nod.

"The recombinants."

I nod again.

"Then you understand that much?"

Another nod.

He grabs my right hand. Despite the fact that it is larger than when I'm in human form, more rounded like a paw, Dad's big hand still fits around it. He holds it gently, the old way that American Indians always shake hands with one another.

"I guess I don't have to tell you how proud I am of you, Son."

"It's okay." I growl. "Tell . . . me."

That brings a smile to Dad's face, as I'd hoped it would.

"Hari's job was to see what was what here. He wasn't part of the team making those monsters. He'd been brought in as window dressing, the reputable research scientist who could be the public face of their biochem business. But even though he didn't have clearance to the inner labs, he managed to get close enough to put two and two together. Things being done with DNA that indicated somehow they'd gotten hold of . . . one of us. He never found out who, but I thought it had to be . . . Cal. After all, his body was never found."

Dad pauses again and swallows hard. "So Hari did everything he could to slow things down until a decision was made to take direct action. Little acts of sabotage that could be passed off as accidents or human error. Like contaminating samples when no one was looking, losing shipments of chemicals. Whew!"

Dad bends over and takes a hard breath. Talking this much is tiring for him. His body is still suffering from whatever they put into him.

"Dad," I growl, "Don't . . . wear yourself . . . out."

He forces himself to stand up straight, pats my back. "No, you got to hear this, Son. Hari was put here because we knew that something very hinky was going on. As soon as Rogan Machescou showed up, we knew. If he hadn't been wealthy enough to buy his way out of it, Machescou would have been on trial at the Hague for war crimes after what he did in Bosnia. Torture, mass murder, experiments on prisoners. That man is pure evil."

Dad pauses. "Strange thing, though, soon after Machescou showed up, he just vanished. Didn't leave the country, just went deep into the Maxico complex and never came out again. Even Hari hasn't seen him for weeks. Only one running the show now seems to be Kesselring."

"You know . . . who Kessel-rrring is?" I growl.

"We do now," Dad says. "I just got the dossier from Interpol three days ago. Just before they sent that team to snatch me." He shakes his head. "My guess is that someone, a mole in Interpol, tipped them off. As soon as I knew Kesselring's real identity, there was no way they could ignore me. I was a danger." He pounds his fist against his leg. "I can't believe I let them catch me. I . . ." His weight on my shoulder increases as he legs give way.

"Dad," I say. "Sit . . . rest."

He doesn't protest, lets me lean him against the wall. He puts down the AK-47, shrugs off the bulky shoulder pack he took out of the cabinet, a pack that is very heavy from the various armaments he stuffed into it. He slides down into a sitting position. He takes a labored breath, shakes his head. "Man, I just don't think I'm going to work out as a spokesman for Maxico's patented weight-loss program."

"Harrr . . . harr."

I growl out a laugh. But I don't know if his weak joke is a good sign or not. Cracking ironic jokes like that—that's just what he and Uncle Cal always did when things were at their worst. Like now.

"I was dumb, Luke," Dad says. "You read my . . . instructions, right? Remember that arrogance I told you about? That's one of my weaknesses. I thought they'd never figure out who and what I was. I'd never used the name King or any of the ID that goes with it when I was on any of the jobs I did. Didn't think it was even in the databases. Shows how much I knew, eh?"

"Are . . . others on your team . . . coming now?" I'm imagining highly trained soldiers in midnight-hued body armor dropping in from helicopters to stage a daring last minute rescue—just like in the movies.

Dad looks sad. He shakes his head. "Son, even though I work for the government, this op is not even a black one. It is off the radar, rogue. It was just Cal and Hari and me. We thought we'd be enough. Arrogance again. One of those little special missions like the ones we'd do in the past when we were supposed to be on leave. We might have been able to bring more help in with the intel that Hari got to me, but I never had a chance to send it on up the chain. I got taken before I could do that."

"You . . . mean?" My growling voice is deeper as I say those words.

"Uh-huh. We are on our own."

"Not . . . all . . . alone."

"Oh," Dad says, "Who?"

It takes me a while, my speech being labored at best while I'm in this form. He listens intently, nodding now and then as I fill him in on the fact that an equally unusual team of Russian secret agents, my *druzhoks,* my bloodsucking best buddies, had been working from their end on an identical mission.

It helps that it has always been the case that when Dad is really listening to me, I need fewer words to get something across to him than anyone else. It's like our minds are one and he can anticipate what I'm going to say next.

When I finish he doesn't say anything for a while.

Finally I break the silence. "Uncle Cal . . . said . . . not to . . . trrrust them."

Dad surprises me by smiling. "Trust but verify," he says.

"Hunnrrh?"

"An old Russian saying, Son. But in this case it's trumped by an equally old English one. Any old port in a storm. Any allies are better than none. And one thing about Russians—of whatever stripe—is that they're not short of courage. Remember Leningrad? And when they say they're going to do something, they do it. And they do have some of the best biochemists and hackers in the world. Your buddies—Boris and Vlad, right?"

I nod.

"If they get to the main systems with their little devices, Maxico's operation here is toast."

Dad pulls the pack toward him, opens it, pulls out a roll of metallic tape, tears off one long strip and two short ones and hands them to me. "Use these to make an arrow on the wall the way we're going. We do this each time we take a turn. If they're coming in behind us, they'll know where we've gone."

Dad puts back the tape, takes out a heavy-duty screwdriver. I reach a paw hand out to him, but he stands up unaided. It's as if what I told him has given him new strength. He walks over to the still-open portal we just passed through. Sticking the screwdriver into a slot inside the jamb, he leans hard, twists it, and there's a snapping sound.

"Amazing how easy it is to wreck the locking mechanism of one of these things after it's been opened," he smiles. "Don't want your sunglass-wearing *druzhoks* to feel left out."

DOWN THE RABBIT HOLE

We've gone through two more sets of sealed doors. This place is like a twenty-first-century cross between Alice's rabbit hole and the semimythical underground White House—the one built years ago deep under an undisclosed mountain in case of a nuclear hit on D.C. The long corridors here are all slightly rounded, twenty feet wide and ten feet high, sheathed in metal.

If it weren't for my sense of smell, we wouldn't have had a clue which way to go at any of the branching tunnels we've encountered. Another reason why Yuri sent me in ahead of them.

Be a good dog, Rover, and lead us.

If Yuri and his crew are following us, they'll probably be glad for the dozen tape arrows we've now stuck to the walls. Millions of Kesselring's and Rogan Machescou's Euros and dollars must have gone into building this maze. We haven't run into a single living—or dead—soul since I freed my father from his restraints.

Ahead of us, though, is one sign of life. It's a cafeteria for human workers. And a good thing. Food is something Dad needs now to restore some of his strength.

"Ah," he says, "midnight snack time." He grabs a cup, fills it with water from a tap, dumps two teaspoons of instant coffee into it, puts it into a microwave, hits three minutes. Then he opens one of the fridges, pulls out some of the food.

"Luke?" he asks as he puts together a Dagwood-sized ham sandwich.

I shake my head. "I . . . prefer . . . rrrare."

That earns me a big grin from him.

"Right," he says.

As he eats, I can see he's starting to feel stronger.

"Man," he says, "I could eat a horse."

"Me . . . too . . . forr . . . rreal."

Another chuckle from him. The microwave dings and he pulls out the steaming cup, dumps in half a bowl of sugar, stirs it, and gulps it down. By the time he finishes drinking, the color has returned to his face.

"Okay," Dad says, wiping his mouth with the back of his hand. "Back down the rabbit hole."

He no longer leans on me as we leave the cafeteria. The scent trail leads to a left-hand tunnel corridor.

"So," Dad says as we walk, "you told your friend Meena to warn her father."

"Rrrr . . . yes," I growl, feeling guilty as I answer. It's my fault she got caught up in this.

"I don't see it being your fault that she got caught up in this, Son," Dad says, reading my mind as he so often does. "Hari was taking chances. Once they caught on to me, even if they didn't know we were working together, my guess is that they started looking around for leaks. They just took him to see how much he knows."

"I see," I say. His words make me feel a little better. But not much. The girl I love is still a prisoner of some of the worst people in the world.

"If Meena and her father are lucky," Dad says, talking to himself as much as to me, "Kesselring and his cohorts haven't caught on that Hari's an agent. Maybe they just think he was getting too curious. I'm guessing that's why they've taken his daughter. Or maybe she just happened to be there when they snatched him and they took her along. I doubt they'll hurt her, at least not right away. She'll be leveraged to make him cooperate, tell them what he knows. Then they'll decide what to do to . . . minimize risk."

Dad checks the clips and grenades he's hung on his belt, the Magnum revolver he's belted around his waist.

"Find her, we find him," he says. "Right? Then we do . . . whatever we have to do."

"Rrright," I growl.

We make a right turn and then it starts to go wrong. The tunnel is suddenly filled with a confusion of odors. It does to my sense of smell the same thing that being sprayed with mace would do to a normal human's eyes. I cough, paw at my muzzle.

Dad grabs hold of the thick fur on the nape of my neck with both hands, shakes me. I snarl, almost attack him.

"Luke!" he's saying. "Son, calm down. Think."

I manage to control myself, even though I feel like fighting, howling, clawing at my nose until it bleeds. The corridor has been flooded with a mixture of smells, harsh, chemical, overwhelming. Probably through the air vents and not by accident. A measure just in case someone like Uncle Cal—or me—escaped their control and started coming after them. If I was merely a wolf this would have driven me mad. I come close to doing so. I snap my jaws, biting at the air in front of me.

"Think!" Dad says again, shaking me a second time. His voice is like a lifeline for a drowning swimmer. I hold onto it. I open my eyes, look at his face, dangerously close to my gaping jaws but trusting me. I am more than a wolf. More than a wolf! I take a breath, relax the muscles of my neck.

"Dad . . . I'm . . . all *rrright.*"

"Good," he says, letting go of me.

But it's not good . . . and I'm not really all right. The sense of smell that has been with me all of my life, guiding me more during the last few days than almost any other sense, is not working for me. The rank, confusing miasma that has filled this corridor is preventing me from picking out any one trail, especially the one that I was following. Maybe I'll be able to adjust to this with time. But time isn't something we have much of right now. And it is for sure not on our side.

I shake my head again, trying to clear my sinuses. This is like the world's worst head cold, flu, and sore throat combined and all of it located in my olfactory lobes.

"Want me to lead?" Dad asks.

I nod. Even speaking is hard right now.

"Okay." Dad studies the intersecting corridors ahead of us. "Now let's see. In that partial schematic I saw . . ." he says in a soft voice, talking to himself. He nods, jerks his chin toward the right. "This way."

It's like walking through heavy mist. Even though whatever has been pumped into the air isn't visible to human eyes, I feel half-blinded. Like my father, I've never had a cold—or any kind of illness for that matter. I've never thought anything about it before, just figured we had unusually good health, rather than that we had a special genetic inheritance that made us resistant to such germs—among other things. As a result, I've never suffered a stuffy nose or anything that diminished my sense of smell. Not until now.

Focus, Luke.

You still have your eyes and ears. Use them.

We move down the hall.

The air is a little clearer now, but my nose is still not fully working. The lights in the corridor have all dimmed to the point of almost going out and we're moving through near darkness. Even with my wolf vision, it's hard to make out anything beyond my father's broad back ahead of me. That's why I don't see or smell them until they come boiling out at us.

RATS

"Look out!" Dad yells.

Though I'm in my skinwalking shape, Dad's eyes are quicker than mine.

He steps back and fires the AK-47 from his hip at something close to the floor in the shadows ahead of us. The rattling sounds of the shots and the whine of ricocheting bullets mix with angry squeals and the thud of bullets hitting flesh.

I still don't see anything. The smell of cordite from the gun barrel is strong enough for me to catch its odor along with another ranker stench that makes me want to puke.

My father kicks at something, fires another burst. A blurred black shape the size of a Labrador retriever squeezes past him. There's a sharp pain in my thigh, like a searing knife tearing at me. I drop down on all fours, bite the beast attacking me, and shake hard. The satisfying sound of a neck breaking is recompense enough for the bad taste of its blood and flesh.

I see out of the corner of my eye that my father has dropped the AK-47. He's now pulled out the long heavy Bowie knife he'd taken from the weapons chest. He's spinning, striking, slashing with the kind of efficiency only one who's worked with such weapons for years can master.

But I have just a split second to take that in. More of those black creatures, giant rats, are swarming over me. Snapping their teeth, drooling yellow saliva.

Rats, the animals I hate the most. I grab one by its snaky three-foot-long tail with a paw hand, spin it once, then smash it so hard against the wall that it falls in a limp heap. Another red-eyed rat claws up my shoulder, trying to sink its yellow teeth into my throat. I roll to crush it beneath my weight.

I don't know how many my father's gunshots took down or how many are engaged with him right now, but I have at least six more of these slimy creatures to deal with. Their teeth are slashing, their long claws scratching. My furred skin is thick, but I may be bleeding in a hundred places. However, I'm no longer feeling any pain. Adrenaline has kicked in, as well as all those hours of martial arts training my parents gave me. I'm fighting both like a wolf and a black belt. Blocking and striking, clawing and biting. Turn in a circle so that the attack goes past us, use each opponent's momentum against it. All that my mind can focus on right now is the fight. I'm turning, throwing them off me, hurling them through the air, following to leap and get in a killing bite. Biting, shaking, killing.

"Luke."

It's my father's voice that cuts through the crimson cloud surrounding me.

"Luke! We got them all."

I drop the last body, but not before giving it one final, satisfying shake.

I rise to two legs. There's blood all over me, but not that much of it is mine after all. I look myself over. There's only that wound in my thigh and a couple of smaller slashes on my shoulder and my right forearm.

Dad's clothing is torn, but he seems to have fared even better than I did. The only wound I see is a gash on his cheek. He bends to wipe the Bowie knife off on one of the dead creatures then sheathes the blade.

"Rats," he growls. His voice is almost as wolfish as mine. He's no more a fan of rodents than I am. One of the creatures twitches. Dad steps forward and stomps hard on its chest, cracking ribs and stopping whatever heartbeat was left.

"There," he says, motioning with his head toward an opening in the wall that doesn't look large enough for a house cat to squeeze through. A normal rat can push its way through a crack that looks smaller than its head, so I'm not surprised. "That's where they came from, all thirty of them."

"*Thirrrty?*"

"Count 'em."

I look around. Yup. There's thirty of them. Thirty more little obstacles that Yuri and his cohorts will not have to worry about as they follow our trail. But they've not caught up with us yet. I suspect that they may be encountering some other equally delightful delays.

Dad smiles as he wipes the cut on his face with a cloth he's taken from the pack. "You done good, Son."

The cut on his face has already stopped bleeding, just as my wounds have.

It hits me then that Dad doesn't have any scars. I never thought much about the fact that my own healing—even before I found my second skin—was quicker than most. Dad also doesn't have any tattoos, unlike most military men. Does that mean his skin would get rid of a tattoo as easily as it heals itself? I'd always planned to get a tattoo or two myself. I even had a few neat designs sketched out, including a line of wolf tracks around my upper arm and a rising sun on my back. I may have to give up that plan. Of course, there is one little additional detail—I have to survive this hellhole to have any future plans at all.

"*Rrrats*," I say. "I hate *rrrats*."

Dad's grin gets wider. "But at least it's not as bad as . . ."

"Snakes . . . on a . . . plane," I reply, grinning back at him.

"There," Dad says, indicating a door at the end of this latest left-hand turn. "That looks likely."

My sense of smell has returned to me. And the scent I've been following now, as easily as Theseus followed Ariadne's string, is that of Meena. And despite the joke Dad and I just shared, I'm more and more worried. We've been walking ever deeper into the warren of tunnels, taking one turn and then another. Luckily, we've not encountered any further genetically modified obstacles. But there has to be at least one more giant rat in this labyrinth, if not a minotaur.

The door my father is referring to is different than any of the previous ones. For one, it's slightly larger and the Maxico symbol on it, that exaggerated M with the golden circle and lightning bolts around it, is bigger. The door is closed, of course, just as the ones behind us were before we opened them and jammed their locking mechanisms. That way we can always beat a quick retreat if we walk into yet another ambush—as we fully expect. Plus the way is open, we hope, for Yuri and his crew to catch up to us.

This final door has a portal in the top third of it so you can see through to the other side. The glass may be thick as that in a bathysphere, a diving bell made to withstand tons of pressure per square inch miles underwater.

There's no wheel on this door, though, only a control panel next to it with a keypad. Whatever is on the other side of that door is important. Perhaps it's what we've been hoping to find. The nerve center that is hidden deep in the heart of the complex. This is where Boris's serum and Vlad's virus would be most effective. This is where they must have taken Meena and her father. And this is where the ones who run this place—

"Hello, doggies," an urbane voice booms in through a hidden loudspeaker. "I have you both now."

A round smug face appears in the window in front of us, smirking at us from the other side. Dr. Kesselring.

I hear something behind us, a mechanism being activated, something moving. I turn to look. Fifty feet behind a seemingly solid section of the wall we just passed has just opened to allow a concealed door to slide swiftly out across the passageway. The *thunk* as it presses against the other wall tells me that it has now sealed us into an airtight chamber.

As simple as that. We're trapped.

I throw my body against the door, bounce off it. It's as solid as a wall of granite.

There's a hissing sound. Even with my overwhelmed sense of smell I start to detect another odor, one that is sickeningly sweet, making my head swim.

"Nighty-night, my pets," Kesselring intones, adjusting his glasses with his left hand as he peers through at us. "May flights of angels sing thee to thy rest."

68 UNNATURAL SELECTION

I drop down to all fours snarling. My father is digging into the pack with one arm while holding his other arm over his nose and mouth. He's trying to find the .45 Colt he stuffed in there. The AK-47 fires a small round. Nowhere near powerful enough. It would just bounce off rather than punch through the thick glass of the portal through which Kesselring is leering at us like a demented jack-o-lantern. Even the .45 may not have enough mass and velocity. Despite the gas hissing around us, the desperate nature of our situation, there's a part of me that is thinking. Not just thinking about what we can do, but also about how we got here.

Why is our blood, our DNA that Dr. Kesselring and his cohorts covet to make them into wealthy, powerful, and possibly immortal rulers of the earth, so unlike that of others? Where did we come from? Why are we so different from other human beings? Or are we human beings at all?

Only a week ago when I was in the school library—a place and time that seem as long ago and far away from me now as a distant galaxy—I read an article in *Discovery* magazine about the human brain that surprised me. It discussed recent research that has proven there've been significant changes in the human brain over the last four thousand years.

I'll bet you already think you know what those changes are. Human brains have gotten larger than those of our ancestors from millennia ago, right? Wrong. The brains of our Cro-Magnon grandparents ten thousand years ago were bigger. And until about four thousand years ago they stayed big. Then they began to shrink to the point that they're, on average, smaller by about the size of a baseball. A loss of about twenty-five percent.

How to explain that? One scientist theorized it was like the difference between our docile domestic animals and their wild forebears. A wolf has a bigger brain than a dog's and is better at solving problems involving its survival in the natural world, including things like avoiding human traps that a dog will stumble into. There was another theory, too, that tied into that one. The reason for the change is capital punishment. That bigger brain held more capacity for aggression and when humans showed too much of that aggression other humans would either kick them out into the cold—where they'd be less likely to survive—or condemn them to death. So those aggressive big-brain genes would not get passed down. Unnatural deselection. And if a man could turn into a wolf, it's a no-brainer what would happen to him.

Except there were a select few who learned they had to hide such difference, control their aggression, mask their true nature. Band together and stay alive. Shape-shifters, upyrs . . .

My brain is moving so fast that I've thought all of that in less time than it has taken for my father to try a dozen different combinations on that keypad. None of them have worked. The door is not moving. Kesselring's predatory face is still floating in it, gloating, round and pale as a malignant moon.

The moon. The real moon. The thought of that celestial body that has always drawn me like nothing else, that must still be high in the sky somewhere far above gives me strength. I raise myself up onto my hind legs. I'm in the body of a beast, but I am more than a beast. I'm also a human and not just any human. For the last decade and more I've been trained by my father and Uncle Cal to focus, to concentrate my strength, to do things that most people never believe they can do.

There's a power at our center that is call *ki* in Japanese, *chi* in Chinese. If you concentrate it, you can generate supernatural strength. A human hand, with its weak flesh and fragile bones, can smash a pile of concrete blocks. If you focus.

Chi, the moon, Dad, my mother, Meena, all that has ever inspired love in me. I blend that with the anger and frustration, all the loss and disappointment. I turn it into a single white-hot point, a flow of power and breath that comes from the center of my being.

"Ayyy-arrhh!"

My hammer-fist blow strikes the exact center of that glass window. Dr. Kesselring's face disappears from view as the double panes shatter into pebbles of bulletproof glass. I reach through, find the door handle.

Coughing, his arm still over his nose and mouth, my father stumbles through the door behind me. Some of the gas comes with us, swirling around us, but the sizable room we've entered is well-ventilated enough to dissipate its power.

My father lowers his arm and nods at me. "You have done well, Grasshopper."

Kung-fu humor. I bow my wolfish head. "Thank you . . . Miyagi-san."

A mixing of martial arts movie metaphors, I know, but Dad gets it.

But even as we are joking, we've moved so that we're standing back-to-back, able to scan the space around us for the further threats that we have no doubt are about to make themselves known.

What do I see? This room is not unusually large, maybe ten thousand square feet. No bigger than a midsize corporation's central area with a corridor leading to executive offices against the back wall. There's a bank of computer towers. To the right is laboratory space, including another of those glassed-in operating rooms, although this one looks bigger than the others I found on the floor far above us.

Aside from the air in the room being rippled by the whispering blower vents, nothing is moving. And apart from a pair of glasses with broken lenses and a small spatter of blood on the floor near the door, there's no sign of Kesselring.

I sniff the air. He's here. Not far away.

And he's not alone.

Far from it.

NOT DONE YET

"Not done yet," Dad says.

"I . . . know," I growl. I'm on all fours now, sniffing the air. I'm expecting to see Dr. Kesselring appear in the classic villain's pose—holding a gun to Meena's head, telling us to surrender or the girl gets it.

Get real, Luke. There's no reason for him to do that. Why would Kesselring think that a pitiless four-legged horror such as myself would have any feelings for a Pakistani girl just kidnapped to put pressure on her father? The only ones who know about my hopeless puppy love for her are my father and me and Renzo—who is home peacefully sleeping right now.

If what my nose tells me is right, Meena and her father are being held in a cell or a room connected to this one, far back there to the left. Kesselring's scramble away from us led him to the right. Toward attempted escape? Or to gather further reinforcements?

Which way to go?

"No, not us. They weren't done, Son. Look."

He raises the .45 in his right hand and nods to the left.

I see what he means. This nerve center is only half complete. Wires are still exposed, walls half built, floor areas empty where workstations might be installed. It's like the vast room upstairs that had only a few control modules in working order. Our invasion has come before this center for terror could go completely online or be fully staffed. Just as Yuri said, this was the time to attack—before Maxico's strength was at the max, before its power was so over-whelming we wouldn't have stood a chance. Those simulacra that attacked Yuri and his crew in the high school were only the first of what was meant to have been many using Uncle Cal's DNA—and my Dad's. The devil dogs and recombinant beasts we killed have not yet been joined by a large legion of brethren. If we'd come here a month later, there would have been an army of creatures ready to defend this place. It explains why Dad and I have met only sporadic resistance as we've made our way to this nerve center.

The Sunglass Mafia haven't reached us yet. I wonder what is taking them so long. Did they not see the signs we left for them, the doors propped open? They must have met some remaining human or recombinant pawns that delayed them. Probably the bulk of Maxico's remaining forces.

A smile curls my lips. I doubt that any of those defenders enjoyed their encounter with my bloodthirsty teenage upyr allies. Or survived it.

It's about time to start singing "Hail, hail, the gang's all here."

Come on guys, where are you? I think. Alda. *Let's roll.*

In response to that last thought of mine something touches me. It's like a strand from a spider's thread, a soundless sardonic whisper.

Vsyo po tikhonku, no worries. We will be there soon after we finish . . . dessert.

The image of Yuri and the others over the lifeless bodies of foes that failed to do more than slow their progress is one that might have disturbed me before I found my other self and became at least as deadly as they are.

My lips curl back from my teeth as I remember what Yuri said.

Kill them all, and let God sort out the innocent.

Hah! I doubt that, aside from Meena, there's any innocent person here. Alive, dead, or in-between.

"Heads up!" Dad yells.

He's already pivoted, dropped to one knee, and started firing before finishing those words of warning. Each .45 slug takes down one of the half-dozen devil dogs that have come silently out of nowhere.

Bullets from other guns are striking around us.

One round sears my cheek. I see red. I leap toward the armed sable-clad attackers coming from the other side. There's four of them, but I barrel into the first two, taking them down so hard that I hear the crack of breaking bones. These armed simulacra have appeared as suddenly as the dog creatures. But they haven't just materialized out of thin air. Dogs and semihumans alike have charged in from panels that opened in the walls. I slash at an arm, a leg, pull down the second two. Crunch bone, rend flesh. Tear out a throat, spit out rank flesh, stand growling over the pile of bodies.

The human part of me is still thinking even as the wolf part grabs one of the still-stirring simulacra by its neck to give it a final killing shake. Only four of them? No more coming?

Only four.

Is that all?

More, I want more!

But no more appear to attack us.

That may mean either of two things. The first is that there may be no more of these semihuman pawns to be put into play. I don't know how long it takes to manufacture them or how much DNA or blood they needed from Uncle Cal. They kept him a prisoner since his capture—almost two years ago. But I'm guessing that it was only recently that they finally had advanced their research to the point where they could start to use his vital fluids for their task of making monsters. And even after they started sucking his life from him, they'd needed to allow him to recover between their drainings—or they would lose their source. That had meant that he was able to stay alive. But he was their only source—it wasn't until they identified my father and me that they decided he was expendable and pulled so much from him that he couldn't recover.

Our arrival, I realize, growling as the thought comes to me, didn't save Cal. It killed him. I want to start howling.

The second thing that this seeming lack of further attackers may mean is that there are only a few sets of human hands down here to operate the simulacra from workstations hidden somewhere behind Kesselring. I study the scents in the air. The strongest is the rank odor, both animal and other, that comes from the dead creatures at our feet. Then there are the odors coming from those still living—Meena's, her father's, Kesselring's . . . and four other men. I smell them all, but I don't see them yet.

Dad has risen to his feet, reloaded, and then put the .45 into his belt. He unslings the AK-47 from his shoulder, pulls a new clip from the back and clicks it into the gun. Along with me, he's scanning the room, his left hand on the trigger of the rifle.

"Don't shoot." It's a human voice.

Those words are followed by the appearance of the one who said them. Hands over his head, a blue-clad man steps out from behind the main bank of computers. It's Rangerville Police Chief Roger Frank.

No, why shoot? Just rip out his throat.

I tense my muscles to leap, a growl building deep in my chest.

"Luke," Dad says.

He doesn't say no or tell me to stop, but I understand and hold myself back.

Dad gestures with his free right hand at Chief Frank.

"On your knees," Dad says. "Lace your fingers together on top of your head."

"Okay," Chief Frank says, his voice fast and nervous. "Okay, okay. Whatever you say!"

It's not easy for him to go down on his knees with his hands over his head. He has the body of a former football lineman after years of inactivity have allowed his muscles to settle into fat. He's staring at us with wide eyes. Well, more at me than us. I can smell the fear in him. But the look on his face, whose drooping jowls are only accentuated by his mustache, is not that of anyone I'd trust. If he was an animal, he'd be a hyena.

"He's crazy," Chief Frank says. "He don't care who he gets killed. You gotta protect me or he'll kill me for giving up. Honest Injun."

He's edging his way toward us on his knees as he keeps talking. Dad is noticing that, as am I.

"Where are the others?" Dad asks, his voice cold.

"There's just Kesselring, tha's all. Him and the Paki girl and her father. Tha's all, I swear," Chief Frank babbles. "We din't know what he was doing here. We was innocent. Tha's the truth. Once he brought us here and we saw it, we was going to tell. Honest Injun. That's why he had Phil and Jerry and Joe kilt."

He means, of course, his other policemen. Innocent men who had been trained to operate simulacra. How admirable that they were able to remain innocent after months of training to operate inhuman murder machines. After the accepted promises of wealth and power that must have led to their corruption. Innocent, all right. As innocent as concentration camp guards.

Frank's eyes are now almost bugging out of his head. Sweat is pouring down his face. I can smell something in that sweat. And it's not just his lying, which I could have detected even without my nose. It's amazing how many liars have to accompany their fabrications with such repeated protestations as "That's the truth," and "Honest Injun." That one little racist remark alone is enough to make me want to rip out his throat. I can also detect in his perspiration the scent of a synthetic drug of some kind, one that may be giving him the courage to do what he's trying to do. He doesn't know that I can smell the drug, the other three not-quite deceased policemen now attempting to flank us, the gun that he has concealed in a holster. He also doesn't know who he's dealing with—either my father or me. Even though the sight of me is making him nervous, this policeman thinks he has seen worse. And he's about to act.

"Dad," I growl.

"I know," Dad says. His voice is quiet, but there's iron in it. "Let me do this, Son." He holds out his open right hand and gestures palm down.

I drop down to all fours, get as low as I can to the floor.

My father lowers the barrel of the AK-47 as he takes a step forward. It's what Frank was waiting for. Moving faster than you'd think an overweight man could, the police chief rolls to one side as he reaches behind his neck to pull out a Glock.

Dad is faster. The .45 is back in his hand as if it leaped out of its belt by itself. The first shot hits the police chief center mass, the second opens a third eye in Frank's forehead. His eyes are filled with darkness before he stops rolling.

My father's hand speed may have thrown off the other three police officers. As they step out from three directions, they open fire wildly. Dad doesn't try to dodge. He once told me that standing still can be just as effective in a firefight as trying to duck and ruin your own aim. In the heat of battle, there's at least a hundred shots fired for every one that hits home. Stay calm and make every shot count. That, he said, was how some of the best gunfighters in the Old West won their battles.

Four more shots from the .45 in his right hand, three quick bursts from the AK-47 in his left.

That's all it takes. And now there are five fewer live human beings in this room.

I stand back up. More of the smell of smokeless powder and fresh blood now fills the air. But it doesn't dull my other sense. As the echoes of the gun blasts die, I hear something else. A new sound.

Dad lifts the hand holding the Colt. He hears it too.

70

I HAVE YOUR FRIEND

It's a whooshing, pneumatic sound coming from above and to the right of us. Another section of wall has opened thirty feet above our heads. A balcony is being pushed out. Standing behind something that looks like a cross between a keyboard and a ship's wheel is Dr. Kesselring. He's put on another pair of glasses, identical to the broken ones lying at our feet. Just the type to always keep a few spare pairs on hand. There's blood on his cheek, but other than that he looks unharmed.

I should have punched farther through that porthole window.

His face looks triumphant. And this is the point in the movie when the villain gloats over the hero and his pals, certain he has them where he wants them.

"You!" he screams down at us. "You . . ."

A stream of invective comes from his mouth regarding our origins and suggesting several anatomical impossibilities. Dad and I just look up at him. It's a little too high for me to reach with one jump. And the Plexiglas shield in front of Kesselring will probably stop any bullets from Dad's guns. Kesselring finally runs out of either insults or wind. He stands there, breathing hard, spittle coming out of his mouth. For sure not ready for a photo op.

He takes one final deep breath, then adjusts his glasses. He taps the screen in front of him and leans slightly forward.

"I have your friend," he says. The microphone he's just activated amplifies his whiny voice so that it echoes through the room. "And his daughter." He looks to his left and points theatrically. "Back there."

He slides his hand across the screen in front of him and yet another wall panel opens. I can see through the thick Plexiglas a small room—a prison cell more like. It's perhaps seven feet tall, four feet wide and four feet deep. There, sitting on the floor and looking exhausted, his face bruised and bloodied, is Dr. Kureshi. Meena stands next to him, one hand on her father's shoulder. The look on her face is not one of fear. She looks concerned, but also defiant. She doesn't seem to have been hurt.

There's a rumbling sound building. It is coming from my own throat.

I am going to kill Dr. Kesselring, whose wild laughter is now filling the room. He's so out of control and close to the mike that a shrill shriek of feedback is added to his hysteria.

Dad lifts his right hand and turns it palm up toward the side. American Indian sign language for no. He wants to me wait.

For what? But I hold the beast part of me in check, though my growl keeps building and my muscles are tensed, my jaws aching to crush his bones.

Professor Kureshi lifts his head and looks out of his cell at us. He's been hurt, but there's the same strength left in him that I can see in Meena. He reaches up, takes her hand, and stands. He mouths my father's name, then points as me. I can lipread what he says next.

Luke? Your boy?

My father nods.

Meena looks up at her father in surprise. She's heard what he said. She's looking at me now. What is she seeing? A terrible nightmare? Something that her mind cannot grasp? A beast to scream and hide from?

I want to look away, whimper and bury my head in my paws. But I can't. I may never see her again. It's not melodramatic to fear that we may both perish here, that her last memory of me will be of Luke, the monster. But I have to look at her.

My eyes meet her beautiful eyes.

Can she see me here within my second skin?

Meena doesn't look away. She reaches up her hand and brushes back her long, dark hair. She takes a breath and then leans forward. Close to the glass wall that holds her prisoner. I lip-read what she is saying.

Luke. Luke. Save us.

71
YOU'RE MINE NOW

Dr. Kesselring has calmed down now. He's studying us over the top of his glasses. The superior smirk is back on his face but I can also sense that he's a bit disappointed my father has not said anything. He nods, leans back toward the microphone.

Looks like we are going to get the megalomaniac evil mastermind's rant after all.

"NOW," Kesselring says. The screech of feedback that interrupts him spoils the effect. He taps the panel in front of him to turn down the volume.

"Now," he repeats, "you're mine. You're alone. By now the traps we set have eliminated those other intruders you invited into my facility. All you've done is cause a minor setback in my plans. And, thanks to you"—he points at me—"I'm going to have more than enough of a . . . supply to progress even further toward my goal. You're not going to die. Oh no, you're going to keep on living for a very long time while we extract all that we need from you."

He pauses to smile mirthlessly at me. "It will not be at all comfortable for you. However, I shall be quite comfortable as I build and build my power and finances, thanks to you. I shall be able to manufacture as many totally loyal lethal HKUs—humanoid killing units, of course—as the market needs." Another smirk. "And the market is already demanding more than I can provide, and will be growing even further as other . . . clients . . . realize they need what I can supply. Even better, this time I shall surely accomplish my goal of using your freakish mutation to make something of even greater value. A means of cellular regeneration that shall both stop and reverse the aging process." Kesselring chuckles. "Did you ever think of yourself, my little fanged horror, as a furry fountain of youth?"

Kesselring pauses. Is he about to say what I think he is, about to complete the cliché?

"And as I continue to live without aging, year after year, decade after decade, I will be able to continue building my wealth, my power, my influence. Then, finally, I SHALL RULE THE WORLD."

Yup, he said it.

A sound comes from somewhere else in this room. It's a combination of a moan of despair and a muted throaty roar. Kesselring looks in the direction of that sound. Off to his left and below him. A visible shiver goes down his back. He shakes his head.

"Poor Rogan," he says, talking to himself with not a trace of sympathy in his voice. "So sad. No, we shall not hurry this time as my, ah, unfortunate colleague did." Kesselring shakes his head. "Poor foolish Rogan with his Balkan impatience."

Whatever happened to Rogan is not something Kesselring is happy about. But neither my father nor I are about to ask him. My father has his right hand out, palm down.

Wait. I keep waiting.

And I sense something. A presence behind us just outside the door. I smell them and also feel them with that sixth sense that speaks inside my mind.

We are here.

I curl my lips back showing my teeth in a wolfish grin. Maybe Yuri will tell me later just what traps had been set for them and how they got through them. Or maybe not. It really doesn't matter. The final act in this drama is about to be played out.

The roaring moan is repeated, louder this time. Kesselring is looking in that direction, his eyes turned away from us.

Come in now, I think.

I watch their entrance out of the corner of my eye. They move so fast that they've reached the wall below Kesselring's extruded balcony before he can turn his gaze back in the direction of Dad and me. Dad takes no more notice of them than to slightly raise one eyebrow in my direction.

They've protected themselves better than in the high school gym. Helmets that protect their heads and necks, plexi-shields to stop any missiles fired at them. There are rips in their clothing, cracks in their shields. Whatever was thrown at them may have delayed their arrival, but it didn't stop them. Vlad, the biggest target among them, has so many wood-tipped bolts still stuck in his armored body that he looks like a porcupine. He nods at me and gives me a thumbs-up as he smiles, a grin that displays the blood on his lips and his long canines.

Boris, the biochemist, is holding a gun with a compact suppressor screwed onto its barrel. With his other hand he pulls the small black canister out of his pocket, shows it to me. It contains the virus to contaminate and destroy the biological medium used to produce Maxico's monsters. Now Boris just has to find the source—somewhere in this nerve center.

Yuri has his back to me. He's found a keypad on the wall,

places something that looks like a refrigerator magnet on it. A wide door slides open and stays open. It discloses yet another room, one with more computers and devices. The seven enter. As I watch out of the corner of one eye, Vlad approaches a computer terminal. Boris, a large smile on his face, stands in front of something that looks from my vantage point like a large washing machine. Boris puts down his guns, spreads out his hands in a sort of "Ah, now!" gesture, and then leans over the machine.

It's taken no longer than a few seconds. Kesselring hasn't noticed. He's looking down at us again, poised to say something. Neither Dad nor I make a sound. We just stand here, my father on his two legs and me on all fours, looking up at him.

Kesselring takes a breath, seems to be lost in thought. Then he turns his attention to the control panel in front of him.

For a brief second, the lights in the room flicker. Kesselring looks back over his shoulder then shrugs, unaware what that brief loss of power really means. Vlad has plugged in his program. Suddenly, silently, the door in the wall that the Sunglass Mafia passed through into that control room has now closed behind them. I can no longer see my upyr allies.

"Now," Kesselring says, "enough of the pleasantries and chit-chat. Time to conclude this conversation, doggies."

He taps the screen in front of him. Waits. Looks up, looks left and then right. Nothing happens. He taps it again, sweeps his hand across it. Still nothing. Apparently whatever he expected to occur as a result doesn't. Knockout gas sprayed over us? A net dropped from the ceiling? Kesselring adjusts his glasses, taps the panel again, harder this time. Not working for sure. His face is troubled. It's almost as if he's forgotten we're here.

With a visible effort, he manages to control himself.

"A minor glitch," he says to himself, his nasal voice a bit higher.

"Let's see if this works." He looks down at us. "Something to keep you occupied, doggies. You've already seen the Lady." He looks over at Meena, peering out from the cell where she and her father are held captive. Meena's eyes widened slightly at the silent entrance of the upyrs. Maybe she recognized them as the Sunglass Mafia, despite their bloodied and armored appearance. But she was careful not to stare in their direction, not to give anything away in case Kesselring was looking at her. There's no expression other than defiance on her face or the face of her father. Nothing that might give away to the good doctor that anything even more out of the ordinary than the insanity of this hellhole is happening. Just as there was no terror, no disgust on her face when she saw me and knew me. I can't believe how self-contained she is in this awful situation. It makes me even more determined to do anything I can to save her, even if it means sacrificing my life.

"Now," Kesselring says. "it is time to meet the Tiger!"

He reaches over and flicks a switch. The electric relay to that actually works. Yet another panel in the wall opens, perhaps forty feet to the left of the small door that the upyrs just used and right next to the cell where Meena and her father are held.

I take a step back in horror at what it discloses.

It's the grue.

72

DEAD SOULS

One of the greatest books in Russian literature is Nicolai Gogol's
Dead Souls. It explores human nature in a way that lays bare the
potential for love and hate, for pain and loss that is in every human
being.

Everything, Gogol says, can happen to a man.

It also depends on who that man is, what is at the core of that
man's being. I've put on the skin of a wolf, become a mixture of
human and something other than human. But, like my father, I
haven't sacrificed my humanity by doing that. Pity, empathy, and
even love are still with me, guiding me, holding me back from giving in to rage or bloodlust or a callous indifference to all other life.
I didn't become the grue.

But what if I'd already been one, even though I was walking
around in human form? What if I'd already killed others or ordered
their deaths? What if all I really cared about was dominance and my
own self-interest?

"Behold the Beast." Kesselring's voice flutes down at us triumphantly as he gestures at the once-human creature that stares at us from behind the thick glass of its cage. It's standing on two feet, but its resemblance to a human being ends there. Like the grue, it's massive, at least seven feet tall. Its furred skin is mottled like the pelt of a jaguar. It has the heavy musculature and the fangs and claws of a great predatory cat. But it's not its size, or its teeth and claws that are so terrible to see. It's the whole demeanor of the creature, the mad look in its eyes.

Kill, that look says. *Kill.*

The creature hears Kesselring's words, turns to look up at him on his perch above us.

"Hello, Rogan," the doctor says. "I told you that it wasn't ready, didn't I? But you just had to go and do it? Impulsive as always. I warned you that you were going too fast with your treatments. *Nicht* so? Just as I told you that you were draining too much from our subject, that it was going to kill him. Didn't I? And now look at you. What shall I call you now? ManCat? *Nein*, you haven't changed all that much, have you? We can just use your old nickname from Bosnia, *ja*? Rogan the Beast. That will do, won't it?"

The soulless being that was once Rogan Machescou strikes the glass in front of it with a huge taloned paw.

The doctor points toward me. "Now the DNA of that one there, that might have suited you better. I am sure it will suit me. But you, ah, alas, too late." He holds his hand over a second switch. "Shall I press this one? Set you free so that you can amuse yourself with them?" He shakes his head. "No, enjoyable as that might be to watch, I do not want to waste any of my little doggy's valuable blood."

The lights suddenly flicker again, then they go out entirely and we are plunged into stygian darkness. Whatever Vlad did to the system with his virus is continuing to affect the mainframe insofar as it controls the facility's power. The blackout lasts only for a second before I hear a deep hum from somewhere beneath us as backup generators turn on and the lights return. But a second was all that it took. The heavy glass doors that front the two cells slide open.

"Get . . . back," I snarl at Meena. She hears me, pulls her father by the arm, drawing him back with her into the corner of their cell.

"I'll draw it off," Dad shouts. "Hey! Hey!" He steps forward, waving one arm to attract the attention of the beast while aiming his heavy automatic at it.

However, the creature that was Rogan Machescou pays no attention to him. It stalks slowly and silently out of its cell, its eyes fixed on the doctor above us.

Dad holds his fire, seeing that what is about to happen might not have to involve us. He begins to slowly back up toward Meena and her father. I place myself in front of the entrance to the cell with Meena and her father.

"Luke, are you all right?" Meena whispers from behind me.

"Quiet," I growl.

"Rogan," Kesselring is pleading, his voice high and thin, "I'm sorry about what happened. Go back into your room, *ja?* We will do something to reverse what you've, ah, become. Be patient, *mein freund.* I help you, *nicht wahr?*"

The beast is now directly below the balcony. It's opening and closing its paws, flexing the long claws on them. My father looks over at us from the place where he stands. I eye the AK-47 over his shoulder, the .45 in his hand. Dad shakes his head. Bullets might distract it, but they probably won't kill this creature. Like me, it's almost invulnerable to such puny human weapons.

Kesselring is reaching down under the control panel, trying to find something while he keeps his eyes glued on his former partner.

"Ja, gut," he says. He pulls it out with some effort. It's a long-barreled gun. He lifts it awkwardly to his shoulder, steps to the side of the clear shield so that he can lean over the railing and point it down.

His tone changes now. He begins speaking as if he was an adult dealing with a difficult and not very bright child.

"Sehen sie? See the big gun? Remember this, Rogan? Explosive rounds, you know. *Ja.* You don't want me to use this on you, do you? *Nein.* It will hurt you. So just go back to your room, *mein guter freund."*

The creature stares up at him with unblinking eyes. I can see that it is slowly beginning to crouch, gathering itself for a leap that might just take it high enough to reach that balcony.

"Isvini, excuse me," says an ironic Russian voice from behind Kesselring. Yuri glides out onto the balcony from the doorway behind him.

Startled, the doctor tries to turn his gun toward Yuri. The barrel, though, catches on the edge of the plastic shield. The gun is knocked out of Kesselring's hands. It falls toward the beast below—who swats the weapon off to the side. It clatters away across the floor. Meanwhile, in his futile attempt to grab the rifle, Dr. Kesselring has lost his balance. As Yuri watches, face impassive, the doctor windmills his arms and then, almost in slow motion, topples back over the railing.

It might have killed him had he hit the floor. But he doesn't. The creature that had been his cohort gathers the doctor's heavy body out of the air as easily as an adult catching a small child. Then it lifts him, clawed hands under Kesselring's arms so that they are face-to-face.

"Good man, Rogan," Kesselring squeaks. "Now put me down and . . ."

He never finishes that sentence. The beast opens its jaws wide, thrusts forward, bites . . . and drops the dead doctor's headless body onto the floor.

Kesselring's story may have just reached the end of its final chapter, but ours is not yet over. The creature looks up at the balcony. Yuri is gone. So, perhaps, are all of his friends. They've done their job. Why stick around?

But we're still here. The beast sniffs the air, turns in our direction, and then screams. It's not a roar like that of the lion creature I killed. It is far more human and thus far more bloodcurdling. It's full of not just anger, but soul-dead torment. Nothing will satisfy it other than killing and more killing. One step at a time, like a tiger stalking its prey, it moves toward us. Maybe all it has is power, but not speed.

It's between us and the gun that Kesselring dropped. That might be the only thing that can stop it. It takes a slow step in our direction, lowers its head. My father raises the Colt .45, steps forward, drops into a classic shooter's stance.

Blam!Blam!Blam!Blam!Blam!Blam!

Despite the speed of his shooting and the fact that the creature is a hundred feet away, every shot hits home in a tight pattern.

The man-beast pauses for a moment, rubs at its chest the way a man might when he's been stung by a wasp. But it had no more effect than that. It raises its head and roars, readies itself to rush at us with the speed of a runaway locomotive.

My father tosses the .45 to the side, raises the AK-47 as he backs toward the cell where I'm guarding the entrance.

I snarl, brace myself for a leap at the monster's throat.

Ka-boom! The heavy concussive sound of a big gun is almost deafening in this room. The explosive round that thuds into the beast's shoulder unbalances it and halts its charge. It spins to the side and snarls back at the one who just picked up the long gun dropped by the late doctor.

I'm wrong, it seems, on two counts. My first error was assuming that my Russian *druzhoks* has deserted us. The one holding the rifle is Vlad. Great. Not so great is my second mistake. The expectation that the big gun would seriously injure the Rogan-beast. That explosive round had only a minimal effect.

Ka-boom. The second shot Vlad lets go hits the creatures in its belly. It might as well have been fired at body armor. Vlad doesn't have time for a third shot. The beast has covered the ground between them in two swift leaps. Vlad tries to step to the side, use the rifle butt as a club. No time for that. A clawed talon rakes his arm, stripping away the gun as the other paw engulfs his face. He's down and the snarling beast is on top of him, about to tear out his throat.

I understand now why Yuri was afraid of me, why the upyrs as a whole have little love for my kind. We're that much stronger than they are. One of us could probably tear apart seven of them. But I don't stop to ponder that.

I attack. I hit the creature with my whole body so hard that it's knocked off Vlad, who lays there limp. Unconscious or dead, I can't tell—and don't have time to check. I'm a mite too busy just now.

Somehow the beast ends up on top of me. Its massive jaws are clamped on my right front leg. Even over its mad snarl and my own angry growl, I can hear the creak of bones about to break. My own—though I'm not feeling the pain yet. Its shoulder is between my jaws. I'm trying to work my teeth up to its throat, but its weight on me is too heavy. Things are beginning to turn black.

Suddenly a muscular arm reaches around the beast's throat, pulls it back. Is it my father's arm? No, that arm is as hairy as my own legs, but the pattern of fur is mottled like that of the cat creature on top of me. A head, half human, half animal, thrusts itself over the beast's shoulder. For just a second those familiar eyes meet mine. Eyes that I never thought to see again in this life.

"Gimme back my blood, you son of Satan," Uncle Cal snarls as he sinks his teeth into the throat of the creature that was once Rogan Machescou. Their weight rolls off me. I manage to pull myself up, rising to two feet because my right front leg can't seem to bear any weight. The two werebeasts are tearing at each other with their claws, but Uncle Cal's throat hold on the creature that was Rogan Machescou is too tight for it to break, even though it is larger and stronger than he is. All it has is power and anger. Uncle Cal still has his soul to give him strength.

The struggle is no longer so furious. The beast isn't yet dead; it's still digging its claws into Uncle Cal's side and his belly, though it's almost a reflex motion now. Cal is terribly wounded, but I know he won't let go until it's dead or he is. My father steps close to them. He has the heavy rifle in his hands. He lifts it and aims at one of the staring rage-filled eyes of Rogan Machescou.

"Go to hell," he says and pulls the trigger. The explosive round penetrates the beast's brain and it goes limp. Dad puts down the gun slowly, kneels by Uncle Cal's side. I stumble over to them. I can hear and smell Meena and her father coming to join us. Meena's hand gently falls on my shoulder. But all I can look at is Uncle Cal.

Cal smiles up at me. Even in this shape it's the same old smile. "Mine own Telemachus," he whispers. "What can I say now? Already done used my best line for dying."

"How?" I growl.

"Your blood, Nephew. It fell on my skin, it brought me back, gave me just enough life to put it on one more time, follow after you. Sorry it took me so long to get here."

My dad is holding Cal's big paw in his hand. His other hand rests on Cal's chest. "I love you, Brother," he says.

Cal closes his eyes. His body goes limp.

There are tears running down my father's face as he looks over at me. Can a wolf cry? Maybe not, but a man wearing his second skin can. Meena is sobbing softly behind me and I love her that much more for sharing the pain we're feeling.

Cal's left eye opens and he looks up at us.

"Why you all crying like that? This is stupid. I'm just fine."

Then, leaving none of us quite sure what to do, he does close his eyes and he really does die, with the quiet satisfaction of having played one last joke.

73

HAPPY ENDINGS?

Happy endings. Isn't that how it is supposed to be resolved? That's the way it is in the big budget movies, the sappy television shows, and the YA novels I used to read in the school library—even the ones with vampires and werewolves as main love interests. Love conquers all. The bad guys defeated, the heroine rescued. And the good guy always gets the girl.

But what if he's not really good? Or, for that matter, a guy in the sense of being a normal human being? And what if the girl, even if she was crazy enough to accept someone who can transform himself into a beast out of your worst nightmare, is someone whose real home is half a world away?

Why don't I feel like I've won?

Yes, Maxico is no more. But the bad guys are never really defeated. There's just one batch beaten and another waiting in the wings to carry on the fight. Jobs and food and even water may be in increasingly short supply all around the world. But there's never any scarcity of hatred or greed. And there were, according to my father, other backers of Maxico beyond the late, lamented Machescou and Kesselring. Though we may have destroyed all that was done here, others may be attempting something similar elsewhere in the world. In North Korea, maybe, or the mountains of Yemen.

Dad doesn't seem to be in that much better of a mood than I am. We're each sitting on the end of the twin beds in the motel room we've been living in for the past week on the eastern outskirts of Rangerville, a good seven miles away from the Drake House and on the other side of town from where Maxico used to be. Even though we're the owners of a mansion, Dad thinks it's still not safe to openly go there. He's hinted that there may be more secrets there beyond that room where my second skin is safely stashed. I'm looking out the window and he's holding a picture in his hand and staring at it. I don't have to look to see whose picture it is. Mom's.

Dad sighs and turns to look at me. "You okay, Luke?"

I don't even try to lie. "No."

How can I be, thinking of all that's been lost, no matter what victory we may have achieved?

"Uh-huh," Dad says. "They say it's always darkest before the dawn. But what do you do when the sun comes up and it's still not a new day? Come here."

I move over to sit next to him and he puts an arm around my shoulder like he used to do when I was little. "Too much to process, eh, Son?"

"More than enough," I answer. I hold out a hand. "But, like Uncle Cal used to say, at least it's not raining."

The clap of thunder that sounds from outside—like an ironic reply to my remark—startles us both. Then we both start laughing. It's a deep laugh, as painful as it is funny. But it's what we've needed to do. We laugh so hard that we end up rolling on the floor, holding our sides. And when the laughter passes, there are tears in both our eyes.

"Somehow," Dad says, "it's going to be all right." He stands up in one graceful, fluid motion. His old strength has come back quickly during the days of recuperation we've both had. He may have deliberately shed his wolf skin to be more human, but he still has far more physical strength than most normal humans. Plus, what Uncle Cal said makes me think that story of Dad's burning his second skin may not have been the entire truth. There's so much I still have to learn about my father and his life—especially now that my own is more like his.

About a week has passed since the four of us—Meena, her father, my dad, and me—left Maxico behind us in one of those black cars left parked outside the wall. Dad and me in the front. Meena and her father in the back. None of us saying anything. Our first stop was that high hill where Dad left me that message. That was where we took Uncle Cal's body out of the trunk of the car and buried him at the foot of the old tree.

We didn't remain together long after that. We dropped Meena and her father at their home on the better side of town. Before we drove off and left them there, though, Meena pulled me out of the car to hug me hard and then kiss me—on the lips. There was no protest from Professor Kureshi. Probably because he figured it was the last time she'd ever see me. I'm sure they're well on their way back to Pakistan by now.

Dad and me, after contacting the authorities to let them know he was back in town and available to handle whatever else needed to be done regarding the destruction of our trailer, retreated to the Best Suites Motel. We checked in a full two hours before the explosions that lit up the sky to the west of the town. This week of rest and isolation has helped my own wounds heal too. Even the broken bones. There's just a tiny bit of residual stiffness here and there to remind me of that awful last battle.

When I called Renzo, to find out how much he remembered of what he'd seen and what I'd told him, I was relieved to find that his memory seemed to have been wiped clean of every dangerous fact I'd shared with him, from my Dad's abduction to the Sunglass Mafia and everything that had to do with Maxico.

"So," he said, "want to get together, seeing as how we got a week off from school? Make some music."

"Sorry," I replied, adding a theatrical cough, "I'm laid up with the flu. Contagious."

"Later, then?"

"Later."

But does later mean never?

"Luke?" Dad's voice brings me out of my reverie. He holds out his hand. I take it with my left hand, let him pull me erect.

Dad looks me up and down. "Is it possible for you to have grown two inches taller overnight?" he asks.

"What isn't possible . . . overnight?" I ask, purposely lowering my voice into a near growl. "Aside from a normal life?"

Dad raises one eyebrow.

"What do you want, Luke?" He lifts both hands as he asks this and holds them palm out with a shrug. It's a gesture that means he is asking that question in the context of who I am, who he is, what we've both done.

What does any teenager want, normal or abnormal? To just not get hassled? To feel good about myself? To have friends and be liked? To find love, somehow, crazy as that seems? Especially now after having lost Meena forever, most likely. To figure out what I want to do with my life? To do something that means something?

To be like my Uncle Cal. Like my father?

"All of the above," I answer, figuring that Dad already knows what I'm thinking.

Dad presses the picture of my mother against his head for a second with the palm of his hand before slipping it into the breast pocket of his shirt. I'm not sure he even is aware when he does that. He purses his lips together as he looks at me.

"Tell you what, Luke. There's a lot ahead of you. A lot of decisions you're going to have to make. Especially if you take," he looks into the palms of his hands as if reading a map, "this road." A smile comes to his face, a truly pleased look. "But you don't have to make all those decisions yet. There's more possible than you think, Son. The first thing you need to do is stay on the path of education. Get as much of it as you can."

"Where?" I ask. "Where are we going?"

"For now," Dad says, that hint of a smile becoming broader, "nowhere."

"Huh?"

"Here," he says. "Monday morning tomorrow. School. Remember?"

That's right.

Though I've not given it much thought (seeing as how I'd assumed the two of us would be on the road again, heading for some new town and new names), life is finally more or less getting back to normal in Rangerville.

The mysterious explosions that destroyed the Maxico facility had been so enormous that they damaged the entire power grid for fifty miles around. It was the lead story on the national news for two days. Blamed on the rupture of a gas line and the resultant secondary explosions of "various volatile substances used in manufacturing that were stored in great quantities at the plant," it turned the giant main building into an inferno. It also led to the weeklong total shutdown of the local schools until the restoration of power and order.

The total loss of life, the local news reported, may never be known due to the severity of the blaze which seems to have left no identifiable human remains. What seems certain is that it included not only an as yet undetermined number of outside contract employees domiciled at the plant, but apparently also Chief Roger Frank of the Rangerville Police. Further, Rangerville's beloved supervisor, the well-known philanthropist Dr. Edmund O. Kesselring, is assumed to have perished in the tragic accident, along with the international investor and Maxico CEO Rogan Machescou. The only fortunate aspect of the tragedy, according to Professor Hari Kureshi, who was not present at the event, but is the most senior surviving employee of the corporation, is that it occurred late at night, when only those residing in the central facility were present. Thus the mortality rate was lessened.

I'd smiled grimly and found myself growling deep in my throat as I listened to the TV announcer read those words.

"I'm going back to school . . . here?"

"Why not?" Dad asked. "Of course, some of your new friends won't be there."

Yuri, Boris, Natasha, Marina, Ekaterina, Igor, and Vlad. They'd actually come—quite late at night—to bid me farewell here in this motel room, the day after we'd checked in here. Dad had gone out to pick up a pizza for us and I was alone.

I'd sensed them before they knocked and limped over to open the door.

The seven of them slid into the room.

I limped back to the bed, propped a pillow behind my back, and looked at them, ranged in the familiar semicircle with Yuri at the head. They seemed to have healed faster than me—though it looked as if the marks on Vlad's cheek from Rogan's talons were going to be permanent, like Prussian dueling scars.

"*Nam pora*," Yuri said. "Time for us to go."

"I miss you, *lyubov moya*," Marina whispered as she leaned over to kiss my cheek. My love, eh. But there was less sultriness than usual in her tone and maybe a little actual regret.

Boris and Igor each held out a fist and I bumped them with my own, despite the fact that it jarred the still-healing bones in my left forearm.

"*Do skorovo. Do vstryechi.*"

See ya later. See ya soon.

Natasha and Ekaterina merely nodded and said "*Koka. Koka.*" Bye.

But Vladimir, my *druzhok*, was not that standoffish. Far from it. He placed a hand the size of a grizzly's paw on my shoulder.

"Kino lives, *da*? You keep making music?"

"*Da*," I agreed.

Vlad lifted me up off the bed in a bear hug that threatened to rebreak every bone that had started to mend.

"You saved my life, *bratan*," he rumbled. "Friends till death."

"*Da, Vova*," I managed to grunt out. "Just don't kill me now."

All seven of them had laughed at that. So had I. So hard that I closed my eyes for a moment. And when I opened them again the upyrs were gone. The only signs they'd ever been there were resting on my bedside table. Marina's collection of Ahkmatova's poems and a CD of *Kinoproby*, the Viktor Tsoi tribute album released in Leningrad in 2000 that I'd heard about but never seen before.

"You listening, Luke?" Dad asks, bringing me out of my Russian reverie. I'm wondering why his grin has gotten wide enough to split a jack-o-lantern.

"Yes," I said. "I'm going back to school."

Big deal, I'm thinking.

But then there's a knock on the door.

Dad looks at the clock on the wall. "Ten minutes late," he says. "Typical teenagers."

He stands up and opens the door.

Renzo is standing there. Meena is next to him.

"Hari," Dad is saying, "has decided to stick around here for at least the next year. There's clean-up work for both him and me to do and as long as . . ."

He's still talking, but I'm not listening. Renzo has grabbed my hand and Meena has just wrapped her arms around me and put her head on my shoulder.

"Are you ready to finally take me for that ride with you on your motorcycle?" Meena whispers.

This is as close to a happy ending as I'm going to get.

AUTHOR'S NOTE

There's a long and far from sinister connection between American Indian tribal nations and the wolves they often saw as relatives and as nations of their own—Wolf People. Lakota traditions tell how a long-ago wolf made the Milky Way—the great path across the sky that leads the way to the spirit land, and is called the Wolf Trail by more than one American Indian nation. When one becomes a scout—one who seeks out the enemy and defends his people— among many of the indigenous nations of the American continent, that man is often referred to as a Wolf. The Haudenosaunee (Iroquois) nations speak of how the wolf people have taught many things to humans, among them the lesson that all adults in a community must care for their children as do all of the grown animals in a wolf pack. The Wolf Clan, in fact, is one of the three main Haudenosaunee Clans. Among my own Abenaki people, our culture hero Gluskonba was often accompanied by two faithful companions, a black wolf and a white wolf. Rather than a vicious beast, the wolf is usually viewed as a creature that models cooperation, calm, and proper behavior.

I mention all this at the start because the most popular

European folk traditions often seem to view the wolf in a drastically different way—as an adversary, a deceiver, a dangerous beast to be exterminated. And when a human allies with the wolves—or becomes one—monstrous behavior seems to be the only result. Thus, the European conception of the shape shifter known as a werewolf nearly always seems to be of a being that is out of control and consumed by blood lust. It's an image that permeates popular culture. You would have to look long and hard to find any werewolf in the movies or on television that does not exhibit such mindlessly bestial behavior.

Having said all that, like many other Americans of every racial background, I grew up watching those films and TV shows, was entertained and fascinated by stories of werewolves in books and on the silver screen. I've always loved fantasy and science fiction and have even taught courses in it on the college level. And I've been researching the subject of werewolves for years. (One of the books I often referred to while writing *Wolf Mark* is *The Werewolf Book*, Visible Ink, 1999, a truly encyclopedic look at shape-shifting beings from ancient times to the end of the 20th century.) Thus, there is an awareness of that heritage of horror in my story.

However, what I wanted to do in *Wolf Mark* was to approach the idea of a man becoming a wolf in a very different way—from a modern American Indian point of view. Part of what I ended up doing draws from various native traditions, but just as much of it came to me in the way many of my stories in the past have—from my dreams and my imagination. Further, I wanted to do what one of my non-Native writing heroes John Irving did decades ago in his book Grendel, tell the story from the point of view of the "monster." As a result, I hope readers will agree that Luke is a very different sort of werewolf than they've encountered before.

Two other things need to be mentioned. The first is the martial arts that are of such importance to my main character. My sons James and Jesse and I owe a great debt of gratitude to the warrior ways we have been privileged to study for the last three decades and more—Korean and Okinawan karate, kung fu wu su, tai chi, capoeira, tae kwon do, Brazilian jiu jitsu, and pentjak silat. Both of my sons are dedicated teachers and it was my honor to recently be raised to the rank of Master in pentjak-karate. I could not have written this book without all that I have learned over the years from the mental, physical, emotional, and spiritual training offered by those Ways.

The second thing to be mentioned is the presence in this book of my Russian characters. Half of my own heritage is Eastern European and my Slovak ancestors have much in common with the Slavic peoples of Russia. It saddens me that, all too often, Russian people are still presented as stereotyped, humorless, colorless caricatures. I hope that my wise-cracking, poetry-loving, modern Russian slang-speaking drughs in *Wolf Mark* succeed in breaking outside that mold. I have a great love for the literature and the contemporary popular music of Russia and great admiration for the ordinary folk of that nation—some of the most resilient people in the world.

My wish is that this book may, as my favorite fantasy novels by such wonderful writers as Guy Gavriel Kay, Ursula Le Guin, and Neil Gaiman have done for me, afford both enjoyment and escape to its readers. I also hope that it may also, like our old traditional tales, if not teach a lesson then at least make readers stop and think.